The Cit

A.J. Cronin

The Citadel
Copyright © 1937, 2015 by A.J. Cronin

Cover design by Peter Clark
ISBN: 978-0-7953-0039-4
www.RosettaBooks.com

To my wife

Book I

i

Late one October afternoon in the year 1921, a shabby young man gazed with fixed intensity through the window of a third-class compartment in the almost empty train labouring up the Penowell valley from Swansea. All that day Manson had travelled from the North, changing at Carlisle and Shrewsbury, yet the final stage of his tedious journey to South Wales found him strung to a still greater excitement by the prospects of his post, the first of his medical career, in this strange, disfigured country.

Outside, a heavy rainstorm came blinding down between the mountains which rose on either side of the single railway track. The mountain tops were hidden in a grey waste of sky, but their sides, scarred by ore workings, fell black and desolate, blemished by great heaps of slag on which a few dirty sheep wandered in vain hope of pasture. No bush, no blade of vegetation was visible. The trees, seen in the fading light, were gaunt and stunted spectres. At a bend of the line the red glare of a foundry flashed into sight, illuminating a score of workmen stripped to the waist, their torsos straining, arms upraised to strike. Though the scene was swiftly lost behind the huddled top gear of a mine, a sense of power persisted, tense and vivid. Manson drew a long breath. He felt an answering surge of effort, a sudden overwhelming exhilaration springing from the hope and promise of the future.

Darkness had fallen, emphasizing the strangeness and remoteness of the scene when, half an hour later, the engine panted into Blaenelly, the end township of the Valley, and the terminus of the line. He had arrived at last. Gripping his bag, Manson leaped from the train and walked quickly down the platform, searching eagerly for some sign of welcome. At the station exit, beneath a wind-blown lamp, a yellow-faced old man in a square hat and a long nightshirt of a mackintosh stood waiting. He inspected Manson with a jaundiced eye and his voice, when it came, was reluctant.

"You Doctor Page's new assistant?"

"That's right. Manson. Andrew Manson is the name."

"Huh! Mine's Thomas; 'Old Thomas' they mostly call me, dang 'em! I got the gig here. Set in—unless you'd rayther swim."

Manson slung his bag up and climbed into the battered gig behind a tall, angular black horse. Thomas followed, took the reins and addressed the horse.

"Hue-up, Taffy!" he said.

They drove off through the town, which, though Andrew tried keenly to discern its outline, presented in the slashing rain no more than a blurred huddle of low grey houses ranged beneath the high and ever-present mountains. For several minutes the old groom did not speak, but continued to dart pessimistic glances at Andrew from beneath the dripping brim of his hat. He bore no resemblance to the smart coachman of a successful doctor, but was, on the contrary, wizened and slovenly, and all the time he gave off a peculiar yet powerful odour of stale cooking-fat.

At last he said: "Only jest got your parchment, eh?"

Andrew nodded.

"I knowed it." Old Thomas spat. His triumph made him more gravely communicative. "Last assistant went ten days ago. Mostly they don't stop."

"Why?" Despite his nervousness, Andrew smiled.

"Work's too hard for one thing, I reckon."

"And for another?"

"You'll find out!" A moment later, as a guide might indicate a fine cathedral, Thomas lifted his whip and pointed to the end of a row of houses where, from a small lighted doorway, a cloud of steam was emerging. "See that! That there's the missus and my chip petato shop. We fry twice a week. Wet fish." A secret amusement twitched his long upper lip. "Reckon you might want to know, shortly."

Here the main street ended and, turning up a short uneven side road, they boggled across a piece of waste ground, and entered the narrow drive of a house which stood isolated from the adjacent rows behind three monkey-puzzle trees. On the gate was the name BRYNGOWER.

"This is us," said Thomas, pulling up the horse.

Andrew descended. The next minute, while he was gathering himself for the ordeal of his entrance, the front door was flung open and he was in the lighted hall being welcomed effusively by a short, plump, smiling woman of about forty with a shining face and bright bold twinkling eyes.

"Well! Well! This must be Doctor Manson. Come in, my dee-ar, come in. I'm the Doctor's wife, Mrs. Page. I do hope you didn't have a tryin' journey. I am pleased to see you. I been out my mind, nearly, since that last awful feller we had left us. You ought to have seen him. He was a waster if ever I met one, I can tell you. Oh! But never mind. It's all right now you're here. Come along, I'll show you to your room myself."

Upstairs, Andrew's room was a small camsiled apartment with a brass bed, a yellow varnished chest of drawers, and a bamboo table bearing a basin and ewer.

Glancing round it, while her black button eyes searched his face, he said with anxious politeness: "This looks very comfortable, Mrs. Page."

"Yes, indeed." She smiled and patted his shoulder maternally. "You'll do famous here, my dee-ar. You treat me right and I'll treat you right. I can't say fairer nor that, can I? Now come along before you're a minute older and meet Doctor." She paused, her gaze still questioning his, her tone striving to be off-hand. "I don't know if I said so in my letter but, as a matter of fact—Doctor 'asn't been too well, lately."

Andrew looked at her in sudden surprise.

"Oh, it's nothing much," she went on quickly, before he could speak. "He's been laid up a few weeks. But he'll soon be all right. Make no mistake about that."

Perplexed, Andrew followed her to the end of the passage, where she threw open a door, exclaiming blithely:—

"Here's Doctor Manson, Edward—our new assistant. He's come to say 'ow do."

As Andrew went into the room, a long fustily furnished bedroom with chenille curtains closely drawn and a small fire burning in the grate, Edward Page turned slowly upon the bed, seeming to do so by a great effort. He was a big, bony man of perhaps sixty with harshly lined features and tired, luminous eyes. His whole expression was stamped with suffering and a kind of weary patience. And there was something more. The light of the oil lamp, falling across the pillow, revealed one half of his face expressionless and waxen. The left side of his body was equally paralyzed and his left hand, which lay upon the patchwork counterpane, was contracted to a shiny cone.

Observing these signs of a severe and far from recent stroke, Andrew was conscious of a sudden shock of dismay. There was an odd silence.

"I hope you'll like it here," Doctor Page remarked at length, speaking slowly and with difficulty, slurring his words a little. "I hope you'll find the practice won't be too much for you. You're very young."

"I'm twenty-four, sir," Andrew answered awkwardly. "I know this is the first job I've had, and all that—but I'm not afraid of work."

"There, now!" Mrs. Page beamed. "Didn't I tell you, Edward, we'd be lucky with our next one?"

An even deeper immobility settled on Page's face. He gazed at Andrew. Then his interest seemed to fade.

He said in a tired voice: "I hope you'll stay."

"My goodness gracious!" cried Mrs. Page. "What a thing to say!" She turned to Andrew, smilingly and apologetic. "It's only because he's a morsel down to-day. But he'll soon be up and doing again. Won't you, ducky?" Bending, she kissed her husband heartily. "There now! I'll send your supper up by Annie whenever we've 'ad ours."

Page did not answer. The stony look on his one-sided face made his mouth seem twisted. His good hand strayed to the book that lay on the table beside his bed. Andrew saw that it was entitled *The Wild Birds of Europe*. Even before the paralyzed man began to read he felt himself dismissed.

As Andrew went down to supper his thoughts were painfully confused. He had applied for this assistantship in answer to an advertisement in the *Lancet*. Yet in the correspondence, conducted at this end by Mrs. Page, which had led to his securing the post, there had been no mention whatsoever of Doctor Page's illness. But Page was ill; there could be no question of the gravity of the cerebral haemorrhage which had incapacitated him. It would be months before he was fit for work, if, indeed, he were ever fit for work again.

With an effort Andrew put the puzzle from his mind. He was young, strong, and had no objection to the extra work in which Page's illness might involve him. Indeed, in his enthusiasm, he yearned for an avalanche of calls.

"You're lucky, my dee-ar," remarked Mrs. Page brightly as she bustled into the dining room. "You can have your bit of snap straight off to-night. No surgery. Dai Jenkins done it."

"Dai Jenkins?"

"He's our dispenser," Mrs. Page threw out casually. "A handy little feller. An' willin' too. 'Doc' Jenkins some folks even call him, though of course he's not to be compared in the same breath with Doctor Page. He's done the surgery and visits also, these last ten days."

Andrew stared at her in fresh concern. All that he had been told, all the warnings he had received regarding the questionable ways of practice in these remote Welsh Valleys, flashed into his recollection. Again it cost him an effort to be silent.

Mrs. Page sat at the head of the table with her back to the fire. When she had wedged herself comfortably into her chair with a cushion she sighed in pleasant anticipation and tinkled the little cowbell in front of her. A middle-aged servant with a pale, well-scrubbed face brought in the supper, stealing a glance at Andrew as she entered.

"Come along, Annie," cried Mrs. Page, buttering a wedge of soft bread and stuffing it in her mouth. "This is Doctor Manson."

Annie did not answer. She served Andrew in a contained, silent fashion with a thin slice of cold boiled brisket. For Mrs. Page, however, there was a hot beefsteak and onions with a pint bottle of oatmeal stout. As the doctor's wife lifted the cover from her special dish and cut into the juicy meat, her teeth watering in expectation, she explained:—

"I didn't have much lunch, Doctor. Besides, I got to watch my diet. It's the blood. I have to take a drop of porter for the blood."

Andrew chewed his stringy brisket and drank cold water determinedly. After a momentary indignation his main difficulty lay with his own sense of humour. Her pretence of invalidism was so blatant he had to struggle to conquer a wild impulse to laugh.

During the meal Mrs. Page ate freely but said little. At length, sopping up the gravy with her bread, she finished her steak, smacked her lips over the last of the stout, and lay back in her chair, breathing a trifle heavily, her round little cheeks flushed and shiny. Now she seemed disposed to linger at table, inclined to confidences—perhaps trying, in her own bold way, to sum Manson up.

Studying him, she saw a spare and gawky youngster, dark, rather tensely drawn, with high cheekbones, a fine jaw and blue eyes. These eyes, when he raised them, were, despite the nervous tensity of his brow, extraordinarily steady and inquiring. Although Blodwen Page knew nothing of it, she was looking at a Celtic type. Though she admitted the vigour and alert intelligence in Andrew's face, what pleased her most of all was his acceptance, without demur, of that scanty cut from the three-days-old heel of brisket. She reflected that, though he looked hungry, he might not be hard to feed.

"I'm sure we'll get on famous, you and me," she again declared genially, picking her teeth with a hairpin. "I do need a bit o' luck for a change." Mellowed, she told him of her troubles, and sketched a vague outline of the practice and its position. "It's been awful, my dee-ar. You don't know. What with Doctor Page's illness, wicked bad assistants, nothin' comin' in and everythin' goin' out—well! you wouldn't believe it! And the job I've 'ad to keep the manager and mine officials sweet—it's them the practice money comes through—what there is of it," she added hurriedly. "You see, the way they work things in Blaenelly is like this: the Company has three doctors on its list, though mind you Doctor Page is far and away the cleverest doctor of the lot. And besides—the time he's been 'ere! Nearly thirty years and more; that's something, I should think! Well, then, these doctors can have as many assistants as they like,—Doctor Page has you, and Doctor Lewis has a would-be feller called Denny,—but the assistants don't ever get on the Company's list. Anyway, as I was sayin', the Company deducts so much from every man's wages they employ at the mines and the quarries, and pays that out to the listed doctors according to 'ow many of the men signs on with them."

She broke off under the strain of her illiteracy and an overloaded stomach.

"I think I see how the system works, Mrs. Page."

"Well, then!" She heaved out her jolly laugh. "You don't have to bother about it no more. All you got to remember is that you're workin' for Doctor Page. That's the main thing, Doctor. Just remember you're workin' for Doctor Page and you and poor little me'll get on a treat."

It seemed to Manson, silent and observant, that she tried at the same time to excite his pity and to establish her authority over him, all beneath that manner of breezy affability. Perhaps she felt she had unbent too far. With a glance at the clock, she straightened herself, restored the hairpin to her greasy black hair. Then she rose. Her voice was different, almost peremptory.

"By the way, there's a call for Number 7 Glydar Place. It come in the back of five o'clock. You better do it straight away."

ii

Andrew went out to the call immediately, with a queer sensation, almost of relief. He was glad of the opportunity to disentangle himself from the curious and conflicting emotions stirred up by his arrival at Bryngower. Already he had a glimmer of a suspicion as to how matters stood and of how he would be made use of by Blodwen Page to run the practice for his disabled principal. It was a strange situation, and very different from any romantic picture which his fancy might have painted. Yet, after all, his work was the important thing; beside it all else was trivial. He longed to begin it. Insensibly he hastened his pace, taut with anticipation, exulting in the realization—this, this was his first case.

It was still raining when he crossed the smeary blackness of the waste land and struck along Chapel Street in the direction vaguely indicated by Mrs. Page. Darkly, as he traversed it, the town took shape before him. Shops and chapels—Zion, Capel, Hebron, Bethel, Bethesda; he passed a round dozen of them—then the big Cooperative Stores, and a branch of the Western Counties Bank, all lining the main thoroughfare, lying deep in the bed of the Valley. The sense of being buried, far down in this cleft of the mountains, was singularly oppressive. There were few people about. At right angles, reaching up a short distance on either side of Chapel Street, were rows and rows of blue-roofed workers' houses. And, beyond, at the head of the gorge, beneath a glow that spread like a great fan into the opaque sky, the Blaenelly Haematite Mine and Ore Works.

He reached 7 Glydar Place, knocked breathlessly upon the door, and was at once admitted to the kitchen, where, in a recessed bed, the patient lay. She was a young woman, wife of a steel puddler named Williams, and as he approached the bedside with a fast-beating heart he felt, overwhelmingly, the significance of this, the real starting-point of his life. How often had he envisaged it as, in a crowd of students, he had watched a demonstration in Professor Lamplough's wards! Now there was no sustaining crowd, no easy exposition. He was alone, confronted by a case which he must diagnose and treat unaided. All at once, with a quick pang, he was conscious of his nervousness, his inexperience, his complete unpreparedness, for such a task.

While the husband stood by in the cramped, ill-lit stone-floored room, Andrew Manson examined the patient with scrupulous care. There was no doubt about it, she was ill. She complained that her head ached intolerably. Temperature, pulse, tongue, they all spoke of trouble, serious trouble. What was it? Andrew asked himself that question with a strained intensity as he went over her again. His first case. Oh, he knew that he was overanxious! But suppose he made an error, a frightful blunder? And worse —suppose he found himself unable to make a diagnosis? He had missed nothing. Nothing. Yet he still found himself struggling towards some solution of the problem, striving to group the symptoms under the heading of some recognized disease. At last, aware that he could protract his investigation no longer, he straightened himself slowly, folding up his stethoscope, fumbling for words.

"Did she have a chill?" he asked, his eyes upon the floor.

"Yes, indeed," Williams answered eagerly. He had looked scared during the prolonged examination. "Three, four days ago. I made sure it was a chill, Doctor."

Andrew nodded, attempting painfully to generate a confidence he did not feel. He muttered. "We'll soon have her right. Come to the surgery in half an hour. I'll give you a bottle of medicine."

He took his leave of them and with his head down, thinking desperately, he trudged back to the surgery, a ramshackle wooden erection standing at the entrance to Page's drive. Inside, he lit the gas and began to pace backwards and forwards beside the blue and green bottles on the dusty shelves, racking his brains, groping in the darkness. There was nothing symptomatic. It must, yes, it must be a chill. But in his heart he knew that it was not a chill. He groaned in exasperation, dismayed and angry at his own inadequacy. He was forced, unwillingly, to temporize. Professor Lamplough, when confronted by obscurity in his wards, had a neat little ticket, which he tactfully applied: P.U.O.—pyrexia of unknown origin—it was noncommittal and exact, and it had such an admirable scientific sound!

Unhappily, Andrew took a six-ounce bottle from the recess beneath the dispensary counter and began with a frown of concentration to compound an antipyretic mixture. Spirits of nitre, salicylate of sodium—where the dickens was the soda sal.? Oh, there it was! He tried to cheer himself by reflecting that they were all splendid, all excellent drugs, bound to get the temperature down, certain to do good. Professor Lamplough had often declared there was no drug so generally valuable as salicylate of sodium.

He had just finished his compounding and with a mild sense of achievement was writing the label when the surgery bell went *ping*, the outer door swung open, and a short, powerfully thickset red-faced man of thirty strolled in, followed by a dog. There was a silence while the black-and-tan mongrel squatted on its muddy haunches, and the man—who wore an old velveteen suit, pit stockings, and hobnail boots, with a sodden oilskin cape over his shoulders—looked Andrew up and down. His voice, when it came, was politely ironic and annoyingly well-bred.

"I saw a light in your window as I was passing. Thought I'd look in to welcome you. I'm Denny, assistant to the esteemed Doctor Lewis, L.S.A. That, in case you haven't met it, is the Licentiate of the Society of Apothecaries, the highest qualification known to God and man."

Andrew stared back doubtfully. Philip Denny lit a cigarette from a crumpled paper packet, threw the match on the floor, and strolled forward insolently. He picked up the bottle of medicine, read the address, the directions, uncorked it, sniffed it, recorked it and put it down, his morose red face turning blandly complimentary.

"Splendid! You've begun the good work already! One tablespoon every three hours. God Almighty! It's reassuring to meet the dear old mumbo-jummery. But, Doctor, why not three times a day? Don't you realize, Doctor, that in strict orthodoxy the tablespoonfuls should pass down the œsophagus three times a day?" He paused, becoming, with his assumed air of confidence, more blandly offensive than ever. "Now tell me, Doctor, what's in it? Spirit of nitre, by the smell. Wonderful stuff, sweet spirit of nitre. Wonderful, wonderful, my dear Doctor! Carminative, stimulant, diuretic, and you can swill it by the tubful. Don't you remember what it says in the little red book? When in doubt give spirit of nitre—or is it *pot. iod.*? Tut! Tut! I seem to have forgotten some of my essentials."

Again there was a silence in the wooden shed, broken only by the drumming of the rain upon the tin roof. Suddenly Denny laughed, a mocking appreciation of the blank expression on Andrew's face.

He said derisively: "Science apart, Doctor, you might satisfy my curiosity. Why have you come here?"

By this time Andrew's temper was rising rapidly. He answered grimly: "My idea was to turn Blaenelly into a health resort—a sort of spa, you know."

Again Denny laughed. His laugh was an insult, which made Andrew long to hit him.

"Witty, witty, my dear Doctor. The true Scots steam-roller humour. Unfortunately I can't recommend the water here as being ideally suited for a spa. As to the medical gentlemen—my dear Doctor, in this Valley they're the rag, tag, and bobtail of a glorious, a truly noble profession."

"Including yourself?"

"Precisely!" Denny nodded. He was silent a moment, contemplating Andrew from beneath his sandy eyebrows. Then he dropped his mocking irony; his ugly features turned morose again. His tone, though bitter, was serious.

"Look here, Manson! I realize you're just passing through on your way to Harley Street, but in the meantime there are one or two things about this place you ought to know. You won't find it conforms to the best traditions of romantic practice. There's no hospital, no ambulance, no X rays, no anything. If you want to operate you use the kitchen table. You wash up afterwards at the scullery bosh. The sanitation won't bear looking at. In a dry summer the kids die like flies with infantile cholera. Page, your boss, was a damn good old doctor, but he's finished now, bitched by Blodwen, and'll never do a hand's turn again. Lewis, my owner, is a tight little money-chasing midwife. Bramwell, the Silver King, knows nothing but a few sentimental recitations and the Songs of Solomon. As for myself, I'd better anticipate the gay tidings—I drink like a fish. Oh! and Jenkins, your tame druggist, does a thriving trade, on the side, in little lead pills for female ills. I think that's about all. Come, Hawkins, we'll go." He called the mongrel and moved heavily towards the door. There he paused, his eyes ranging again from the bottle on the counter to Manson. His tone was flat, quite uninterested. "By the way, I should look out for enteric in Glydar Place, if I were you. Some of these cases aren't exactly typical."

Ping! went the door again. Before Andrew could answer, Doctor Philip Denny and Hawkins disappeared into the wet darkness.

iii

It was not his lumpy flock mattress which caused Andrew to sleep badly that night, but growing anxiety about the case in Glydar Place. Was it enteric? Denny's parting remark had started a fresh train of doubt and misgiving in his already uncertain mind. Dreading that he had overlooked some vital symptom, he restrained himself with difficulty from rising and revisiting the case at an unearthly hour of the morning. Indeed, as he tossed and turned through the long restless night, he came to ask himself if he knew anything of medicine at all.

Manson's nature was extraordinarily intense. Probably he derived this from his mother, a Highland woman who, in her childhood, had watched the northern lights leap through the frosted sky from her home in Ullapool. His father, John Manson, a small Fifeshire farmer, had been solid, painstaking, and steady. He had never made a success of the land, and when he was killed in the Yeomanry in the last year of the War, he had left the affairs of the little steading in a sad muddle. For twelve months Jessie Manson has struggled to run the farm as a dairy, even driving the float upon the milk-round herself when she felt Andrew was too busy with his books to do so. Then the cough which she had unsuspectingly endured for a period of years turned worse and suddenly she surrendered to the lung complaint which ravages that soft-skinned, dark-haired type.

At eighteen Andrew found himself alone, a first-year student at St. Andrews University, carrying a scholarship worth forty pounds a year, but otherwise penniless. His salvation had been the Glen Endowment, that typically Scottish foundation, which in the naïve terminology of the late Sir Andrew Glen "invites deserving and necessitous students of the baptismal name of Andrew to apply for loans not exceeding fifty pounds a year for five years provided they are conscientiously prepared to reimburse such loans whenever they have qualified."

The Glen Endowment, coupled with some gay starvation, had sent Andrew through the remainder of his course at St. Andrews, then on to the Medical Schools in the city of Dundee. And gratitude to the Endowment, allied to an inconvenient honesty, had sent him hurrying down to South Wales—where newly qualified assistants could command the highest remuneration—to a salary of two hundred and fifty pounds a year, when in his heart he would have preferred a clinical appointment at the Edinburgh Royal and an honorarium of one tenth that sum.

And now he was in Blaenelly, rising, shaving, dressing, all in a haze of worry over his first patient. He ate his breakfast quickly, then ran up to his room again. There he opened his bag and took out a small blue leather case. He opened the case and gazed earnestly at the medal inside—the Hunter Gold Medal, awarded annually at St. Andrews to the best student in clinical medicine. He, Andrew Manson, had won it. He prized it beyond everything, had come to regard it as his talisman, his inspiration for the future. But this morning he viewed it less with pride than with a queer, secret entreaty, as though trying to restore his confidence in himself. Then he hurried out for the morning surgery.

Dai Jenkins was already in the wooden shanty when Andrew reached it, running water from the tap into a large earthenware pipkin. He was a quick little whippet of a man with purple-veined, hollow cheeks, eyes that went everywhere at once, and the tightest pair of trousers on his thin legs that Andrew had ever seen.

He greeted Manson ingratiatingly:—

"You don't have to be so early, Doctor. I can do the repeat mixtures and the certificates before you come in. Mrs. Page had a rubber stamp made with Doctor's signature when he was taken bad."

"Thanks," Andrew answered. "I'd rather see the cases myself." He paused, shaken momentarily from his anxiety by the dispenser's procedure. "What's the idea?"

Jenkins winked. "Tastes better out of here. We know what good old *aqua* means, eh, Doctor, *bach*? But the patients don't. I'd look a proper fool too, wouldn't I, them standin' there watchin' me fillin' up their bottles out the tap."

Plainly the little dispenser wished to be communicative, but here a loud voice rang out from the back door of the house forty yards away.

"Jenkins! *Jenkins!* I want you—*this minnit.*"

Jenkins jumped like an overtrained dog at the crack of the ring master's whip. He quavered: "Excuse me, Doctor. There's Mrs. Page callin' me. I'll... I'll have to run."

Fortunately there were few people at the morning surgery, which was over at half-past ten, and Andrew, presented with a list of visits by Jenkins, set out at once with Thomas in the gig. With an almost painful expectancy he told the old groom to drive direct to 7 Glydar Place.

Twenty minutes later he came out of Number 7, pale, with his lips tightly compressed and an odd expression on his face. He went two doors down, into Number 11, which was also on his list. From Number 11 he crossed the street to Number 18. From Number 18 he went round the corner to Radnor Place, where two further cases were marked by Jenkins as having been seen the day before. Altogether, within the space of an hour, he made seven such calls in the immediate vicinity. Five of them, including Number 7 Glydar Place, which was now showing a typical rash, were clear cases of enteric. For the last ten days Jenkins had been treating them with chalk and opium. Now, whatever his own bungling efforts of the previous night had been, Andrew realized with a shiver of apprehension that he had an outbreak of typhoid fever on his hands.

The remainder of his round he accomplished as quickly as possible in a state dithering towards panic. At lunch, during which Mrs. Page dealt exclusively with a nicely browned sweetbread, which she explained merrily, "I ordered it for Doctor Page but he don't seem to fancy it somehow," he brooded upon the problem in frozen silence. He saw that he would get little information and no help from Mrs. Page. He decided he must speak to Doctor Page himself.

But when he went up to the doctor's room the curtains were drawn and Edward lay prostrate with a pressure headache, his forehead deeply flushed and furrowed by pain. Though he motioned his visitor to sit with him a little Andrew felt it would be cruelty to thrust this trouble upon him at present.

As he rose to go, after remaining seated by the bedside for a few minutes, he had to confine himself to asking: "Doctor Page, if we get an infectious case, what's the best thing to do?"

There was a pause. Page replied with closed eyes, not moving, as though the mere act of speech were enough to aggravate his migraine.

"It's always been difficult. We've no hospital, let alone an isolation ward. If you should run into anything very nasty ring up Griffiths at Toniglan. That's fifteen miles down the Valley. He's the District Medical Officer." Another pause, longer than before. "But I'm afraid he's not very helpful."

Reinforced by this information, Andrew hastened down to the hall and rang up Toniglan. While he stood with the receiver to his ear he saw Annie, the servant, looking at him through the kitchen door.

"Hello! Hello! Is that Doctor Griffiths of Toniglan?" He got through at last.

A man's voice answered very guardedly. "Who wants him?"

"This is Manson of Blaenelly. Doctor Page's assistant." Andrew's tone was overpitched. "I've got five cases of typhoid up here. I want Doctor Griffiths to come up immediately."

There was the barest pause, then with a rush the reply came back in a singsong intonation, very Welsh and apologetic. "I'm powerful sorry, Doctor, indeed I am, but Doctor Griffiths has gone to Swansea. Important official business."

"When will he be back?" shouted Manson. The line was bad.

"Indeed, Doctor, I couldn't say for certain."

"But, listen…"

There was a click at the far end. Very quietly the other had rung off. Manson swore out loud with nervous violence. "Damn it, I believe that was Griffiths himself."

He rang the number again, failed to get a connection. Yet, persisting doggedly, he was about to ring again when, turning, he found that Annie had advanced into the hall, her hands folded upon her apron, her eyes contemplating him soberly. She was a woman of perhaps forty-five, very clean and tidy, with a grave, enduring placidity of expression.

"I couldn't help but hear, Doctor," she said. "You'll never find Doctor Griffiths in Toniglan this hour of day. He do go to the golf at Swansea afternoons mostly."

He answered angrily, swallowing a lump that hung in his throat.

"But I think that was him I spoke to."

"Maybe." She smiled faintly. "When he don't go to Swansea I've 'eard tell he do say 'e 'ave gone." She considered him with tranquil friendliness before turning away. "I wouldn't waste my time on him if I was you."

Andrew replaced the receiver with a deepening sense of indignation and distress. Cursing, he went out and visited his cases once more. When he got back it was time for evening surgery. For an hour and a half he sat in the little back-shop cubicle which was the consulting room, wrestling with a packed surgery until the walls sweated and the place was choked with the steam of damp bodies. Miners with beat knee, cut fingers, nystagmus, chronic arthritis. Their wives, too, and their children with coughs, colds, sprains—all the minor ailments of humanity. Normally he would have enjoyed it, welcomed the quiet appraising scrutiny of these dark, sallow-skinned people with whom he felt he was on probation. But now, obsessed by the major issue, his head reeled with the impact of these trifling complaints. Yet all the time he was reaching his decision, thinking, as he wrote prescriptions, sounded chests and offered words of advice, "It was he who put me on to the thing. I hate him. Yes, I loathe him—superior devil—like hell. But I can't help that; I'll have to go to him."

At half-past nine, when the last patient had left the surgery, he came out of his den with resolution in his eyes.

"Jenkins, where does Doctor Denny live?"

The little dispenser, hastily bolting the outer door for fear another straggler might come in, turned with a look of horror on his face that was almost comic.

"You aren't goin' to have anything to do with that feller, Doctor? Mrs. Page—she don't like him."

Andrew asked grimly: "Why doesn't Mrs. Page like him?"

"For the same reason everybody don't. 'E's been so damn rude to her." Jenkins paused then; reading Manson's look he added, reluctantly, "Oh, well, if you 'ave to know, it's with Mrs. Seager he stops, Number 49 Chapel Street."

Out again. He had been going the whole day long, yet any tiredness he might have felt was lost in a sense of responsibility, the burden of those cases pressing, pressing urgently upon his shoulders. His main feeling was one of relief when, on reaching Chapel Street, he found that Denny was at his lodgings. The landlady showed him in.

If Denny was surprised to see him he concealed it. He merely asked, after a prolonged and aggravating stare, "Well! Killed anybody yet?"

Still standing in the doorway of the warm untidy sitting-room, Andrew reddened. But, making a great effort, he conquered his temper and his pride.

He said abruptly: "You were right. It was enteric. I ought to be shot for not recognizing it. I've got five cases. I'm not exactly overjoyed at having to come here. But I don't know the ropes. I rang the M.O., and couldn't get a word out of him. I've come to ask your advice."

Denny, half-slewed round in his chair by the fire, listening, pipe in mouth, at last made a grudging gesture.

"You'd better come in." With sudden irritation: "Oh! and for God's sake take a chair. Don't stand there like a Presbyterian parson about to forbid the banns. Have a drink? No! I thought you wouldn't."

Though Andrew stiffly complied with the request, seating himself and even, defensively, lighting a cigarette, Denny seemed in no hurry. He sat prodding the dog Hawkins with the toe of his burst slipper.

But at length, when Manson had finished his cigarette, Denny said with a jerk of his head: "Take a look at that, if you like!"

On the table indicated a microscope stood,—a fine Zeiss,—and some slides. Andrew focussed a slide, then slid round the oil-immersion and immediately picked up the rod-shaped clusters of the bacteria.

"It's very clumsily done, of course," Denny said quickly and cynically, as though forestalling criticism. "Practically botched, in fact. I'm no lab. merchant, thank God! If anything, I'm a surgeon. But you've got to be jack-of-all-trades under our bloody system. There's no mistake, though, even to the naked eye. I cooked them on agar in my oven."

"You've got cases too?" Andrew asked with tense interest.

"Four! All in the same area as yours." He paused. "And these bugs come from the well in Glydar Place."

Andrew gazed at him, alert, burning to ask a dozen questions, realizing something of the genuineness of the other man's work, and, beyond everything, overjoyed that he had been shown the focus of the epidemic.

"You see," Denny resumed with that same cold and bitter irony, "paratyphoid is more or less endemic here. But one day soon, very soon, we're going to have a pretty little blaze-up. It's the main sewer that's to blame. It leaks like the devil, and seeps into half the low wells at the bottom of the town. I've hammered at Griffiths about it till I'm tired. He's a lazy, evasive, incompetent, pious swine. Last time I rang him I said I'd knock his block off next time I met him. Probably that's why he welshed on you today."

"It's a damned shame," Andrew burst out, forgetting himself in a sudden rush of indignation.

Denny shrugged his shoulders. "He's afraid to ask the Council for anything in case they dock his wretched salary to pay for it."

There was a silence. Andrew had a warm desire that the conversation might continue. Despite his hostility towards Denny, he found a strange stimulus in the other's pessimism, in his scepticism, his cold and measured cynicism. Yet now he had no pretext on which to prolong his stay. He got up from his seat at the table and moved towards the door, concealing his feelings, striving to express a formal gratitude, to give some indications of his relief.

"I'm much obliged for the information. You've let me see how I stand. I was worried about the origin, thought I might be dealing with a carrier; but since you've localized it to the well it's a lot simpler. From now on every drop of water in Glydar Place is going to be boiled."

Denny rose also. He growled: "It's Griffiths who ought to be boiled." Then, with a return of his satiric humour: "Now, no touching thanks, Doctor, if you please. We shall probably have to endure a little more of each other before this thing is finished. Come and see me any time you can bear it. We don't have much social life in this neighbourhood." He glanced at the dog and concluded rudely: "Even a Scots doctor would be welcome. Isn't that so, Sir John?"

Sir John Hawkins flogged the rug with his tail, his pink tongue lolling derisively at Manson.

Yet, going home via Glydar Place, where he left strict instructions regarding the water supply, Andrew realized that he did not detest Denny so much as he had thought.

iv

Andrew threw himself into the enteric campaign with all the fire of his impetuous and ardent nature. He loved his work and he counted himself fortunate to have such an opportunity so early in his career. During these first weeks he slaved joyfully. He had all the ordinary routine of the practice on his hands, yet somehow he got through with it, then turned exultantly to his typhoid cases.

Perhaps he was lucky in this, his first assault. As the end of the month drew near, all his enteric patients were doing well and he seemed to have confined the outbreak. When he thought of his precautions, so rigidly enforced—the boiling of the water, the disinfection and isolation, the carbolic-soaked sheet on every door, the pounds of chloride of lime he had ordered to Mrs. Page's account and himself shot down the Glydar drains, he exclaimed in elation: "It's working. I don't deserve it. But by God! I'm *doing* it!" He took a secret, detestable delight in the fact that his cases were mending quicker than Denny's.

Denny still puzzled, exasperated him. They naturally saw each other often because of the proximity of their cases. It pleased Denny to exert the full force of his irony upon the work which they were doing. He referred to Manson and himself as "grimly battling with the epidemic" and savoured the cliché with vindictive relish. But for all his satire, his sneers of "Don't forget, Doctor, we're upholding the honour of a truly glorious profession," he went close to his patients, sat on their beds, laid his hands upon them, spent hours in their sickrooms.

At times Andrew came near to liking him for a flash of shy, self-conscious simplicity, then the whole thing would be shattered by a morose and sneering word. Hurt and baffled, Andrew turned one day in the hope of enlightenment to the *Medical Directory*. It was a five-year-old copy on Doctor Page's shelf; but it held some startling information. It showed Philip Denny as an honours scholar of Cambridge and Guy's, an M.S. of England, holding—at that date—a practice with an honorary surgical appointment in the ducal town of Leeborough.

Then, on the tenth day of November, Denny unexpectedly rang him up.

"Manson! I'd like to see you. Can you come to my place at three o'clock? It's important."

"Very well. I'll be there."

Andrew went into lunch thoughtfully. As he ate the cottage pie that was his portion he felt Blodwen Page's eye fastened on him in a bright and overbearing stare.

"Who was that on the phone? So it was Denny, eh? You don't have to go around with that feller. He's no use at all."

He faced her coldly. "On the contrary, I've found him a great deal of use."

"Go on with you, Doctor!" As usual, when opposed, Blodwen sparked out spitefully. "He's reg'lar quee-ar. Mostly he don't give medicine at all. Why, when Megan Rhys Morgan, what's had to have medicine all her life, went to him, he told her to walk two mile up the mountain every day and stop boggin' herself with hog-wash. These was his very words. She came to us after, I can tell you, and has had bottles and bottles of splendid medicine from Jenkins ever since. Oh! he's a low insultin' devil. 'E's got a wife somewhere by all accounts. Not livin' with him. See! Mostly he's drunk also. You leave him alone, Doctor, and remember you're workin' for Doctor Page."

As she flung the familiar injunction at his head Andrew felt a quick rush of anger sweep over him. He was doing his utmost to please her, yet there seemed no limit to her demands. Her attitude, whether of suspicion or jollity, seemed always designed to get the last ounce out of him and to give as little as possible in return. His first month's pay was already three days overdue, perhaps an oversight upon her part, yet one which had worried and annoyed him considerably. At the sight of her there, greasily buxom, tight with good living, sitting in judgment upon Denny, his feelings got the better of him.

He said with sudden heat: "I'd be more likely to remember that I'm working for Doctor Page if I had my month's salary, Mrs. Page."

She reddened so quickly that he was sure the matter lay in the forefront of her mind. Then she tossed her head defiantly. "You shall have it. The idea!"

For the rest of the meal she sat in a huff, not looking at him, as though he had insulted her. But after lunch, when she called him into the sitting-room, her mood was affable, smiling, merry.

"Here's your money then, Doctor. Sit down and be friendly. We can't get along if we don't pull together proper."

She herself was seated in the green plush armchair, and in her pudgy lap were twenty pound notes and her black leather purse. Taking up the notes she began to count them slowly into Manson's hand—"One, two, three, four!" As she approached the end of the bundle she went slower and slower, her sly black eyes twinkling ingratiatingly, and when she came to eighteen she stopped altogether and gave a self-commiserating little gasp.

"Dear, oh dear, Doctor, it's a lot of money in these hard times. What d'you say. Give and take's always been my motto. Shall I keep the odd two for luck?"

He simply kept silent. The situation created by her meanness was abominable. He knew that the practice was paying her handsomely.

For a full minute she sat there, searching his face; then, finding no response but a stony blankness, with a peevish gesture she slapped over the rest of the notes and said sharply: "See you earn it, then!"

She rose abruptly and made to quit the room, but Andrew stopped her before she reached the door.

"Just a moment, Mrs. Page." There was nervous determination in his voice. Hateful though this might be, he was determined not to let her, or her cupidity, get the better of him. "You've only given me twenty pounds, which works out at two hundred and forty a year, whereas we both definitely agreed that my salary should be two-fifty. You owe me another sixteen shillings and eightpence, Mrs. Page."

She went dead-white with temper and disappointment.

"So!" she panted. "You're goin' to let the silver come between us. I always heard the Scotch was mean. And now I know it. Here! Take your dirty shillin's, and your coppers too."

She counted out the money from her bulging purse, her fingers trembling, her eyes snapping at him. Then, with a final glare, she bounced out and slammed the door.

Andrew left the house smouldering with anger. Her taunt had stung him more deeply because he felt it to be unfair. Couldn't she see that it was not the paltry sum which was at stake but the whole principle of justice? Besides, apart from any high-sounding morality, he had an inborn trait: a Northern resolution never, while he breathed, to allow anyone to make a fool of him.

Only when he had reached the post office, bought a registered envelope, and posted the twenty pounds to the Glen Endowment—he kept the silver as pocket money for himself—did he feel better. Standing on the steps of the post office, he saw Doctor Bramwell approaching and his expression lightened further.

Bramwell came slowly, his large feet pressing down the pavement majestically, his seedy black figure erect, uncut white hair sweeping over the back of his soiled collar, eyes fixed on the book he held at arm's length. When he reached Andrew, whom he had seen from halfway down the street, he gave a theatrical start of recognition.

"Ah! Manson, my boy! I was so immersed, I almost missed you!"

Andrew smiled. He was already on friendly terms with Doctor Bramwell, who, unlike Lewis, the other "listed" doctor, had given him a cordial welcome on his arrival. Bramwell's practice was not extensive, and did not permit him the luxury of an assistant, but he had a grand manner, and some attitudes worthy of a great healer.

He closed his book, studiously marking the place with one dirty forefinger, then thrust his free hand picturesquely into the breast of his faded coat. He was so operatic he seemed hardly real. But there he was, in the main street of Blaenelly. No wonder Denny had named him "the Silver King."

"And how, my dear boy, are you liking our little community? As I told you when you called upon my dear wife and myself at The Retreat, it isn't so bad as it might appear at first sight. We have our talent, our culture. My dear wife and I do our best to foster it. We carry the torch, Manson, even in the wilderness. You must come to us one evening. Do you sing?"

Andrew had an awful feeling that he must laugh.

Bramwell was continuing with unction:—

"Of course, we have all heard of your work with the enteric cases. Blaenelly is proud of you, my dear boy. I only wish the chance had come my way. If there is any emergency in which I can be of service to you, call upon me!"

A sense of compunction—who was he that he should be amused by the older man?—prompted Andrew to reply:—

"As a matter of fact, Doctor Bramwell, I've got a really interesting secondary mediastinitis in one of my cases, very unusual. You may care to see it with me if you're free."

"Yes?" queried Bramwell with a slight fall in his enthusiasm. "I don't wish to trouble you."

"It's just round the corner," Andrew said hospitably. "And I've got half an hour to spare before I meet Doctor Denny. We'll be there in a second."

Bramwell hesitated, looked for a minute as though he might refuse, then made a damped gesture of assent. They walked down to Glydar Place and went in to see the patient.

The case was, as Manson had inferred, one of unusual interest, involving a rare instance of persistence of the thymus gland. He was genuinely proud to have diagnosed it and he experienced a warm sense of communicative ardour as he invited Bramwell to share the thrill of his discovery.

But Doctor Bramwell, despite his protestations, seemed unattracted by the opportunity. He followed Andrew into the room haltingly, breathing through his nose, and in ladylike fashion approached the bed. Here he drew up and, at a safe range, made a cursory investigation. Nor was he disposed to linger. Only when they left the house, and he had inhaled a long breath of the pure fresh air, did his normal eloquence return. He glowed towards Andrew.

"I'm glad to have seen your case with you my boy, firstly because I feel it part of a doctor's calling never to shrink from the danger of infection, and secondly because I rejoice in the chance of scientific advancement. *Believe it or not, this is the best case of inflammation of the pancreas I have ever seen!*"

He shook hands and hurried off, leaving Andrew utterly nonplussed. The pancreas, thought Andrew dazedly. It was no mere slip of the tongue which had caused Bramwell to make that crass error. His entire conduct at the case betrayed his ignorance. He simply did not know. Andrew rubbed his brow. To think that a qualified practitioner, in whose hands lay the lives of hundreds of human beings, did not know the difference between the pancreas and the thymus, when one lay in the belly and the other in the chest—why, it was nothing short of staggering!

He walked slowly up the street towards Denny's lodgings, realizing once again how his whole orderly conception of the practice of medicine was toppling about him. He knew himself to be raw, inadequately trained, quite capable of making mistakes through his inexperience. But Bramwell was not inexperienced and because of that his ignorance was inexcusable. Unconsciously Andrew's thoughts returned to Denny, who never failed in his derision towards this profession to which they belonged. Denny at first had aggravated him intensely by his weary contention that all over Britain there were thousands of incompetent doctors distinguished for nothing but their sheer stupidity and an acquired capacity for bluffing their patients. Now he began to question if there were not some truth in what Denny said. He determined to reopen the argument this afternoon.

But when he entered Denny's room, he saw immediately that the occasion was not one for academic discussion. Philip received him in morose silence with a gloomy eye and a darkened forehead.

Then, after a moment, he said: "Young Jones died this morning at seven o'clock. Perforation." He spoke quietly, with a still, cold fury. "And I have two new enterics in Ystrad Row."

Andrew dropped his eyes, sympathizing, yet hardly knowing what to say.

"Don't look so smug about it," Denny went on bitterly. "It's sweet for you to see my cases go wrong and yours recover. But it won't be so pretty when that cursed sewer leaks your way."

"No, no! Honestly, I'm sorry," Andrew said impulsively. "We'll have to do something about it. We must write to the Ministry of Health."

"We could write a dozen letters," Philip answered, with grim restraint. "And all we'd get would be a doddering commissioner down here in six months' time. No! I've thought it all out. There's only one way to make them build a new sewer."

"How?"

"Blow up the old one!"

For a second Andrew wondered if Denny had taken leave of his senses. Then he perceived something of the other's hard intention. He stared at him in consternation. Try as he might to reconstruct his changing ideas, Denny seemed fated to demolish them.

Manson muttered: "There'll be a heap of trouble—if it's found out."

Denny glanced up arrogantly.

"You needn't come in with me, if you don't want to."

"Oh, I'm coming in with you," Andrew answered slowly. "But God only knows why!"

All that afternoon Manson went about his work fretfully regretting the promise he had given. He was a madman, this Denny, who would, sooner or later, involve him in serious trouble. It was a dreadful thing that he now proposed, a breach of the law which, if discovered, would bring them into the police court and might even cause them to be scored off the Medical Register. A tremor of sheer horror passed over Andrew at the thought of his beautiful career, stretching so shiningly before him, suddenly cut short, ruined. He cursed Philip violently, swore inwardly, a dozen times, that he would not go.

Yet, for some strange and complex reason, he would not, could not draw back.

At eleven o'clock that night Denny and he started out in company with the mongrel Hawkins for the end of Chapel Street. It was very dark with a gusty wind and a fine spatter of rain which blew into their faces at the street corners. Denny had made his plan and timed it carefully. The late shift at the mine had gone in an hour ago. A few lads hung about old Thomas' fish shop at the top end, but otherwise the street was deserted.

The two men and the dog moved quietly. In the pocket of his heavy overcoat, Denny had six sticks of dynamite especially stolen for him that afternoon from the powder shed at the quarry by Tom Seager, his landlady's son. Andrew carried six cocoa tins, each with a hole bored in the lid, an electric torch, and a length of fuse. Slouching along, coat collar turned up, one eye directed apprehensively across his shoulder, his mind a whirl of conflicting emotions, he gave only the curtest answers to Denny's brief remarks. He wondered grimly what Lamplough—bland professor of the orthodox—would think of him, involved in this outrageous nocturnal adventure.

Immediately above Glydar Place they reached the main manhole of the sewer, a rusty iron cover set in rotten concrete, and there they set to work. The gangrenous cover had not been disturbed for years but, after a struggle, they prised it up. Then Andrew shone the torch discreetly into the odorous depths, where on the crumbled stonework a dirty stream flowed slimily.

"Pretty, isn't it?" Denny rasped. "Take a look at the cracks in that pointing. Take a *last* look, Manson."

No more was said. Inexplicably, Andrew's mood had changed and he was conscious now of a wild upswing of elation, a determination equal to Denny's own. People were dying of this festering abomination, and petty officialdom had done nothing. It was not the moment for the bedside manner and a niggling bottle of physic!

They began to deal swiftly with the cocoa tins, slipping a stick of dynamite in each. Fuses of graduated lengths were cut and attached. A match flared in the darkness, startling in its harsh illumination of Denny's pale hard face, his own shaking hands. Then the first fuse spluttered. One by one the live cocoa tins were floated down the sluggish current, those with the longest fuses going first.

Andrew could not see clearly. His heart was thudding with excitement. It might not be orthodox medicine, but it was the best moment he had ever known.

As the last tin went in with its short fuse fizzing, Hawkins took it into his head to hunt a rat. There was a breathless interlude, filled with the yapping of the dog and the fearful possibilities of an explosion beneath their feet, while they chased and captured him. Then the manhole cover was flung back and they raced frantically thirty yards up the street.

They had barely reached the corner of Radnor Place and stopped to look round when *bang!* the first can went off.

"By God!" Andrew gasped, exultantly. "We've done it, Denny!" He had a sense of comradeship with the other man, he wanted to grip him by the hand, to shout aloud.

Then swiftly, beautifully, the muffled explosions followed: two, three, four, five, and the last a glorious detonation that must have been at least a quarter of a mile down the Valley.

"There!" said Denny in a suppressed voice, as though all the secret bitterness of his life escaped into that single word. "That's the end of one bit of rottenness!"

He had barely spoken before the commotion broke. Doors and windows were flung open, shedding light upon the darkened roadway. People ran out of their houses. In a minute the street was thronged. At first the cry went up that it was an explosion at the mine. But this was quickly contradicted—the sounds had come from down the Valley. Arguments arose, and shouted speculations. A party of men set out with lanterns to explore. The hubbub and confusion made the night ring. Under cover of the darkness and the noise, Denny and Manson started to dodge home by the back ways. There was a singing triumph in Andrew's blood.

Before eight o'clock next morning Doctor Griffiths arrived upon the scene by car—fat, veal-faced, and verging upon panic, summoned from his warm bed with much blasphemy by Councillor Glyn Morgan. Griffiths might refuse to answer the calls of the local doctors, but there was no denying the angry command of Glyn Morgan. And, indeed, Glyn Morgan had cause for anger. The Councillor's new villa, half a mile down the Valley, had, overnight, become surrounded by a moat of more than mediaeval squalor.

For half an hour the Councillor, supported by his adherents, Hamar Davies and Deawn Roberts, told the Medical Officer, in voices audible to many, exactly what they thought of him.

At the end of it, wiping his forehead, Griffiths tottered over to Denny who, with Manson, stood amongst the interested and edified crowd. Andrew had a sudden qualm at the approach of the Health Officer. A troubled night had left him less elated. In the cold light of morning, abashed by the havoc of the torn-up road, he was again uncomfortable, nervously perturbed.

But Griffiths was in no condition to be suspicious.

"Man, man," he quavered to Philip, "we'll have to get that new sewer for you straight off now."

Denny's face remained expressionless.

"I warned you about that months ago," he said frigidly. "Don't you remember?"

"Yes, yes, indeed! But how was I to guess the wretched thing would blow up this way? It's a mystery to me how it all happened."

Denny looked at him coolly.

"Where's your knowledge of public health, Doctor? Don't you know these sewer gasses are highly inflammable?"

The construction of the new sewer was begun on the following Monday.

V

It was three months later, and a fine March afternoon. The promise of spring scented the soft breeze blowing across the mountains where vague streaks of green defied the dominating, heaped, and quarried ugliness. Under the crisp blue sky even Blaenelly was beautiful.

As he went out to pay a call, which had just come in, at 3 Riskin Street, Andrew felt his heart quicken to the day. Gradually he was becoming acclimatized to this strange town,—primitive and isolated, entombed by the mountains, with no places of amusement, not even a cinema, nothing but its grim mine, its quarries and ore works, its string of chapels and bleak rows of houses,—a queer and silently contained community.

And the people, they also were strange; yet Andrew, though he saw them so alien to himself, could not but feel stirrings of affection towards them. With the exception of the tradesfolk, the preachers, and a few professional people, they were all directly in the employment of the Company. At the end and beginning of each shift, the quiet streets would suddenly awake, re-echoing to steelshod footfalls, unexpectedly alive with an army of marching figures. The clothing, boots, hands, even the faces of those from the haematite mine, bore a bright red powdering of ore dust. The quarrymen wore moleskins with pads and gartered knees. The puddlers were conspicuous in their trousers of blue twill.

They spoke little, and much of what they said was in the Welsh tongue. They had the air, in their self-contained aloofness, of being a race apart. Yet they were a kindly people. Their enjoyments were simple, and were found usually in their own homes, in the chapel halls, on the foreshortened Rugby football ground at the top of the town. Their prevailing passion was, perhaps, a love of music—not the cheap melodies of the moment, but stern, classical music. It was not uncommon for Andrew, walking at night along the rows, to hear the sound of a piano coming from one of these poor homes, a Beethoven sonata or a Chopin prelude, beautifully played, floating through the still air, rising to these inscrutable mountains and beyond.

The position in regard to Doctor Page's practice was now clear to Andrew. Edward Page would never see another patient again. But the men did not like to "go off" Page, who had served them faithfully for over thirty years. And the bold Blodwen, by uniting bluff and cajolery towards Watkins, the mine manager, through whom the workmen's medical contributions were paid, had succeeded in keeping Page on the Company's list, and was in consequence receiving a handsome income—perhaps one sixth of which she paid out to Manson, who did all the work.

Andrew was profoundly sorry for Edward Page. Edward, a gentle, simple soul, had married plump, trim, pert little Blodwen—not knowing what lay behind those dancing sloe-black eyes—out of an Aberystwyth tea-room. Now, broken and bedridden, he was at her mercy, subjected to a treatment which combined blandishment with a kind of jolly bullying. It was not that Blodwen did not love him. She was, in some extraordinary fashion fond of Edward. He, Doctor Page, was hers. Coming into the room while Andrew sat with the sick man, she would advance, smiling apparently, yet with a queer jealous sense of exclusion, exclaiming: "Hey! What are you two talkin' about?"

It was impossible not to love Edward Page, he had so manifestly the spiritual qualities of sacrifice and unselfishness. He would lie there, helpless in bed, a worn-out man, submissive to all the blustering attentions of this bold, dark-faced, impatient woman who was his wife, the victim of her greediness, her persistent and shameless importunity.

There was no need for him to remain in Blaenelly, and he longed to get away to a warmer, kindlier place. Once, when Andrew asked, "Is there anything you'd like, sir?" he had sighed: "I'd like to get out of here, my boy. I've been reading about that island—Capri—they're going to make a bird sanctuary there." Then he had turned his face sideways on the pillow. The longing in his voice was very sad.

The children irritated him. He never spoke of the practice except to say occasionally in a spent voice: "I daresay I didn't know a great deal. Yet I did my best." But he would spend hours lying absolutely still, watching his window sill where Annie every morning devotedly placed crumbs, bacon rind, and grated coconut. On Sunday forenoons an old miner, Enoch Davies, came in, very stiff in his rusty black suit and celluloid dickey, to sit with Page. The two men watched the birds in silence.

On one occasion Andrew met Enoch stamping excitedly downstairs.

"Man alive," burst out the old miner, "we've had a rare fine mornin'! Two bluetits playin' pretty as you please on the sill for the best part of an hour."

Enoch was Page's only friend. He had great influence with the miners. He swore staunchly that not a man would come off the doctor's list so long as he drew breath. He little knew how great a disservice his loyalty was to poor Edward Page.

Another frequent visitor to the house was the manager of the Western Counties Bank, Aneurin Rees, a long dry bald-headed man whom Andrew at first sight distrusted. Rees was a highly respected townsman who never by any chance met anyone's eye. He came to spend a perfunctory five minutes with Doctor Page, and was then closeted for an hour at a time with Mrs. Page. These interviews were perfectly moral. The question under discussion was money. Andrew judged that Blodwen had a great deal of it invested in her own name and that under the admirable direction of Aneurin Rees she was from time to time shrewdly increasing her holdings. Money, at this period, held no significance for Andrew. It was enough that he was regularly paying off his obligation to the Endowment. He had a few shillings in his pocket for cigarettes. Beyond that he had his work.

Now, more than ever, he appreciated how much his clinical work meant to him. It existed, the knowledge, as a warm everpresent inner consciousness which was like a fire at which he warmed himself when he was tired, depressed, perplexed. Lately, indeed, even stranger perplexities had formed and were moving more strongly than before within him. Medically, he had begun to think for himself. Perhaps Denny, with his radical destructive outlook, was mainly responsible for this. Denny's codex was literally the opposite of everything which Manson had been taught. Condensed and framed, it might well have hung, textlike, above his bed: "I do not believe."

Turned out to pattern by his medical school, Manson had faced the future with a well-bound textbook confidence. He had acquired a smattering of physics, chemistry, and biology—at least he had slit up and studied the earthworm. Thereafter he had been dogmatically fed upon the accepted doctrines. He knew all the diseases, with their tabulated symptoms, and the remedies thereof. Take gout, for instance. You could cure it with colchicum. He could still see Professor Lamplough blandly purring to his class, "*Vinum colchici*, gentlemen, twenty to thirty minimum doses, an absolute specific in gout." But was it? That was the question he now asked himself. A month ago he had tried colchicum, pushing it to the limit in a genuine case of "poor man's" gout—a severe and painful case. The result had been dismal failure.

And what about half, three quarters of the other "remedies" in the pharmacopœia? This time he heard the voice of Doctor Eliot, lecturer on *Materia Medica*: "And now, gentlemen, we pass to *elemi*—a concrete resinous exudation, the botanical source of which is undetermined, but is probably *Canarium commune*, chiefly imported from Manila; employed in ointment form, one in five, an admirable stimulant and disinfectant to sores and issues."

Rubbish! Yes, absolute rubbish. He knew that now. Had Eliot ever tried *Unguentum elemi*? He was convinced that Eliot had not. All of that erudite information came out of a book; and that, in its turn, came out of another book; and so on, right back, probably to the Middle Ages. The word "issues," now dead as mutton, confirmed this view.

Denny had sneered at him, that first night, for naïvely compounding a bottle of medicine: Denny always sneered at the medicine compounders, the medicine swillers. Denny held that only half a dozen drugs were any use, the rest he cynically classed as "muck." It was something, that view of Denny's, to wrestle with in the night—a shattering thought, the ramifications of which Andrew could as yet only vaguely comprehend.

At this point in his reflections he arrived at Riskin Street and entered Number 3. Here he found the patient to be a small boy of nine years of age, named Joey Howells, who was exhibiting a mild, seasonal attack of measles. The case was of little consequence; yet, because of the circumstances of the household, which was a poor one, it promised inconvenience to Joey's mother. Howells himself, a day labourer at the quarries, had been laid up three months with pleurisy, for which no compensation was payable; and now Mrs. Howells, a delicate woman, already run off her feet attending to one invalid in addition to her work of cleaning Bethesda Chapel, was called upon to make provision for another.

At the end of his visit, as Andrew stood talking to her at the door of her house, he remarked with regret:—

"You have your hands full. It's a pity you must keep Idris home from school." Idris was Joey's younger brother.

Mrs. Howells raised her head quickly. She was a resigned little woman with shiny red hands and work-swollen finger-knuckles.

"But Miss Barlow said I needn't have him back."

In spite of his sympathy Andrew felt a throb of annoyance.

"Oh?" he inquired. "And who is Miss Barlow?"

"She's the teacher at Bank Street School," said the unsuspecting Mrs. Howells. "She come round to see me this morning. And seein' how hard put I was, she's let little Idris stop on in her class. Goodness knows what I'd have done if I'd had him fallin' over me as well!"

Andrew had a sharp impulse to tell her that she must obey his instructions and not those of a meddling schoolmistress. However, he saw well enough that Mrs. Howells was not to blame. For the moment he made no comment, but as he took his leave and came down Riskin Street his face wore a resentful frown. He hated interference, especially with his work, and beyond everything he hated interfering women. The more he thought of it the angrier he became. It was a distinct contravention of the regulations to keep Idris at school when Joey, his brother, was suffering from measles.

He decided suddenly to call upon this officious Miss Barlow and have the matter out with her.

Five minutes later he ascended the incline of Bank Street, walked into the school, and, having inquired his way of the janitor, found himself outside the classroom of Standard I. He knocked at the door, entered.

It was a large detached room, well-ventilated, with a fire burning at one end. All the children were under seven and, as it was the afternoon break when he entered, each was having a glass of milk—part of an assistance scheme introduced by the local branch of the M. W. U. His eyes fell upon the mistress at once. She was busy writing out sums upon the blackboard, her back towards him, and she did not immediately observe him. But suddenly she turned round.

She was so different from the intrusive female of his indignant fancy that he hesitated. Or perhaps it was the surprise in her brown eyes which made him immediately ill at ease.

He flushed and said: "Are you Miss Barlow?"

"Yes." She was a slight figure in a brown tweed skirt, woollen stockings, and small stout shoes. His own age, he guessed; no, younger—about twenty-two. She inspected him, a little doubtful, faintly smiling, as though, weary of infantile arithmetic, she welcomed distraction on this fine spring day. "Aren't you Doctor Page's new assistant?"

"That's hardly the point," he answered stiffly; "though, as a matter of fact, I am Doctor Manson. I believe you have a contact here: Idris Howells. You know his brother has measles."

There was a pause. Her eyes, though questioning now, were persistently friendly.

Brushing back untidy hair she answered: "Yes, I know."

Her failure to take his visit seriously was sending his temper up again.

"Don't you realize it's quite against the rules to have him here?"

At his tone her colour rose and she lost her air of comradeship. He could not help thinking how clear and fresh her skin was, with a tiny brown mole, exactly the colour of her eyes, high on her right cheek. She was very fragile in her white blouse, and ridiculously young. Now she was breathing rather quickly, yet she spoke slowly:—

"Mrs. Howells was at her wits' end. Most of the children here have had measles. Those that haven't are sure to get it sooner or later. If Idris had stopped off, he'd have missed his milk, which is doing him such a lot of good."

"It isn't a question of his milk," he snapped. "He ought to be isolated."

She answered stubbornly. "I have got him isolated—in a kind of way. If you don't believe me, look for yourself."

He followed her glance. Idris, aged five, at a little desk all by himself near the fire, was looking extraordinarily pleased with life. His pale blue eyes goggled contentedly over the rim of his milk mug.

The sight infuriated Andrew. He laughed contemptuously, offensively.

"That may be your idea of isolation. I'm afraid it isn't mine. You must send that child home at once."

Tiny points of light glinted in her eyes.

"Doesn't it occur to you that I'm the mistress of this class? You may be able to order people about in more exalted spheres. But here it's my word that counts."

He glared at her, with raging dignity.

"You're breaking the law! You can't keep him here. If you do, I'll have to report you."

A short silence followed. He could see her hand tighten on the chalk she held. That sign of her emotion added to his anger against her—yes, against himself.

She said disdainfully: "Then you had better report me. Or have me arrested. I've no doubt it will give you immense satisfaction."

Furious, he did not answer, feeling himself in an utterly false position. He tried to rally himself, raising his eyes, attempting to beat down hers, which now sparkled frostily towards him. For an instant they faced each other, so close he could see the soft beating in her neck, the gleam of her teeth between her parted lips.

Then she said: "There's nothing more, is there?" She swung round tensely to the class. "Stand up children, and say: 'Good morning, Doctor Manson. Thank you for coming.'"

There was a clatter of chairs as the infants rose and chanted her ironic bidding. His ears were burning as she escorted him to the door. He had an exasperating sense of discomfiture, and added to it the wretched suspicion that he had behaved badly in losing his temper while she had so admirably controlled hers. He sought for a crushing phrase, some final intimidating repartee. But before that came the door closed quietly in his face.

vi

Manson, after a furious evening during which he composed and tore up three vitriolic letters to the Medical Officer of Health, tried to forget about the episode. His sense of humour, momentarily lost in the vicinity of Bank Street, made him impatient with himself because of his display of petty feeling. Following a sharp struggle with his stiff Scots pride, he decided he had been wrong, he could not dream of reporting the case, least of all to the ineffable Griffiths. Yet, though he made the attempt, he could not so easily dismiss Christine Barlow from his mind.

It was absurd that a juvenile schoolmistress should so insistently occupy his thoughts or that he should be concerned by what she might think of him. He told himself that it was a stupid case of injured pride. He knew that he was shy and awkward with women. Yet no amount of logic could alter the fact that he was now restless and a little irritable. At unguarded moments, as for example when he was falling off to sleep, the scene in the classroom would flash back to him with renewed vividness and he would find himself frowning in the darkness. He still saw her, crushing the chalk, her brown eyes warm with indignation. There were three small pearly buttons on the front of her blouse. Her figure was thin and agile, with a firm economy of line which spoke to him of much hard running and dauntless skipping in her childhood. He did not ask himself if she were pretty. It was enough that she stood, spare and living, before the screen of his sight. And his heart would turn unwillingly, with a kind of sweet oppression which he had never known before.

A fortnight later he was walking down Chapel Street in a fit of abstraction when he almost bumped into Mrs. Bramwell at the corner of Station Road. He would have gone on without recognizing her. She, however, stopped at once, and hailed him, dazzling him with her smile.

"Why, Doctor Manson! The very man I'm looking for. I'm giving one of my little social evenings to-night. You'll come, won't you?"

Gladys Bramwell was a corn-haired lady of thirty-five, showily dressed, with a full figure, baby-blue eyes and girlish ways. Gladys described herself romantically as a man's woman. The gossips of Blaenelly used another word. Doctor Bramwell doted upon her, and it was rumoured that only his blind fondness prevented him from observing her more than skittish preoccupation with Doctor Gabell, the "coloured" doctor from Toniglan.

As Andrew scanned her, he sought hurriedly for an evasion.

"I'm afraid, Mrs. Bramwell, I can't possibly get away to-night."

"But you must, silly. I've got such nice people coming. Mr. and Mrs. Watkins from the mine and," a conscious smile escaped her, "Doctor Gabell from Toniglan—oh, and I almost forgot, the little schoolteacher, Christine Barlow."

A shiver passed over Manson.

He smiled foolishly.

"Why, of course I'll come, Mrs. Bramwell. Thank you very much for asking me." He managed to sustain her conversation for a few moments until she departed. But for the remainder of the day he could think of nothing but the fact that he was going to see

Christine Barlow again.

Mrs. Bramwell's "evening" began at nine o'clock, the late hour being chosen out of consideration for the medical gentlemen who might be detained at their surgeries. It was, in fact, quarter-past nine when Andrew finished his last consultation. Hurriedly, he splashed himself in the surgery sink, tugged back his hair with the broken comb, and hastened to The Retreat. He reached the house—which, belying its idyllic name, was a small brick dwelling in the middle of the town—to find that he was the last arrival. Mrs. Bramwell, chiding him brightly, led the way, followed by her five guests and her husband, into supper.

It was a cold meal, spread out on paper doilies on the fumed-oak table. Mrs. Bramwell prided herself upon being a hostess, something of a leader in style in Blaenelly, which permitted her to shock public opinion by "doing herself up," and her idea of "making things go" was to talk and laugh a great deal. She always implied that her background, before her marriage to Doctor Bramwell, had been one of excessive luxury.

To-night, as they sat down, she glittered: "Now! Has everybody got what they want?"

Andrew, breathless from his haste, was at first deeply embarrassed. For a full ten minutes he dared not look at Christine. He kept his eyes lowered, overpoweringly conscious of her sitting at the far end of the table between Doctor Gabell—a dark-complexioned dandy in spats, striped trousers, and pearl pin—and Mr. Watkins, the elderly scrubby-headed mine manager who, in his blunt fashion, was making much of her. At last, driven by a laughing allusion from Watkins,—"Are ye still my Yorkshire lass, Miss Christine?"—Andrew lifted his head jealously, looked at her, found her so intimately there, in a soft grey dress with white at the neck and cuffs, that he was stricken and withdrew his eyes lest she should read them.

Defensively, scarcely knowing what he said, he began to devote himself to his neighbour, Mrs. Watkins, a little wisp of a woman who had brought her knitting.

For the remainder of the meal he endured the anguish of talking to one person when he longed to talk to another.

He could have sighed with relief when Doctor Bramwell, presiding at the top of the table, viewed the cleared plates benevolently and made a Napoleonic gesture.

"I think, my dear, we have all finished. Shall we adjourn to the drawing-room?"

In the drawing-room, when the guests were variously disposed,—chiefly upon the three-piece suite,—it was plain that music was expected in the order of the evening. Bramwell beamed fondly on his wife and led her to the piano.

"What shall we oblige with first to-night, my love?" Humming, he fingered amongst the music on the stand.

"'Temple Bells'," Gabell suggested. "I never get tired of that one, Mrs. Bramwell."

Seating herself on the revolving music-stool, Mrs. Bramwell played and sang while her husband, one hand behind his back, the other advanced as in the motion of snuff-taking, stood beside her and deftly turned the sheets. Gladys had a full contralto voice, bringing all her deep notes up from her bosom with a lifting motion of her chin. After the Love Lyrics she gave them "Wandering By" and "Just a Girl."

There was generous applause. Bramwell murmured absently, in a pleased undertone: "She's in fine voice to-night."

Doctor Gabell was then persuaded to his feet. Fiddling with his ring, smoothing his well-oiled but still traitorous hair, the olive-skinned buck bowed affectedly towards his hostess, and, clasping his hands well in front of him, bellowed fruitily "Love in Sweet Seville." Then, as an encore, he gave "Toreador."

"You sing these songs about Spain with real go, Doctor Gabell," commented the kindly Mrs. Watkins.

"It's my Spanish blood, I suppose," laughed Gabell modestly, as he resumed his seat.

Andrew saw an impish glint in Watkins' eye. The old mine manager, a true Welshman, knew music, had last winter helped his men to produce one of Verdi's more obscure operas, and now, dormant behind his pipe, was enjoying himself enigmatically. Andrew could not help thinking that it must afford Watkins deep amusement to observe these strangers to his native town affecting to dispense culture in the shape of worthless, sentimental ditties. When Christine smilingly refused to perform, Watkins turned to her with a twitch to his lips.

"You're like me, I reckon, my dear. Too fond of the piano to play it."

Then the high light of the evening shone. Doctor Bramwell took the centre of the stage. Clearing his throat, he struck out one foot, threw back his head, placed his hand histrionically inside his coat. He announced: "Ladies and gentlemen—'The Fallen Star. A Musical Monologue.'" At the piano, Gladys started to vamp a sympathetic accompaniment, and Bramwell began.

The recitation, which dealt with the pathetic vicissitudes of a once-famous actress now come to dire poverty, was glutinous with sentiment, and Bramwell gave it with soulful anguish. When the drama rose Gladys pressed bass chords. When the pathos oozed she tinkled on the treble. As the climax came, Bramwell drew himself up, his voice breaking on the final line, "There she was"—A pause—"starving in the gutter..." A long pause. "Only a fallen star!"

Little Mrs. Watkins, her knitting fallen to the floor, turned damp eyes towards him.

"Poor thing, poor thing! Oh, Doctor Bramwell, you always do that most beautiful."

The arrival of the claret-cup created a diversion. By this time it was after eleven o'clock, and, on the tacit understanding that anything following Bramwell's effort would be sheer anticlimax, the party prepared to break up. There were laughter, polite expressions of thanks, and a movement towards the hall. As Andrew pulled on his coat, he reflected miserably that he had not exchanged a word with Christine all night.

Outside, he stood at the gate. He felt that he must speak to her. The thought of the long wasted evening, in which he had meant so easily, so pleasantly, to put things right between them, weighed on him like lead. Though she had not seemed to look at him, she had been there, near him, in the same room, and he had kept his eyes doltishly upon his boots. "Oh, Lord!" he thought wretchedly, "I'm worse than the fallen star. I'd better get home and go to bed."

But he did not. He remained there, his pulse racing suddenly as she came down the steps and walked towards him, alone.

He gathered all his strength and stammered: "Miss Barlow—May I see you home?"

"I'm afraid—" She paused. "I've promised to wait for Mr. and Mrs. Watkins."

His heart sank. He felt like turning away, a beaten dog. Yet something still held him. His face was pale, but his chin had a firm line. The words came tumbling one upon another with a rush.

"I only want to say that I'm sorry about the Howells affair. I came round to give a cheap exhibition of authority. I ought to be kicked—hard. What you did about the kid was splendid. I admire you for it. After all, it's better to observe the spirit than the letter of the law. Sorry to bother you with all this, but I had to say it. Good night!"

He could not see her face. Nor did he wait for her answer. He swung round and walked down the road. For the first time in many days he felt happy.

vii

The half-yearly return of the practice had come in from the Company offices, giving Mrs. Page matter for serious reflection and another topic to discuss with Aneurin Rees, the bank manager. For the first time in eighteen months the figures showed an upward jump. There were over seventy more men on "Doctor Page's list" than there had been before Manson's arrival.

Delighted with the increase in her cheque, Blodwen nevertheless nursed a most disturbing thought. At mealtimes Andrew caught her unguardedly fixing him with an inquiring, suspicious stare.

On the Wednesday following Mrs. Bramwell's social evening, Blodwen came bustling into lunch with a great display of gaiety.

"I declare!" she remarked. "I just been thinkin'. It's near on four months since you been here, Doctor. And you 'aven't done too bad, neither. I'm not complainin'. Mind you, it isn't like Doctor Page himself. Oh, dear, no! Mr. Watkins was only sayin' the other day how they was all lookin' forward to Doctor Page comin' back. Doctor Page is so clever, says Mr. Watkins to me, we wouldn't never dream of havin' anybody in his place."

She laid herself out to describe, in picturesque detail, the extraordinary skill and ability of her husband. "You wouldn't believe it," she exclaimed, widening her eyes. "There's nothing he can't do or hasn't done. Operations! You ought to have seen them. Let me tell you this, Doctor, once he took a man's brains out and put them back again. Yes! look at me if you like, Doctor Page scraped these brains and put them back again."

She lay back in her chair and gazed at him, trying to read the effect of her words. Then she smiled confidently.

"There'll be great rejoicings in Blaenelly when Doctor Page gets back to work. And it'll be soon, too. In the summer, says I to Mr. Watkins, in the summer Doctor Page will be back."

Returning from his afternoon round towards the end of the same week, Andrew was shocked to find Edward huddled in a chair by the front porch, fully dressed, a rug over his knees and a cap stuck rakishly on his shaking head. A sharp wind was blowing and the gleam of April sunshine which bathed the tragic figure was pale and cold.

"There, now," cried Mrs. Page, bustling triumphantly towards Manson from the porch. "You see, don't you? Doctor's *up*! I've just telephoned Mr. Watkins to tell him Doctor's better. He'll soon be back at work, won't you, ducky?"

Andrew felt the blood rush to his brow.

"Who got him down here?"

"I did," said Blodwen defiantly; "and why not? He's my husband. And he's better."

"He's not fit to be up, and you know it." Andrew threw the words at her in a low tone. "Do as I tell you. Help me get him back to bed at once."

"Yes, yes," Edward said feebly. "Get me back to bed. I'm cold. I'm not right. I—I don't feel well." And to Manson's distress the sick man began to whimper.

Instantly Blodwen was in floods of tears beside him.

Down on her knees she flopped, her arms around him, contrite, slobbering: "There,

there now, ducky. You shall go back to bed, poor lamb. Blodwen'll do it for you. Blodwen'll take care of you. Blodwen loves you, ducky."

She smacked wet kisses on his stiff cheek.

Half an hour later, with Edward upstairs and comfortable again, Andrew came to the kitchen, raging.

Annie was now a genuine friend: many a confidence they had exchanged in this same kitchen and many an apple and currant griddlecake the quietly contained middle-aged woman had slipped out of the larder for him when rations were extra tight. Sometimes, indeed, as a last resort, she would run down to Thomas' for a double fish supper and they would banquet sumptuously by candlelight at the scullery table.

Annie had been at Pages' for nearly twenty years. She had many relations in Blaenelly, all tidy folk, and her only reason for remaining so long in service was her devotion to Doctor Page.

"Give me my tea in here, Annie," Andrew now declared. "I can't stand any more of Blodwen at the moment."

He was in the kitchen before he realized that Annie had visitors—her sister Olwen and Olwen's husband, Emrys Hughes. He had met them several times before. Emrys was a shot-firer in the Blaenelly High Levels, a solid good-natured man with pale, thickened features.

As Manson, seeing them, hesitated, Olwen, a spry dark-eyed young woman, took an impulsive breath.

"Don't mind us, Doctor, if you want your tea. As a matter of fact, we were just talkin' about you when you came in."

"Yes?"

"Yes, indeed!" Olwen darted a glance at her sister. "It's no use your lookin' at me that way, Annie, I'll speak what's in my mind. All the men are talkin', Doctor Manson, about how they haven't had such a good young doctor as you for years, about how you take trouble to examine them, and all. You can ask Emrys if you don't believe me. And they're fair mad about how Mrs. Page is puttin' on them. They say you ought to 'ave the practice by rights. And she's 'eard that talk, mind you; that's why she got poor old Doctor Page up this afternoon. Pretendin' he was better, indeed, poor old feller!"

When he had finished his tea Andrew withdrew. Olwen's downright speech made him feel ill at ease. Yet it was flattering to be told that the people of Blaenelly liked him. And he took it as an especial tribute when, a few days later, Joe Morgan, a foreman driller at the haematite mine, came to see him with his wife.

The Morgans were a middle-aged couple, not well-off, but highly thought of in the district; they had been married for nearly twenty years. Andrew had heard that they were leaving shortly for South Africa, where Morgan had the promise of work in the Johannesburg mines. It was not unusual for good drillers to be tempted out to the gold mines on the Rand, where the drill work was similar and the pay much better. Yet no one was more surprised than Andrew when Morgan, seated in the little surgery with his wife, self-consciously explained the purpose of their visit.

"Well, sir, we have done it, at last, it seems. The missus here is goin' to have a baby. After nineteen year, mark you. We are plain delighted, man. And we've decided to put off our leavin' till after the event. For we've been thinkin' about doctors like, and we come to the conclusion that you're the one we must have to handle the case. It means a lot to us, Doctor. It'll be a hard job too, I fancy. Missus here is forty-three. Yes, indeed. But there, now, we know you'll give us every satisfaction."

Andrew entered up the case with a warm sense of having been honoured. It was a strange emotion, clear and without material origin, which in his present state was doubly comforting. Lately he had felt lost, completely desolate. Extraordinary currents were moving within him, disturbing and painful. There were times when his heart held a strange dull ache which, as a mature bachelor of medicine, he had hitherto believed impossible.

He had never before thought seriously of love. At the University he had been too poor, too badly dressed and far too intent on getting through his examinations to come much in contact with the other sex. At St. Andrews one had to be a blood, like his friend and classmate Freddie Hampton, to move in that circle which danced and held parties and exhibited the social graces. All this had been denied him. He had really belonged—his friendship with Hampton apart—to that crowd of outsiders who turned up their coat collars, swotted, smoked, and took their occasional recreation not at the Union but in a downtown billiard saloon.

It is true that the inevitable romantic images had presented themselves to him. Because of his poverty these were usually projected against a lavishly wealthy background. But now, in Blaenelly, he stared through the window of the ramshackle surgery, his clouded eyes fastened upon the dirty slag-heap of the ore works, longing with all his heart for the skimpy junior mistress of a council school. The bathos of it made him want to laugh.

He had always prided himself on being practical, upon his strong infusion of native caution; and he attempted, violently and with determined self-interest, to argue himself out of his emotion. He tried, coldly and logically, to examine her defects. She was not beautiful, her figure was too small and thin. She had that mole upon her cheek, and a slight crinkling, visible when she smiled, in her upper lip. In addition she probably detested him.

He told himself angrily that he was utterly ill-advised to give way to his feelings in this weak fashion. He had dedicated himself to his work. He was still only an assistant. What kind of doctor was he, to form, at the very outset of his career, an attachment which must hamper her future and was even now seriously interfering with his work?

In the effort to take himself in hand, he created loopholes of distraction. Deluding himself that he was missing the old associations of St. Andrews, he wrote a long letter to Freddie Hampton, who had lately gone down to a hospital appointment in London. He fell back, a great deal, upon Denny. But Philip, though sometimes friendly, was more often cold, suspicious, with the bitterness of a man whom life has hurt.

Try as he would Andrew could not get Christine out of his mind, nor that tormenting yearning for her from his heart. He had not seen her since his outburst at the front gate of The Retreat. What did she think of him? Did she ever think of him? It was so long since he had seen her, despite an eager scanning of Bank Street when he passed it, that he despaired of seeing her at all.

Then, on the afternoon of Saturday, May 25, when he had almost given up hope, he received a note which ran as follows:—

Dear Doctor Manson,
   Mr. and Mrs. Watkins are coming to supper with me tomorrow, Sunday evening. If you have nothing better to do, would you care to come too? Half-past seven.
                                                                Sincerely,
                                                    CHRISTINE BARLOW

He gave a cry which brought Annie hurrying from the scullery.

"Eh, Doctor, *bach*,"—reprovingly,—"sometimes you do act sil-ly."

"I have, Annie," he answered, still overcome. "But I—I seem to have got off with it. Listen, Annie, dear. Will you press my trousers for me before to-morrow? I'll sling them outside my door to-night when I go to bed."

On the following evening which, being Sunday, left him free of the evening surgery, he presented himself in tremulous expectation at the house of Mrs. Herbert, with whom Christine lodged, near the Institute. He was early and he knew it, but he could not wait a moment longer.

It was Christine herself who opened the door for him, her face welcoming, smiling towards him.

Yes, she was smiling, actually smiling. And he had felt that she disliked him! He was so overwhelmed he could barely speak.

"It's been a lovely day, hasn't it?" he mumbled as he followed her into her sitting-room.

"Lovely," she agreed. "And I had such a grand walk this afternoon. Right out beyond Pandy. I actually found some celandines."

They sat down. It was on his tongue to inquire nervously if she enjoyed walking, but he nipped the gauche futility in time.

"Mrs. Watkins has just sent word," she remarked. "She and her husband will be a little late. He's had to go down to the office. You don't mind waiting a few minutes on them?"

Mind! A few minutes! He could have laughed out of sheer happiness. If only she knew how he had waited all those days, how wonderful it was to be here with her. Surreptitiously, he looked about him. Her sitting-room, furnished with her own things, was different from any room he had entered in Blaenelly. It held neither plush nor horsehair nor Axminster, nor any of those shiny satin cushions which conspicuously adorned Mrs. Bramwell's drawing-room. The floorboards were stained and polished, with a plain brown rug before the open fireplace. The furniture was so unobtrusive he scarcely noticed it. In the centre of the table, set for supper, was a plain white dish in which floated, like masses of tiny water lilies, the celandines she had gathered. The effect was simple and beautiful. On the window sill stood a wooden confectionery box, now filled with earth, from which thin green seedlings were sprouting. Above the mantelpiece was a most peculiar picture, which showed nothing more than a child's small wooden chair, painted red and, he thought, extremely badly drawn.

She must have noticed the surprise with which he viewed it. She smiled with infectious amusement.

"I hope you don't think it's the original!"

Embarrassed, he did not know what to say. The expression of her personality through the room, the conviction that she knew things which were beyond him, confounded him. Yet his interest was so awakened he forgot his awkwardness, escaped from the stupid banalities of remarks about the weather. He began to ask her about herself.

She answered him simply. She was from Yorkshire. Her mother had died when she was fifteen. Her father had then been under-manager at one of the big Bramwell Main Collieries. Her only brother, John, had been trained in the same colliery as a mining engineer. Five years later, when she was nineteen and her Normal course completed, her father had been appointed manager of the Porth Pit twenty miles down the Valley. She and her brother had come to South Wales with him, she to keep the house, John to assist his father. Six months after their arrival, there had been an explosion in the Porth Pit. John had been underground, killed instantly. Her father, hearing of the disaster, had immediately gone down, only to be met by a rush of black damp. A week later his body and John's were brought out together.

When she concluded there was a silence.

"I'm sorry," Andrew said in a sympathetic voice.

"People were kind to me," she said soberly. "Mr. and Mrs. Watkins especially. I got this job at school here." She paused, her face lighting up again. "I'm like you, though. I'm still strange here. It takes a long time to get used to the Valleys."

He looked at her, searching for something which would even faintly express his feeling for her, a remark which might tactfully dispose of the past and hopefully open out the future.

"It's easy to feel cut off down here, lonely. I know. I do often. I often feel I want someone to talk to."

She smiled. "What do you want to talk about?"

He reddened, with a sense that she had cornered him. "Oh, my work, I suppose." He halted, then felt obliged to explain himself. "I seem just to be blundering about, running into one problem after another."

"Do you mean you have difficult cases?"

"It isn't that." He hesitated, went on. "I came down here full of formulae, the things that everybody believes, or pretends to believe. That swollen joints mean rheumatism... That rheumatism means salicylate... You know, the orthodox things! Well, I'm finding out that some of them are all wrong. Take medicine, too... It seems to me that some of it does more harm than good. It's the system. A patient comes into the surgery. He expects his 'bottle of medicine.' And he gets it, even if it's only burnt sugar, soda bicarb. and good old *aqua*. That's why the prescription is written in Latin—so he won't understand it. It isn't right. It isn't scientific. And another thing: It seems to me that too many doctors treat disease empirically—that's to say, they treat the symptoms individually. They don't bother to combine the symptoms in their own mind and puzzle out the diagnosis. They say—very quick, because they're usually in a rush—'Ah! headache—try this powder!' Or 'You're anaemic, you must have some iron.' Instead of asking themselves what is *causing* the headache or the anaemia—" He broke off sharply. "Oh! I'm sorry! I'm boring you!"

"No, no," she said quickly. "It's awfully interesting."

"I'm just beginning, just feeling my way," he went on tempestuously, thrilled by her interest. "But I do honestly think, even from what I've seen, that the textbooks I was brought up on have too many old-fashioned conservative ideas in them. Remedies that are no use, symptoms that were shoved in by somebody in the Middle Ages. You might say it doesn't matter to the average G.P. But why should the general practitioner be no more than a poultice mixer or a medicine slinger? It's time science was brought into the front line. A lot of people think that science lies in the bottom of a test tube. I don't. I believe that the outlying G.P.'s have all the opportunities to *see* things, and a better chance to observe the first symptoms of new disease, than they have at any of the hospitals. By the time a case gets to hospital it's usually past the early stages."

She was about to answer quickly when the doorbell rang. She rose, suppressing her remark, saying instead, with her faint smile:—

"I hope you won't forget your promise to talk of this another time."

Watkins and his wife came in, apologizing for being late. And almost at once they sat down to supper.

It was a very different meal from that cold collation which had last brought them together. There was veal cooked in a casserole, and there were potatoes mashed with butter, followed by new rhubarb tart with cream, then cheese and coffee. Though plain, every dish was good and there was plenty of it.

After the skimpy meals served to him by Blodwen, it was a great treat to Andrew to find hot appetizing food before him. He sighed:

"You're lucky in your landlady, Miss Barlow. She's a marvellous cook!"

Watkins, who had been observing Andrew's trencherwork with a quizzical eye, suddenly laughed out loud.

"That's a good one." He turned to his wife. "Did you hear him, Mother? He says old Mrs. Herbert's a marvellous cook!"

Christine coloured slightly.

"Don't pay any attention to him," she said to Andrew. "It's the nicest compliment I've ever had—because you didn't mean it as such. At it happens, I cooked the supper. I have the run of Mrs. Herbert's kitchen. I like doing for myself. And I'm used to it."

Her remark served to make the mine manager more jovially boisterous. He was quite changed from the taciturn individual who had stoically endured the entertainment at Mrs. Bramwell's. Blunt and likeably common, he enjoyed his supper, smacked his lips over the tart, put his elbows on the table, told stories which made them laugh.

The evening passed quickly. When Andrew looked at his watch he saw to his amazement that it was nearly eleven o'clock. And he had promised to pay a late visit to a case in Blaina Place before half-past ten!

As he rose, regretfully, to take his leave, Christine accompanied him to the door. In the narrow passage his arm touched her side. A pang of sweetness went over him. She was so different from anyone he had ever known, with her quietness, her fragility, her dark intelligent eyes. Heaven forgive him for daring to have thought her skimpy!

Breathing quickly, he mumbled: "I can't thank you enough for asking me to-night. Please can I see you again? I don't always talk shop. Would you—Christine, would you come to the Toniglan cinema with me, sometime?"

Her eyes smiled up at him, for the first time faintly provocative.

"You try asking me."

A long silent minute on the doorstep under the high stars... The dew scented air was cool on his hot cheek. Her breath came sweetly towards him. He longed to kiss her. Fumblingly he pressed her hand, turned, clattered down the path and was on his way home with dancing thoughts, walking on air along that dizzy path which millions have tritely followed and still believed themselves unique, rapturously predestined, eternally blessed. Oh, she was a wonderful girl! How well she had understood his meaning when he spoke of his difficulties in practice! She was clever, far cleverer than he. What a marvellous cook, too! And he had called her Christine!

viii

Though Christine now occupied his mind more than ever, the whole complexion of his thoughts was altered. He no longer felt despondent, but happy, elated, hopeful. And this change of outlook was immediately reflected in his work. He was young enough to create in fancy a constant situation wherein she observed him at his cases, watched his careful methods, his scrupulous examinations, commended him for the searching accuracy of his diagnosis. Any temptation to scamp a visit, to reach a conclusion without first sounding the patient's chest, was met by the instant thought: "Lord, no! What would she think of me if I did that?"

More than once he found Denny's eye upon him, satirical, comprehensive. But he did not care. In his intense, idealistic way he linked Christine with his ambitions, made her unconsciously an extra incentive in the great assault upon the unknown.

He admitted to himself that he still knew practically nothing. Yet he was teaching himself to think for himself, to look behind the obvious in an effort to find the proximate cause. Never before had he felt himself so powerfully attracted to the scientific ideal. He prayed that he might never become slovenly or mercenary, never jump to conclusions, never come to write "the mixture as before." He wanted to find out, to be scientific, to be worthy of Christine.

In the face of this ingenuous eagerness it seemed a pity that his work in the practice should suddenly and uniformly turn dull. He wanted to scale mountains. Yet for the next few weeks he was presented by a series of insignificant molehills. His cases were trivial, supremely uninteresting, a banal run of sprains, cut fingers, colds in the head. The climax came when he was called two miles down the valley by an old woman who asked him, peering yellow-faced from beneath her flannel mutch, to cut her corns.

He felt foolish, chafed at his lack of opportunity, longed for whirlwind and tempest.

He began to question his own faith, to wonder if it were really possible for a doctor in this out-of-the-way place to be anything more than a petty, common hack. And then, at the lowest ebb of all, came an incident which sent the mercury of his belief soaring once again towards the skies.

Towards the end of the last week in June, as he came over the station bridge, he encountered Doctor Bramwell. The Silver King was slipping out of the side door of the Railway Inn, stealthily wiping his upper lip with the back of his hand. He had the habit, when Gladys departed, gay and dressed in her best, upon her enigmatic "shopping" expeditions to Toniglan, of soothing himself unobtrusively with a pint or two of beer.

A trifle discomfited at being seen by Andrew, he nevertheless carried off the situation with a flourish.

"Ah, Manson! Glad to see you. I just had a call to Pritchard."

Pritchard was the proprietor of the Railway Inn—and Andrew had seen him five minutes ago, taking his bull terrier for a walk. But he allowed the opportunity to pass. He had an affection for the Silver King, whose high-flown language and mock heroics were offset in a very human way by his timidity, and the holes in his socks which the gay Gladys forgot to darn.

As they walked up the street together they began to talk shop. Bramwell was always ready to discuss his cases and now, with an air of gravity, he told Andrew that Emrys Hughes, Annie's brother-in-law, was on his hands. Emrys, he said, had been acting strangely lately, getting into trouble at the mine, losing his memory. He had turned quarrelsome and violent.

"I don't like it, Manson," Bramwell nodded sagely. "I've seen mental trouble before. And this looks uncommonly like it."

Andrew expressed his concern. He had always thought Hughes a stolid and agreeable fellow. He recollected that Annie had looked worried lately and when questioned had implied vaguely—for despite her proclivity for gossip she was reticent upon family affairs—that she was anxious about her brother-in-law. When he parted from Bramwell he ventured the hope that the case might quickly take a turn for the better.

But on the following Friday, at six o'clock in the morning, he was awakened by a knocking on his bedroom door. It was Annie, fully dressed and very red about the eyes, offering him a note.

Andrew tore open the envelope. It was a message from Doctor Bramwell:—

Come round at once. I want you to help certify a dangerous lunatic.

Annie struggled with her tears.

"It's Emrys, Doctor, *bach*. A dreadful thing has happened. I do hope you'll come down quick, like."

Andrew threw on his things in three minutes. Accompanying him down the road, Annie told him as best she could about Emrys. He had been ill and unlike himself for three weeks, but during the night he had turned violent, and gone clean out of his mind. He had set upon his wife with a breadknife. Olwen had just managed to escape by running into the street in her nightgown. The sensational story was sufficiently distressing as Annie brokenly related it, hurrying beside him in the grey light of morning, and there seemed little he could add, by way of consolation, to alter it. They reached the Hughes's house. In the front room Andrew found Doctor Bramwell, unshaven, without his collar and tie, wearing a serious air, seated at the table, pen in hand. Before him was a bluish paper form, half filled in.

"Ah, Manson! Good of you to come so quickly. A bad business this. But it won't keep you long."

"What's up?"

"Hughes has gone mad. I think I mentioned to you a week ago I was afraid of it. Well! I was right. Acute mania." Bramwell rolled the words over his tongue with tragic grandeur. "Acute homicidal mania. We'll have to get him into Pontynewdd straight away. That means two signatures on the certificate, mine and yours—the relatives wanted me to call you in. You know the procedure, don't you?"

"Yes." Andrew nodded. "What's your evidence?"

Bramwell began, clearing his throat, to read what he had written upon the form. It was a full, flowing account of certain of Hughes's actions during the previous week, all of them conclusive of mental derangement. At the end of it Bramwell raised his head. "Clear evidence, I think!"

"It sounds pretty bad," Andrew answered slowly. "Well! I'll take a look at him."

"Thanks, Manson. You'll find me here when you're finished." And he began to add further particulars to the form.

Emrys Hughes was in bed, and seated beside him—in case restraint should be necessary—were two of his mates from the mine. Standing by the foot of the bed was Olwen, her pale face, ordinarily so pert and lively, now ravaged by weeping. Her attitude was so overwrought, the atmosphere of the room so dim and tense, that Andrew had a momentary thrill of coldness, almost of fear.

He went over to Emrys, and at first he hardly recognized him. The change was not gross; it was Emrys true enough, but a blurred and altered Emrys, his features coarsened in some subtle way. His face seemed swollen, the nostrils thickened, the skin waxy, except for a faint reddish patch that spread across the nose. His whole appearance was heavy, apathetic. Andrew spoke to him. He muttered an unintelligible reply. Then, clenching his hands, he came out with a tirade of aggressive nonsense, which, added to Bramwell's account, made the case for his removal only too conclusive.

A silence followed. Andrew felt that he ought to be convinced. Yet, inexplicably, he was not satisfied. Why, why, he kept asking himself, *why* should Hughes talk like this? Supposing the man had gone out of his mind, what was the cause of it all? He had always been a happy, contented man—no worries, easygoing, amicable. Why, without apparent reason, had he changed to *this*?

There must be a reason, Manson thought doggedly; symptoms don't just happen of themselves. Staring at the swollen features before him, puzzling, puzzling for some solution of the conundrum, he instinctively reached out and touched the swollen face, noting subconsciously, as he did so, that the pressure of his finger left no dent in the oedematous cheek.

All at once, electrically, a terminal vibrated in his brain. *Why* didn't the swelling pit on pressure? Because—now it was his heart which jumped!—because it was not true oedema, but myxoedema. He had it, by God, he *had* it! No, no, he must not rush. Firmly, he caught hold of himself. He must not be a plunger, wildly leaping to conclusions. He must go cautiously, slowly, be sure!

Curbing himself, he lifted Emrys' hand. Yes, the skin was dry and rough, the fingers slightly thickened at the ends. Temperature—it was subnormal. Methodically he finished the examination, fighting back each successive wave of elation. Every sign and every symptom—they fitted as superbly as a complex jigsaw puzzle. The clumsy speech, dry skin, spatulate fingers, the swollen inelastic face, the defective memory, slow mentation, the attacks of irritability culminating in an outburst of homicidal violence. Oh! the triumph of the completed picture was sublime.

Rising, he went down to the parlour, where Doctor Bramwell, standing on the hearthrug with his back to the fire, greeted him:—

"Well? Satisfied? The pen's on the table."

"Look here, Bramwell—" Andrew kept his eyes averted, battling to keep impetuous triumph from his voice. "I don't think we ought to certify Hughes."

"Eh, what?" Gradually the blankness left Bramwell's face. He exclaimed in hurt astonishment: "But the man's out of his mind!"

"That's not my view," Andrew answered in a level tone, still stopping down his excitement, his elation. It was not enough that he had diagnosed the case. He must handle Bramwell gently, try not to antagonize him. "In my opinion Hughes is only sick in mind because he's sick in body. I feel that he's suffering from thyroid deficiency—an absolutely straight case of myxœdema."

Bramwell stared at Andrew glassily. Now, indeed, he was dumbfounded. He made several efforts to speak—a queer sound, like snow falling off a roof.

"After all," Andrew went on persuasively, his eyes on the hearthrug, "Pontynewdd is such a sink of a place. Once Hughes gets in there he'll never get out. And if he does he'll carry the stigma of it all his life. Suppose we try pushing thyroid into him first?"

"Why, Doctor," Bramwell quavered, "I don't see—"

"Think of the credit for you," Andrew cut in quickly. "If you should get him well again. Don't you think it's worth it? Come on now, I'll call in Mrs. Hughes. She's crying her eyes out because she thinks Emrys is going away. You can explain we're going to try a new treatment."

Before Bramwell could protest Andrew went out of the room. A few minutes later, when he came back with Mrs. Hughes, the Silver King had recovered himself. Planted on the hearthrug he informed Olwen in his best manner "that there might still be a ray of hope" while, behind his back, Andrew made a neat tight ball of the certificate and threw it in the fire. Then he went out to telephone to Cardiff for thyroid.

There was a period of quivering anxiety, several days of agonized suspense, before Hughes began to respond to the treatment. But once it had started, that response was magical. Emrys was out of bed in a fortnight, and back at his work at the end of two months. He came round one evening to the surgery at Bryngower, lean and active, accompanied by the smiling Olwen, to tell Andrew he had never felt better in his life.

Olwen said:—

"We owe everything to you, Doctor. We want to change over to you from Bramwell. Emrys was on his list before I married him. He's just a silly old woman. He's have had my Emrys in the—well, you know what—if it hadn't been for you and all you've done for us."

"You *can't* change, Olwen," Andrew answered. "It would spoil everything." He dropped his professional gravity and broke into genuine youthful glee. "If you even try to—I'll come after you with that breadknife."

Bramwell, meeting Andrew in the street, remarked airily:—

"Hello, Manson! You've seen Hughes about, I suppose. Ha! They're both very grateful. I flatter myself I've never had a better case."

Annie said:—

"That ol' Bramwell, struttin' about the town like he was somebodee. He don't know nothing. And his wife, bah! She can't keep her servants no time."

Mrs. Page said:—

"Doctor, don't forget you're workin' for Doctor Page."

Denny's comment was:—

"Manson! At present you're too conceited to live with. You're going to make a most hell of a bloomer. Soon. Very soon."

But Andrew, hurrying to Christine full of the triumph of the scientific method, kept everything he had to say for her.

ix

In July of that year the Annual Conference of the British Medical Union was held in Cardiff. The Union, to which, as Professor Lamplough always informed his students in his final address, every reputable medical man ought to belong, was famous for its Annual Conferences. Splendidly organized, these Conferences offered sporting, social, and scientific enjoyments to members and their families, reduced terms at all but the best hotels, free charabanc trips to any ruined Abbey in the neighbourhood, a memento art brochure, souvenir diaries from the leading Surgical Appliance Makers and Drug Houses, and pumproom facilities at the nearest spa. The previous year, at the end of the week's festivity, generous free sample boxes of Non-Adipo Biscuits had been sent to each doctor and his wife.

Andrew was not a member of the Union, since the five-guinea subscription was, as yet, beyond his means, but he viewed it a little enviously from a distance. Its effect was to make him feel isolated and out of touch in Blaenelly. Photographs in the local newspapers of an array of doctors receiving addresses of welcome on a beflagged platform, driving off at the first tee of the Penarth Golf Course, flocking upon the steamer for a sea trip to Weston-super-Mare, served to intensify his sense of exclusion.

But midway through the week a letter arrived bearing the address of a Cardiff hotel which caused Andrew a more pleasurable sensation. It was from his friend Freddie Hampton. Freddie, as might be expected, was attending the Conference, and he asked Manson to run down and see him. He suggested Saturday, for dinner.

Andrew showed the letter to Christine. It was instinctive now for him to take her into his confidence. Since that evening, nearly two months before, when he had gone round to supper, he was more than ever in love. Now that he could see her frequently, and be reassured by her evident pleasure in these meetings, he was happier than ever he had been in his life before. Perhaps it was Christine who had this stabilizing effect upon him. She was a very practical little person, perfectly direct and entirely without coquetry. Often he would join her in a state of worry or irritation and come away soothed and tranquillized. She had a way of listening to what he had to say, quietly, then of making some comment which was usually apropos or amusing. She had a lively sense of humour. And she never flattered him.

Occasionally, despite her calmness, they had great arguments, for she had a mind of her own. She told him, with a smile, that her argumentativeness came from a Scottish grandmother. Perhaps her independent spirit came from that source too. He often felt that she had great courage, which touched him, made him long to protect her. She was really quite alone in the world except for an invalid aunt in Bridlington.

When it was fine on Saturday or Sunday afternoons they took long walks along the Pandy Road. Once they had gone to see a film, Chaplin in "The Gold Rush," and again to Toniglan, at her suggestion, to an orchestral concert. But most of all he enjoyed the evenings when Mrs. Watkins was visiting her and he was able to enjoy the intimacy of her companionship in her own sitting-room. It was then that most of their discussions took place, with Mrs. Watkins—knitting placidly yet primly resolved to make her wool last out the session—no more than a respectable buffer state between them.

Now, with this visit to Cardiff in prospect, he wished her to accompany him. Bank Street School broke up for the summer holidays at the end of the week, and she was going to Bridlington to spend her vacation with her aunt. He felt that some special celebration was needed before she took her leave.

When she had read the letter he said, impulsively:—

"Will you come with me? It's only an hour and a half in the train. I'll get Blodwen to unchain me on Saturday evening. We might manage to see something of the Conference. And in any case I'd like you to meet Hampton."

She nodded.

"I'd love to come."

Excited by her acceptance, he had no intention of being baulked by Mrs. Page. Before he approached her upon the matter he placed a conspicuous notice in the surgery window:—

CLOSED SATURDAY EVENING

He went into the house gaily.

"Mrs. Page! According to my reading of the Sweated Medical Assistants Act, I'm entitled to one half-day off a year. I'd like mine on Saturday. I'm going to Cardiff."

"Now look you here, Doctor!" She bristled at his demand, thinking that he was very full of himself, uppish; but after staring at him suspiciously, she grudgingly declared: "Oh, well—you can go, I suppose." A sudden idea struck her. Her eye cleared. She smacked her lips. "Anyhow, I'll have you bring me some pastries from Parry's. There's nothing I fancy better nor Parry's pastries."

On Saturday, at half-past four, Christine and Andrew took the train for Cardiff. Andrew was in high spirits, boisterous, hailing porter and booking clerk by their first names. With a smile he looked across at Christine, seated on the opposite seat. She wore a navy blue coat and skirt which intensified her usual air of trimness. Her black shoes were very neat. Her eyes, like her whole appearance, conveyed a sense of appreciation of the expedition. They were shining.

At the sight of her there, a wave of tenderness came over him, and a fresh sense of desire. It was all very well, he thought, this comradeship of theirs. But he wanted more than that. He wanted to take her in his arms, to feel her, warm and breathing, close to him.

Involuntarily he said, "I'll be lost without you—when you're away this summer."

Her cheek coloured slightly. She looked out of the window.

He asked impulsively, "Shouldn't I have said that?"

"I'm glad you said it, anyway," she answered, without looking round.

It was on his tongue to tell her that he loved her, to ask her, in spite of the ridiculous insecurity of his position, if she would marry him. He saw, with sudden lucid insight, that this was the only, the inevitable solution for them. But something, an intuition that the moment was not apt, restrained him. He decided he would speak to her in the train coming home.

Meanwhile he went on, rather breathlessly:—

"We ought to have a grand time this evening. Hampton's a good chap. He was rather a blade at the Royal. He's a smart lad. I remember once,"—his eyes became reminiscent, —"there was a charity matinee in Dundee for the hospitals. All the stars were appearing, you know, regular artistes, at the Lyceum. Hanged if Hampton didn't go on and give a turn, sang and danced, and by George! he brought the house down!"

"He sounds more like a matinee idol than a doctor," she said, smiling.

"Now don't be highbrow, Chris! You'll like Freddie."

The train ran into Cardiff at quarter-past six, and they made directly for the Palace Hotel. Hampton had promised to meet them there at half-past, but he had not arrived when they entered the lounge.

They stood together watching the scene. The place was crowded with doctors and their wives, talking, laughing, generating immense cordiality. Friendly invitations flew back and forth.

"Doctor! You and Mrs. Smith must sit next to us to-night."

"Hey! Doctor! How about these theatre tickets?"

There was a great deal of excited coming and going, and gentlemen with red tabs in their buttonholes sped importantly across the tessellated floor with papers in their hands. In the alcove opposite an official kept up a booming monotone: "Section of O-tology and Larin-gology *this* way please." Above a passage leading to the Annex was the notice: MEDICAL EXHIBITION. There were also palms and a string orchestra.

"Pretty social, eh?" Andrew remarked, feeling that they were rather outlawed by the general hilarity. "And Freddie's late as usual, hang him. Let's take a look round the Exhibition."

They walked interestedly around the Exhibition. Andrew soon found his hands full of elegant literature. He showed one of the leaflets to Christine with a smile. *Doctor! Is your surgery empty? We can show you how to fill it!* Also there were nineteen folders, all different, offering the newest sedatives and analgesics.

"It looks like the latest trend in medicine is dope," he remarked, frowning.

At the last stand, on their way out, a young man tactfully engaged them, producing a shiny watchlike contraption.

"Doctor! I think you'd be interested in our new indexometer. It has a multiplicity of uses, is absolutely up to the minute, creates an admirable impression by the bedside, and the price is only two guineas. Allow me, Doctor! You see, on the front, an index of incubation periods. One turn of the dial, and you find the period of infectivity. Inside," he clicked open the back of the case, "you have an excellent haemoglobin colour index, while on the back in tabulated form—"

"My grandfather had one of these," Andrew interrupted him firmly. "But he gave it away."

Christine was smiling as they came back through the alcove again.

"Poor man," she said, "nobody ever dared laugh at his lovely meter before!"

At that moment, as they re-entered the lounge, Freddie Hampton arrived, leaping from his taxi and entering the hotel with a page boy carrying his golf clubs behind him. He saw them at once and advanced with a wide and winning smile.

"Hello! Hello! Here you are! Sorry I'm late. I had my tie to play off in the Lister Cup. I never saw such luck as that fellow had! Well, well! It's good to see you again, Andrew. Still the same old Manson. Ha! Ha! Why don't you buy yourself a new hat, my boy!" He clapped Andrew on the back, affectionate, hail fellow well met, his glance smilingly including Christine. "Introduce me, stick in the mud! What are you dreaming about?"

They sat down at one of the round tables. Hampton decided they must all have a drink. With a crack of his fingers he had a waiter running for them. Then, over the sherry, he told them all about his golf match, how he was absolutely set to win when his opponent had started sinking his mashie shots at every hole.

Fresh-complexioned, with blond brilliantine-plastered hair, a nicely cut suit, and black opal links in his projecting cuffs, Freddie was a well-turned-out figure, not good-looking—his features were very ordinary—but good-natured, smart. He looked a trifle conceited perhaps; yet, when he exerted himself, he had an attractive way. He made friends with ease, in spite of which, at the University, Doctor Muir, pathologist and cynic, had once glumly addressed him in the presence of the class: "You know nothing, Mr. Hampton. Your balloon-like mind is entirely filled with egotistical gas. But you're never at a loss. If you are successful in cribbing your way through the nursery games known here as examinations, I prophesy for you a great and shining future."

They went into the grillroom for dinner, since none of them was dressed, though Freddie informed them he would have to get into tails later in the evening. There was a dance, a confounded nuisance, but he must show up at it.

Having nonchalantly ordered from a menu gone wildly medical—*potage Pasteur, sole Madame Curie, tournedos à la Conférence Médicale*—he began recalling the old days with dramatic ardour.

"I'd never have thought, then," he ended with a shake of his head, "that old Manson would have buried himself in the South Wales Valleys!"

"Do you think he's quite buried?" Christine asked, and her smile was rather forced. There was a pause. Freddie surveyed the crowded grillroom, grinned at Andrew.

"What do you think of the Conference?"

"I suppose," Andrew answered doubtfully, "it's a useful way of keeping up-to-date."

"Up-to-date, my uncle! I haven't been to one of their ruddy sectional meetings all week. No, no, old man, it's the contacts you make that matter, the fellows you meet, mix up with. You've no idea the really influential people I've got in with this week. That's why I'm here. When I get back to town, I'll ring them up, go out and play golf with them. Later on—you mark my words—that means business."

"I don't quite follow you, Freddie," Manson said.

"Why, it's as simple as falling off a log. I'm holding down an appointment in the meantime, but I've got my eye on a nice little room up West where a smart little brass plate with Freddie Hampton, M.B. on it would look dashed well. When the plate does go up these fellows, my pals, will send me cases. You know how it happens. Reciprocity. You scratch my back and I'll scratch yours." Freddie took a slow, appreciative sip of hock. He went on: "And apart from that it pays to push in with the small suburban fellows. Sometimes they can send you stuff. Why, in a year or two, you old dog, you'll be sending patients up to me in town from your stick in the mud Blaen—whatever you call it."

Christine glanced quickly at Hampton, made as if to speak, then checked herself. She kept her eyes fastened upon her plate.

"And now tell me about yourself, Manson, old son," Freddie continued, smiling.

"What's been happening to you?"

"Oh, nothing out of the ordinary. I consult in a wooden surgery, average thirty visits a day—mostly miners and their families."

"Doesn't sound too good to me." Freddie shook his head again, condolingly.

"I enjoy it," Andrew said mildly.

Christine interposed, "And you get in some real work."

"Yes, I did have one rather interesting case lately," Andrew reflected. "As a matter of fact I sent a note of it to the *Journal*."

He gave Hampton a short account of the case of Emrys Hughes. Though Freddie made a great show of interested listening, his eyes kept rolling round the room.

"That was pretty good," he remarked when Manson concluded. "I thought you only got goitre in Switzerland or somewhere. Anyhow, I hope you socked in a whacking good bill. And that reminds me. A fellow was telling me to-day the best way to handle this fee question…" He was off again, full of a scheme, which someone had suggested to him, for the cash payment of all fees. They had reached the end of the dinner before his voluble dissertation was over. He rose, flinging down his napkin.

"Let's have coffee outside. We'll finish our powwow in the lounge."

At quarter to ten, his cigar burned down, his stock of stories temporarily exhausted, Freddie yawned slightly and looked at his platinum wrist-watch.

But Christine was before him. She glanced at Andrew brightly, sat up straight and remarked: "Isn't it almost our train time?"

Manson was about to protest that they had another half-hour yet when Freddie said: "And I suppose I must think about this confounded dance. I can't let the party I'm going with down."

He accompanied them to the swing doors, taking prolonged and affectionate farewell of them both.

"Well, old man," he murmured with a final shake of the hand and a confidential pat on the shoulder, "when I put the little plate up in the West End I'll remember to send you a card."

Out in the warm evening air Andrew and Christine walked along Park Street in silence. Vaguely, he was conscious that the evening had not been the success he had anticipated, that it had, at least, fallen short of Christine's expectations. He waited for her to speak, but she did not.

At last, diffidently, he said: "It was pretty dull for you, I'm afraid, listening to all these old hospital yarns."

"No," she answered. "I didn't find that dull in the least."

There was a pause.

He asked: "Didn't you like Hampton?"

"Not a great deal." She turned, losing her restraint, her eyes sparking with honest indignation. "The idea of him, sitting there, all evening, with his waxed hair and his cheap smile, patronizing you."

"Patronizing me?" he echoed in amazement.

She nodded hotly.

"It was unbearable. 'A fellow was telling me the best way to handle the fee question.' Just after you'd told him about your wonderful case! Calling it a goitre, too. Even I know it was exactly the opposite. And that remark about your sending him patients—" her lip curled, "it was simply superb." She finished quite fiercely: "Oh! I could hardly stand it, the way he put himself above you."

"I don't think he put himself above me," reasoned Andrew puzzled. He paused. "I admit he seemed rather full of himself to-night. May have been a mood. He's the best-natured fellow you could hope to meet. We were great friends at College. We had digs together."

"Probably he found you useful to him," Christine said, with unusual bitterness. "Got you to help him with his work."

He protested unhappily: "Now, don't be mean, Chris."

"It's you," she flared, bright tears of vexation in her eyes. "You must be blind not to see the kind of person he is. And he's ruined our little expedition. It was lovely till he arrived and started talking about himself. And there was a wonderful concert at the Victoria Hall we could have gone to. But we've missed it, we're too late for anything—though he's just in time for his idiotic dance!"

They trudged towards the station some distance apart. It was the first time he had seen Christine angry. And he was angry too: angry at himself, at Hampton—yes, at Christine. Yet she was right when she said that the evening had not been a success. Now, in fact, secretly observing her pale constrained face, he felt it had been a dismal failure.

They entered the station. Suddenly, as they made their way towards the Up platform, Andrew caught sight of two people on the other side. He recognized them at once: Mrs. Bramwell and Doctor Gabell. At that moment the Down train came in, a local which ran out to the seaside at Porthcawl. Gabell and Mrs. Bramwell entered the Porthcawl train together, smiling at one another. The whistle blew. The train steamed off.

Andrew experienced a sudden sensation of distress. He glanced quickly at Christine, hoping she had not observed the incident. Only that morning he had encountered Bramwell—who, commenting on the fineness of the day, had rubbed his bony hands with satisfaction, remarking that his wife was going to spend the week end with her mother at Shrewsbury.

Andrew stood with his head bent, silent. He was so much in love that the scene he had just witnessed, with all its implications hurt him like a physical pain. He felt slightly sick. It had only wanted this conclusion to make the day thoroughly depressing. His mood seemed to undergo a complete revulsion. A shadow had fallen on his joyfulness. He longed with all his soul to have a long quiet talk with Christine, to open his heart to her, to straighten out their stupid little disagreement. He longed, above everything, to be quite alone with her. But the Up Valley train, when it came in, was overcrowded. They had to be content with a compartment packed with miners, loudly discussing the City football match.

It was late when they reached Blaenelly, and Christine looked very tired. He was convinced that she had seen Mrs. Bramwell and Gabell. He could not possibly speak to her now. There was nothing for it but to see her to Mrs. Herbert's and unhappily bid her good night.

x

Though it was nearly midnight when Andrew reached Bryngower, he found Joe Morgan waiting on him, walking up and down with short steps between the closed surgery and the entrance to the house. At the sight of him the burly driller's face expressed relief.

"Eh, Doctor, I'm glad to see you. I been back and forward here this last hour. The missus wants ye—before time, too."

Andrew, abruptly recalled from the contemplation of his own affairs, told Morgan to wait. He went into the house for his bag, then together they set out for Number 12 Blaina Terrace. The night air was cool and deep with quiet mystery. Usually so perceptive, Andrew now felt dull and listless. He had no premonition that this night call would prove unusual, still less that it would influence his whole future in Blaenelly.

The two men walked in silence until they reached the door of Number 12, then Joe drew up short.

"I'll not come in," he said, and his voice showed signs of strain. "But, man, I know ye'll do well for us."

Inside, a narrow stair led up to a small bedroom, clean but poorly furnished, and lit only by an oil lamp. Here Mrs. Morgan's mother, a tall grey-haired woman of nearly seventy, and the stout elderly midwife waited beside the patient, watching Andrew's expression as he moved about the room.

"Let me make you a cup of tea, Doctor, *bach*," said the former quickly, after a few moments.

Andrew smiled faintly. He saw that the old woman, wise in experience, realized there must be a period of waiting, that she was afraid he would leave the case, saying he would return later.

"Don't fret, Mother. I'll not run away."

Down in the kitchen he drank the tea which she gave him. Overwrought as he was, he knew he could not snatch even an hour's sleep if he went home. He knew, too, that the case here would demand all his attention. A queer lethargy of spirit came upon him. He decided to remain until everything was over.

An hour later he went upstairs again, noted the progress made, came down once more, sat by the kitchen fire. It was still, except for the rustle of a cinder in the grate and the slow tick-tock of the wall clock. No, there was another sound—the beat of Morgan's footsteps as he paced in the street outside. The old woman opposite him sat in her black dress, quite motionless, her eyes strangely alive and wise, probing, never leaving his face.

His thoughts were heavy, muddled. The episode he had witnessed at Cardiff station still obsessed him morbidly. He thought of Bramwell, foolishly devoted to a woman who deceived him sordidly, of Edward Page, bound to the shrewish Blodwen, of Denny, living unhappily, apart from his wife. His reason told him that all these marriages were dismal failures. It was a conclusion which, in his present state, made him wince. He wished to consider marriage as an idyllic state; yes, he could not otherwise consider it with the image of Christine before him. Her eyes, shining towards him, admitted no other conclusion. It was the conflict between his level, doubting mind and his overflowing heart which left him resentful and confused. He let his chin sink upon his chest, stretched out his legs, stared broodingly into the fire. He remained like this so long, and his thoughts were so filled with Christine, that he started when the old woman opposite suddenly addressed him. Her meditation had pursued a different course.

"Susan said not to give her the chloroform if it would harm the baby. She's awful set upon this child, Doctor, *bach.*" Her old eyes warmed at a sudden thought. She added in a low tone: "Ay, we all are, I fancy."

He collected himself with an effort.

"It won't do any harm, the anaesthetic," he said kindly. "They'll be all right."

Here the nurse's voice was heard calling from the top landing. Andrew glanced at the clock, which now showed half-past three. He rose and went up to the bedroom. He perceived that he might now begin his work.

An hour elapsed. It was a long, harsh struggle. Then, as the first streaks of dawn strayed past the broken edges of the blind, the child was born, lifeless.

As he gazed at the still form a shiver of horror passed over Andrew. After all that he had promised! His face, heated with his own exertions, chilled suddenly. He hesitated, torn between his desire to attempt to resuscitate the child, and his obligation towards the mother, who was herself in a desperate state. The dilemma was so urgent he did not solve it consciously. Blindly, instinctively, he gave the child to the nurse and turned his attention to Susan Morgan, who now lay collapsed, almost pulseless, and not yet out of the ether, upon her side. His haste was desperate, a frantic race against her ebbing strength. It took him only an instant to smash a glass ampule and inject pituitrin. Then he flung down the hypodermic syringe and worked unsparingly to restore the flaccid woman. After a few minutes of feverish effort, her heart strengthened; he saw that he might safely leave her. He swung round, in his shirt sleeves, his hair sticking to his damp brow.

"Where's the child?"

The midwife made a frightened gesture. She had placed it beneath the bed.

In a flash Andrew knelt down. Fishing amongst the sodden newspapers below the bed, he pulled out the child. A boy, perfectly formed. The limp warm body was white and soft as tallow. The cord, hastily slashed, lay like a broken stem. The skin was of a lovely texture, smooth and tender. The head lolled on the thin neck. The limbs seemed boneless.

Still kneeling, Andrew stared at the child with a haggard frown. The whiteness meant only one thing: asphyxia pallida, and his mind, unnaturally tense, raced back to a case he once had seen in the Samaritan, to the treatment that had been used. Instantly he was on his feet.

"Get me hot water and cold water," he threw out to the nurse. "And basins too. Quick! Quick!"

"But, Doctor—" she faltered, her eyes on the pallid body of the child.

"*Quick!*" he shouted.

Snatching a blanket he laid the child upon it and began the special method of respiration. The basins arrived, the ewer, the big iron kettle. Frantically he splashed cold water into one basin; into the other he mixed water as hot as his hand could bear.

Then, like some crazy juggler, he hurried the child between the two, now plunging it into the icy, now into the steaming bath.

Fifteen minutes passed. Sweat was now running into Andrew's eyes, blinding him. One of his sleeves hung down, dripping. His breath came pantingly. But no breath came from the lax body of the child.

A desperate sense of defeat pressed on him, a raging hopelessness. He felt the midwife watching him in stark consternation, while there, pressed back against the wall where she had all the time remained,—her hand pressed to her throat, uttering no sound, her eyes burning upon him,—was the old woman. He remembered her longing for a grandchild, as great as had been her daughter's longing for this child. All dashed away now; futile, beyond remedy...

The floor was now a draggled mess. Stumbling over a sopping towel, Andrew almost dropped the child, which was now wet and slippery in his hands, like a strange white fish.

"For mercy's sake, Doctor," whimpered the midwife. "It's stillborn."

Andrew did not heed her. Beaten, despairing, having laboured in vain for half an hour, he still persisted in one last effort, rubbing the child with a rough towel, crushing and releasing the little chest with both his hands, trying to get breath into that limp body.

And then, as by a miracle, the pigmy chest, which his hands enclosed, gave a short convulsive heave. Another... And another... Andrew turned giddy. The sense of life, springing beneath his fingers after all that unavailing striving, was so exquisite it almost made him faint. He redoubled his efforts feverishly. The child was gasping now, deeper and deeper. A bubble of mucus came from one tiny nostril, a joyful iridescent bubble. The limbs were no longer boneless. The head no longer lay back spinelessly. The blanched skin was slowly turning pink. Then, exquisitely, came the child's cry.

"Dear Father in Heaven," the nurse sobbed hysterically, "it's come—it's come alive."

Andrew handed her the child. He felt weak and dazed. About him the room lay in a shuddering litter: blankets, towels, basins, soiled instruments, the hypodermic syringe impaled by its point in the linoleum, the ewer knocked over, the kettle on its side in a puddle of water. Upon the huddled bed the mother still dreamed her way quietly through the anaesthetic. The old woman still stood against the wall. But her hands were together, her lips moved without sound. She was praying.

Mechanically Andrew wrung out his sleeve, pulled on his jacket.

"I'll fetch my bag later, Nurse."

He went downstairs, through the kitchen into the scullery. His lips were dry. At the scullery he took a long drink of water. He reached for his hat and coat.

Outside he found Joe standing on the pavement with a tense, expectant face.

"All right, Joe," he said thickly. "Both all right."

It was quite light. Nearly five o'clock. A few miners were already in the streets: the first of the night shift moving out. As Andrew walked with them, spent and slow, his footfalls echoing with the others under the morning sky, he kept thinking blindly, oblivious to all other work he had done in Blaenelly: "I've done something; oh, God! I've done something real at last."

xi

After a shave and a bath—thanks to Annie there was always plenty of boiling water in the tap—he felt less tired. But Mrs. Page, finding his bed unslept in, was facetiously sarcastic at the breakfast table, the more so as he received her shafts in silence.

"Ha! You lookin' bit of a wreck this mornin', Doctor. Bit dark under the eyes like! Didn't get back from Swansea till this mornin', eh? And forgot my pastries from Parry's too, like. Been out on the tiles, my boy? Tee-hee! You can't deceive *me*! I thought you was too good to be true. You're all the same, you assistants. I never found one yet that didn't drink or go wrong some'ow!"

After morning surgery and his forenoon round, Andrew dropped in to see his case. It had just gone half-past twelve as he turned up Blaina Place. There were little knots of women talking at their open doorways, and as he passed they stopped talking to smile and give him a friendly "Good morning." Approaching Number 12 he fancied he saw a face at the window. And it was so. They had been waiting on him. The instant he placed his foot on the newly pipe-clayed doorstep, the door was swung open and the old woman, beaming unbelievably all over her wrinkled face, made him welcome to the house.

Indeed, she was so eager to make much of him she could barely frame the words. She asked him to come first for some refreshment to the parlour. When he refused, she fluttered:—

"All right, all right, Doctor, *bach*. It's as *you* say. Maybe you'll have time, though, on your way down for a drop of elderberry wine and a morsel of cake." She patted him upstairs with tremulous old hands.

He entered the bedroom. The little room, lately a shambles, had been scoured and polished until it shone. All his instruments, beautifully arranged, gleamed upon the varnished deal dresser. His bag had been carefully rubbed with goose-grease, the snib catches cleaned with metal polish, so that they were as silver. The bed had been changed, spread with fresh linen; and there, upon it, was the mother, her plain middle-aged face gazing in dumb happiness towards him, the babe sucking quiet and warm at her full breast.

"Ay!" The stout midwife rose from her seat by the bedside, unmasking a battery of smiles. "They do look all right now, don't they, Doctor, *bach*? They don't know the trouble they gave us. They don't *care*, either, do they?"

Moistening her lips, her soft eyes warmly inarticulate, Susan Morgan tried to stammer out her gratitude.

"Ay, you may well say," nodded the midwife, extracting the last ounce of credit from the situation. "An' don't you forget, my gal, you wouldn't never have another at your age. It was this time or *never*, so far as you was concerned!"

"We know that, Mrs. Jones," interrupted the old woman meaningly, from the door. "We know we do owe everything here to *Doctor*."

"Has my Joe been to see you yet, Doctor?" asked the mother timidly. "No? Well he's comin', you may be sure. He's fair overjoyed. He was only sayin' though, Doctor, that's the thing we will miss when we're in South Africa, not havin' you to 'tend to us."

Leaving the house, duly fortified with seedcake and homemade elderberry wine,—it would have broken the old woman's heart had he refused to drink her grandson's health,—Andrew continued on his round with a queer warmth round his heart. "They couldn't have made more of me," he thought self-consciously, "if I'd been the King of England." This case became somehow the antidote to that scene he had witnessed upon Cardiff platform. There was something to be said for marriage and the family life, when it brought such happiness as filled the Morgan home.

A fortnight later, when Andrew had paid his last visit at Number 12, Joe Morgan came round to see him. Joe's manner was solemnly portentous. And, having laboured long with words, he said explosively:—

"Dang it all, Doctor, *bach*, I'm no hand at talkin'. Money can't repay what you done for us. But all the same the missus and I want to make you this little present."

Impulsively, he handed over a slip to Andrew. It was an order on the Building Society, made out for five guineas.

Andrew stared at the cheque. The Morgans were, in the local idiom, tidy folk; but they were far from being well-off. This amount, on the eve of their departure, with expenses of transit to be faced, must represent a great sacrifice, a noble generosity.

Touched, Andrew said: "I can't take this, Joe, lad."

"You must take it," Joe said with grave insistence, his hand closing over Andrew's, "or Missus and me'll be mortal offended. It's a present for yourself. It's not for Doctor Page. He's had my money now for years and years, and we've never troubled him but this once. He's *well* paid. This is a present—for *yourself*—Doctor, *bach*. You understand."

"Yes, I understand, Joe," Andrew nodded, smiling.

He folded the order, placed it in his waistcoat pocket and for a few days forgot about it. Then, the following Tuesday, passing the Western Counties Bank, he paused, reflected a moment, and went in. As Mrs. Page always paid him in notes, which he forwarded by registered letter to the Endowment offices, he had never had occasion to deal through the bank. But now, with a comfortable recollection of his own substance, he decided to open a deposit account with Joe's gift.

At the grating he endorsed the order, filled in some forms, and handed them to the young cashier, remarking with a smile: "It's not much, but it's a start anyhow."

Meanwhile he had been conscious of Aneurin Rees hovering in the background, watching him. And, as he turned to go, the longheaded manager came forward to the counter. In his hands he held the order. Smoothing it gently, he glanced sideways across his spectacles.

"Afternoon, Doctor Manson. How are you?" Pause… Sucking his breath in over his yellow teeth… "Eh—you want this paid into your new account?"

"Yes." Manson spoke in some surprise. "Is it too small an amount to open with?"

"Oh, no, no, Doctor. 'Tisn't the amount, like. We're very glad to have the business." Rees hesitated, scrutinizing the order; then, raising his small suspicious eyes to Andrew's face: "Eh—you want it in your *own* name?"

"Why—certainly."

"All right, all right, Doctor." His expression broke suddenly into a watery smile. "I only wondered, like. Wanted to make sure. What lovely weather we're havin' for the time of year. Good day to you, Doctor Manson. Go-od day!"

Manson came out of the bank puzzled, asking himself what that bald, buttoned-up devil meant. It was some days before he found an answer to the question.

xii

Christine had left on her vacation more than a week before. He had been so occupied by the Morgan case that he had not succeeded in seeing her for more than a few moments, on the day of her departure. He had not spoken to her. But now that she was gone he longed for her with all his heart.

The summer was exceptionally trying in the town. The green vestiges of spring had long been withered to a dirty yellow. The mountains wore a febrile air, and when the daily shot-firing from the mines or quarries re-echoed on the still spent air they seemed to enclose the valley in a dome of burnished sound. The men came out from the mine with the ore dust smeared upon their faces like rust. Children played listlessly. Old Thomas, the groom, had been taken with jaundice and Andrew was compelled to make his rounds on foot. As he slogged through the baking streets he thought of Christine. What was she doing? Was she thinking of him, perhaps, a little? And what of the future, her prospects, their chance of happiness together?

And then, quite unexpectedly, he received a message from Watkins asking him to call at the Company offices.

The mine manager received him in agreeable fashion, invited him to sit down, pushed over the packet of cigarettes on his desk.

"Look here, Doctor," he said in a friendly tone, "I've been wantin' to talk to you for some time—and we better get it over afore I make up my annual return." He paused to pick a yellow shred of tobacco off his tongue. "There's been a number of the lads at me, Emrys Hughes and Ed Williams are the leadin' spirits, askin' me to put you up for the Company's list."

Andrew straightened in his chair, pervaded by a swift glow of satisfaction, of excitement.

"You mean—arrange for me to take over Doctor Page's practice?"

"Why, no, not exactly, Doctor," Watkins said slowly. "You see the position is difficult. I've got to watch how I handle my labour question 'ere. I can't put Doctor Page off the list; there's a number of the men wouldn't have *that*. What I was meanin', in the best interests of yourself, was to squeeze you, quiet like, on to the Company's list; then them that wanted to slip away from Doctor Page to yourself could easily manage it."

The eagerness faded from Andrew's expression. He frowned, his figure still braced.

"But surely you see I couldn't do that? I came here as Page's assistant. If I set up in opposition—no decent doctor could do a thing like that!"

"There isn't any other way."

"Why don't you let me take over the practice?" Andrew said urgently. "I'd willingly pay something for it, out of receipts—that's another way."

Watkins shook his head bluntly.

"Blodwen won't 'ave it. I've put it up to her afore. She knows she's in a strong position. Nearly all the older men here, like Enoch Davies, for instance, are on Page's side. They believe he'll come back. I'd have a strike on my hands if I even tried to shift him." He paused. "Take till to-morrow to think it over, Doctor. I send the new list to Swansea Head Office then. Once it's gone in we can't do anything for another twelve months."

Andrew stared at the floor a moment, then slowly made a gesture of negation. His hopes, so high a minute ago, were now dashed completely to the ground.

"What's the use? I couldn't do it—if I thought it over for weeks."

It cost him a bitter pang to reach this decision, and to maintain it in the face of Watkins's partiality towards him. Yet there was no escaping the fact that he had gained his introduction to Blaenelly as Doctor Page's assistant. To set up against his principal, even in the exceptional circumstances of the case, was quite unthinkable. Suppose Page did, by some chance, resume active practice—how well he would look, fighting the old man for patients! No, no. He could not, and would not, accept.

Nevertheless, for the rest of the day he was sadly cast-down, resentful of Blodwen's barefaced extortion, aware that he was caught in an impossible position, wishing the offer had not been made to him at all. In the evening, about eight o'clock, he went dejectedly to call on Denny. He had not seen him for some time, and he felt that a talk with Philip, perhaps some reassurance that he had acted correctly, would do him good. He reached Philip's lodgings about half-past eight, and, as was now his custom, walked into the house without knocking. He entered the sitting-room.

Philip lay on the sofa. At first, in the fading light, Manson thought that he was resting after a hard day's work. But Philip had done no work that day. He sprawled there on his back, breathing heavily, his arm flung across his face. He was dead-drunk.

Andrew turned to find the landlady at his elbow, watching him sideways, her eyes concerned, apprehensive.

"I heard you come in, Doctor. He's been like this all day. He's eaten nothing. I can't do a thing with him."

Andrew simply did not know what to say. He stood staring at Philip's senseless face, recollecting that first cynical remark, uttered in the surgery on the night of his arrival.

"It's ten months now since he had his last bout," the landlady went on. "And he don't touch it in between. But when he do begin he goes at it wicked. I can tell you it's more nor awkward, with Doctor Lewis bein' away on holiday. It looks like I must wire him."

"Send Tom up," Andrew said at last. "And we'll get him into bed."

With the help of the landlady's son, a young miner who seemed to regard the matter as something of a joke, they got Philip undressed and into his pyjamas. Then they carried him, dull and heavy as a sack, through to the bedroom.

"The main thing is to see that he doesn't get any more of it, you understand. Turn the key in the door if necessary," Andrew addressed the landlady as they came back into the sitting-room. "And now—you'd better let me have to-day's list of calls."

From the child's slate hanging in the hall he copied out the visits which Philip should have made that day. He went out. By hurrying round he could get most of them done before eleven.

Next morning, immediately after surgery, he went round to the lodgings. The landlady met him, wringing her hands.

"I don't know where he's got it. I 'aven't done it, I've only done my best for him."

Philip was drunker than before, heavy, insensible. After prolonged shakings and an effort to restore him with strong coffee, which in the end was upset and spilled all over the bed, Andrew took the list of calls again. Cursing the heat, the flies, Thomas' jaundice, and Denny, he again did double work that day.

In the late afternoon he came back, tired out, angrily resolved to get Denny sober. This time he found him astride one of the chairs in his pyjamas, still drunk, delivering a long address to Tom and Mrs. Seager. As Andrew entered Denny stopped short and gave him a lowering, derisive stare. He spoke thickly.

"Ha! The Good Samaritan. I understand you've done my round for me. Extremely noble. But why should you? Why should that blasted Lewis clear out and leave us to do the work?"

"I can't say." Andrew's patience was wearing thin. "All I know is it would be easier if you did your bit of it."

"I'm a surgeon. I'm not a blasted general practitioner—G.P. Huh! What does that mean? D'you ever ask yourself? You didn't? Well, I'll tell you. It's the last and most ster —stereotyped anachronism, the worst, the stupidest system ever created by God-made man. Dear old G.P.! And dear old B.P.!—that's the British Public. Ha! Ha!" He laughed derisively. "They made him. They love him. They weep over him." He swayed in his seat, his inflamed eye again bitter and morose, lecturing them drunkenly. "What can the poor devil do about it? Your G.P.—your dear old quack of all trades! Maybe it's twenty years since he qualified. How can he know medicine and obstetrics and bacteriology and all the modern scientific advances, and surgery as well? Oh, yes! Oh, yes! Don't forget the surgery! Occasionally he tries a little operation at the cottage hospital. Ha! Ha!" Again the sardonic amusement. "Say a mastoid. Two hours and a half by the clock. When he finds pus he's a saviour of humanity. When he doesn't, they bury the patient." His voice rose. He was angry, wildly, drunkenly angry. "Damn it to hell, Manson. It's been going on for hundreds of years. Don't they ever want to *change* the system? What's the use? What's the *use*? I ask you. Give me another whisky. We're all cracked. And it seems I'm drunk as well."

There was silence for a few moments; then, suppressing his irritation, Andrew said: "Oughtn't you to get back to bed now? Come on, we'll help you."

"Let me alone," said Denny sullenly. "Don't use your blasted bedside manner on me. I've used it plenty in my time. I know it too well." He rose abruptly, staggering, and, taking Mrs. Seager by the shoulder, he thrust her into the chair. Then, swaying on his feet, his manner a savage assumption of bland suavity, he addressed the frightened woman. "And how are you to-day, my dear lady? A leetle better, I fancy. A little more strength in the pulse. Sleep well? Ha! Hum! Then we must prescribe a leetle sedative."

There was, in the ludicrous scene, a strange, alarming note—the stocky, unshaven, pyjama-clad figure of Philip aping the society physician, swaying in servile deference before the shrinking miner's wife. Tom gave a nervous gulp of laughter. In a flash Denny turned on him and violently cuffed his ears.

"That's right! Laugh! Laugh your blasted head off. But I spent five years of my life doing that. God! When I think of it I could die." He glared at them, seized a vase that stood on the mantelpiece, and dashed it hard upon the floor. The next instant the companion piece was in his hands and he sent it shattering against the wall. He started forward, red destruction in his eye.

"For mercy's sake," whimpered Mrs. Seager. "Stop him, stop him—"

Andrew and Tom Seager flung themselves on Philip, who struggled with the wild intractability of intoxication. Then, perversely, he suddenly relaxed and was sentimental, fuddled.

"Manson," he drooled, hanging on Andrew's shoulder, "you're a good chap. I love you better than a brother. You and I—if we stuck together we could save the whole bloody medical profession."

He stood, his gaze wandering, lost. Then his head dropped. His body sagged. He allowed Andrew to help him to the next room and into bed. As his head rolled over on the pillow he made a last maudlin request:—

"Promise me one thing, Manson! For Christ's sake, don't marry a lady!"

Next morning he was drunker than ever. Andrew gave it up. He half-suspected young Seager of smuggling in the liquor, though the lad, when confronted, swore, pale-faced, that he had nothing to do with it.

All that week Andrew struggled through Denny's calls in addition to his own. On Sunday, after lunch, he visited the Chapel Street lodgings. Philip was up, shaved, dressed, and immaculate in his appearance; also, though drawn and shaky, cold sober.

"I understand you've been doing my work for me, Manson." Gone was the intimacy of these last few days. His manner was constrained, icily stiff.

"It was nothing," Andrew answered clumsily.

"On the contrary, it must have put you to a great deal of trouble."

Denny's attitude was so objectionable that Andrew flushed. Not a word of gratitude, he thought; nothing but that stiff, hidebound arrogance.

"If you do want to know the truth," he blurted out, "it put me to a hell of a lot of trouble!"

"You may take it from me something will be done about it."

"What do you think I am?" Andrew answered hotly. "Some damned cabby that expects a tip from you? If it hadn't been for me, Mrs. Seager would have wired Doctor Lewis and you'd have been thrown out on your neck. You're a supercilious, half-baked snob. And what you need is a damned good punch on the jaw."

Denny lit a cigarette, his fingers shaking so violently he could barely hold the match.

He sneered: "Nice of you to choose this moment to offer physical combat. True Scottish tact. Some other time I may oblige you."

"Oh, shut your bloody mouth!" said Andrew. "Here's your list of calls. Those with a cross should be seen on Monday."

He flung out of the house in a fury. Damn it, he raged, wincing, what kind of man is he to behave like God Almighty! It's as if he had done *me* the favour, *allowing* me to do his work!

But, on the way home, his resentment slowly cooled. He was genuinely fond of Philip, and he had by now a better insight into his complex nature: shy, inordinately sensitive, vulnerable. It was this alone which made him secrete a shell of hardness round himself. The memory of his recent bout, of how he had exposed himself during it, must even now be causing him excruciating torture.

Again Andrew was struck by the paradox of this clever man, using Blaenelly as a bolt-hole from convention. As a surgeon, Philip was exceptionally gifted. Andrew, administering the anaesthetic, had seen him perform a resection of the gall bladder on the kitchen table of a miner's house, the sweat dripping from his red face and hairy forearms, a model of swiftness and accuracy. It was possible to make allowances for a man who did such work.

Nevertheless, when Andrew reached home he still smarted from his impact with Philip's coldness. And so, as he came through the front door and hung his hat on the stand, he was scarcely in the mood to hear Mrs. Page's voice exclaiming:—

"Is that you, Doctor? Doctor Manson! I want you!"

Andrew ignored her call. Turning, he prepared to go upstairs to his own room. But as he placed his hand on the banister Blodwen's voice came again, sharper, louder.

"Doctor! Doctor Manson! I *want* you."

Andrew swung round, to see Mrs. Page sail out of the sitting-room, her face unusually pale, her black eyes sparking with some violent emotion. She came up to him.

"Are you deaf? Didn't you 'ear me say I *wanted* you?"

"What is it, Mrs. Page?" he asked irritably.

"What is it, indeed!" She could scarcely breathe. "I like that. You askin' me! It's me that wants to ask you somethin', my fine Doctor Manson!"

"What, then?" Andrew snapped.

The shortness of his manner seemed to excite her beyond endurance.

"It's *this*. Yes, my smart young gentleman! Maybe you'll be kind enough to explain this." From her pudgy bosom she produced a slip of paper and, without relinquishing it, fluttered it menacingly before his eyes. He saw it was Joe Morgan's cheque. Then, raising his head, he saw Rees behind Blodwen, skulking in the doorway of the sitting-room.

"Ay, you may well look!" Blodwen went on. "I see you recognize it. But you better tell us quick how you come to bank that money for yourself, when it's Doctor Page's money and you know it."

Andrew felt the blood rise behind his ears in quick surging waves.

"It's mine. Joe Morgan made me a present of it."

"A *present*! Ho! Ho! I like that. He's not 'ere now to deny it."

He answered between his shut teeth.

"You can write to him if you doubt my word."

"I've more to do than write letters all over the place." Losing the last of her restraint she shouted: "I do doubt your word. You think you're a wise one. Huh! Comin' down here and thinkin' you can get the practice into your own hands when you should be workin' for Doctor Page! But this shows what you are, all right. You're a thief, that's what you are, a common thief."

She spat the word at him, half-turning for support to Rees—who, in the doorway, was making sounds of expostulation in his throat, his face sallower than usual. Andrew, indeed, saw Rees as the instigator of the whole affair, dallying a few days in indecision, then scurrying to Blodwen with the story. His hands clenched fiercely. He came down the two bottom steps and advanced towards them, his eyes fixed on Rees's thin bloodless mouth with threatening intensity. He was livid with rage and thirsting for battle.

"Mrs. Page," he said, in a laboured tone, "you've made a charge against me. Unless you take it back and apologize within two minutes, I'll sue you for damages for defamation of character. The source of your information will come out in Court. I've no doubt Mr. Rees's board of governors will be interested to hear how he discloses his official business."

"I—I only did my duty," stuttered the bank manager, his complexion turning muddier than before.

"I'm waiting, Mrs. Page." The words came with a rush, choking him. "And if you don't hurry up, I'll give your bank manager the worst hiding he's ever had in his life."

She saw she had gone too far—had said more, far more than she had intended. His threat, his ominous attitude, frightened her. It was almost possible to follow her swift reflection: *Damages! Heavy damages! Oh, Lord, they might take a lot o' money off 'er!*

She choked, swallowed, stammered: "I—I take it back. I apologize."

It was almost comic, the plump little termagant so suddenly and unexpectedly subdued. But Andrew found it singularly humourless. He realized, all at once, with a great flood of bitterness, that he had reached the limit of his endurance. He could not put up with this nagging, importunate creature any longer. He took a quick deep breath. He forgot everything but his loathing of her. There was a wild and savage joy in letting himself go.

"Mrs. Page, there are just one or two things I want to tell you. In the first place I know for a fact that you are making one thousand, five hundred pounds a year because of the work which I do for you here. Out of this you pay me a miserable two hundred and fifty, and in addition you've done your best to starve me. It may interest you to know, also, that last week a deputation of the men approached the manager, who invited me to put my name on the Company's list. It may further interest you to know that on ethical grounds—which you couldn't possibly know anything about—I definitely refused. And now, Mrs. Page, I'm so absolutely sick of you, I couldn't stay on. You're a mean, guzzling, mercenary bitch. In fact, you're a pathological case. I give you a month's notice here and now."

She gaped at him, her little button eyes nearly bursting from her head. Then suddenly she shrilled:—

"No, you don't. No, you don't. It's all lies. You couldn't get near the Company's list. And you're *sacked*, that's what you are. No assistant 'as ever given me notice in his life. The idea, the impudence, the insolence, talkin' to me like that. I said it first. You're sacked, you are, that's what you are, sacked, sacked, sacked—"

The outburst was loud, hysterical, degrading. And at the height of it, there was an interruption. Upstairs, the door of Edward's room swung slowly open and, a moment later, Edward himself appeared, a strange gaunt figure, his wasted shanks showing beneath his nightshirt.

So strange and unexpected was this apparition that Mrs. Page stopped dead in the middle of a word. From the hall she gazed upwards, as also did Rees and Andrew, while the sick man, dragging his paralyzed leg behind him, came slowly, painfully, to the topmost stair.

"Can't I have a little peace?" His voice, though agitated, was stern. "What's the matter?"

Blodwen took another gulp, launched into a tearful diatribe against Manson. She concluded: "And so—and so I gave him his notice."

Manson did not contradict her version of the case.

"You mean he's going?" Edward asked, trembling all over with agitation and the exertion of keeping himself upright.

"Yes, Edward." She sniffed. "Any'ow, you'll soon be back."

There was a silence. Edward abandoned all that he wished to say. His eyes dwelt on Andrew in mute apology, moved to Rees, passed quickly on to Blodwen, then came to rest sorrowfully on nothing at all. A look of hopelessness yet of dignity formed upon his stiff face.

"No," he said at last. "I'll never be back. You know that—all of you."

He said nothing more. Turning slowly, holding on to the wall, he dragged his way back into his room. The door closed without sound.

xiii

Remembering the joy, the pure elation which the Morgan case had given him and which, with a few ugly words, Blodwen Page had turned to something sordid, Andrew brooded angrily, wondering if he should not take the matter further, write to Joe Morgan, demand something more than a mere apology. But he dismissed the idea as one worthy of Blodwen.

In the end he picked out the most useless charity in the district and in a mood of determined bitterness posted five guineas to the home and asked them to send the receipt to Aneurin Rees. After that he felt better. But he wished he might have seen Rees reading that receipt.

And now, realizing that his work must terminate here at the end of a month, he began immediately to look for another position, combing the back pages of the *Lancet*, applying for everything which seemed suitable. There were numerous advertisements inserted in the "Assistants Wanted" column. He sent in good applications, copies of his testimonials, and even, as was frequently requested, photographs of himself. But at the end of the first week, and again at the conclusion of the second, he had received not a single answer to his applications. He was disappointed and astounded.

Then Denny offered him the explanation in one terse phrase: "You've been in Blaenelly."

It dawned upon Andrew, with a pang of dismay, that his having been in practice in this remote Welsh mining town condemned him. No one wanted assistants from "the Valleys"—they had a reputation.

When a fortnight of his notice had expired Andrew really began to worry. What on earth was he to do? He still owed over fifty pounds to the Glen endowment. They would allow him to suspend payments, of course. But apart from that, if he could not find another job, how was he to live? He had two or three pounds in ready cash, no more. He had no equipment, no reserves. He had not even bought himself a new suit since coming to Blaenelly, and his present garments had been shabby enough when he arrived. He had moments of sheer terror when he saw himself sinking to destitution.

Surrounded by difficulties and uncertainty, he longed for Christine. Letters were no use; he had no talent for expressing himself on paper; anything he could write would undoubtedly convey a wrong impression. Yet she was not returning to Blaenelly until the first week in September. He turned a fretful, hungry eye upon the calendar, counting the days that intervened. There were still twelve of them to run. He felt, with growing despondency, that they might as well be past, for all the prospect which they held for him.

On the evening of the thirtieth of August, three weeks after Manson had given Mrs. Page his notice and at about the time he had begun, from stark necessity, to entertain the idea of trying for a dispenser's post, he was walking dispiritedly along Chapel Street when he met Denny. They had remained on terms of slightly strained civility during the past few weeks, and Andrew was surprised when the other man stopped him.

Knocking out his pipe on the heel of his boot, Philip inspected it as though it demanded all his attention.

"I'm rather sorry you're going, Manson. It's made quite a difference, your being here." He hesitated. "I heard this afternoon that the Aberalaw Medical Aid Society are looking for a new assistant. Aberalaw—that's just thirty miles across the Valleys. It's quite a decent Society, as these things go. I believe the head doctor—Llewellyn—is a useful man. And as it's a Valley town, they can't very well object to a Valley man. Why don't you try?"

Andrew gazed at him doubtfully. His expectations had recently been raised so high and dashed so hopelessly that he had lost all faith in his ability to succeed.

"Well, yes," he agreed slowly. "If that's the case, I may as well try."

A few minutes later he walked home, through the now heavy rain, to apply for the post.

On the sixth of September there took place a full meeting of the Committee of the Aberalaw Medical Aid Society for the purpose of selecting a successor to Doctor Leslie, who had recently resigned in order to take up an appointment on a Malay rubber plantation. Seven candidates had applied for the position and all seven candidates had been asked to attend.

It was a perfect summer afternoon and the time, by the big Cooperative Stores clock, was close on four o'clock. Prowling up and down on the pavement outside the Medical Aid offices in Aberalaw Square, darting anxious glances at the six other candidates, Andrew nervously awaited the first stroke of the hour. Now that his foreboding had proved incorrect and he was here, actually being considered for the post, he longed with all his heart to be successful.

From what he had seen of it he liked Aberalaw. Standing at the extreme end of the Gethely Valley, the town was less in the Valley than on top of it. High, bracing, considerably larger than Blaenelly,—nearly twenty thousand inhabitants was his guess, —with good streets and shops, two cinemas, and a sense of spaciousness conveyed by green fields on its outskirts, Aberalaw appeared to Andrew, after the sweltering confines of the Penelly ravine, as a perfect paradise.

"But I'll never get it," he fretted as he paced up and down—never, never, *never*. No, he couldn't be so lucky! All the other candidates looked far more likely to be successful than himself, better turned-out, more confident. Doctor Edwards, especially, radiated confidence. Andrew found himself hating Edwards, a stoutish, prosperous, middle-aged man who had freely intimated, in the general conversation a moment ago in the office doorway, that he had just sold his own practice down the Valley in order to "apply" for this position. Damn him, grated Andrew inwardly; he wouldn't have sold out of a safe berth if he hadn't been sure of this one!

Up and down, up and down, head bent, hands thrust in his pockets. What would Christine think of him if he failed? She was returning to Blaenelly either to-day or to-morrow—in her letter she had not been quite sure. Bank Street School reopened on the following Monday. Though he had written her no word of his application here, failure would mean his meeting her gloomily, or worse, with a fictitious brightness, at that very moment when he wished, above everything in the world, to stand well with her, to win her quiet, intimate, exciting smile!

Four o'clock at last. As he turned towards the entrance a fine saloon motor car swept silently into the Square and drew up at the offices. From the back seat a short, dapper man emerged, smiling briskly, affably, yet with a sort of careless assurance, at the candidates. Before mounting the stairs he recognized Edwards, nodding casually.

"How do, Edwards." Then, aside: "It'll be all right, I fancy."

"Thank you, thank you ever so, Doctor Llewellyn," breathed Edwards with tremendous deference.

"Finish!" said Andrew to himself bitterly.

Upstairs, the waiting-room was small, bare, and sour-smelling, situated at the end of a short passage leading to the committee room. Andrew was the third to go in for interview. He entered the big committee room with nervous doggedness. If the post was already promised he was not going to cringe for it. He took the seat offered him with a blank expression.

About thirty miners filled the room, seated, and all of them smoking, gazing at him with blunt but not unfriendly curiosity. At the small side table was a pale, quiet man with a sensitive, intelligent face who looked, from his blue pitted features, as if he had once been a miner. He was Owen, the secretary. Lounging on the edge of the table, smiling good-naturedly at Andrew, was Doctor Llewellyn.

The interview began. Owen, in a quiet voice, explained the conditions of the post.

"It's like this, you see, Doctor. Under our scheme, the workers in Aberalaw—there are two anthracite mines here, a steel works, and one coal mine in the district—pay over a certain amount to the Society out of their wages every week. Out of this the Society administers the necessary medical services, provides a nice little hospital, surgeries, medicines, splints, et cetera. In addition, the Society engages doctors,—Doctor Llewellyn, the head physician and surgeon, and four assistants, together with a surgeon dentist,—and pays them a capitation fee—so much per head, according to the number on their list. I believe Doctor Leslie was making something like five hundred pounds a year when he left us." He paused. "Altogether, we find it a good scheme." There was a mutter of approval from the thirty committee men. Owen raised his head and faced them. "And now, gentlemen, have you any questions to ask?"

They began to fire questions at Andrew. He tried to answer calmly, without exaggeration, truly. Once he made a point.

"Do you speak Welsh, Doctor?" This from a persistent, youngish miner by the name of Chenkin.

"No," said Andrew. "I was brought up on the Gaelic."

"A lot o' good that would be 'ere!"

"I've always found it useful for swearing at my patients," said Andrew coolly, and a laugh went up against Chenkin.

It was over at last. "Thank you very much, Doctor Manson," Owen said. And Andrew was out again in the sour little waiting-room, feeling as if he had been buffeted by heavy seas, watching the rest of the candidates go in.

Edwards, the last man called, was absent a long, a very long time. He came out smiling broadly, his look plainly saying: "Sorry for you, fellows. This is in my pocket."

Then followed an interminable wait. But at last the door of the committee room opened and out of the smoke-swirling depths came Owen the secretary, a paper in his hands. His eyes, searching, rested finally with real friendliness upon Andrew.

"Would you come in a minute, Doctor Manson? The Committee would like to see you again."

Pale-lipped, his heart pounding in his side, Andrew followed the secretary back into the committee room. It couldn't be—no, no, it couldn't be that they were interested in him.

Back in the prisoner's chair again he found smiles and encouraging nods thrown in his direction. Doctor Llewellyn, however, was not looking at him.

Owen, spokesman of the meeting, commenced:—

"Doctor Manson, we may as well be frank with you. The Committee is in some doubt. The Committee, in fact, on Doctor Llewellyn's advice, had a strong bias in favour of another candidate, who has considerable knowledge of practice in the Gethely Valley."

"'E's too bloody fat, that Edwards," came an interruption from a grizzled member at the back. "I'd like to see 'im climb to the houses on Mardy Hill!"

Andrew was too tense to smile. Breathlessly, he waited on Owen's words.

"But to-day," the secretary went on, "I must say that the Committee have been very taken with you. The Committee—as Tom Kettles poetically expressed it a minute ago—want young, active men."

Laughter, with cries of "'Ear! 'Ear!" and "Good old Tom!"

"Moreover, Doctor Manson," continued Owen, "I must tell you that the Committee have been exceedin'ly struck by two testimonials, I might even say testimonials *unsolicited* by yourself, which makes them of more value in the eyes of the Committee and which reached us by post only this mornin'. These are from two practitioners in your own town, I mean Blaenelly. One is a Doctor Denny, who has the M.S., a very high degree, as Doctor Llewellyn, who should know, admits. The other, enclosed with Doctor Denny's, is signed by Doctor Page, whose assistant I believe you now are. Well, Doctor Manson, the Committee has experience of testimonials, and these two refer to your good self in such genuine terms that the Committee has been much impressed."

Andrew bit his lip, his eye lowered, aware for the first time of this generous thing that Denny had done for him.

"There is just one difficulty, Doctor Manson." Owen paused, diffidently moving the ruler on his table. "While the Committee is now unanimously disposed in your favour, this position with its—responsibilities—is more or less one for a married man. You see, apart from the fact that the men prefer a married doctor when it comes to attendin' their families, there's a house, Vale View, and a good house too, that goes with the position. It wouldn't—no, it wouldn't be very suitable for a single man."

A tumultuous silence. Andrew drew a tense breath, his thoughts focussed, a bright white light, upon the image of Christine. They were all, even Doctor Llewellyn, looking at him, awaiting his answer. Without thinking, entirely independent of his own volition, he spoke. He heard himself declaring calmly:—

"As a matter of fact, gentlemen, I'm engaged to someone in Blaenelly. I've—I've just been waiting on a suitable appointment—such as this—to get married."

Owen slapped down the ruler in satisfaction. There was approval, signified by a tapping of heavy boots.

And the irrepressible Kettles exclaimed: "Good enough, lad! Aberalaw's a rare fine place for an 'oneymoon!"

"I take it you're agreed then, gentlemen?" Owen's voice rose above the noise. "Doctor

Manson is unanimously appointed?"

There was a vigorous murmur of assent. Andrew experienced a wild thrill of triumph.

"When can you take up your duties, Doctor Manson? The earlier the better, so far as the Committee is concerned."

"I could start the beginning of next week," Manson answered. Then he turned cold as he thought: "Suppose Christine won't have me. Suppose I lose her, and this wonderful job as well."

"That's settled then. Thank you, Doctor Manson. I'm sure the Committee wishes you—and Mrs. Manson that's to be—every success in your new appointment."

Applause. They were all congratulating him now, the members, Llewellyn, and, with a very cordial clasp, Owen. Then he was out in the waiting-room, trying not to show his elation, trying to appear unconscious of Edwards' incredulous, crestfallen face.

But it was no use, no use at all. As he walked from the Square to the station his heart swelled with excited victory. His step was quick and springy. On his right, as he strode down the hill, was a small green public park with a fountain and a bandstand. Think of it! A bandstand—when the only elevation, the only feature of the landscape in Blaenelly was a slag-heap! Look at that cinema over there, too; those fine big shops; the hard good road—not a rocky mountain track—under his feet! And hadn't Owen said something about a hospital too, a "nice little" hospital? Ah! Thinking of what the hospital would mean to his work, Andrew drew a deep, excited breath. He hurled himself into an empty compartment in the train for Cardiff. And as it bore him thither he exulted wildly.

xiv

Though the distance was not great across the mountains, the railway journey from Aberalaw to Blaenelly was circuitous. The Down train stopped at every station, the Penelly Valley train into which he changed at Cardiff would not, simply would not go fast enough. Manson's mood had altered now. Sunk in the corner seat, chafing, burning to be back, his thoughts tormented him.

For the first time he saw how selfish he had been, these last few months, in considering only his side of the case. All his doubts about marriage, his hesitation in speaking to her, had centred on his own feelings and had preconceived the fact that she would take him. But suppose he had made a frightful mistake? Suppose Christine did not love him? He saw himself, rejected, dismally writing a letter to the Committee telling them that "owing to circumstances over which he had no control" he could not accept the position.

He saw her now, vividly before him. How well he knew her, the faint inquiring smile, the way in which she rested her hand against her chin, the steady candour in her dark brown eyes. A pang of longing shot through him. Dear Christine! If he had to forgo her he did not care what happened to him.

At nine o'clock the train crawled into Blaenelly. In a flash he was out on the platform and moving up Railway Road. Though he did not expect Christine until the morning, there was just the chance that she might already have arrived. Into Chapel Street... Round the corner of the Institute... A light in the front room of her lodgings sent a pang of expectation through him. Telling himself that he must contain himself, that it was probably only her landlady preparing the room, he swept into the house, burst into the sitting-room.

Yes! it was Christine. She was kneeling over some books in the corner, arranging them on the lowest shelf. Finished, she had begun to tidy up the string and paper which lay beside her on the floor. Her suitcase with her jacket and hat upon it lay in a chair. He saw she had not long returned.

"Christine!"

She swung round, still kneeling, a strand of hair fallen over her brow, then with a little cry of surprise and pleasure she rose.

"Andrew! How nice of you to come round."

Advancing towards him, her face alight, she held out her hand. But he took both her hands in his and held them tightly. He gazed down at her. He loved her especially in that skirt and blouse which she was wearing. It somehow increased her slightness, the tender sweetness of her youthfulness. Again his heart was throbbing.

"Chris! I've got to tell you something."

Concern swept into her eyes. She studied his pale and travel-grimed face with real anxiety.

She said quickly: "What has happened? Is it more trouble with Mrs. Page? Are you going away?"

He shook his head, enslaving her small hands more tightly in his.

And then, all at once, he broke out:—

"Christine! I've got a job, the most wonderful job. At Aberalaw. I was up seeing the Committee to-day. Five hundred a year, and a house. A house, Christine! Oh, darling—Christine—could you—would you marry me?"

She went very pale. Her eyes were lustrous in her pale face. Her breath seemed to catch in her throat.

She said faintly: "And I thought—I thought it was bad news you were going to tell me."

"No, no!"—impulsively. "It's the most marvellous news, darling. Oh! if you'd just seen the place. All open and clean, with green fields and decent shops and roads and a Park and—oh, Christine, actually a hospital! If only you'll marry me, darling, we can start there straight away."

Her lips were soft, trembling.

But her eyes smiled, smiled with that strange and shining lustre towards him.

"Is this because of Aberalaw, or because of me?"

"It's you, Chris. Oh, you know I love you; but then—perhaps you don't love me."

She gave a little sound in her throat, came towards him so that her head was buried in his breast.

As his arms went round her she said brokenly:—

"Oh, darling, darling. I've loved you ever since—" smiling through her happy tears —"oh, ever since I saw you walk into that stupid classroom."

Book II

i

Gwilliam John Lossin's decrepit motor van banged and boiled its way up the mountain road. Behind, an old tarpaulin drooped over the ruined tailboard, the rusted number-plate, the oil lamp that was never lit, dragging a smooth pattern in the dust. At the sides, the loose wings flapped and clattered to the rhythm of the ancient engine. And in front, jammed gaily in the driving seat with Gwilliam John, were Doctor Manson and his wife.

They had been married that morning. This was their bridal carriage. Underneath the tarpaulin were Christine's few pieces of furniture, a kitchen table bought secondhand in Blaenelly for twenty shillings, several new pots and pans, and their suitcases. Since they were without pride they had decided that the best, the cheapest way to bring this grand summation of their worldly goods, and themselves, to Aberalaw was in Gwilliam John's pantechnicon.

The day was bright, with a fresh breeze blowing, burnishing the blue sky. They had laughed and cracked jokes with Gwilliam John, who obliged occasionally with his special rendering of Handel's "Largo" upon the motor horn. They had stopped at the solitary inn high on the mountain at Ruthin Pass, to make Gwilliam John toast them in Rhymney beer. Gwilliam John, a scatterbrained little man with a squint, toasted them several times and then had a drop o' gin on his own account. Thereafter their career down Ruthin—with its two hairpin bends edging a sheer precipice of five hundred feet —had been demonic.

At last they crested the final rise and coasted down into Aberalaw. It was a moment tinged with ecstasy. The town lay before them with its long and undulating lines of roofs reaching up and down the Valley, its shops, churches, and offices clustered at the upper end and, at the lower, its mines and oreworks, the chimneys smoking steadily, the squat condenser belching clouds of steam—and all, all spangled by the midday sun.

"Look! Chris, look!" Andrew whispered, pressing her arm tightly. He had all the eagerness of the cicerone. "It's a fine place, isn't it? There's the Square up there. We've come in the back way. And look! No more oil lamps, darling. There's the gasworks. I wonder where our house is."

They stopped a passing miner, and were soon directed to Vale View, which lay, he told them, in this very road, on the fringe of the town. Another minute and they were there.

"Well!" said Christine. "It's—it's nice, isn't it?"

"Yes, darling. It looks—it looks a lovely house."

"By Gor!" Gwilliam John said, shoving his cap to the back of his head. "That's a rum-lookin' shop!"

Vale View was, indeed, an extraordinary edifice, at first sight something between a Swiss châlet and a Highland shooting-box, with a great profusion of little gables; the whole rough-cast, and standing in a half-acre of desolate garden choked with weeds and nettles, through which a stream tumbled over a variety of tin cans, to be surmounted midway in its course by a mouldering rustic bridge. Though they were not then aware of it, Vale View was their first introduction to the diverse power, the variegated omniscience, of the Committee—who, in the boom year of 1919, when contributions were rolling in, had said largely that they would build a house, a fine house that would do the Committee credit, something stylish, a "reglar smarter." Every member of the Committee had had his own positive idea as to what a reglar smarter should be. There were thirty members. Vale View was the result.

Whatever their impression of the outside, however, the new owners were speedily comforted within. The house was sound, well-floored, and cleanly papered. But the number of rooms was alarming. They both perceived instantly, though neither of them mentioned it, that Christine's few pieces would barely furnish two of these apartments.

"Let's see, darling," Chris said, counting practically on her fingers as they stood in the hall after their first breathless tour. "I make it a dining-room, drawing-room, and library, oh, or morning-room—whatever we like to call it—downstairs; and five bedrooms upstairs."

"That's right," Andrew smiled. "No wonder they wanted a married man!" His smile faded to compunction. "Honestly, Chris, I feel rotten about this—me, without a bean, using your nice furniture, like I was sponging on you, taking everything for granted, dragging you over here at a minute's notice—hardly giving them time to get your deputy into the school! I'm a selfish ass. I ought to have come over first and got the place decently ready for you."

"Andrew Manson! If you'd dared to leave me behind!"

"Anyhow I'm going to do something about it," he frowned at her doggedly. "Now listen, Chris—"

She interrupted with a smile.

"I think, darling, I'm going to make you an omelette—according to Madame Poulard. At least, the cookery book's idea of it."

Cut off at the outset of his declamation, his mouth open, he stared at her. Then gradually his frown vanished. Smiling again he followed her into the kitchen. He could not bear her out of his sight. Their footsteps made the empty house sound like a cathedral.

The omelette—Gwilliam John had been sent for the eggs before he took his departure—came out of the pan hot, savoury, and a delicate yellow. They ate it sitting together on the edge of the kitchen table. He exclaimed vigorously:—

"By God!—Sorry, darling; forgot I was a reformed character. By Jove! You *can* cook! That calendar they've left doesn't look bad on the wall. Fills it up nicely. And I like the picture on it—these roses. Is there a little more omelette? Who was Poulard? Sounds like a hen. Thanks, darling. Gosh! You don't know how keen I am to get started. There ought to be opportunities here. *Big* opportunities!" He broke off suddenly, his eyes resting on a varnished wooden case which stood beside their baggage in the corner. "I say, Chris! What's that?"

"Oh, that!" She made her voice sound casual. "That's a wedding present—from Denny!"

"Denny!" His face changed. Philip had been stiff and off-hand when he had charged down upon him to thank him for his help in getting the new job and to tell him he was marrying Christine. This morning he had not even come to see them off. It had hurt Andrew, made him feel that Denny was too complex, too incomprehensible to remain his friend. He advanced slowly, rather suspiciously, to the case; thinking, probably an old boot inside—that was Denny's idea of humour. He opened the case.

Then he gave a gasp of sheer delight. Inside was Denny's microscope, the exquisite Zeiss, and a note: "I don't really need this, I told you I was a sawbones. Good luck."

There was nothing to be said. Thoughtful, almost subdued, Andrew finished his omelette, his eye fixed all the time upon the microscope. Then, reverently, he took it up and, accompanied by Christine, went into the room behind the dining-room. He placed the microscope solemnly in the middle of the bare floor.

"This isn't the library, Chris—or the morning-room or the study or anything like that. Thanks to our good friend, Philip Denny, I hereby christen it the Lab."

He had just kissed her, to make the ceremony really effective, when the phone rang—a persistent shrilling which, coming from the empty hall, was singularly startling. They gazed at each other questioningly, excitedly.

"Perhaps it's a call, Chris! Think of it! My first Aberalaw case."

He dashed into the hall.

It was not a case, however, but Doctor Llewellyn, telephoning his welcome from his home at the other end of the town. His voice came over the wire, distinct and urbane, so that Chris, on her toes at Andrew's shoulder, could hear the conversation perfectly.

"Hel-*lo*, Manson. How are you? Don't fret, now; it isn't work this time. I only wanted to be the first to welcome you and your missus to Aberalaw."

"Thanks; thanks, Doctor Llewellyn. It's awfully good of you. I don't mind if it is work, though?"

"Tut! Tut! Wouldn't dream of it till you get straight," Llewellyn gushed. "And look here, if you're not doing anything to-night come over and have dinner with us, you and your missus, no formality, half-past seven, we'll be delighted to see you both. Then you and I can have a chat. That's settled, then. Good-by, in the meantime."

Andrew put down the receiver, his expression deeply gratified.

"Wasn't that decent of him, Chris? Asking us over bang off like that! The head doctor, mind you! He's a well-qualified man, too, I can tell you. I looked him up. London hospital—M.D., F.R.C.S., and the D.P.H. Think of it—all these star degrees! And he sounded so friendly. Believe me, Mrs. Manson, we're going to make a big hit here."

Slipping his arm round her waist, he began jubilantly to waltz her round the hall.

ii

That night, at seven o'clock, they set out through the brisk and busy streets for Doctor Llewellyn's house, Glynmawr. It was a stimulating walk. Andrew viewed his new fellow townsmen with enthusiasm.

"See that man coming, Christine? Quick! That fellow coughing over there."

"Yes, dear—but why—?"

"Oh, nothing!"—nonchalantly. "Only, he's probably going to be my patient."

They had no difficulty in finding Glynmawr, a solid villa with well-tended grounds, for Doctor Llewellyn's beautiful car stood outside and Doctor Llewellyn's beautifully polished plate, his qualifications displayed in small chaste letters, was bolted to the wrought-iron gate. Suddenly nervous, in the face of such distinction, they rang the bell and were shown in.

Doctor Llewellyn came out of the drawing-room to meet them, more dapper than ever in frock coat and stiff gold-linked cuffs, his expression beamingly cordial.

"Well, well! This is splendid. Delighted to meet you, Mrs. Manson. Hope you'll like Aberalaw. It's not a bad little place, I can tell you. Come along in here. Mrs. Llewellyn'll be down in a minute."

Mrs. Llewellyn arrived immediately, as beaming as her husband. She was a reddish-haired woman of about forty-five, with a palish freckled face; and, having greeted Manson, she turned towards Christine with an affectionate gasp.

"Oh, my de-ar, you lovely little thing! I declare I've lost my heart to you already. I must kiss you. I must. You don't mind, my dear, do you?"

Without pausing, she embraced Christine, then held her at arm's length, still viewing her glowingly. At the end of the passage a gong sounded. They went in to dinner.

It was an excellent meal—tomato soup, two roast fowls with stuffing and sausages, sultana pudding. Doctor and Mrs. Llewellyn talked smilingly to their guests.

"You'll soon get the hang of things, Manson," Llewellyn was saying. "Yes, indeed. I'll help you all I can. By the way, I'm glad that feller Edwards didn't get himself appointed. I couldn't have stuck him at any price, though I did half-promise I'd put a word in for him. What was I sayin'? Oh, yes! Well, you'll be at the West Surgery—that's your end—with old Doctor Urquhart—he's a card I can tell you—and Gadge the dispenser. Up here at the East Surgery we've got Doctor Medley and Doctor Oxborrow. Oh! They're all good chaps. You'll like them. Do you play golf? We might run out sometimes to the Fernley Course—that's only nine miles down the Valley. Of course I have a lot to do here. Yes, yes, indeed. Myself, I don't bother about the surgeries. I have the hospital on my hands, I do the compensation cases for the Company, I'm Medical Officer for the town, I have the gasworks appointment, I'm surgeon to the workhouse, and public vaccinator as well. I do all the approved Society examinations, with a good deal of County Court work. Oh! and I'm coroner, too. And besides," a gleam escaped his guileless eye, "I do a goodish bit of private practice odd times."

"It's a full list," Manson said.

Llewellyn beamed. "We got to make ends meet, Doctor Manson. That little car you saw outside cost a little matter of twelve hundred pound. As for—oh, well, never mind.

There's no reason why you shouldn't make a good livin' here. Say a round three to four hundred for yourself, if you work hard and watch your *p's* and *q's*." He paused—confidential, humidly sincere. "There's just one thing I think I ought to put you up to. It's been all settled and agreed amongst the assistant doctors that they each pay me a fifth of their incomes." He went on quickly, guilelessly: "That's because I see their cases for them. When they get worried they have me in. It's worked very well for them, I may tell you."

Andrew glanced up in some surprise. "Doesn't that come under the Medical Aid Scheme?"

"Well, not exactly," Llewellyn said, corrugating his brow. "It was all gone into and arranged by the doctors themselves a long time ago."

"But—?"

"Doctor Manson!" Mrs. Llewellyn was calling him sweetly from her end of the table. "I'm just telling your dear little wife we must see a lot of each other. She must come to tea sometime. You'll spare her to me, won't you, Doctor? And sometime she must run down to Cardiff with me in the car. That'll be nice, won't it, my de-ar?"

"Of course," Llewellyn proceeded glossily, "where you'll score—Leslie, that's the feller that was here before you, was a slack devil. Oh, he was a rotten doctor, nearly as bad as old Edwards. He couldn't give a decent anaesthetic anyhow! You're a good anaesthetist, I hope, Doctor? When I have a big case, especially my private cases, I must have a good anaesthetic. But, bless my soul! We'll not talk about that at present. Why, you've hardly started; it isn't fair to bother you."

"Idris!" cried Mrs. Llewellyn to her husband with a kind of delighted sensationalism. "They were only *married* this morning! Mrs. Manson just told me. She's a little bride! Why, would you believe it, the dear innocents!"

"Well, well, well, now!" beamed Llewellyn.

Mrs. Llewellyn patted Christine's hand. "My poor lamb! To think of the work you'll have getting straight in that stupid Vale View! I must come sometime and give you a hand."

Manson reddened slightly, collecting his scattered wits. He felt as though Christine and he had somehow become moulded into a soft little ball, played back and forth, with deft ease, between Doctor and Mrs. Llewellyn. However he judged the last remark propitious.

"Doctor Llewellyn," he said, with nervous resolution, "it's quite true what Mrs. Llewellyn says. I was wondering—I hate asking it—but could I have a couple of days off to take my wife to London to see about furnishings for our house and—and one or two other things?"

He saw Christine's eyes widen in surprise. But Llewellyn was graciously nodding his head.

"Why not? Why not? Once you start it won't be so easy to get off. You take to-morrow and the next day, Doctor Manson. You see! That's where I'm useful to you. I can help the assistants a lot. I'll speak to the Committee for you."

Andrew would not have minded speaking to the Committee, to Owen, himself. But he let the matter pass.

They drank their coffee in the drawing-room from, as Mrs. Llewellyn pointed out, "hand-painted" cups. Llewellyn offered cigarettes from his gold cigarette case.

"Take a look at that, Doctor Manson. There's a present for you! Grateful patient! Heavy, isn't it? Worth twenty pounds if it's worth a penny."

Towards ten o'clock Doctor Llewellyn looked at his fine half-hunter watch—actually he beamed at the watch, for he could contemplate even inanimate objects, particularly when they belonged to him, with that bland cordiality which was especially his own. For a moment Manson thought he was going into intimate details about the watch.

But instead he remarked: "I've got to go to the hospital. Gastro-duodenal I did this morning. How about runnin' round with me in the car and taking a look at it?"

Andrew sat up eagerly. "Why, I'd love to, Doctor Llewellyn."

Since Christine was included in the invitation also, they said good night to Mrs. Llewellyn, who waved them tender farewells from the front door, and stepped into the waiting car, which moved with silent elegance along the main street, then up the incline to the left.

"Powerful headlights, aren't they?" Llewellyn remarked, switching them on for their benefit. "Luxite! They're an extra. I had them fitted specially."

"Luxite!" said Christine suddenly, in a meek voice. "Surely they're very expensive, Doctor?"

"You bet they were," Llewellyn nodded emphatically, appreciative of the question. "Cost me every penny of thirty pounds."

Andrew, hugging himself, dared not meet his wife's eye.

"Here we are, then," said Llewellyn two minutes later. "This is my spiritual home."

The hospital was a red brick building, well-constructed and approached by a gravel drive flanked with laurel bushes. Immediately they entered Andrew's eyes lit up. Though small, the place was modern, beautifully equipped. As Llewellyn showed them round the theatre, the X-ray room, the splintroom, the two fine airy wards, Andrew kept thinking exultantly, this is perfect, perfect—what a difference from Blaenelly! God! I'll get my cases well, in here!

They picked up the matron on their travels, a tall, raw-boned woman who ignored Christine, greeted Andrew without enthusiasm, then melted into adoration before Llewellyn.

"We get pretty well all we want here, don't we, Matron?" Llewellyn said. "We just speak to the Committee. Yes, yes, they're not a bad lot, take them all in all. How's my gastro-enterostomy, Matron?"

"Very comfortable, Doctor Llewellyn," murmured the matron.

"Good! I'll see it in a minute!" He escorted Christine and Andrew back again to the vestibule.

"Yes, I do admit, Manson, I'm rather proud of this place. I regard it as my own. Can't blame me, either. You'll find your own way home, won't you? And look here, when you get back on Wednesday, ring me up. I might want you for an anaesthetic."

Walking down the road together they kept silence for a while; then Christine took Andrew's arm.

"Well?" she inquired.

He could feel her smiling in the darkness.

"I like him," he said quickly. "I like him a lot. Did you spot the matron, too—as if she was going to kiss the hem of his garment. But by Jove! That's a marvellous little hospital. It was a good dinner they gave us, too. They're not mean. Only—oh! I don't know—why should we pay him a fifth of our salary? It doesn't sound fair, or even ethical! And somehow—I feel as if I'd been smoothed and petted and told to be a good boy."

"You were a very good boy to ask for these two days. But really, darling—how can we do it? We've no money to buy furniture with—yet?"

"You wait and see," he answered cryptically.

The lights of the town lay behind now, and an odd silence fell between them as they approached Vale View. The touch of her hand upon his arm was precious to him. A great wave of love swept over him. He thought of her, married off-hand in a mining village, dragged in a derelict lorry across the mountains, dumped into a half-empty house where their wedding couch must be her own single bed—and sustaining these hardships and makeshifts with courage and a smiling tenderness. She loved him, trusted him, believed in him. A great determination swelled in him. He would repay it, he would show her, by his work, that her faith in him was justified.

They crossed the wooden bridge. The murmur of the stream, its littered banks hidden by the soft darkness of night, was sweet in their ears. He took the key from his pocket, the key of their house, and fitted it in the lock.

In the hall it was almost dark. When he had closed the door he turned to where she waited for him. Her face was faintly luminous, her slight figure expectant yet defenceless. He put his arm round her gently. He whispered, strangely:

"What's your name, darling?"

"Christine," she answered wondering.

"Christine what?"

"Christine Manson." Her breath came quickly, quickly, and was warm upon his lips.

iii

The following afternoon their train drew into Paddington Station. Adventurously, yet conscious of their inexperience in the face of this great city which neither of them had seen before, Andrew and Christine descended to the platform.

"Do you see him?" Andrew asked anxiously.

"Perhaps he'll be at the barrier," Christine suggested.

They were looking for the Man with the Catalogue.

On the journey down Andrew had explained, in detail, the beauty, simplicity, and extraordinary foresight of his scheme; of how, realizing their needs even before they left Blaenelly, he had placed himself in touch with the Regency Plenishing Company and Depositaries, of London, E. It wasn't a colossal establishment, the Regency—none of your department store nonsense—but a decent, privately owned emporium which specialized in hire purchase. He had the recent letter from the proprietor in his pocket. Why, in point of fact...

"Ah!" he now exclaimed with satisfaction. "There he is!"

A seedy little man in a shiny blue suit and a bowler hat, holding a large green catalogue like a Sunday School prize, seemed, by some obscure feat of telepathy, to single them out from the crowd of travellers. He sidled towards them.

"Doctor Manson, sir? And Mrs. Manson?" Deferentially raising his hat: "I represent the Regency. We had your telegram this morning, sir. I have the car waiting. May I offer you a cigar?"

As they drove through the strange, traffic-laden streets, Andrew betrayed perhaps the faintest glimmer of disquiet, the corner of one eye on the presentation cigar, still unlighted, in his hand.

He grunted: "We're doing a lot of driving about in cars these days. But this must be all right. They guarantee everything, including free transport to and from the station, *also* our railway fares."

Yet, despite this assurance, their transit along bewilderingly complex and often mean thoroughfares was perceptibly anxious. At length, however, they were there. It was a showier establishment than either of them had expected, and there was a good deal of plate glass and shiny brass about the frontage. The door of the car was opened for them; they were bowed into the Regency Emporium.

Again they were expected, made royally welcome by an elderly salesman in a frock coat and high collar, who with his striking air of probity bore some resemblance to the late Prince Albert.

"This way, sir. This way, madam. Very happy to serve a medical gentleman, Doctor Manson. You'd be surprised the number of 'Arley Street specialists I've had the honour of attending to. The testimonials I've 'ad from them! And now, Doctor, what would you be requiring?"

He began to show them furniture, padding up and down the aisles of the emporium with a stately tread. He named prices that were inconveniently large. He used the words "Tudor," "Jacobean," and "Looez Sez." And what he showed them was fumed and varnished rubbish.

Christine bit her lip and her worried look increased. She willed with all her strength that Andrew would not be deceived, that he would not burden their home with this awful stuff.

"Darling," she whispered swiftly, when Prince Albert's back was turned, "no good—no good at all."

A barely perceptible tightening of his lips was her answer. They inspected a few more pieces. Then quietly, but with surprising rudeness, Andrew addressed the salesman.

"Look here, you! We've come a long way to buy furniture. I said *furniture*. Not this kind of junk." Violently with his thumb he pressed the front of an adjoining wardrobe, which, being of plywood, caved in with an ominous cracking.

The salesman almost collapsed. This, his expression said, simply cannot be true.

"But, Doctor," he gulped, "I've been showing you and your lady the best in the 'ouse."

"Then show us the worst," Andrew raged. "Show us old secondhand stuff—so long as it's *real!*"

A pause. Then, muttering under his breath, "The guv'ner'll give me what for, if I don't sell you!" the salesman padded disconsolately away. He did not return. Four minutes later, a short red-faced common man came bustling towards them.

He shot out: "What d'you want?"

"Good secondhand furniture—cheap!"

The short man fired a hard glance at Andrew. Without further speech he spun round and led them to a trade lift at the back, which, when manipulated, dropped them to a large chilly basement, crammed to the ceiling with secondhand goods.

For an hour Christine probed amongst the dust and cobwebs, finding a stout chest here, a good plain table there, a small upholstered easy chair beneath a pile of sacking, while Andrew, following behind, wrangled long and stubbornly with the short man over prices.

Their list was complete at last, and Christine, her face smudged but happy, pressed Andrew's hand with a thrilling sense of triumph as they ascended in the lift.

"Just what we wanted," she whispered.

The red-faced man took them to the office, where, laying down his order book on the proprietor's desk with the air of a man who has laboured to do his best, he said: "That's the lot then, Mr. Isaacs."

Mr. Isaacs caressed his nose. His eyes, liquid against his sallow skin, were sorrowful as he studied the order book.

"I'm afraid we can't give you E.P. terms on this, Doctor Manson. You see, it's all secondhand goods." A deprecating shrug. "We don't do our business like that."

"Oh, yes you do, Mr. Isaacs. At least it says so in your letter. Printed in black and white on the top of your notepaper. 'New and secondhand furniture supplied on easy terms.'"

There was a pause. The red-faced man, bending over Mr. Isaacs, made rapid mutterings accompanied by gesticulations in his ear. Christine plainly caught impolite words which testified to the toughness of her husband's fibre, the power of his racial persistence.

"Well, Doctor Manson," smiled Mr. Isaacs, with an effort. "You shall have your way.

Don't say the Regency wasn't good to you. And don't forget to tell your patients. All about how well you were treated here... Smith! Make out that bill on the H.P. sheet and see that Doctor Manson has a copy posted to him first thing to-morrow morning!"

"Thank you, Mr. Isaacs."

Another pause. Mr. Isaacs said, by way of closing the interview: "That's right, then, that's right. The goods will reach you on Friday."

Christine made to leave the office. But Andrew still remained fast to his chair. He said slowly: "And now, Mr. Isaacs? What about our railway fares?"

It was as if a bomb had exploded into the office. Smith, the red-faced man, looked as though his veins would burst.

"My God, Doctor Manson!" exclaimed Isaacs. "What d'you mean? We can't do business like that. Fair's fair, but I ain't a camel! *Railway fares!*"

Inexorably Andrew produced his pocketbook. His voice, though it wavered slightly, was measured.

"I have a letter here, Mr. Isaacs, in which you say in plain black and white that you will pay customers' railway fares from England and Wales on orders over fifty pounds."

"But I tell you," Isaacs expostulated wildly, "you only bought fifty-five pounds' worth of goods—and all secondhand stuff—"

"In your letter, Mr. Isaacs—"

"Never mind my letter." Isaacs threw up his hands. "Never mind anything. The deal's off. I never had a customer like you in all my life! We're used to nice young married people which we can talk to. First you insult my Mr. Clapp, then my Mr. Smith can't do nothing with you, then you come here breakin' my heart with talk of *railway fares*. We can't do business, Doctor Manson. You can go try if you can do better somewhere else!"

Christine, in a panic, glanced at Andrew, her eyes holding a desperate appeal. She felt that all was lost. This terrible husband of hers had thrown away all the benefits he had so hardly won. But Andrew, appearing not to see her even, was dourly folding up his pocketbook and placing it in his pocket.

"Very well, then, Mr. Isaacs. We'll say good afternoon to you. But I'm telling you—this won't make very good hearing to all my patients and their friends. I have a large practice. And this is bound to get round. How you brought us up to London, promising to pay our fares, and when we—"

"Stop! Stop!" Isaacs wailed in something like a frenzy. "How much was your fares? Pay them, Mr. Smith! Pay them, pay them, *pay* them. Only don't say the Regency didn't ever do what it promised. *There* now! Are you satisfied?"

"Thank you, Mr. Isaacs. We're very satisfied. We'll expect delivery on Friday. Good afternoon, Mr. Isaacs."

Gravely, Manson shook him by the hand and, taking Christine's arm, hastened her to the door. Outside, the antique limousine which had brought them was waiting and, as though he had given the largest order in the history of the Regency, Andrew exclaimed:
—

"Take us to the Museum Hotel, driver!"

They were off immediately, without interference, swinging out of the East End in the direction of Bloomsbury. And Christine, tensely clutching Andrew's arm, allowed herself gradually to relax.

"Oh, darling," she whispered. "You managed that wonderfully. Just when I thought
—"

He shook his head, his jaw still stubbornly set.

"They didn't want trouble, that crowd. I had their promise, their *written promise—*"
He swung round to her, his eyes burning. "It wasn't these idiotic fares, darling. You
know that. It was the principle of the thing. People ought to keep their word. It put my
back up too, the way they were waiting for us, you could see it a mile away—here's a
couple of greenhorns—easy money—Oh, and that cigar they dumped on me too, the
whole thing reeked of swindle."

"We managed to get what we wanted, anyhow," she murmured tactfully.

He nodded. He was too strung-up, too seething with indignation, to see the humour
of it then. But in their room at the Museum the comic side became apparent. As he lit a
cigarette and stretched himself on the bed, watching her as she tidied her hair, he
suddenly began to laugh. He laughed so much that he set her laughing too.

"That look on old Isaacs' face—" he wheezed, his ribs aching. "It was—it was
screamingly funny."

"When you," she gasped weakly, "when you asked him for the fares!"

"'Business,' he said, 'we can't do business—'" He went off into another paroxysm.
"'Am I a camel,' he said. Oh, lord!—*a camel—*"

"Yes, darling." Comb in hand, tears running down her cheeks, she turned to him,
scarcely able to articulate. "But the funniest thing—to me—was the way you kept saying
'I've got it here in black and white' when I—when I—oh, dear!—*when I knew all the time
you'd left the letter on the mantelpiece at home.*"

He sat up, staring at her, then flung himself down with a yell of laughter. He rolled
about, stuffing the pillow into his mouth, helpless, out of all control, while she clung to
the dressing table, shaking, sore with laughter, begging him, deliriously, to stop or she
would expire.

Later, when they had managed to compose themselves, they went to the theatre. Since
he gave her free choice, she selected "Saint Joan." All her life, she told him, she had
wanted to see a play by Shaw.

Seated beside her in the crowded pit he was less engaged by the play—too historical,
he told her afterwards, who does this fellow Shaw think he is, anyway?—than by the
faint flush upon her eager, entranced face. Their first visit to the theatre together... Well,
it wouldn't be the last by a long way. His eyes wandered round the full house. They
would be back here again some day—not in the pit, in one of those boxes there. He
would see to it; he would show them all a thing or two! Christine would wear a low-
necked evening dress, people would look at him, nudge each other; that's Manson—you
know, that doctor who did that marvellous work on lungs... He pulled himself up
sharply, rather sheepishly, and bought Christine an ice cream at the interval.

Afterwards he was reckless in the princely manner. Outside the theatre they found
themselves completely lost, baffled by the lights, the buses, the teeming crowds.
Peremptorily Andrew held up his hand. Safely ensconced, being driven to their hotel,
they thought themselves, blissfully, pioneers in discovering the privacy afforded by a
London taxi.

iv

After London the breeze of Aberalaw was crisp and cool. Walking down from Vale View on Thursday morning to commence his duties, Andrew felt it strike invigoratingly on his cheek. A tingling exhilaration filled him. He saw his work stretching out before him here, work well and cleanly done, work always guided by his principle, the scientific method.

The West Surgery, which lay not more than four hundred yards from his house, was a high vaulted building, white-tiled and with a vague air of sanitation. Its main and central portion was the waiting-room. At the bottom end, cut off from the waiting-room by a sliding hatch, was the dispensary. At the top were two consulting rooms, one bearing the name of Doctor Urquhart and the other, freshly painted, the mysteriously arresting name, DOCTOR MANSON.

It gave Andrew a thrill of pleasure to see himself identified, already, with his room, which though not large had a good desk and a sound leather couch for examinations. He was flattered too by the number of people waiting on him—such a crowd, in fact, that he thought it better to begin work immediately without first making himself known, as he had intended, to Doctor Urquhart and the dispenser, Gadge.

Seating himself, he signed for his first case to come in. This was a man who asked simply for a certificate—adding, as a kind of afterthought, "Beat knee." Andrew examined him, found him suffering from beat knee, gave him the certificate of incapacity for work.

The second case came in. He also demanded his certificate; nystagmus. The third case: certificate, bronchitis. The fourth case: certificate, beat elbow.

Andrew got up, anxious to know where he stood. These certificative examinations took a great deal of time.

He went to his door and asked: "How many more men for certificates? Will they stand up, please?"

There were perhaps forty men waiting outside. They all stood up. Andrew reflected quickly. It would take him the best part of the day to examine them all properly—an impossible situation. Reluctantly, he made up his mind to defer the more exacting examinations until another time.

Even so, it was half-past ten when he got through his last case. Then, as he glanced up, there stamped into his room a medium-sized, oldish man with a brick-red face and a small pugnacious grey imperial. He stooped slightly, so that his head had a forward, belligerent thrust. He wore cord breeches, gaiters, and a tweed jacket, the side pockets stuffed to bursting with pipe, handkerchief, an apple, a gum-elastic catheter. About him hung the odour of drugs, carbolic, and strong tobacco. Andrew knew before he spoke that it was Doctor Urquhart.

"Dammit to hell, man," said Urquhart without a handshake or a word of introduction, "where were ye these last two days? I've had to lump your work for ye. Never mind, never mind! We'll say no more about it. Thank God ye look sound in mind an' limb now ye have arrived. Do ye smoke a pipe?"

"I do."

"Thank God for that also! Can ye play the fiddle?"

"No."

"Neither can I—but I can make them bonny. I collect china too. They've had my name in a book. I'll show ye some day when ye come ben my house. It's just at the side of the surgery, ye'll have observed. And now, come away and meet Gadge. He's a miserable devil. But he knows his incompatibles."

Andrew followed Urquhart through the waiting-room into the dispensary, where Gadge greeted him with a gloomy nod. He was a long, lean, cadaverous man with a bald head streaked with jet black hair and drooping whiskers of the same colour. He wore a short alpaca jacket, green with age and the stains of drugs, which showed his bony wrists and death's door shoulder blades. His air was sad, caustic, tired; his attitude that of the most disillusioned man in the whole universe. As Andrew entered he was serving his last client, flinging a box of pills through the hatch as though it were rat poison. "Take it or leave it," he seemed to say. "You've got to die in any case!"

"Well," said Urquhart spryly, when he had effected the introduction. "Ye've met Gadge and ye know the worst. I warn ye he believes in nothing except maybe castor oil and Charles Bradlaugh. Now—is there anything I can tell ye?"

"I'm worried about the number of certificates I had to sign. Some of these chaps this morning looked to me quite capable of work."

"Ay, ay. Leslie let them pile up on him anyhow. His idea of examining a patient was to take his pulse for exactly five seconds by the clock. He didn't mind a docken."

Andrew answered quickly: "What can anyone think of a doctor who hands out certificates like cigarette coupons?"

Urquhart darted a glance at him. He said bluntly:—

"Be careful how you go. They're liable not to like it if you sign them off."

For the first and last time that morning Gadge made gloomy interjection.

"That's because there's nothing wrong wi' half o' them, ruddy scrimshankers!"

All that day as he went on his visits Andrew worried about these certificates. His round was not easy, for he did not know the neighbourhood, the streets were unfamiliar, and more than once he had to go back and cover the same ground twice. His district, moreover, or the greater part of it, lay on the side of that Mardy Hill to which Tom Kettles had referred, and this meant stiff climbing between one row of houses and the next.

Before afternoon his cogitation had forced him to an unpleasant decision. He could not, on any account, give a slack certificate. He went down to his evening surgery with an anxious yet determined line fixed between his brows.

The crowd, if anything, was larger than at the morning surgery. And the first patient to enter was a great lump of a man, rolling in fat, who smelled strongly of beer and looked as if he had never done a full day's work in his life. He was about fifty and had small pig eyes which blinked down at Andrew.

"Certificate," he said, without minding his manners.

"What for?" Andrew asked.

"'Stagmus." He held out his hand. "The name's Chenkin. Ben Chenkin."

The tone alone caused Andrew to look at Chenkin with quick resentment. Even from a cursory inspection he felt convinced that Chenkin had no nystagmus. He was well aware, apart from Gadge's hint, that some of these old pitmen "swung the lead on 'stagmus," drawing compensation money to which they were not entitled for years on end. However, he had brought his ophthalmoscope with him this evening. He would soon make sure. He rose from his seat.

"Take your things off."

This time it was Chenkin who asked: "What for?"

"I'm going to examine you."

Ben Chenkin's jaw dropped. He had not been examined, so far as he could remember, in the whole of Doctor Leslie's seven years of office. Unwillingly, sulkily, he pulled off his jacket, his muffler, his red-and-blue-striped shirt, revealing a hairy torso swathed in adiposity.

Andrew made a long and thorough examination, particularly of the eyes, searching both retinae carefully with his tiny electric bulb.

Then, sharply, he said: "Dress up, Chenkin." He sat down and, taking his pen, he began to write out a certificate.

"Ha!" sneered old Ben. "I thought you'd let us 'ave it."

"Next, please," Andrew called out.

Chenkin almost snatched the pink slip from Andrew's hand. Then he strode triumphantly from the surgery.

Five minutes later he was back, his face livid, bellowing like a bull, thrusting his way between the men seated waiting on the benches.

"Look what he's done on us! Let us in, will ye? Hey! What's the meanin' of this?"

He flourished the certificate in Andrew's face.

Andrew affected to read the slip. It said, in his own handwriting:—

This is to certify that Ben Chenkin is suffering from the effects of overindulgence in malt liquors but is perfectly fit to work.

Signed: A. MANSON, M.B.

"Well?" he asked.

"'Stagmus," shouted Chenkin. "Certificate for 'stagmus. You can't play the bloody fool on us. Fifteen year us got 'stagmus!"

"You haven't got it now," Andrew said.

A crowd had gathered round the open door. He was conscious of Urquhart's head popping out curiously from the other room, of Gadge inspecting the tumult with relish through his hatch.

"For the last time—are ye going to give us 'stagmus certificate?" Chenkin bawled.

Andrew lost his temper.

"No, I'm not," he shouted back. "And get out of here before I put you out."

Ben's stomach heaved. He looked as if he might wipe the floor with Andrew. Then his eyes dropped; he turned and, muttering profane threats, walked out of the surgery.

The minute he was gone Gadge came out of the dispensary and shuffled across to Andrew. He rubbed his hands with melancholy delight.

"You know who that was you just knocked off? Ben Chenkin. His son's a big man on the Committee."

V

The sensation of the Chenkin case was enormous; it hummed round Manson's district in a flash. Some people said it was "a good job"—a few went so far as "a damned good job"—that Ben had been pulled up in his swindling and signed fit for work. But the majority were on Ben's side. All the "compo cases"—those drawing compensation money for disabilities—were especially bitter against the new doctor. As he went on his rounds Andrew was conscious of black looks directed towards him. And at night, in the surgery, he had to face an even worse manifestation of unpopularity.

Although nominally every assistant was allotted a district, the workmen in that district had still the right of free choice of doctor. Each man had a card and by demanding that card and handing it to another doctor he could effect a change. It was this ignominy which now began for Andrew. Every night that week men whom he had never seen dropped into his surgery—some who were disinclined for the personal encounter even sent their wives—to say, without looking at him: "If you don't mind, Doctor, I'll 'ave my card."

The wretchedness, the humiliation of rising to extract these cards from the box on his desk was intolerable. And every card he gave away meant ten shillings subtracted from his salary.

On Saturday night Urquhart invited him into his house. The old man, who had gone about all week with an air of self-justification on his choleric features, began by exhibiting the treasures of his forty years of practice. He had perhaps a score of yellow violins, all made by himself, hung up on his walls, but these were as nothing compared with the choice perfection of his collection of old English china.

It was a superb collection—Spode, Wedgwood, Crown Derby, and best of all, old Swansea—they were all there. His plates and mugs, his bowls, cups, and jugs—they filled every room in the house and overflowed into the bathroom where it was possible for Urquhart, when making his toilet, to survey with pride an original willow pattern tea service.

China was, in fact, the passion of Urquhart's life, and he was an old and cunning master in the gentle art of acquiring it. Whenever he saw a "nice bit"—his own phrase—in a patient's house he would call and call with unwearying attention, meanwhile fixing his eye, with a kind of wistful persistence, upon the coveted piece; until at last in desperation the good woman of the house would exclaim: "Doctor, you seem awful struck on that bit. I can't see but what I'm goin' to let you 'ave it!"

Thereupon Urquhart would make a virtuous protest; then, bearing his trophy, wrapped up in newspaper, he would dance home in triumph and place it tenderly on his shelves.

The old man passed, in the town, as a character. He gave his age as sixty but was probably over seventy, and possibly near to eighty. Tough as whalebone, his sole vehicle shoe leather, he covered incredible distances, swore murderously at his patients, and could yet be tender as a woman; lived by himself—since the death of his wife eleven years before—and existed almost entirely upon tinned soup.

This evening, having proudly displayed his collection, he suddenly remarked to

Andrew with an injured air:—

"Dammit, man! I don't want any of your patients. I've got enough of my own. But what can I do if they come pestering me? They can't all go to the East Surgery; it's too far away."

Andrew reddened. There was nothing that he could say.

"You want to be more careful, man," Urquhart went on in an altered tone. "Oh, I know, I know. You want to tear down the walls of Babylon—I was young myself once. But all the same, go slow, go easy, look before you leap! Good night. My compliments to your wife."

With Urquhart's words sounding in his ear, Andrew made every effort to steer a cautious course. But, even so, a greater disaster immediately overtook him.

On the Monday following he went to the house of Thomas Evans in Cefen Row. Evans, a hewer at the Aberalaw colliery, had upset a kettle of boiling water over his left arm. It was a serious scald, covering a large area and particularly bad in the region of the elbow. When Andrew arrived he found that the District Nurse, who had been in the Row at the time of the accident, had dressed the scald with carron oil and had then continued on her round.

Andrew examined the arm, carefully suppressing his horror of the filthy dressing. Out of the corner of his eye he observed the carron oil bottle, corked with a plug of newspaper, holding a dirty whitish liquid, in which he could almost see bacteria seething in shoals.

"Nurse Lloyd done it pretty good, eh, Doctor?" said Evans nervously. He was a dark-eyed, highly strung youngster and his wife, who stood near, closely observing Andrew, was nervous too and not unlike him in appearance.

"A beautiful dressing," Andrew said with a great show of enthusiasm. "I've rarely seen a neater one. Only a first dressing, of course. Now I think we'll try some picric."

He knew that if he did not quickly use the antiseptic the arm would almost certainly become infected. And then, he thought, heaven help that elbow joint!

They watched him dubiously while, with scrupulous gentleness, he cleansed the arm and slipped on a moist picric dressing.

"There now," he exclaimed. "Doesn't that feel easier?"

"I don't know as how it does," Evans said. "Are you sure it's goin' to be all right, Doctor?"

"Positive!" Andrew smiled reassuringly. "You must leave this to Nurse and me."

Before he left the house he wrote a short note to the District Nurse, taking extra pains to be tactful, considerate of her feelings, wise. He thanked her for her splendid emergency treatment and asked her, as a measure against possible sepsis, if she would mind continuing with the picric dressings. He sealed the envelope carefully.

Next morning, when he arrived at the house, his picric dressings had been thrown in the fire and the arm was redressed with carron oil. Waiting upon him, prepared for battle, was the District Nurse.

"What's all this about, I'd like to know? Isn't my work good enough for you, Doctor Manson?" She was a broad, middle-aged woman with untidy iron-grey hair and a harassed, over-wrought face. She could barely speak for the heaving of her bosom.

Andrew's heart sank. But he took a rigid grip upon himself. He forced a smile.

"Come now, Nurse Lloyd, don't misunderstand me. Suppose we talk this over together in the front room."

The nurse bridled, swept her eye to where Evans and his wife, who clutched a little girl of three to her skirts, were listening wide-eyed and alarmed.

"No, indeed, we'll talk it over here. I got nothing to hide. My conscience is clear. Born and brought up in Aberalaw I was; went to school here; married here; 'ad children here; lost my 'usband here; and worked here twenty year as District Nurse. And nobody ever told me not to use carron oil on a burn or scald."

"Now listen, Nurse," Andrew pleaded. "Carron oil is all right in its way, perhaps. But there's a great danger of contracture here." He stiffened up her elbow by way of illustration. "That's why I want you to try my dressing."

"Never 'eard of the stuff. Old Doctor Urquhart don't use it. And that's what I told Mr. Evans. I don't hold with newfangled ideas of somebody that's been here no more nor a week!"

Andrew's lips were dry. He felt shaky and ill at the thought of further trouble, of all the repercussions of this scene; for the nurse, going from house to house, and talking her mind in all of them, was a person with whom it was dangerous to quarrel. But he could not, he dared not, risk his patient with that antiquated treatment.

He said in a low voice: "If you won't do the dressing, Nurse, I'll come in morning and evening and do it myself."

"You can then, for all I care," Nurse Lloyd declared, moisture flashing to her eyes. "And I 'ope Tom Evans lives through it."

The next minute she had flounced out of the house.

In dead silence Andrew removed the dressing once again. He spent nearly half an hour patiently bathing and attending to the damaged arm. When he left the house he promised to return at nine o'clock that night.

That same evening, as he entered his consulting-room, the first person to enter was Mrs. Evans, her face white, her dark frightened eyes avoiding his.

"I'm sure, Doctor," she stammered, "I do hate to trouble you; but can I have Tom's card?"

A wave of hopelessness passed over Andrew. He rose without a word, searched for Tom Evans' card, handed it to her.

"You understand, Doctor, you—you won't be callin' any more!"

He said unsteadily: "I understand, Mrs. Evans." Then as she made for the door he asked—he had to ask—the question: "Is the carron oil on again?"

She gulped, nodded, and was gone.

After surgery, Andrew, who usually tore home at top speed, made the passage to Vale View wearily. A triumph, he thought bitterly, for the scientific method! And again, am I honest or am I simply clumsy? Clumsy and stupid, stupid and clumsy!

He was very silent during supper. But afterwards, in the sitting-room, now comfortably furnished, while they sat together on the couch before the cheerful fire, he laid his head close to her soft young breasts.

"Oh, darling," he groaned, "I've made an awful muddle of our start!"

As she soothed him, gently stroking his brow, he felt tears smarting behind his eyes.

vi

Winter set in early and unexpectedly with a heavy fall of snow. Though it was only mid-October, Aberalaw lay so high that hard and bitter frosts gripped the town almost before the leaves had fallen from the trees. The snow came silently through the night, soft drifting flakes, and Christine and Andrew woke to a great glittering whiteness. A herd of mountain ponies had come through a gap in the broken wooden palings at the side of the house and were gathered round the back door. Upon the wide uplands, stretches of rough grass land all around Aberalaw, these dark wild little creatures roamed in large numbers, starting away at the approach of man. But in snowy weather, hunger drove them down to the outskirts of the town.

All winter Christine fed the ponies. At first they backed from her, shy and stumbling, but in the end they came to eat from her hand. One especially became her friend, the smallest of them all, a black, tangle-maned, roguish-eyed creature, no larger than a Shetland, whom they named Darkie.

The ponies would eat any kind of food, scraps of loaf, potato and apple rinds, even orange peel. Once, in fun, Andrew offered Darkie an empty matchbox. Darkie munched it down, then licked his lips like a gourmet eating pâté.

Though they were so poor, though they had to bear many things, Christine and Andrew knew happiness. Andrew had only pence to jingle in his pockets, but the Endowment debt was almost settled and the furniture instalments were being paid. Christine, for all her fragility and look of inexperience, had the attribute of the Yorkshire woman: she was a housewife. With the help only of a young girl named Jenny, a miner's daughter from the Row behind who came daily for a few shillings each week, she kept the house shining. Although four of its rooms remained unfurnished, and discreetly locked, she made Vale View a home. When Andrew came in tired, almost defeated by a long day, she would have a hot meal on the table which quickly restored him.

The work of the practice was desperately hard—not, alas! because he had many patients, but because of the snow, the difficult "climbs" to the high parts of his district, the long distances between his calls. When it thawed and the roads turned to slush, before freezing hard again at night, the going was heavy and difficult. He came in so often with sodden trouser-ends that Christine bought him a pair of leggings. At night when he sank into a chair exhausted she would kneel and take off these leggings, then his heavy boots, before handing him his slippers. It was not an act of service but of love.

The people remained suspicious, difficult. All Chenkin's relations—and they were numerous, since intermarriage was common in the Valleys—had become welded into a hostile unit. Nurse Lloyd was openly and bitterly his enemy, and would run him down as she sat drinking tea in the houses which she visited, listened to by a knot of women from the Row.

In addition he had to contend with an ever-increasing irritation. Doctor Llewellyn was using him for anaesthetics far oftener than he judged fair. Andrew hated giving anaesthetics—it was mechanical work which demanded a specialized type of mind, a slow and measured temperament which he certainly did not possess. He did not in the least object to serving his own patients. But when he found himself requisitioned three days a week for cases he had never seen before, he began to feel that he was shouldering a burden which belonged to someone else. Yet he simply dared not risk a protest, for fear of losing his job.

One day in November, however, Christine noticed that something unusual had upset him. He came in that evening without hailing her gaily and, though he made pretence of unconcern, she loved him too well not to detect, from the deepened line between his eyes and a score of other minute signs, that he had received an unexpected blow.

She made no comment during supper, and afterwards she began to busy herself with some sewing beside the fire.

He sat beside her, biting on his pipe; then all at once he declared:—

"I hate grousing, Chris! And I hate bothering you. God knows I try to keep things to myself!"

This, considering that he poured his heart out to her every night, was highly diverting. But Christine did not smile as he continued:—

"You know the hospital, darling. You remember going over it our first night. Remember how I loved it and raved about opportunities and chances of doing fine work there, and everything? I thought a lot about that, didn't I, darling? I had great ideas about our little Aberalaw Hospital?"

"Yes, I know you did."

He said stonily:—

"I needn't have deluded myself. It isn't the Aberalaw Hospital. It's Llewellyn's Hospital."

She was silent, her eyes concerned, waiting for him to explain.

"I had a case this morning, Chris!" He spoke quickly now, at white heat. "You'll note that I say *had!*—a really early apical pneumonia, in one of the anthracite drillers, too. I've told you often how terribly interested I am in their lung conditions. I'm positive there's a big field for research work there. I thought to myself: Here's my first case for hospital—genuine chance for charting and scientific recording. I rang up Llewellyn, asked him to see the case with me, so that I could get it into the ward."

He stopped to take a swift breath, then rushed on:—

"Well! Down came Llewellyn, limousine and all. Nice as you please, and damned thorough in his examination. He knows his work inside-out, mind you; he's an absolute topnotch man. He confirmed the diagnosis, after pointing out one or two things I'd missed, and absolutely agreed to take the case into hospital there and then. I began to thank him, saying how much I would appreciate coming into the ward and having such good facilities for this particular case." He paused again, his jaw set. "Llewellyn gave me a look at that, Chris, very friendly and nice. 'You needn't bother about coming up, Manson,' he said, '*I'll* look after him now. We couldn't have you assistants clattering around the wards'—he took a look at my leggings—'in your hobnail boots.'" Andrew broke off with a choking exclamation. "Oh! What's the use going over what he said? It all boils down to this: I can go tramping into miners' kitchens, in my sopping raincoat and dirty boots, examining my cases in a bad light, treating them in bad conditions, but when it comes to the hospital—ah! I'm only wanted there to give the ether!"

He was interrupted by the ringing of the telephone. Gazing at him with sympathy she rose, after a moment, to answer it. He could hear her speaking in the hall. Then, very hesitatingly, she returned.

"It's Doctor Llewellyn on the phone. I'm—I'm terribly sorry, darling. He wants you to-morrow at eleven for—for an anaesthetic."

He did not answer, but remained with his head bowed despondently between his clenched fists.

"What shall I tell him, darling?" Christine murmured anxiously.

"Tell him to go to hell!" he shouted; then, passing his hand across his brow: "No, no. Tell him I'll be there at eleven." He smiled bitterly. "At eleven *sharp*."

When she came back she brought him a cup of hot coffee—one of her effectual devices for combating his moods of depression.

As he drank it he smiled at her wryly.

"I'm so dashed happy here with you, Chris. If only the work would go right. Oh! I admit there's nothing personal or unusual in Llewellyn's keeping me out of the wards. It's the same in London, in all the big hospitals everywhere. It's the system. But why should it be, Chris? Why should a doctor be dragged off his case when it goes into hospital? He loses the case as completely as if he'd lost the patient. It's part of our damn Specialist-G.P. system, and it's wrong, all wrong! Lord! why am I lecturing you, though? As if we hadn't enough worries of our own. When I think how I started here! What I was going to do! And instead—one thing after another—all gone wrong!"

But at the end of the week he had an unexpected visitor. Quite late, when he and Christine were upon the point of going upstairs, the doorbell rang. It was Owen, the secretary to the Society.

Andrew paled. He saw the secretary's visit as the most ominous event of all, the climax of these struggling unsuccessful months. Did the Committee want him to resign? Was he to be sacked, thrown out with Christine into the street, a wretched failure? His heart contracted as he gazed at the secretary's thin, diffident face, then suddenly expanded with relief and joy as Owen produced a yellow card.

"I'm sorry to call so late, Doctor Manson, but I've been detained late at the office; I didn't have time to look in at the surgery. I was wondering if you would care to have my medical card. It's strange, in a way, me being secretary to the Society, that I haven't ever bothered to fix up. The last time I visited a doctor I was down in Cardiff. But now, if you'll have me, I'd greatly appreciate to be on your list."

Andrew could scarcely speak. He had handed over so many of these cards, wincing as he did so, that now to receive one, and from the secretary himself, was overwhelming.

"Thank you, Mr. Owen. I'll—I'll be delighted to have you."

Christine, standing in the hall, was quick to interpose.

"Won't you come in, Mr. Owen? Please."

Protesting that he was disturbing them, the secretary seemed nevertheless willing to be persuaded into the sitting-room. Seated in an armchair, his eyes fixed reflectively upon the fire, he had an air of extraordinary tranquillity. Though in his dress and speech he seemed no different from an ordinary workingman, he had the contemplative stillness, the almost transparent complexion, of the ascetic. He appeared for some moments to be arranging his thoughts. Then he said:—

"I'm glad to have the opportunity of talking to you, Doctor. Don't be downhearted if you're havin' a bit of a setback to begin with, like! They're a little stiff, the folks here, but they're all right at heart. They'll come, after a bit, they'll come!"

Before Andrew could intervene he continued:—

"You haven't heard of Tom Evans, like? No? His arm has turned out very bad. Ay, that stuff you warned them against did exactly what you was afraid of. His elbow's gone all stiff and crooked, he can't use it, he's lost his job at the pit over it. Ay, and since it was at home he scalded himself, he don't get a penny piece of compo."

Andrew muttered an expression of regret. He had no rancour against Evans, merely a sense of sadness at the futility of this case which had so needlessly gone wrong.

Owen was again silent, then in his quiet voice he began to tell them about his own early struggles, of how he had worked underground as a boy of fourteen, attended night school and gradually "improved himself," learned typing and shorthand, and finally secured the secretaryship of the Society.

Andrew could see that Owen's whole life was dedicated to improving the lot of the men. He loved his work in the Society because it was an expression of his ideal. But he wanted more than mere medical services. He wanted better housing, better sanitation, better and safer conditions, not only for the miners, but for their dependents. He quoted the maternity mortality rate amongst miners' wives, the infantile mortality rate. He had all the figures, all the facts at his finger-ends.

But, besides talking, he listened. He smiled when Andrew related his experience with the sewer in the typhoid epidemic at Blaenelly. He showed a deeper interest in the view that the anthracite workers were more liable to lung troubles than other underground workers.

Stimulated by Owen's presence, Andrew launched into this subject with great ardour. He had been struck, as the result of many painstaking examinations, by the large percentage of the anthracite miners who suffered from insidious forms of lung disease. In Blaenelly many of the drillers who came to him complaining of a cough or "a bit of phlegm in the tubes" were in reality incipient or even open cases of pulmonary tuberculosis. And he was finding the same thing here. He had begun to ask himself if there was not some direct connection between the occupation and the disease.

"You see what I mean?" he exclaimed eagerly. "These men are working in dust all day, bad stone dust in the hard headings—their lungs get choked with it. Now I have my suspicion that it's injurious. The drillers, for instance, who get most of it—they seem to develop trouble more frequently than, say, the hauliers. Oh! I may be on the wrong track. But I don't think so! And what excites me so much is—oh, well! it's a line of investigation nobody has covered much. There's no mention in the Home Office list of any such industrial disease. When these men are laid up they don't get a penny piece of compensation!"

Roused, Owen bent forward, a vivid animation kindling his pale face.

"My goodness, Doctor. You're really talkin'! I never heard anything so important for a long time."

They fell into a lively discussion of the question. It was late when the secretary rose to go. Apologizing for having stayed so long, he pressed Andrew wholeheartedly to proceed with his investigation, promising him all the help in his power.

As the front door closed behind Owen, he left a warm impression of sincerity. And

Andrew thought, as at the Committee meeting when he had been given the appointment: "That man is my friend."

The news that the secretary had lodged his card with Andrew spread quickly through the district, and did something to arrest the run of the new doctor's unpopularity.

Apart from this material gain both Christine and he felt better for Owen's visit. So far, the social life of the town had completely passed them by. Though Christine never spoke of it there were moments during Andrew's long absences upon his rounds when she felt her loneliness. The wives of the higher officials of the Company were too conscious of their own importance to call upon the wives of medical aid assistants. Mrs. Llewellyn, who had promised undying affection, and delightful little motor trips to Cardiff, left cards when Christine was out and was not heard of again. While the wives of Doctors Medley and Oxborrow of the East Surgery—the former a faded white rabbit of a woman, the latter a stringy zealot who talked West African missions for one hour by the secondhand Regency clock—had proved singularly uninspiring. There seemed, indeed, to be no sense of unity or social intercourse amongst the medical assistants or their wives. They were indifferent, unresistant, and even downtrodden in the attitude they presented to the town.

One December afternoon, when Andrew was returning to Vale View by the back road which led along the brow of the hill, he saw approaching a lanky yet erect young man of his own age whom he recognized at once as Richard Vaughan. His first impulse was to cross to the other side to avoid the oncoming figure. And then, doggedly, came the thought: "Why should I? I don't care a damn who he is!"

With his eyes averted, he prepared to trudge past Vaughan—when, to his surprise, he heard himself addressed in a friendly, half-humorous tone.

"Hello! You're the chap who put Ben Chenkin back to work, aren't you?"

Andrew stopped, his gaze lifting warily, his expression saying: "What of it? I didn't do it for you." Though he answered civilly enough, he told himself he was not prepared to be patronized even by the son of Edwin Vaughan. The Vaughans were the virtual owners of the Aberalaw Company; they drew all the royalties from the adjacent pits, were rich, exclusive, unapproachable. Now that old Edwin had retired to an estate near Brecon, Richard, the only son, had taken over the managing directorship of the Company. Recently married, he had built himself a large modern house overlooking the town.

Now, considering Andrew and tugging at his spare moustache, Vaughan said:—

"I'd have enjoyed seeing old Ben's face."

"I didn't find it particularly amusing."

Vaughan's lip twitched behind his hand at the stiff Scots pride.

He said easily: "You're by way of being our nearest neighbours. My missus—she's been away in Switzerland these last weeks—will be calling on yours, now that you're settled in."

"Thanks!" Andrew said curtly, walking on.

At tea that night he related the incident sardonically to Christine.

"What was his idea? Tell me that! I've seen him pass Llewellyn in the street and barely throw him a nod. Perhaps he thought he'd mug me into sending a few more men back to work at his dashed mines!"

"Now, don't, Andrew," Christine protested. "That's one thing about you! You're suspicious, frightfully suspicious of people."

"Think I would be suspicious of him. Stuck up blighter, rolling in money, old school tie under his ugly phiz—'My missus'—been yodelling on the Alps while you pigged it on Mardy Hill 'will be calling on yours'! Huh! I can *see* her looking near us, darling! And if she does,"—he was suddenly fierce,—"take jolly good care you don't let her patronize you."

Chris answered—more shortly than he had ever heard her in all the tenderness of those first months—"I think I know how to behave."

Despite Andrew's premonitions Mrs. Vaughan did call upon Christine and remained, apparently, much longer than the bare period demanded by convention. When Andrew came in that evening he found Christine gay, slightly flushed, with every appearance of having enjoyed herself. She was reticent to his ironic probings but admitted that the occasion had been a success.

He mocked her. "I suppose you had out the family silver, the best china, the gold plated samovar. Oh! and a cake from Parry's."

"No. We had bread and butter," she answered equably, "and the brown teapot."

He raised his brows derisively.

"And she liked it?"

"I hope so!"

Something rankled queerly in Andrew after this conversation, an emotion which, had he tried, he could not quite have analyzed. Ten days later when Mrs. Vaughan rang him up and asked Christine and him to dinner he was shaken. Christine was in the kitchen at the time baking a cake, and he answered the phone himself.

"I'm sorry," he said. "I'm afraid it's impossible. I have surgery till nearly nine every evening."

"But not on Sunday, surely!" Her voice was light, charming. "Come to supper next Sunday. That's settled, then. We'll expect you!"

He stormed into Christine.

"These dashed high-blown friends of yours have raked us in to supper. We can't go! I've got a positive conviction I'm having a midder case next Sunday evening!"

"Now you listen to me, Andrew Manson!" Her eyes had sparkled at the invitation, but nevertheless she lectured him severely. "You've got to stop being silly. We're poor, and everybody knows it. You wear old clothes and I do the cooking. But that doesn't matter. You're a doctor and a good doctor, too; and I'm your wife." Her expression relaxed momentarily. "Are you listening to me? Yes; it may surprise you, but I have my marriage lines tucked away in my bottom drawer. The Vaughans have got a lot of money, but that's just a detail beside the fact that they're kind and charming and intelligent people. We're marvellously happy together here, darling; but we must have friends. Why shouldn't we be friendly with them if they'll let us? Now don't you be ashamed of being poor. Forget about money and position and everything, and learn to take people for what they really are!"

"Oh, well—" he said grudgingly.

He went, on Sunday, expressionless and with apparent docility, merely using the corner of his mouth to remark, as they walked up the well-laid-out drive beside a new hard tennis court: "Probably won't let us in, seeing I haven't got on a fish-and-soup."

Contrary to his expectation, they were well received. Vaughan's bony, ugly face smiled hospitably over a silver canister which, for a reason unexplained, he shook heartily. Mrs. Vaughan greeted them with effortless simplicity. There were two other guests, Professor and Mrs. Challis, who were staying over the week end with the Vaughans.

Over the first cocktail he had ever dealt with in his life Andrew took stock of the long fawn-carpeted room with its flowers, books, strangely beautiful old furniture. Christine was talking lightheartedly with Vaughan and his wife and Mrs. Challis, an elderly woman with humorous wrinkles around her eyes. Feeling isolated and conspicuous, Andrew gingerly approached Challis who, despite a large white beard, was successfully and cheerfully dispatching his third short drink.

"Will some bright young physician kindly undertake an investigation," he smiled at Andrew, "as to the exact function of the olive in the Martini? Mind you I warn you beforehand—I have my suspicions. But what do you think, Doctor?"

"Why—" Andrew stammered. "I—I hardly know—"

"My theory!" Challis took pity on him. "A conspiracy of bartenders and inhospitable fellows like our friend Vaughan. An exploitation of the law of Archimedes." He blinked rapidly under his black bushy brows. "By the simple action of displacement they hope to save the gin!"

Andrew could not smile for thinking of his own awkwardness. He had no social graces and he had never been in so grand a house in all his life. He did not know what to do with his empty glass, his cigarette ash, his own—actually his own hands! He was glad when they went into supper. But here again he felt himself at a disadvantage.

It was a simple but beautifully set-out meal—hot bouillon, followed by a chicken salad, all white breast and heart of lettuce and strange delicate flavours.

Andrew was next to Mrs. Vaughan. "Your wife is charming, Doctor Manson," she quietly remarked as they sat down. She was a tall, thin, elegant girl, very delicate in her appearance, not in the least pretty but with wide intelligent eyes and a manner of distinguished ease. Her mouth had a kind of upturned crookedness, a mobility which somehow conveyed a sense of wit and breeding.

She began to talk to him about his work, saying that her husband had heard of his thoroughness on more than one occasion. She tried kindly to draw him out, asking, in an interested fashion, how he felt the conditions of practice could be improved in the district.

"Well—I don't know—" clumsily spilling some soup—"I suppose—I'd like to see more scientific methods used."

Stiff and tongue-tied upon his favourite subject,—with which he had entranced Christine for hours,—he kept his eyes upon his plate until, to his relief, Mrs. Vaughan slipped into conversation with Challis, on her other side.

Challis—presently revealed as Professor of Metallurgy at Cardiff, lecturer on the same subject at London University, and a member of the exalted Mines Fatigue Board—was a gay and gusty talker. He talked with his body, his hands, his beard, arguing, laughing, exploding, gurgling, meanwhile throwing great quantities of food and drink into himself like a stoker deliriously raising steam. But his talk was good; and the rest of the table seemed to like it.

Andrew, however, refused to admit the value of the conversation; he listened grudgingly as it turned to music, to the qualities of Bach, and then, by one of Challis' prodigious leaps, to Russian literature. He heard mentioned the names of Tolstoy, Chekhov, Turgenev, Pushkin with his teeth on edge.

Tripe, he raged to himself, all unimportant tripe. Who does this old beaver think he is? I'd like to see him tackle a tracheotomy, say, in a black kitchen in Cefen Row. He wouldn't get far with his Pushkin there!

Christine, however, was enjoying herself thoroughly. Glaring sideways, Andrew saw her smiling at Challis, heard her take her part in the discussion. She made no pretence, she was perfectly natural. Once or twice she referred to her council schoolroom in Bank Street. It amazed him how well she stood up to the professor, how quickly, unselfconsciously she made her points. He began to see his wife as for the first time, and in a strange new light. Seems to know all about these Russian bugs, he grated inwardly; funny she never talks to me about them! And later, as Challis approvingly patted Christine on the hand: Can't old Bird's-nest keep his paws to himself? Hasn't he got a wife of his *own*?

Once or twice he caught Christine's eyes offering him a bright interchange of intimacy, and several times she diverted the conversation in his direction.

"My husband is very interested in the anthracite workers, Professor Challis. He's started a line of investigation. On dust inhalation."

"Yes, yes," puffed Challis, turning an interested glance on Manson.

"Isn't that so, darling?" Christine encouraged. "You were telling me all about it the other night."

"Oh, I don't know," Andrew growled. "There's probably nothing in it. I haven't enough data yet. Perhaps this T.B. doesn't come from the dust at all."

He was furious with himself, of course. Perhaps this man Challis might have helped him, not that he would have asked him for assistance, yet the fact that he was connected with the Mines Fatigue Board certainly seemed to offer a wonderful opportunity. For some incomprehensible reason his anger became directed towards Christine.

As they walked home towards Vale View at the end of the evening he was jealously silent. And in the same silence he preceded her to the bedroom.

While they undressed, usually a communicative and informal proceeding when, with his braces hanging and a toothbrush in his hand, he would dilate upon the doings of the day, he kept his gaze studiously averted.

When Christine pleaded, "We did have a nice time, didn't we, darling?" he answered with great politeness, "Oh! An excellent time!" In bed he kept well to the edge, away from her, resisting the slight movement which he felt her make towards him, with a long and heavy snore.

Next morning the same sense of constraint persisted between them. He went about his work sulking, stupidly unlike himself. About five o'clock in the afternoon, while they were having tea, a ring came to the front door. It was the Vaughan chauffeur with a pile of books and a great bunch of pheasant's eye narcissi laid on top of them.

"From Mrs. Vaughan, madam," he said smiling, touching his peaked cap as he retreated.

Christine returned to the sitting-room with heaped arms and a glowing face.

"Look, darling," she cried excitedly. "Isn't that too kind? The whole of Trollope loaned me by Mrs. Vaughan. I've always wanted to read him right through! And such lovely—lovely flowers."

He stood up stiffly, sneering: "Very pretty! Books and flowers from the lady of the manor! You've got to have them, I suppose, to help you to endure living with me! I'm too *dull* for you. I'm not one of those flash talkers that you seemed to like so much last night. I don't know the Russian for boloney! I'm just one of these bloody ordinary medical aid assistants!"

"Andrew!" All the colour had gone out of her face. "How can you?"

"It's true, isn't it? I could see while I was gawking my way through that blasted supper. I've got eyes in my head. You're sick of me already. I'm only fit for slogging round in the slush, turning over dirty blankets, collecting fleas. I'm too much of a lout for your taste now!"

Her eyes were dark and pitiful in her pale face. But she said steadily: "How can you talk like that? It's because you *are* yourself that I love you. And I'll never love anybody else."

"Sounds like it," he snarled, and banged out of the room.

For five minutes he skulked in the kitchen, tramping up and down, biting his lip. Then all at once he turned, dashed back to the sitting-room where she stood, her head bent forlornly, staring into the fire. He took her fiercely in his arms.

"Chris, darling!" he cried, in hot repentance. "Darling, darling! I'm sorry! For heaven's sake forgive me. I didn't mean a word of it. I'm just a crazy, jealous fool. I adore you!"

They clung to each other wildly, closely. The scent of the narcissi was in the air.

"Don't you know," she sobbed, "that I'd just die without you!"

Afterwards, as she sat with her cheek pressed against his, he said sheepishly, reaching forward for a book:—

"Who is this chap Trollope anyway? Will you teach me, darling? I'm just an ignorant hog!"

viii

The winter passed. He had now the added incentive of his work on dust inhalation which he had begun by planning and conducting a systematic examination of every anthracite worker upon his list. Their evenings together were even happier than before. Christine helped him to transcribe his notes, working before the fine coal fire—it was one advantage of the district that they never lacked an abundance of cheap coal—when he came home from his late surgery. Often they had long talks in which the extent of her knowledge, though she never obtruded it, and her acquaintance with books, astounded him. He began, moreover, to discern in her a fineness of instinct, an intuition which made her judgment of literature, of music, and especially of people, uncannily correct.

"Hang it all," he would tease her. "I'm just getting to know my wife. In case you're getting swelled head we'll take half an hour off and I'll beat you at piquet." They had learned the game from the Vaughans.

As the days lengthened, without speaking of it to him, she began on the wilderness that was the garden. Jenny, the maid, had a great-uncle,—she was proud of the unique relationship,—an elderly, disabled miner who for tenpence an hour became Christine's assistant. Manson, crossing the dilapidated bridge, found them down by the stream-bed one March afternoon, starting an assault on the rusty salmon-tins that lay there.

"Hey, you below!" he shouted from the bridge. "What are you doing? Spoiling my fishing?"

She answered his gibes with a brisk nod:

"You wait and see."

In a few weeks she had grubbed out the weeds and cleared the neglected paths. The bed of the stream was clean, its edges were cut and trimmed. A new rockery, made from loose stones lying about, stood at the foot of the glen. Vaughan's gardener, John Roberts, kept coming over, bringing bulbs and cuttings, offering advice. With real triumph she led Andrew by the arm to view the first daffodil.

Then, on the last Sunday in March, without warning, Denny came over to visit them. They fell upon him with open arms, belaboured him with their delighted welcome. To see the squat figure, that red sandy-browed face again, gave Manson a rare pleasure. When they had shown him round, fed him on their best, and thrust him into their softest chair, they eagerly demanded news.

"Page is gone," Philip announced. "Yes, the poor chap died a month ago. Another haemorrhage. And a good thing too!" He drew on his pipe, the familiar cynicism puckering his eyes. "Blodwen and your friend Rees seem all set for matrimony."

"A golden wedding from the start," Andrew said with unusual bitterness. "Poor Edward!"

"Page was a fine fellow. A good old G.P.," Denny reflected. "You know I hate the very sound of those fatal letters and all that they stand for. But Page let them down lightly."

There was a pause while they thought of Edward Page, who had longed for Capri with its birds and sunshine through all those drudging years amidst the slag-heaps of Blaenelly.

"And how about you, Philip?" Andrew asked at last.

"Oh, I don't know! I'm getting restless." Denny smiled drily. "Blaenelly hasn't seemed quite the same since you people cleared out. I think I'll take a trip abroad somewhere. Ship's surgeon, maybe—if some cheap cargo boat will have me."

Andrew was silent, distressed once again by the thought of this clever man, this really talented surgeon, wasting his life, deliberately, with a kind of self-inflicted sadism. Yet was Denny really wasting his life? Christine and he had often spoken of Philip, trying to solve the enigma of his career. Vaguely they knew that he had married a woman, socially his superior, who had tried to mould him to the demands of a county practice where there was no credit in operating well four days of the week if one did not hunt the other three. After five years of effort on Denny's part she had rewarded him by leaving him, quite casually, for another man. It was no wonder that Denny had fled to the backwoods, despising convention and hating orthodoxy. Perhaps, one day, he would return to civilization.

They talked all afternoon and Philip waited till the last train. He was interested in Andrew's account of the conditions of practice in Aberalaw. As Andrew came, indignantly, to the question of Llewellyn's percentage deducted from the assistants' salaries, Denny said, with an odd smile:—

"I can't see you sitting down under that for long!"

When Philip had gone Andrew became gradually aware, as the days passed, of a gap, an odd vacancy existing in his work. In Blaenelly with Philip near him he had always been aware of a common bond, a definite purpose shared between them. But in Aberalaw he had no such bond, felt no such purpose amongst his fellow doctors.

Doctor Urquhart, his colleague in the West Surgery, was, for all his fiery humour, a kindly man. Yet he was old, rather automatic, and absolutely without inspiration. Though long experience enabled him, as he put it, to smell pneumonia the moment he "put his nose in" the sickroom, though he was deft in his application of splints and plasters and an adept in the cruciform treatment of boils, though occasionally he delighted to prove that he could perform some small operation, he was, nevertheless, in many directions, shatteringly antiquated. He stood out plainly, in Andrew's view, as Denny's "good old type" of family doctor—shrewd, painstaking, experienced, a doctor sentimentalized by his patients and by the public at large, who had not opened a medical book for twenty years and was almost dangerously out-of-date. Though Andrew was always eager to start discussions with Urquhart, the old man had little time for "shop." When his day's work was over he would drink his tinned soup,—tomato was his favourite,—sandpaper his new violin, inspect his old china, them clump off to the Masonic Club to play draughts and smoke.

The two assistants at the East Surgery were equally unencouraging. Doctor Medley, the elder of the two, a man of nearly fifty, with a clever sensitive face, was unhappily almost stone deaf. But for this affliction, which for some reason the vulgar always found amusing, Charles Medley would have been a very long way from an assistantship in the mining Valleys. He was, like Andrew, essentially a physician. As a diagnostician he was remarkable. But when his patients spoke to him he could not hear a word. Of course, he was a practiced lip-reader. Yet he was timid, for he often made laughable mistakes. It was quite painful to see his harassed eyes fastened, in a kind of desperate inquiry, upon the moving lips of the person speaking to him. Because he was so fearful of making a grave error he never prescribed anything but the smallest doses of any drug. He was not well off, for he had met with trouble and expense over his grownup family, and like his faded wife he had become an ineffectual, strangely pathetic being who went in dread of Doctor Llewellyn and the Committee lest he should be suddenly dismissed.

The other assistant, Doctor Oxborrow, was a very different character from poor Medley and Andrew did not like him nearly so well. Oxborrow was a large pasty man with pudgy fingers and a jerky heartiness. Andrew often felt that with more blood in him Oxborrow would have made an admirable bookmaker. As it was Oxborrow, accompanied by his wife, who played the portable harmonium, betook himself on Saturday afternoons to the near-by town of Fernley—etiquette precluding his appearing in Aberalaw—and there, in the Market, he would set up his little carpet-covered stand and hold an open-air religious meeting. Oxborrow was an evangelist. As an idealist, a believer in a supreme quickening force in life, Andrew could have admired this fervour. But Oxborrow, alas! was embarrassingly emotional. He wept unexpectedly and prayed even more disconcertingly. Once when confronted by a difficult confinement which defeated his own straining skill, he plumped suddenly upon his knees beside the bed and, blubbering, implored God to work a miracle upon the poor woman. Urquhart, who detested Oxborrow, told Andrew of this incident, for it was Urquhart who, arriving, had got upon the bed in his boots, and successfully delivered the patient with high forceps.

The more Andrew considered his fellow assistants and the system under which they worked the more he desired to bring them together. As it was they had no unity, no sense of co-operation, and little friendliness amongst themselves. They were simply set up, one against the other, in the ordinary competitive way existing in general practice all over the country, each trying to secure as many patients for himself as he could. Downright suspicion and bad feeling were often the result. Andrew had seen Urquhart, for instance, when a patient of Oxborrow's transferred his card to him, take the half-finished bottle of medicine from the man's hand in the surgery, uncork it, smell it with contempt, and explode: "So *this* is what Oxborrow's been givin' ye! Damn it to hell! He's been slowly poisonin' ye!"

Meanwhile, in the face of this diversity, Doctor Llewellyn was quietly taking his cut from each assistant's pay cheque. Andrew burned under it, longed to create a different arrangement, to institute a new and better understanding which would enable the assistants to stand together—without subsidizing Llewellyn. But his own difficulties, the sense of his own newness to the place, and above all the mistakes he had made at the start in his own district, caused him to be cautious.

It was not until he met Con Boland that he decided to make the great attempt.

ix

One day early in April Andrew discovered a cavity in a back tooth and went, in consequence, upon an afternoon of the following week, in search of the Society's dentist. He had not yet met Boland and did not know his hours of consultation. When he reached the Square, where Boland's little surgery stood, he found the door closed and, pinned upon it, this red-inked notice: *Gone to Extraction. If Urgent Apply at House.*

On a moment's reflection Andrew decided that since he was here, he might at least call to make an appointment; so, having inquired the way from one of the group of youths lounging outside the Valley Ice Cream Saloon, he set out for the dentist's house.

This was a small semidetached villa on the upper outskirts of the East side of the town. As Andrew walked up the untidy path to the front door he heard a loud hammering and, glancing through the wide-open doors of a dilapidated wooden shed situated at the side of the house, he saw a red-haired rangy man in his shirt sleeves, violently attacking the dismembered body of a car with a hammer. At the same time the man caught sight of him.

"Hello!" he said.

"Hello!" Andrew answered a trifle warily.

"What are ye after?"

"I want to make an appointment with the dentist. I'm Doctor Manson."

"Come in," said the man, hospitably waving the hammer.

He was Boland.

Andrew entered the wooden shed, which was littered with portions of an incredibly old motor car. In the middle stood the chassis, supported on wooden egg-boxes, and actually presenting the evidence of having been sawn in half. Andrew glanced from this extraordinary spectacle of engineering to Boland.

"Is this the extraction?"

"It is," Con agreed. "When I'm inclined to be slack in the surgery I just up to my garage and put a little bit in on my car."

Apart from his brogue, which was thick enough to be cut with a knife, he used the words "garage," meaning the falling down shed, and "car," as applied to the fallen-down vehicle, with an accent of unmistakable pride.

"You wouldn't believe what I'm doing now," he went on; "that's to say, unless you're mechanical-minded like myself. I've had her five year this little car of mine and, mind ye, she was three year old when I got her. Ye mightn't believe seeing her *sthripped* but she goes like a hare. But she's small, Manson, she's small by the size of my family now. So I'm in the process of extendin' her. I've cut her, ye see, right across her middle, and that's where I'll slip in a good two feet of insertion. Wait till ye see her finished, Manson!" He reached for his jacket. "She'll be long enough to take a regiment. Come away now, to the surgery, and I'll fix your tooth."

At the surgery, which was almost as untidy as the garage and, it must be confessed, equally dirty, Con filled the tooth, talking all the time. Con talked so much and so violently that his bushy red moustache was always dewed with beads of moisture. His shock of chestnut hair, which badly needed cutting, kept getting into Andrew's eyes, as he bent over, using the amalgam filling which he had tucked under his oily fingernail. He had not bothered to wash his hands—that was a trifle with Con!

He was a careless, impetuous, good-natured, generous fellow. The more Andrew knew Con, the more he was utterly captivated by his humour, simplicity, wildness, and improvidence. Con, who had been six years in Aberalaw, had not a penny to his name. Yet he extracted a vast amount of fun from life. He was mad on "mechanics," was always making gadgets, and he idolized his motor car. The fact that Con should possess a motor car was in itself a joke. But Con loved jokes, even when they were against himself. He told Andrew of the occasion when, called to extract the decayed molar of an important Committee man, he had gone to the patient's house with, as he imagined, his forceps in his pocket—only to find himself reaching for the tooth with a six-inch spanner.

The filling completed, Con threw his instruments into a jelly jar containing Lysol, which was his light-hearted notion of asepsis, and demanded that Andrew should return to the house with him to tea.

"Come on, now," he insisted hospitably. "You've got to meet the family. And we're just in time. It's five o'clock."

Con's family were, in fact, in the process of having tea when they arrived, but were obviously too accustomed to Con's eccentricities to be disturbed by his bringing in a stranger. In the warm, disordered room Mrs. Boland sat at the head of the table with the baby at her breast. Next came Mary, fifteen, quiet, shy—"the only dark-haired one and her dad's favourite" was Con's introduction—who was already earning a decent wage as a clerk to Joe Larkins, the bookmaker, in the Square. Beside Mary was Terence, twelve, then three other younger children sprawling about, crying out to be taken notice of by their father.

There existed about this family, except perhaps for the shyly conscious Mary, a careless gaiety which entranced Andrew. The room itself spoke with a gorgeous brogue. Above the fireplace, beneath the coloured picture of Pope Pius X which bore a strip of palm, the baby's napkins were drying. The canary's cage, uncleaned but bursting with song, stood on the dresser beside Mrs. Boland's rolled-up stays—she had previously removed them in the cause of comfort—and a split bag of puppy biscuits. Six bottles of stout, newly in from the grocer, were upon the chest of drawers, also Terence's flute. And in the corner were broken toys, odd boots, a Japanese parasol, two rusty skate, two slightly battered prayer-books and a copy of *Photo-Bits*.

But, as he drank his tea, Andrew was most fascinated by Mrs. Boland—he simply could not keep his eyes from her. Pale, dreamy, unperturbed, she sat silently imbibing endless cups of black boiled tea while the children squabbled about her and the baby openly drew his nourishment from her generous fount. She smiled and nodded, cut bread for the children, poured out the tea, drank and gave suck, all with a kind of abstracted placidity, as though years of din, dirt, drabness—and Con's ebullience—had in the end exalted her to a plane of heavenly lunacy where she was isolated and immune.

He almost upset his cup when she addressed him, gazing over the top of his head, her voice meek, apologetic.

"I meant to call on Mrs. Manson, Doctor. But I was so busy—"

"In the name of God!" Con rolled with laughter. "Busy, indeed! She hadn't a new dress—that's what she means. I had the money laid by—but damn it all, Terence or one of them had to have new boots. Never mind, Mother, wait till I get the car lengthened and we'll whirl ye up in style." He turned to Andrew with perfect naturalness. "We're hard up, Manson. It's the devil! We've plenty of grub, thank God, but sometimes we're not so fancy with the duds. They're a stingy lot on the Committee. And of course the big chief gets his whack!"

"Who?" Andrew asked, astonished.

"Llewellyn! He takes his fifth from me as well as you."

"But what on earth for?"

"Oh! he sees a case or two for me occasionally. He's taken a couple of dentigerous cysts out for me in the last six years. And he's the X-ray expert when that's needed. But it's a bugger." The family had bundled out to play in the kitchen, so Con could speak freely. "Him and his big saloon. The damn thing's all paint. Let me inform ye, Manson, once I was comin' up Mardy Hill behind him in my own little bus when I make up my mind to step on the gas. Bejasus! Ye should have seen his face when I give him my dust."

"Look here, Boland," Andrew said quickly. "This business of Llewellyn's cut is a shocking imposition. Why don't we fight it?"

"Eh?"

"Why don't we fight it?" Andrew repeated in a louder voice. Even as he spoke he felt his blood rise. "It's a damned injustice. Here are we hard up, trying to make our way— Listen, Boland, you're the very man I've been wanting to meet. Will you stand in with me on this? We'll get hold of the other assistants. Make a big united effort—"

A slow gleam irradiated Con's eye.

"Ye mean, ye want to go after Llewellyn?"

"I do."

Con impressively extended his hand.

"Manson my boy," he declared momentously. "We're together from the start."

Andrew raced home to Christine full of eagerness, thirsting for the fight.

"Chris! Chris! I've found a gem of a chap. A redheaded dentist—quite mad—yes, like me, I knew you'd say that. But listen, darling, we're going to start a revolution." He laughed excitedly. "Oh! Lord! If old man Llewellyn only knew what was in store for him!"

He did not require her caution to go carefully. He was determined to proceed with discernment in everything he did. He began, therefore, the following day, by calling upon Owen.

The secretary was interested and emphatic. He told Andrew that the agreement in question was a voluntary one between the head doctor and his assistants. The whole thing lay outside the jurisdiction of the Committee.

"You see, Doctor Manson," Owen concluded, "Doctor Llewellyn is a very clever, well-qualified man. We count ourselves fortunate to have him. But he has a handsome remuneration from the Society for acting as our Medical Superintendent. It is you assistant doctors who think he ought to have more—"

"Do we hell," thought Andrew. He went away satisfied, rang up Oxborrow and

Medley, made them agree to come to his house that evening. Urquhart and Boland had already promised to be there. He knew, from past conversations, that every one of the four loathed losing a fifth of his salary. Once he had them together the thing was done.

His next step was to speak to Llewellyn. He had decided, on reflection, that it would be underhand not to make some disclosure of his intention beforehand. That afternoon he was at the hospital giving an anaesthetic. As he watched Llewellyn go through with the operation, a long and complicated abdominal case, he could not repress a feeling of admiration. Owen's remark was absolutely true: Llewellyn was amazingly clever, not only clever but versatile. He was the exception, the unique instance, which—Denny would have contended—proved the rule. Nothing came amiss to him, nothing floored him. From public health administration, every bylaw of which he knew by heart, to the latest radiological technique, the whole range of his multifarious duties found Llewellyn blandly expert and prepared.

After the operation, while Llewellyn was washing up, Andrew went up to him, jerkily tugging off his gown.

"Excuse me for mentioning it, Doctor Llewellyn—but I couldn't help noticing the way you handled that tumour, it was awfully fine."

Llewellyn's dull skin tinged with gratification. He beamed affably.

"Glad you think so, Manson. Come to speak of it, you're improvin' nicely with your anaesthetics."

"No, no," Andrew muttered. "I'll never be much good at that."

There was a pause. Llewellyn went on soaping his hands equably. Andrew, at his elbow, cleared his throat nervously. Now that the moment had come he found it almost impossible to speak. But he managed to blurt out:—

"Look here, Doctor Llewellyn. It's only right to tell you—all we assistants think our salary percentage payments to you unfair. It's an awkward thing to have to say, but I— I'm going to propose they are done away with. We've got a meeting at my house to-night. I'd rather you knew that now, than afterwards. I—I want you to feel I'm at least honest about it."

Before Llewellyn could reply, and without looking at his face, Andrew swung round and left the theatre. How badly he had said it! Yet anyway, he *had* said it. When they sent him their ultimatum, Llewellyn could not accuse him of stabbing him in the back.

The meeting at Vale View was fixed for nine o'clock that evening. Andrew put out some bottled beer and asked Christine to prepare sandwiches. When she had done this, she slipped on her coat and went round to Vaughans' for an hour. Strung with anticipation, Andrew stumped up and down the hall, striving to collect his ideas. And presently the others arrived—Boland first, Urquhart next, Oxborrow and Medley together.

In the sitting-room, pouring beer and proffering sandwiches, Andrew tried to initiate a cordial note. Since he almost disliked him, he addressed Doctor Oxborrow first.

"Help yourself, Oxborrow! Plenty more in the cellar."

"Thanks, Manson." The evangelist's voice was chill. "I don't touch alcohol in any shape or form. It's against my principles."

"In the name of God!" Con said, out of the froth on his moustache.

As a beginning it was not auspicious. Medley, munching sandwiches, kept his eyes all the time on the alert, his face wearing the stony anxiety of the deaf. Already the beer was increasing Urquhart's natural belligerence; after glaring steadily at Oxborrow for some minutes he suddenly shot out:—

"Now I find myself in your company, *Doctor* Oxborrow, maybe you'll find it convenient to explain how Tudor Evans, Seventeen Glyn Terrace, came off *my* list onto *yours*."

"I don't remember the case," said Oxborrow, pressing his finger tips together aloofly.

"But I do!" Urquhart exploded. "It was one of the cases you stole from me, Your Medical Reverence! And what's more—"

"Gentlemen!" cried Andrew in a panic. "Please, *please*! How can we ever do anything if we quarrel amongst ourselves? Remember what we're here for."

"What *are* we here for?" Oxborrow said womanishly. "I ought to be at a case."

Andrew, standing on the hearthrug, his expression taut and earnest, took a grab at the slippery situation.

"This is the way of it, then, gentlemen!" He drew a deep breath. "I'm the youngest man here and I'm not long in this practice but I—I hope you'll excuse all that! Perhaps it's because I am new that I get a fresh look at things—things you've been putting up with too long. It seems to me in the first place that our system here is all wrong. We just go hacking and muddling through in the antediluvian way, like we were ordinary town and country G.P.'s, fighting each other, not members of the same Medical Society with wonderful opportunities for working together! Every doctor I've met swears that practice is a dog's life. He'll tell you he drudges on, run off his feet, never a minute to himself, no time for meals, always on call! *Why* is that? It's because there's *no attempt at organization in our profession*. Take just one example of what I mean—though I could give you dozens. Night calls! You know how we all go to bed at night, dreading we'll be wakened and called out. We have rotten nights because we *may* be called out. Suppose we knew we *couldn't* be called out. Suppose we arranged, for a start, a co-operative system of night work. One doctor taking all night calls for one week, and then *going* free of all night calls for the rest of that month, while the others take their turn. Wouldn't that be splendid! Think how fresh you'd be for your day's work—"

He broke off, observing their blank faces.

"Wouldn't work," Urquhart snapped. "Dammit to hell! I'd sooner stay up every night of the month than trust old Oxborrow with one of my cases. Hee! Hee! When *he* borrows he doesn't pay back."

Andrew interposed feverishly:

"We'll leave that, then—anyway, till another meeting—seeing that we're not agreed on it. But there's one thing we are agreed on. And that's why we're here. This percentage we pay to Doctor Llewellyn." He paused. They were all looking at him now, touched in their pockets, interested. "We've all agreed it's unjust. I've spoken to Owen about it. He says it has nothing to do with the Committee but is a matter for adjustment between the doctors."

"That's right," threw out Urquhart. "I remember when it was fixed. A matter of nine year ago. We had two rank Jonahs of assistants then. One at the East Surgery and one at my end. They gave Llewellyn a lot of trouble over their cases. So one fine day he called us all together and said it wasn't goin' to be worth his while unless we could make some arrangement with him. That's the way it started. And that's the way it's gone on."

"But his salary from the Committee already covers *all* his work in the Society. And he simply rakes in the shekels from his other appointments. He's rolling in it!"

"I know, I know," said Urquhart testily. "But, mind you, Manson, he's damn useful to us, is the same Llewellyn. And he knows it. If he chose to cut up rough we'd be in a pretty poor way."

"Why should *we* pay him?" Andrew kept on inexorably.

"Hear! Hear!" interjected Con, refilling his glass.

Oxborrow cast one glance at the dentist.

"If I may be allowed to get a word in... I agree with Doctor Manson in that it is unjust for us to have our salaries deducted. But the fact is—Doctor Llewellyn is a man of high standing, excellently qualified, who gives great distinction to the Society. And besides he goes out of his way to take our bad cases off our hands."

Andrew stared at the other.

"Do you *want* your bad cases off your hands?"

"Of course," said Oxborrow pettishly. "Who doesn't?"

"I don't," Andrew shouted. "I want to keep them, see them through!"

"Oxborrow's right," Medley muttered unexpectedly. "It's the first rule of medical practice, Manson. You'll realize it when you're older. Get rid of the bad stuff, get rid of it, rid of it."

"But damn it all!" Andrew protested hotly.

The discussion continued, in circles, for three quarters of an hour.

At the end of that time Andrew, very heated, chanced to exclaim: "We've got to put this through. D'you hear me, we've simply *got* to. Llewellyn knows we're after him. I told him this afternoon."

"What?" The exclamation came from Oxborrow, Urquhart, even from Medley.

"Do you mean to say, Doctor, you *told* Doctor Llewellyn—" Half-rising, Oxborrow bent his startled gaze on Andrew.

"Of course I did! He's got to know sometime. Don't you see, we've only got to stand together, show a united front and *we're bound to win!*"

"Dammit to hell!" Urquhart was livid. "You've got a nerve! You don't know what influence Llewellyn has! He's got a finger in everything! We'll be lucky if we're not all sacked. Think of *me* trying to find another pitch at my time of life." He bullocked his way towards the door. "You're a good fellow, Manson. But you're too *young*. Good *night*."

Medley had already risen hurriedly to his feet. The look in his eyes said he was going straight to his telephone to tell Doctor Llewellyn apologetically that he, Llewellyn, was a superb doctor and he, Medley, could hear him perfectly. Oxborrow was on his heels. In two minutes the room was clear of all but Con, Andrew, and the remainder of the beer.

They finished the beverage in silence. Then Andrew remembered that there were six more bottles in the larder. They finished these six bottles. Then they began to talk. They said things touching the origin, parentage, and moral character of Oxborrow, Medley, and Urquhart. They dwelt especially upon Oxborrow and Oxborrow's harmonium. They did not observe Christine come in and go upstairs. They talked together soulfully, as brothers shamefully betrayed.

Next morning Andrew marched on his rounds with a splitting headache and a scowl. In the Square he passed Llewellyn in his car. As Andrew lifted his head in shamed defiance Llewellyn beamed at him.

x

For a week Andrew went about chafing under his defeat, bitterly cast-down. On Sunday morning, usually devoted to long and peaceful repose, he suddenly broke loose.

"It isn't the money, Chris! It's the principle of the thing! When I think of it—it drives me crazy. Why can't I let it slip? Why don't I like Llewellyn? At least why do I like him one minute and hate him the next? Tell me honestly, Chris. Why don't I sit at his feet? Am I jealous? What is it?"

Her answer staggered him. "Yes, I think you are jealous!"

"What?"

"Don't break my eardrums, dear. You asked me to tell you honestly. You're jealous, frightfully jealous. And why shouldn't you be? I don't want to be married to a saint. There's enough cleaning in this house already without you setting up a halo."

"Go on," he growled. "Give me all my faults when you're about it. Suspicious! Jealous! You've been at me before! Oh, and I'm too *young*, I suppose. Octogenarian Urquhart rammed that in my teeth the other day!"

A pause during which he waited for her to continue the argument. Then, irritably, "Why should I be jealous of Llewellyn?"

"Because he's frightfully good at his work, knows so much, and well—chiefly because he has all these first-class qualifications."

"While I have a scrubby little M.B. from a Scots University! God Almighty! Now I know what you really think of me." Furious, he flung out of bed and began to walk about the room in his pyjamas. "What do qualifications matter anyway? Pure damn swank! It's method, clinical ability that counts. I don't believe all the tripe they serve up in textbooks. I believe in what I hear through the ends of my stethoscope! And in case you don't know it, I hear plenty. I'm beginning to find out real things in my anthracite investigation. Perhaps I'll surprise you one fine day, my lady! Damn it all! It's a fine state of affairs when a man wakes up on Sunday morning and his wife tells him he knows *nothing!*"

Sitting up in bed, she took her manicure set and began to do her nails, waiting till he had finished.

"I didn't say all that, Andrew." Her reasonableness aggravated him the more. "It's just —darling, you're not going to be an assistant *all* your life. You want people to listen to you, pay attention to your work, your ideas—oh, you understand what I mean. If you had a really fine degree—an M.D. or—or the M.R.C.P.—it would stand you in good stead."

"The M.R.C.P.!" he echoed blankly. Then: "So she's been thinking it out all by her little self. The M.R.C.P.—huh!—take *that* from a mining practice!" His satire should have overwhelmed her. "Don't you understand they only give that to the crowned heads of Europe?"

He banged the door and went into the bathroom to shave. Five minutes later he was back again, one half of his chin shaved, the other lathered. He was penitent, excited.

"Do you *think* I could do it, Chris? You're absolutely right. We need a few pips on the good old name plate so we can hold our own up! But the M.R.C.P.—it's the most difficult medical exam. in the whole shoot. It's—it's *murder*! Still—I believe... Wait and I'll get the particulars—"

Breaking off, he dashed downstairs for the *Medical Directory*. When he returned with it his face had fallen to acute dejection.

"Sunk!" he muttered dismally. "Right bang off. I *told* you it was an impossible exam. There's a preliminary paper in languages. Four languages: Latin, French, Greek, German —and two of them are compulsory, before you can even *sit* the cursed thing. I don't know languages. All the Latin I know is dog lingo: *mist. alba—mitte decem.* As for French—"

She did not answer. There was a silence while he stood at the window gloomily considering the empty view. At last he turned, frowning, worrying, unable to leave the bone alone.

"Why shouldn't I—*damn* it all, Chris—why shouldn't I learn these languages *for* the exam.?"

Her manicure things spread themselves upon the floor as she jumped our of bed and hugged him.

"Oh, I did want you to say that, my dear! That's the real *you.* I could—I could help you, perhaps. Don't forget your old woman's a retired schoolmarm!"

They made plans excitedly all day. They bundled Trollope, Chekhov, and Dostoievski into the spare bedroom. They cleared the sitting-room for action. And that evening he went to school with her. The next evening, and the next...

Sometimes Andrew felt the sublime bathos of it, heard from afar off the mocking laughter of the gods. Sitting over the hard table with his wife, in this remote Welsh mining town, muttering after her *caput—capitis,* or *Madame, est-il possible que...,* wading through declensions, irregular verbs, reading aloud from *Tacitus* and a patriotic reader they had picked up, *Pro patria*—he would jerk back suddenly in his chair, morbidly conscious.

"If Llewellyn could see us here—wouldn't he grin? And to think this is only the beginning, that I've got all the medical stuff after!"

Towards the end of the following month, parcels of books began to arrive periodically at Vale View from the London branch of the International Medical Library. Andrew began to read where, at college, he had left off. He discovered, quickly, how early he had left off. He discovered and was swamped by the therapeutic advance of biochemistry. He discovered renal thresholds, blood ureas, basal metabolism, and the fallibility of the albumen test. As this keystone of his student's days fell from him he groaned aloud.

"Chris! I know nothing. And this stuff is killing me!"

He had to contend with the work of his practice, he had only the long nights in which to study. Sustained by black coffee and a wet towel round his head he battled on, reading into the early hours of the morning. When he fell into bed, exhausted, often he could not sleep. And sometimes when he slept he would awake, sweating from a nightmare, his head ablaze with terms, formulae, and some drivelling imbecility of his halting French.

He smoked to excess, lost weight, became thinner in the face. But Chris was there, constantly, silently there, permitting him to talk, to draw diagrams, to explain, in tongue-twisting nomenclature, the extraordinary, the astounding, the fascinating selective action of the kidney tubules. She also permitted him to shout, to gesticulate, and, as his nerves grew more ragged, to hurl abuse at her.

At eleven o'clock as she brought him fresh coffee he became liable to snarl:— "Why can't you leave me alone? What's this slush for, anyway? Caffein—it's only a rotten drug. You know I'm killing myself, don't you? And it's all for you. You're hard! You're damnably hard. You're like a female turnkey, marching in and out with skilly! I'll never get this blasted thing. There are hundreds of fellows trying to get it from the West End of London, from the big hospitals, and me!—from Aberalaw—ha! ha!" His laughter was hysterical. "From the dear old Medical Aid Society! Oh, God! I'm so tired and I know they'll have me out to-night for that confinement in Cefen Row, and…"

She was a better soldier than he. She had a quality of balance which steadied them through every crisis. She also had a temper, but she controlled it. She made sacrifices, refused all invitations from the Vaughans, stopped going to the orchestral concerts in the Temperance Hall. No matter how badly they had slept she was always up early, neatly dressed, ready with his breakfast when he came dragging down, unshaven, the first cigarette of the day already between his lips.

Suddenly, when he had been working six months, her aunt in Bridlington took ill with phlebitis and wrote asking her to come North. Handing him the letter she declared immediately that it was impossible for her to leave him.

But he, hunched sulkily over his bacon and egg, growled out:— "I wish you'd go, Chris! Studying this way, I'd get on better without you. We've been getting on each other's nerves lately. Sorry—but it seems the best thing to do."

She went, unwillingly, at the end of the week. Before she had been gone twenty-four hours, he found out his mistake. It was agony without her. Jenny, though working to carefully prepared instructions, was a perpetual aggravation. But it was not Jenny's cooking, or the lukewarm coffee, or the badly made bed. It was Christine's absence: knowing she was not in the house, being unable to call out to her, missing her. He found himself gazing dully at his books, losing hours, while he thought of her.

At the end of a fortnight he wired that she was returning. He dropped everything and prepared to receive her. Nothing was too good, too spectacular for the celebration of their reunion. Her wire had not given him much time; but he thought rapidly, then sped to the town on a mission of extravagance. He bought first a bunch of roses. In Kendrick's, the fishmonger's, he was lucky to find a lobster, fresh in that morning. He seized it quickly, lest Mrs. Vaughan—for whom Kendrick primarily intended all such delicacies—should ring up and forestall him. Then he bought ice in quantity, called at the greengrocer's for salad, and finally, with trepidation, ordered one bottle of Moselle which Lampert, the grocer in the Square, assured him was "sound."

After tea he told Jenny she might go, for already he could feel her youthful eye fastened inquisitively upon him. He then set to work and lovingly composed a lobster salad. The zinc bucket from the scullery, filled with ice, made an excellent wine pail. The flowers presented an unexpected difficulty, for Jenny had locked up the cupboard under the stairs where all the vases were kept and, to all intents, hidden the key. But he surmounted even this obstruction, placing half the roses in the water jug and the remainder in the toothbrush holder from the toilet set upstairs. This struck quite a note of variety.

At last his preparations were complete—the flowers, the food, the wine upon the ice; his eye surveyed the scene with shining intensity. After surgery, at half-past nine, he raced to meet her train at the Upper Station.

It was like falling in love all over again—fresh, wonderful. Tenderly, he escorted her to the love feast. The evening was hot and still. The moon shone in upon them. He forgot about the intricacies of basal metabolism. He told her they might be in Provence, or some place like that, in a great castle by a lake. He told her she was a sweet, exquisite child. He told her he had been a brute to her but that for the rest of his life he would be a carpet—not red, since she interjected her objection to that colour—on which she might tread. He told her much more than that.

By the end of the week he was telling her to fetch his slippers.

***

August arrived, dusty and scorching. With the finish of his reading in sight, he was confronted with the necessity of brushing up his practical work, particularly histology—an apparently insuperable difficulty in his present situation. It was Christine who thought of Professor Challis and his position at Cardiff University. When Andrew wrote to him, Challis immediately replied stating, with verbosity, that he would rejoice to use his influence with the Department of Pathology. Manson, he said, would find Doctor Glyn-Jones a first-rate fellow. He concluded with a carolling inquiry for Christine.

"I've got to hand it to you, Chris! It does mean something to have friends. And I very nearly stuck away from meeting Challis that night at Vaughans'! Decent old bouncer! But all the same, I hate asking favours. And what's this about sending tender regards to you?"

In the middle of that month a secondhand Red Indian motorcycle—a low, wickedly unprofessional machine, advertised as "too fast" for its previous owner—made its appearance at Vale View. There were, in the slackness of summer, three afternoon hours which Andrew might reasonably regard as his own. Every day, immediately after lunch, a red streak went roaring down the Valley in the direction of Cardiff, thirty miles away. And every day, towards five o'clock, a slightly dustier red streak, moving in the opposite direction, made a target of Vale View.

These sixty miles in the broiling heat, with an hour's work at Glyn-Jones' specimens and slides sandwiched midway—often he used the microscope with hands which still shook from the handlebars' vibration—made heavy going of the next few weeks. For Christine it was the most anxious part of the whole lunatic adventure to see him depart with a swift crackling exhaust, to wait anxiously for the first faint beat of his return, fearing all the time that something must happen to him, bent to the metal of that satanic machine.

Though he was so rushed he found a moment occasionally to bring her strawberries from Cardiff. They saved these till after his surgery. At tea he was always parched from the dust and red-eyed, wondering gloomily if his duodenum had not dropped off at that last pothole in Trecoed, asking himself if he could possibly manage, before the surgery, these two calls which had come in during his absence.

But the final journey was made at last. Glyn-Jones had nothing more to show him. He knew every slide and every single specimen by heart. All that remained was to enter his name and send up the heavy entrance fees for the examination.

On the fifteenth of October Andrew set out alone for London. Christine saw him to the station. Now that the actual event was so close at hand, a queer calmness had settled upon him. All his striving, his frenzied efforts, his almost hysterical outbursts, seemed far away and done with. His brain was inactive, almost dull. He felt that he knew nothing.

Yet, on the following day, when he began the written part of the examination which was held at the College of Physicians, he found himself answering the papers with a blind automatism. He wrote and wrote, never looking at the clock, filling sheet after sheet, until his head reeled.

He had taken a room at the Museum Hotel, where Christine and he had stayed on their first visit to London. Here it was extremely cheap. But the food was vile, adding the final touch to his upset digestion required to produce a bad attack of dyspepsia. He was compelled to restrict his diet to hot malted milk. A tumblerful in an A.B.C. tea-room in the Strand was his lunch. Between his papers he lived in a kind of daze. He did not dream of going to a place of amusement. He scarcely saw the people in the streets. Occasionally, to clear his head, he took a ride on the top of an omnibus.

After the written papers, the practical and *viva voce* part of the examination began; and Andrew found himself dreading this more than anything which had gone before. There were perhaps twenty other candidates, all of them men older than himself, and all with an unmistakable air of assurance and position. The candidate placed next to him, for instance, a man named Harrison whom he had once or twice spoken to, had an Oxford B.Ch., an outpatient appointment at St. John's and a consulting-room in Brook Street. When Andrew compared Harrison's charming manners and obvious standing with his own provincial awkwardness he felt his chances of favourably impressing the examiners to be small indeed.

His practical, at the South London Hospital, went, he thought, well enough. His case was one of bronchiectasis in a young boy of fourteen, which, since he knew lungs so intimately, was a piece of good fortune. He felt he had written a good report. But when it came to the *viva voce* his luck seemed to change completely. The *viva* procedure at the College of Physicians had its peculiarities. On two successive days each candidate was questioned, in turn, by two separate examiners. If at the end of the first session the candidate was found inadequate he was handed a polite note telling him he need not return on the following day. Faced with the imminence of this fatal missive, Andrew found to his horror that he had drawn as his first examiner a man he had heard Harrison speak of with apprehension, Doctor Maurice Gadsby.

Gadsby was a spare, undersized man with a ragged black moustache and small mean eye. Recently elected to his Fellowship, he had none of the tolerance of the older examiners, but seemed to set out deliberately to fail the candidates who came before him. He considered Andrew with a supercilious lift to his brows and placed before him six slides. Five of these slides Andrew named correctly, but the sixth he could not name. It was on this slide that Gadsby concentrated. For five minutes he harassed Andrew on this section,—which, it appeared, was the ovum of an obscure West African parasite,—

then idly, without interest, he passed him on to the next examiner, Sir Robert Abbey.

Andrew rose and crossed the room with a pale face and a heavily beating heart. All the lassitude, the inertia he had experienced at the beginning of the week was gone now. He had an almost desperate desire to succeed. But he was convinced that Gadsby would fail him. He raised his eyes to find Robert Abbey contemplating him with a friendly, half-humorous smile.

"What's the matter?" said Abbey unexpectedly.

"Nothing, sir," Andrew stammered. "I think I've done rather badly with Doctor Gadsby—that's all."

"Never mind about that. Have a look at these specimens. Then just say anything you think about them." Abbey smiled encouragingly. He was a cleanshaven, ruddy-complexioned man of about sixty-five with a high forehead and a long humorous upper lip. Though Abbey was now perhaps the third most distinguished physician in Europe, he had known hardship and bitter struggles in his earlier days when, coming from his native Leeds, with only a provincial reputation to sustain him, he had encountered prejudice and opposition in London. As he gazed, without seeming to do so, at Andrew, observing his ill-cut suit, the soft collar and shirt, the cheap, ill-knotted tie, and above all, the look of strained intensity upon his serious face, the days of his own provincial youth came back to him. Instinctively his heart went out to this unusual candidate, and his eye, ranging down the list before him, noted with satisfaction that his markings, particularly in the recent practical, were above pass level.

Meanwhile Andrew, with his eyes fixed upon the glass jars before him, had been stumbling unhappily through his commentary upon the specimens.

"Good," Abbey said suddenly. He took up a specimen—it was an aneurism of the ascending aorta—and began in a friendly manner to question Andrew. His questions, from being simple, gradually became wider and more searching in their scope, until finally they came to bear upon a recent specific treatment by the induction of malaria. But Andrew, opening out under Abbey's sympathetic manner, answered well.

Finally, as he put down the specimen, Abbey remarked:

"Do you know anything of the history of aneurism?"

"Ambroise Paré," Andrew answered, and Abbey had already begun his approving nod, "is presumed to have first discovered the condition."

Abbey's face expressed surprise.

"Why 'presumed,' Doctor Manson? Paré did discover aneurism."

Andrew reddened, then turned pale as he plunged on:

"Well, sir, that's what the textbooks say. You'll find it in every book—I myself took the trouble to verify that it was in six." A quick breath. "But I happened to be reading Celsus, brushing up my Latin,—which needed brushing up, sir,—when I definitely came across the word *aneurismus*. Celsus knew aneurism. He described it in full. And that was a matter of thirteen centuries before Paré!"

There was a silence. Andrew raised his eyes, prepared for kindly satire. Abbey was looking at him with a queer expression on his ruddy face.

"Doctor Manson," he said at length, "you are the first candidate in this examination hall who has ever told me something original, something true, and something which I did not know. I congratulate you."

Andrew turned scarlet again.

"Just tell me one thing more—as a matter of personal curiosity," Abbey concluded. "What do you regard as the main principle—the, shall I say the basic idea—which you keep before you when you are exercising the practice of your profession?"

There was a pause while Andrew reflected desperately. At length, feeling he was spoiling all the good effect he had created, he blurted out:—

"I suppose—I suppose I keep telling myself never to take anything for granted."

"Thank you, Doctor Manson."

As Andrew left the room Abbey reached for his pen. He felt young again, and suspiciously sentimental. He thought: "If he'd told me he went about trying to heal people, trying to help suffering humanity, I'd have flunked him out of sheer damned disappointment." As it was, Abbey traced the unheard-of maximum, 100, opposite the name of Andrew Manson. Indeed, could Abbey have "got away with it"—his own eloquent reflection—that figure would have been doubled.

A few minutes later Andrew went downstairs with the other candidates. At the foot of the stairs beside his leather-hooded cave a liveried porter stood with a little pile of envelopes before him. As the candidates went past he handed an envelope to each of them. Harrison, walking out next to Andrew, tore his open quickly. His expression altered; he said quietly, "It would appear I'm not wanted to-morrow." Then, forcing a smile, "How about you?" Andrew's fingers were shaking. He could barely read. Dazedly he heard Harrison congratulate him. His chances were still alive. He walked down to the A.B.C. and treated himself to a malted milk. He thought tensely, "If I don't get through now, after all this, I'll—I'll walk in front of a bus."

The next day passed grindingly. Barely half the original candidates remained and it was rumoured that out of these another half would go. Andrew had no idea whether he was doing well or badly: he knew only that his head ached abominably, that his feet were icy, his inside void.

At last it was over. At four o'clock in the afternoon Andrew came out of the cloakroom, spent and melancholy, pulling on his coat. Then he became aware of Abbey standing before the big open fire in the hall. He made to pass. But Abbey, for some reason, was holding out his hand, smiling, speaking to him, telling him—telling him that he was through.

Dear God, he had done it! He had *done* it! He was alive again, gloriously alive, his headache gone, all his weariness forgotten. As he dashed down to the nearest post office his heart sang wildly, madly. He was through, he had done it, not from the West End of London, but from an outlandish mining town. His whole being was a surging exultation. It hadn't been for nothing after all: these long nights, these mad dashes down to Cardiff, these racking hours of study. On he sped, bumping and cannoning through the crowds, missing the wheels of taxis and omnibuses, his eyes shining—racing, racing to wire news of the miracle to Christine.

xi

When the train got in, half an hour late, it was nearly midnight. All the way up the Valley the engine had been battling against a high head wind and at Aberalaw, as Andrew stepped out on the platform, the force of the hurricane almost bowled him off his feet. The station was deserted. The young poplars planted in line at its entrance bent like bows, whistling and shivering at every blast. Overhead the stars were polished to a high glitter.

Andrew started along Station Road, his body braced, his mind exhilarated by the batter of the wind. Full of his success, his contact with the great, the sophisticated medical world, his ears ringing with Sir Robert Abbey's words, he could not reach Christine fast enough to tell her joyously everything, everything which had taken place. His telegram would have given her the good news; but now he wished to pour out in detail the full exciting story.

As he swung, head down, into Talgarth Street he was conscious, suddenly, of a man running. The man came behind him, labouring heavily, the noisy clatter of his boots upon the pavement so lost in the gale he seemed a phantom figure. Instinctively Andrew stopped. As the man drew near he recognized him: Frank Davis, an ambulance man of Anthracite Sinking Number Three, who had been one of his first-aid class the previous spring. At the same moment Davis saw him.

"I was comin' for you, Doctor. Comin' for you to your house. This wind's knocked the wires all to smash." A gust tore the rest of his words away.

"What's wrong?" shouted Andrew.

"There's been a fall-down at Number Three." Davis cupped his hands close to Manson's ear. "A lad got buried there, almost. They don't seem to be able to shift him. Sam Bevan; he's on your list. Better look sharp, Doctor, and get to him."

Andrew took a few steps down the road with Davis; then a sudden reflection brought him up short.

"I've got to have my bag," he bawled to Davis. "You go up to my house and fetch it for me. I'll go on to Number Three." He added: "And Frank! Tell my missus where I've gone."

He was at Sinking Number Three in four minutes, blown there, across the railway siding and along Roath Lane, by the following wind. In the rescue room he found the under-manager and three men waiting on him. At the sight of him the under-manager's worried expression lifted slightly.

"Glad to see you, Doctor. We're all to bits with the storm. And we've had a nasty fall on top of it. Nobody killed, thank God, but one of the lads pinned by his arm. We can't shift him an inch. And the roof's rotten."

They went to the winding shaft, two of the men carrying a stretcher with splints strapped to it and the third a wooden box of first-aid material. As they entered the cage another figure came bundling across the yard. It was Davis, panting, with the bag.

"You've been quick, Frank," Manson said as Davis squatted beside him in the cage.

Davis simply nodded; he could not speak. There was a clang, an instant's suspense, and the cage dropped and rocketed to the bottom. They all got out, moving in single file, the under-manager first, then Andrew, Davis,—still clutching the bag,—then the three men.

Andrew had been underground before; he was used to the high vaulted caverns of the Blaenelly mines, great dark resounding caves, deep down in the earth where the mineral had been gouged and blasted from its bed. But this sinking, Number Three, was an old one with a long and tortuous haulage-way leading to the workings. The haulage was less a passage than a low-roofed burrow, dripping and clammy, through which they crawled, often on their hands and knees for nearly half a mile. Suddenly the light borne by the under-manager stopped just ahead of Andrew, who then knew that they were there.

Slowly, he crept forward. Three men, cramped together on their bellies in a dead end, were doing their best to revive another man who lay in a huddled attitude, his body slewed sideways, one shoulder pointing backwards, lost seemingly in the mass of fallen rock around him. Tools lay scattered behind the men, two overturned bait cans, stripped-off jackets.

"Well then, lads?" asked the under-manager in a low voice.

"We can't shift him, nohow." The man who spoke turned a sweat-grimed face. "We tried everything."

"Don't try," said the under-manager with a quick look at the roof. "Here's the doctor. Get back a bit, lads, and give us room. Get back a tidy bit if I were you."

The three men pulled themselves back from the dead end and Andrew, when they had squeezed their way past him, went forward. As he did so, in one brief moment, there flashed through his head a memory of his recent examination, its advanced biochemistry, high-sounding terminology, scientific phrases. It had not covered such a contingency as this.

Sam Bevan was quite conscious. But his features were haggard beneath their powdering of dust. Weakly, he tried to smile to Manson.

"Looks like you're goin' to 'ave some amb'lance practice on me proper!" Bevan had been a member of that same first-aid class, and had often been requisitioned for bandage practice.

Andrew reached forward. By the light of the under-manager's lamp, thrust across his shoulder, he ran his hands over the injured man. The whole of Bevan's body was free except his left forearm, which lay beneath the fall, so pressed and mangled under that enormous weight of rock that it held him immovably a prisoner.

Andrew saw instantly that the only way to free Bevan was to amputate the forearm. And Bevan, straining his pain-tormented eyes, read that decision the moment it was made.

"Go on, then, Doctor," he muttered. "Only get me out of here quick."

"Don't worry, Sam," Andrew said. "I'm going to send you to sleep now. When you wake up you'll be in bed."

Stretched flat in a puddle of muck under the two-foot roof he slipped off his coat, folded it, and slipped it under Bevan's head. He rolled up his sleeves and asked for his bag.

The under-manager handed forward the bag and as he did so he whispered in Andrew's ear:—

"For God's sake, hurry, Doctor. We'll have this roof down on us before we know where we are."

Andrew opened the bag. Immediately he smelt the reek of chloroform. Almost before he thrust his hand into the dark interior and felt the jagged edge of broken glass he knew what had occurred. Frank Davis, in his haste to reach the mine, had dropped the bag. The chloroform bottle was broken, its contents irretrievably spilled. A shiver passed over Andrew. He had no time to send up to the surface. And he had no anaesthetic.

For perhaps thirty seconds he remained paralyzed. Then automatically he felt for his hypodermic, charged it, gave Bevan a maximum of morphine. He could not linger for the full effect. Tipping his bag sideways so that the instruments were ready to his hand he again bent over Bevan. He said, as he tightened the tourniquet:—

"Shut your eyes, Sam!"

The light was dim and the shadows moved with flickering confusion. At the first incision Bevan groaned between his shut teeth. He groaned again. Then, mercifully, when the knife grated upon the bone, he fainted.

A cold perspiration broke on Andrew's brow as he clipped the artery forceps on spurting, mangled flesh. He could not see what he was doing. He felt suffocated here, in this rat-hole, deep down beneath the surface of the ground, lying in the mud. No anaesthesia, no theatre, no row of nurses to run to do his bidding. He wasn't a surgeon. He was guddling hopelessly. He would never get through. The roof would crash upon them all.

Behind him the hurried breathing of the under-manager... A slow drip of water falling cold upon his neck... His fingers, working feverishly, stained and warm... The grating of the saw... The voice of Sir Robert Abbey, a long way off: "The opportunity for scientific practice..." Oh, God! would he never get through?

At last. He almost sobbed with relief. He slipped a pad of gauze on the bloodied stump. Stumbling to his knees he said:—

"Take him out."

Fifty yards back, in a clearing in the haulage-way, with space to stand up and four lamps round him, he finished the job. Here it was easier. He tidied up, ligatured, drenched the wound with antiseptic. A tube now. Then a couple of holding-sutures. Bevan remained unconscious. But his pulse, though thin, was steady. Andrew drew his hand across his forehead. Finished.

"Go steady with the stretcher. Wrap these blankets round him. We'll want hot bottles whenever we get out."

The slow procession, bent double in the low places, began to sway up the shadows of the haulage. They had not gone sixty paces when a low rumbling subsidence echoed in the darkness down behind them. It was like the last low rumble of a train entering a tunnel. The under-manager did not turn round. He merely said to Andrew with a quiet grimness:—

"That's it. The rest of the roof."

The journey out-bye took close upon an hour. They had to edge the stretcher sideways at the bad places. Andrew could not tell how long they had been under. But at length they came to the shaft bottom.

Up, up they shot, out of the depths. The keen bite of the wind met them, as they stepped out of the cage. With a kind of ecstasy Andrew drew a long breath.

He stood at the foot of the steps, holding on to the guard-rail. It was still dark, but in the mine yard they had hung a big naphtha flare which hissed and leaped with many tongues. Around the flare he saw a small crowd of waiting figures. There were women amongst them, with shawls about their heads.

Suddenly, as the stretcher moved slowly past them, Andrew heard his name called wildly and the next instant Christine's arms were about his neck. Sobbing hysterically she clung to him. Bareheaded, with only a coat above her nightdress, her bare feet thrust into leather shoes, she was a waiflike figure in the gusty darkness.

"What's wrong?" he asked, startled, trying to disengage her arms so that he might see her face.

But she would not let him go. Clinging to him frantically like a drowning woman she said brokenly:—

"They told us the roof was down—that you wouldn't—wouldn't come out."

Her skin was blue, her teeth chattering with cold. He carried her into the fire of the rescue-room, ashamed, yet deeply touched. There was hot cocoa in the rescue-room. They drank from the same scalding cup. It was a long time before either of them remembered about his grand new degree.

xii

The rescue of Sam Bevan was commonplace to a town which had known, in the past, the agony and horror of major mine disasters. Yet in his own district it did Andrew a vast amount of good. Had he returned with the bare success of London behind him he would have earned merely an extra sneer for "more newfangled nonsense." As it was, he received nods and even smiles from people who had never seemed to look at him before. The real extent of a doctor's popularity in Aberalaw could be gauged by his passage down the Rows. And where Andrew had hitherto been met by a line of tight-shut doors he now found them open, the off-shift men smoking in their shirt sleeves ready for a word with him, the women ready to "call him in," as he went by, the children greeting him smilingly by name.

Old Gus Parry, head driller in Number Two and doyen of the West district, summed up the new current of opinion for his mates as he gazed after Andrew's retreating figure.

"Eh, lads! 'E's a bookish chap no doubt. But he can do the real stuff, like, when it's wanted."

Cards began to come back to Andrew, gradually at first and, when it was seen that he did not abuse his returned renegades, with a sudden rush. Owen was pleased at the increase in Andrew's list. Meeting Andrew in the Square one day he smiled: "Didn't I tell you, now?"

Llewellyn had affected great delight at the result of the examination. He congratulated Andrew effusively upon the phone, then blandly raked him in for double duty at the theatre.

"By the way," he remarked, beaming, at the end of the long and ether-ridden session, "did you tell the examiners you were an assistant in a medical aid scheme?"

"I mentioned your name to them, Doctor Llewellyn," Andrew answered sweetly. "And that made it quite all right."

Oxborrow and Medley of the East Surgery took no notice of Andrew's success. But Urquhart was genuinely glad, though his comment took the form of vituperative explosion.

"Dammit to hell, Manson! What d'you think you're doin'? Trying to put my eye out?"

By way of complimenting his distinguished colleague he asked him in consultation to a case of pneumonia he was then attending and demanded to know the prognosis.

"She'll recover," Andrew said, and he gave scientific reasons.

Urquhart shook his old head dubiously.

He said: "I never heard tell of your polyvalent sera or your antibodies or your international units. But she was a Powell before her marriage and when the Powells get a swollen belly with their pneumonias they die before the eighth day. I know that family backwards. She's got a swollen belly, hasn't she?"

The old man went about with an air of sombre triumph over the scientific method when his patient died on the seventh day.

Denny, now abroad, knew nothing of the new degree. But a final and somewhat unexpected congratulation came in a long letter from Freddie Hampton. Freddie had seen the results in the *Lancet*, chided Andrew on his success, invited him to London, and then detailed his own exciting triumphs in Queen Anne Street where, as he had predicted that night at Cardiff, his neat brass plate now shone.

"It's a shame the way we've lost touch with Freddie," Manson declared. "I must write to him oftener. I've a feeling we shall run into him again. Nice letter, isn't it?"

"Yes, very nice," Christine answered drily. "But most of it seems to be about himself."

With the approach of Christmas the weather turned colder—crisp frosty days and still, starry nights. The iron hard roads rang under Andrew's feet. The clear air was like an exhilarating wine. Already shaping in his mind was the next step which he would take in his great assault on the problem of dust inhalation. His findings amongst his own patients had raised his hopes high, and now he had obtained permission from Vaughan to extend the field of his investigation by making a systematic examination of all the workers in the three anthracite sinkings—a marvellous opportunity. He planned to use the pit workers and surfacemen as controls. He would begin at the start of the New Year.

On Christmas Eve he returned from the surgery to Vale View with an extraordinary sense of spiritual anticipation and physical well-being. As he walked up the road it was impossible to escape the signs of the impending festival. The miners made much of Christmas here. For the past week the front room in each house had been locked against the children, festooned with paper streamers; toys were hidden in the drawers of the chest, and a steady accumulation of good things to eat—cake, oranges, sweet sugar biscuits, all bought with the club money paid out at this time of year—was laid upon the table.

Christine had made her own decorations of holly and mistletoe in gay expectation. But to-night as he came into the house he saw at once an extra excitement upon her face.

"Don't say a word," she said quickly, holding out her hand. "Not a single word! Just shut your eyes and come with me!"

He allowed her to lead him into the kitchen. There, on the table, lay a number of parcels, clumsily made up, some merely wrapped in newspaper, but each with a little note attached. In a flash he realized that they were presents from his patients. Some of the gifts were not wrapped up at all.

"Look, Andrew!" Christine cried. "A goose! And two ducks! And a lovely iced cake! And a bottle of elderberry wine! Isn't it kind of them? Isn't it wonderful they should want to give them to you?"

He simply could not speak. It overwhelmed him, this kindly evidence that the people of his district had at last begun to appreciate, to like him. With Christine at his shoulder he read the notes, the handwriting laboured and illiterate, some scrawled in pencil upon old envelopes turned inside out. "Your grateful patient at 3 Cefen Row"; "With thanks from Mrs. Williams"; one lopsided gem from Sam Bevan, "Thanks for getting me out for Christmas Doctor *bach*"—so they went on.

"We must keep these, darling," Christine said in a low voice, "I'll put them away upstairs."

When he had recovered his normal loquacity—a glass of homemade elderberry assisted him—he paced up and down the kitchen while Christine stuffed the goose. He raved beautifully:—

"That's how fees should be paid, Chris. No money, no damned bills, no capitation fee, no guinea-grabbing. Payment in kind. You understand me, don't you, darling? You get your patient right, he sends you something that he has made, produced. Coal if you like, a sack of potatoes from his garden, eggs maybe if he keeps hens—see my point? Then you'd have an ethical ideal! By the way, that Mrs. Williams who sent us the ducks— Leslie had her guzzling pills and physic for five stricken years before I cured her gastric ulcer with five weeks' diet. Where was I? Oh, yes! Don't you see? If every doctor was to eliminate the question of *gain* the whole system would be purer—"

"Yes, dear. Would you mind handing me the currants? Top shelf in the cupboard!"

"Damn it all, woman, why don't you listen? Gosh! That stuffing's going to taste good."

Next morning, Christmas Day, came fine and clear. Tallyn Beacons in the blue distance were pearly, with a white icing of snow. After a few morning consultations, with the pleasant prospect of no surgery in the evening, Andrew went on his round. He had a short list. Dinners were cooking in all the little houses and his own was cooking at home. He did not tire of the Christmas greetings he gave and received, all along the Rows. He could not help contrasting this present cheerfulness with his bleak passage up those same streets only a year ago.

Perhaps it was this thought which made him draw up, with an odd hesitation in his eyes, outside Number 18 Cefen Row. Of all his patients, apart from Chenkin, whom he did not want, the only one who had not come back to him was Tom Evans. To-day, when he was so unusually stirred, perhaps unduly exalted by a sense of the brotherhood of man, he had a sudden impulse to approach Evans and wish him a merry Christmas.

Knocking once, he opened the front door and walked through to the back kitchen. Here he paused, quite taken aback. The kitchen was very bare, almost empty, and in the grate there burned only a spark of fire. Seated before this, on a broken-backed wooden chair, with his crooked arm bent out like a wing, was Tom Evans. The droop of his shoulders was dispirited, hopeless. On his knee sat his little girl, four years of age. They were gazing, both of them, in silent contemplation, at a branch of fir planted in an old bucket. Upon this diminutive Christmas tree, which Evans had walked two miles over the mountain to procure, were three tiny tallow candles, as yet unlighted. And beneath it lay the family's Christmas treat—three small oranges.

Suddenly Evans turned and caught sight of Andrew. He started, and a slow flush of shame and resentment spread over his face. Andrew sensed that it was agony for him to be found—out of work, half his furniture pawned, crippled—by the doctor whose advice he had rejected.

Andrew had known, of course, that Evans was down on his luck, but he had not suspected anything so pitiful as this. He felt upset and uncomfortable, he wanted to turn and go away. At that moment Mrs. Evans came into the kitchen through the back door with a paper bag under her arm. She was so startled at the sight of Andrew that she dropped the paper bag, which fell to the stone floor and burst open—revealing two beef faggots, the cheapest meat that Aberalaw provided. The child, glancing at her mother's face, began suddenly to cry.

"What's like the matter, sir?" Mrs. Evans ventured at last, her hand pressed against her side. "He hasn't done anything?"

Andrew gritted his teeth together. He was so moved and surprised by this scene he had stumbled upon, only one course would satisfy him.

"Mrs. Evans!" He kept his eyes stiffly upon the floor. "I know there was a bit of a misunderstanding between your Tom and me. But it's Christmas—and—oh, well, I want —" he broke down lamely—"I mean, I'd be awfully pleased if the three of you would come round and help us eat our Christmas dinner."

"But, Doctor—" she wavered.

"You be quiet, lass," Evans interrupted her fiercely. "We're not goin' out to no dinner. If faggots is all we *can* have, it's all we *will* have. We don't want any bloody charity from nobody."

"What are you talking about?" Andrew exclaimed in dismay. "I'm asking you as a friend."

"Ah! you're all the same!" Evans answered wretchedly. "Once you get a man down, all you can do is fling some grub in his face. Keep your bloody dinner. We don't want it."

"Now, Tom—" Mrs. Evans protested weakly.

Andrew turned towards her, distressed, yet still determined to carry out his intention.

"You persuade him, Mrs. Evans. I'll be really upset now, if you don't come. Half-past one. We'll expect you."

Before any of them could say another word he swung round and left the house.

Christine made no comment when he blurted out what he had done. The Vaughans would probably have come to them to-day but for the fact that they had gone to Switzerland for the skiing. And now he had asked an unemployed miner and his family! These were his thoughts as he stood with his back to the fire watching her lay the extra places.

"You're cross, Chris?" he said at last.

"I thought I married Doctor Manson," she answered a trifle brusquely. "Not Doctor Bernardo. Really, darling, you're an incorrigible sentimentalist!"

The Evanses arrived exactly upon time, washed and brushed, desperately ill at ease, proud and frightened. Andrew, striving nervously to generate hospitality, had a dreadful premonition that Christine was right, that entertainment would be a dismal failure. Evans, with a queer look at Andrew, proved to be clumsy at the table because of his bad arm. His wife was obliged to break and to butter his roll for him. And then, by good fortune, as Andrew was using the cruet, the top fell off the pepper caster and the entire half-ounce of white pepper shot into his soup. There was a hollow silence; then Agnes, the little girl, gave a sudden delighted giggle. Panic-stricken, the mother bent to rebuke her, when the sight of Andrew's face restrained her. The next minute they were all laughing.

Free of his dread of being patronized, Evans revealed himself a human being, a staunch Rugby football supporter and a great music lover. He had gone to Cardigan three years before, to sing at the Eisteddfod there. Proud to show his knowledge he discussed with Christine the oratorios of Elgar, while Agnes pulled crackers with Andrew.

Later, Christine drew Mrs. Evans and the little girl into the other room. When they were left alone, a strange silence fell between Andrew and Evans. A common thought was uppermost in the mind of each, yet neither knew how to broach it.

Finally with a kind of desperation Andrew said: "I'm sorry about that arm of yours, Tom. I know you've lost your work underground over the head of it. Don't think I'm trying to crow over you or anything like that. I'm just damned sorry."

"You're not any sorrier than I am," Evans said.

There was a pause, then Andrew resumed:—

"I wonder if you'd let me speak to Mr. Vaughan about you. Shut me up if you think I'm interfering—but I've got a little bit of influence with him and I feel sure I could get you a job on the surface—timekeeper—or something—"

He broke off, not daring to look at Evans. This time the silence was prolonged. At length Andrew raised his eyes, only to lower them again immediately. Tears were running down Evans' cheek, his entire body was shaking with his effort not to give way. But it was no use. He laid his good arm on the table, buried his head in it.

Andrew got up and crossed to the window where he remained for a few minutes. At the end of that time Evans had collected himself. He said nothing, absolutely nothing, and his eyes avoided Andrew's with a dumb reticence more significant than speech.

At half-past three the Evans family departed in a mood contrasting cheerfully with the constraint of their arrival. Christine and Andrew went into the sitting-room.

"You know, Chris," Andrew philosophized, "all that poor fellow's trouble—his stiff elbow I mean—isn't *his* fault. He distrusted me because I was new. He couldn't be expected to know about that damn carron oil. But friend Oxborrow—who accepted his card—*he* should have known. Ignorance, ignorance, pure damned ignorance. There ought to be a law to make doctors keep up-to-date. It's all the fault of our rotten system. There ought to be compulsory post graduate classes—to be taken every five years—"

"Darling!" protested Christine, smiling at him from the sofa. "I've put up with your philanthropy all day. I've watched your wings sprouting like an archangel's. Don't give me the Harveian Oration on top of it! Come and sit by me here; I had a really important reason for wanting us to be alone to-day."

"Yes?"—doubtfully; then, indignantly: "You're not complaining, I hope. I thought I had behaved pretty decently. After all—Christmas Day—"

She laughed silently.

"Oh, my dear, you're just too lovely. Another minute there'll be a snowstorm and you'll take out the St. Bernards—muffled to the throat—to bring in somebody off the mountain—late, late at night."

"I know somebody who came down to Number Three Sinking—late, late at night," he grunted in retaliation; "and she wasn't muffled either."

"Sit here." She stretched out her arm. "I want to tell you something."

He went over to seat himself beside her, when suddenly there came the loud braying of a Klaxon from outside.

"*Krr-krr-krr-ki-ki-krr.*"

"Damn!" said Christine concisely. Only one motor horn in Aberalaw could sound like that. It belonged to Con Boland.

"Don't you want them?" Andrew asked in some surprise. "Con half-said they'd be round for tea."

"Oh, well!" Christine said, rising and accompanying him to the door.

They advanced to meet the Bolands, who sat opposite the front gate in the reconstructed motor car—Con upright at the wheel in a bowler hat and enormous new gauntlets, with Mary and Terence beside him; the three other children tucked around Mrs. Boland, who bore the infant in her arms, in the rear, all packed, despite the elongation of the vehicle, like herrings in a tin.

Suddenly the horn began again: *"Krr-krr-krr-krr—"* Con had inadvertently pushed the button in switching off and now it was jammed. The Klaxon would not stop. *"Krr-krr-krr—"* it went, while Con fumbled and swore, and windows went up in the Row opposite, and Mrs. Boland sat with a remote expression on her face, unperturbed, holding the baby dreamily.

"In the name of God," Con cried, his moustache bristling along the dashboard. "I'm wastin' juice. What's happened? Am I short-circuited or what?"

"It's the button, Father," Mary told him calmly. She took her little fingernail and edged it out. The racket ceased.

"Ah! That's better," Con sighed. "How are you, Manson, my boy? How d'you like the old car now? I've lengthened her a good two feet. Isn't she grand? Mind you, there's still a little bother with the gearbox. We didn't quite take the hill in our stride, as ye might say!"

"We only stuck a few minutes, Father," interposed Mary.

"Ah! never mind," said Con. "I'll soon have that right when I sthrip her again. How are ye, Mrs. Manson? Here we all are, to wish ye a merry Christmas and take our tea off ye!"

"Come in, Con," Christine smiled. "I like your gloves!"

"Christmas present from the wife," Con answered, admiring the flapping gauntlets. "Army Surplus. Would ye believe they were still dishin' them out? Ah! What's gone wrong with this door?"

Unable to open the door he threw his long legs over it, climbed out, helped the children and his wife from the back, surveyed the car,—fondly removing a lump of mud from the windscreen,—then tore himself away to follow the others to Vale View.

They had a cheerful tea party. Con was in high spirits, full of his creation—"You'll not know her when she has a lick of paint." Mrs. Boland abstractedly drank six cups of strong black tea. The children began upon the chocolate biscuits and ended with a fight for the last piece of bread. They cleared every plate upon the table.

After tea, while Mary had gone to wash the dishes,—she insisted that Christine looked tired,—Andrew detached the baby from Mrs. Boland and played with it on the hearthrug before the fire. It was the fattest baby he had ever seen, a Rubens infant, with enormous solemn eyes and pads of plumpness upon its limbs. It tried repeatedly to poke a finger into his eye. Every time it failed a look of solemn wonder came upon its face. Christine sat with her hands in her lap, doing nothing—watching him playing with the baby.

But Con and his family could not stay long. Outside the light was fading and Con, worried about his "juice," had doubts which he did not choose to express concerning the functioning of his lamps.

When they rose to go, he delivered the invitation: "Come out and see us start."

Again Andrew and Christine stood at the gate while Con packed the car with his offspring. After a couple of swings the engine obeyed and Con, with a triumphant nod towards them, pulled on his gauntlets and adjusted his derby to a more rakish tilt. Then he heaved himself proudly into the driving seat.

At that moment Con's union broke and the car, with a groan, collapsed. Bearing the entire Boland family, the overextended vehicle sank slowly to the ground like some beast of burden perishing from sheer exhaustion. Before the bedazzled eyes of Andrew and Christine, the wheels splayed outwards. There was the sound of pieces dropping off, a vomit of tools shot from the locker; then the body of the car came to rest, dismembered, on street level. One minute there was a car, and the next a fun-fair gondola. In the forepart was Con clutching the wheel, in the aft part his wife, clutching the baby. Mrs. Boland's mouth had dropped wide open, her dreamy eyes well fixed upon eternity. The stupefaction on Con's face, at his sudden loss of elevation, was irresistible.

Andrew and Christine gave out a shriek of laughter. Once they began they could not stop. They laughed till they were weak.

"In the name of God," Con said, rubbing his head and picking himself up. Observing that none of the children were hurt, that Mrs. Boland remained, pale but undisturbed, in her seat, he considered the wreckage, pondering dazedly. "Sabotage," he declared at last, glaring at the windows opposite as a solution struck him. "Some of them devils in the Rows has tampered with her." Then his face brightened. He took the helpless Andrew by the arm and pointed with melancholy pride to the crumpled bonnet, beneath which the engine still feebly emitted a few convulsive beats. "See that, Manson! She's still runnin'."

Somehow they dragged the remains into the back yard of Vale View. In due course the Boland family went home on foot.

"What a day!" Andrew exclaimed when they had secured peace for themselves at last. "I'll never forget that look on Con's face as long as I live."

They were silent for a moment; then, turning to her, he asked: "You did enjoy your Christmas?"

She replied oddly: "I enjoyed seeing you play with Baby Boland."

He glanced at her.

"Why?"

She did not look at him. "I've been trying to tell you all day. Oh, can't you guess, darling? I don't think you're such a smart physician after all."

xiii

Spring once more... And early summer... The garden at Vale View was a patch of tender colours which the miners often stopped to admire on their way back from their shift. Chiefly these colours came from flowering shrubs which Christine had planted the previous autumn, for now Andrew would allow her to do no heavy work at all.

"You've *made* the place!" he told her, with authority. "Now *sit* in it."

Her favourite seat was at the end of the little glen where, beside a tiny watersplash, she could hear the soothing converse of the stream. An overhanging willow offered protection from the rows of houses above. The difficulty with the rest of the garden of Vale View was that they had only to sit outside the porch for all the front windows of the Rows to be tenanted and the murmur to go round: "Eh! There's nice! Come an' 'ave a look, Fan-ee! Doctor and his missus are havin' bit of sun, like!" Once indeed, in their early days, when Andrew slipped his arm around Christine's waist as they stretched by the bank of the stream, he had seen the gleam of focussed glass from old Glyn Joseph's parlour. "Damn it!" Andrew had realized hotly. "The old dog—he's got his telescope on us!"

But beneath the willow they were completely screened and here Andrew defined his policy.

"You see, Chris,"—fidgeting with his thermometer; it had just occurred to him in a passion of precaution to take her temperature,—"we've got to keep calm. It's not as if we were—oh! well—*ordinary* people. After all you're a doctor's wife and I'm—I'm a doctor. I've seen this happen hundreds, at least scores of times before. It's a very *ordinary affair*. A phenomenon of nature, survival of the race, all that sort of thing, see! Now don't misunderstand me, darling, it's *wonderful* for us, of course. The fact is I'd begun to ask myself if you weren't too slight, too much of a kid ever to—oh, well, I'm *delighted*. But we're not going to get sentimental. Slushy, I mean. No, no! Let's leave that sort of thing to Mr. and Mrs. Smith. It would be rather idiotic, wouldn't it, for me, a doctor, to start—oh, say to start mooning over those little things you're knitting or crocheting, or whatever it is? No! I just look at them and grunt: 'Hope they'll be warm enough!' And all this junk about what colour of eyes she—er—it will have, and what sort of rosy future we'll give her—that's right off the map!" He paused, frowning; then gradually a reflective smile broke over his face. "I say, though, Chris! I wonder if it *will* be a girl!"

She laughed till the tears ran down her cheeks. She laughed so hard that he sat up, concerned.

"Now stop it, Chris! You'll—you might bring on something."

"Oh, my dear," she wiped her eyes. "As a sentimental idealist I adore you. As a hard-boiled cynic—well! I wouldn't have you in the house!"

He did not quite know what she meant. But he knew he was being scientific and restrained. In the afternoons when he felt she ought to have some exercise he took her for walks in the Public Park, climbing to the uplands being severely forbidden. In the Park they strolled about, listened to the band, watched the miners' children who came to picnic there with bottles of liquorice water and sherbet suckers.

Early one May morning as they lay in bed he became aware through his light sleep, of a faint movement. He awoke, again conscious of that gentle thrusting, the first movement of the child within Christine. He held himself rigid, scarcely daring to believe, suffocated by a rush of feeling, of ecstasy. Oh, hell! he thought a moment later, perhaps I'm just a Smith after all. I suppose that's why they make the rule a medico can't attend his own wife.

The following week he felt it time to speak to Doctor Llewellyn who, from the outset, they had both decided must undertake the case. Llewellyn, when Andrew rang him, was pleased and flattered. He came down at once, made a preliminary examination, then chatted to Andrew in the sitting-room:—

"I'm glad to help you, Manson—" accepting a cigarette. "I always felt you didn't like me enough to ask me to do this for you. Believe me, I'll do my best. By the way, it's pretty stifling in Aberalaw at present. Don't you think your little missus ought to have a change of air while she can?"

"What's happening to me?" Andrew asked himself when Llewellyn had gone. "I like that man! He was decent, damned decent. He's got sympathy and tact. He's a wizard at his work. And twelve months ago I was trying to cut his throat. I'm just a stiff, jealous, clumsy Highland stot!"

Christine did not wish to go away, but he was gently insistent.

"I know you don't want to leave me, Chris! But it's for the best. We've got to think of —oh! everything. Would you rather have the seaside? Or maybe you'd like to go up North to your aunt. Dash it all, I can afford to send you, Chris. We're pretty well off now!"

They had paid off the Glen Endowment and the last of the furniture instalments and now they had nearly one hundred pounds saved in the bank. But she was not thinking of this when, pressing his hand, she answered steadily:—

"Yes! We're pretty well off, Andrew."

Since she must go, she decided to visit her aunt in Bridlington and a week later he saw her off at the Upper Station with a long hug and a basket of fruit to sustain her on the journey.

He missed her more than he could have believed; their comradeship had become such a part of his life. Their talks, discussions, squabbles, their silences together, the way in which he would call to her whenever he entered the house and wait, his ear cocked, for her cheery answer—he came to see how much these meant to him. Without her, their bedroom became a strange room in a hotel. His meals, conscientiously served by Jenny according to the programme written out by Christine, were arid snatches behind a propped-up book.

Wandering round the garden she had made, he was struck, suddenly by the dilapidated condition of the bridge. It offended him, seemed an insult to his absent Christine. He had several times spoken to the Committee about this, telling them the bridge was falling to pieces, but they were always hard to move when it came to repairing the assistants' houses. Now, however, in an access of sentiment, he rang up the office and pressed the point strenuously. Owen had gone away upon a few days' leave, but the clerk assured Andrew that the matter had already been passed by the Committee and referred to Richards the builder. It was only because Richards was busy with another contract that the work had not been put in hand.

In the evenings he betook himself to Boland, twice to the Vaughans who made him remain for bridge, and once, greatly to his surprise, he found himself playing golf with Llewellyn. He wrote letters to Hampton and to Denny, who was journeying to Tampico as the surgeon of a tanker. His correspondence with Christine was a model of illuminating restraint. But he sought distraction, chiefly, in his work.

His clinical examinations at the anthracite sinkings were, by this time, well under way. He could not hasten them, since, apart from the demands of his own patients, his opportunity for examining the men came as they went to the mine-head baths at the end of the shift and it was impossible to keep them hanging about for any length of time when they wanted to get home for their dinners. He got through, on an average, two examinations a day; yet already the results were adding further to his excitement. He saw, without jumping to any immediate conclusion, that the incidence of pulmonary trouble amongst the anthracite workers was positively in excess of that existing in the other underground workers in the coal mines.

Though he distrusted textbooks, in self-defence, since he had no wish to find afterwards that he had merely put his feet in footprints made by others, he went through the literature on the subject. Its paucity astounded him. Few investigators seemed to have concerned themselves greatly with the pulmonary occupational diseases. Zenker had introduced a high-sounding term, "pneumonokoniosis," embracing three forms of fibrosis of the lung due to dust inhalation. Anthracosis, of course, the black infiltration of the lungs met with in coal miners, had long been known and was held by Goldman in Germany and Trotter in England to be harmless. There were a few treatises on the prevalence of lung trouble in makers of millstones, particularly the French millstones, and in knife and axe grinders—"grinder's rot"—and stonecutters. There was evidence, mostly conflicting, from South Africa upon that red rag of Rand labour troubles, gold-miners' phthisis, which was undoubtedly due to dust inhalation. It was recorded also that workers in flax and in cotton, and grain shovellers, were subject to chronic changes in the lungs. But beyond that, nothing!

Andrew drew back from his reading with excitement in his eyes. He felt himself upon the track of something definitely unexplored. He thought of the vast numbers of underground workers in the great anthracite mines, the looseness of the legislation upon the disabilities from which they suffered, the enormous social importance of this line of investigation. What a chance, what a wonderful chance! A cold sweat broke over him at the sudden thought that someone might forestall him. But he thrust this from him. Striding up and down the sitting-room before the dead fire long after midnight, he suddenly seized Christine's photograph from the mantelshelf.

"Chris! I really believe I'm going to *do* something!"

In the card-index he bought for the purpose he carefully began to classify the results of his examinations. Though he never considered this, his clinical skill was now quite brilliant. There, in the changing room, the men stood before him, stripped to the waist, and with his fingers, his stethoscope, he plumbed uncannily the hidden pathology of those living lungs: a fibroid spot here, the next an emphysema, then a chronic bronchitis —deprecatingly admitted as "a bit of a cough." Carefully he localized the lesions upon the diagrams printed on the back of every card.

At the same time he took sputum samples from each man and, working till two and three in the morning at Denny's microscope, tabulated his findings on the cards. He found that most of these samples of muco-pus—locally described by the men as "white-spit"—contained bright angular particles of silica. He was amazed at the number of alveolar cells present, at the frequency with which he came upon the tubercule bacillus. But it was the presence, almost constant, of crystalline silicon, in the alveolar cells, the phagocytes, everywhere, which riveted his attention. He could not escape the thrilling idea that the changes in the lungs, perhaps even the coincident infections, were fundamentally dependent on this factor.

This was the extent of his advance when Christine returned at the end of June and flung her arms round his neck.

"It's so good to be back. Yes, I enjoyed myself; but oh! I don't know—and you look pale, darling! I don't believe Jenny's been feeding you!"

Her holiday had done her good, she was well and her cheeks had a fine bloom upon them. But she was concerned about him, his lack of appetite, his perpetual fumbling for a cigarette.

She asked him seriously:—

"How long is this special work going to take?"

"I don't know." It was the day after her return, a wet day, and he was unexpectedly moody. "It might take a year, it might take five."

"Well, listen to me. I'm not reforming you, one in the family is enough; but don't you think, since it's going on so long as that, you'll have to work systematically, keep regular hours, not stay up late and kill yourself?"

"There's nothing the matter with me."

But in some things she had a peculiar insistence. She got Jenny to scrub out the floor of the Lab., brought in an armchair and a rug. It was a room cool on these hot nights and the pine boards had a sweet resinous smell which mingled with the pungent ethereal scent of the reagents he used. Here she would sit, sewing and knitting, while he worked at the table. Bent over the microscope, he quite forgot about her, but she was there; and at eleven o'clock every night she got up.

"Time for bed!"

"Oh, I say!"—blinking at her nearsightedly over the eyepiece. "You go up, Chris! I'll follow you in a minute."

"Andrew Manson, if you think I'm going up to bed alone, *in my condition*—"

This last phrase had become a comic byword in the household. They both used it, indiscriminately, facetiously, as a clincher to all their arguments. He could not resist it. With a laugh he would rise, stretch himself, swing round his lenses, put the slides away.

Towards the end of July a sharp outbreak of chicken pox made him busy in the practice, and on the third of August he had an especially heavy list which kept him out from morning surgery until well after three o'clock. As he came up the road, tired, ready for that combination of lunch and tea which would be his meal, he saw Doctor Llewellyn's car at the gate of Vale View.

The implication of that static object caused him to start suddenly and to hasten, his heart beating rapidly with anticipation, towards his house. He ran up the porch steps, threw open the front door and there, in the hall, he found Llewellyn.

Gazing at the other man with nervous eagerness he stammered: "Hello, Llewellyn. I—I didn't expect to see you here so soon."

"No," Llewellyn answered.

Andrew smiled. "Well?" In his excitement he could find no better words, but the question in his bright face was plain enough.

Llewellyn did not smile. After the faintest pause he said: "Come in here a minute, my dear chap." And he drew Andrew into the sitting-room. "We've been trying to find you, on your rounds, all morning."

Llewellyn's manner, his hesitation, the strange sympathy in his voice, shot a wave of coldness over Andrew.

He faltered: "Is anything wrong?"

Llewellyn looked through the window, his glance travelling towards the bridge, as if searching for the best, the kindest explanation. Andrew could bear it no longer. He could scarcely breathe, his breast was filled with a stifling agony of suspense.

"Manson," Llewellyn said gently, "this morning, as your wife was going over the bridge—one of the rotten planks gave way. *She's* all right now, quite all right; but I'm afraid—"

He understood even before Llewellyn finished. A great pulse of anguish beat within him.

"You might like to know," Llewellyn went on, in a tone of quiet compassion, "that we did everything. I came at once, brought Matron from the hospital, we've been here all day—"

There was a bar of silence. A sob broke in Andrew's throat, another, then another. He covered his eyes with his hand.

"Please, my dear fellow—" Llewellyn entreated—"who could help an accident like that? I beg of you—go up and console your wife."

His head lowered, holding to the banister, Andrew went upstairs. Outside the door of the bedroom he paused, scarcely breathing; then, stumblingly, he went in.

xiv

By the year 1927 Doctor Manson of Aberalaw had a somewhat unusual reputation. His practice was not prodigious—numerically his list had not greatly increased since those first nervous days of his arrival in the town. But everyone upon that list had a convincing belief in him. He used few drugs—indeed, he had the incredible habit of advising his patients against medicine—but when he did use them he prescribed in shattering style. It was no uncommon sight to see Gadge drooping across the waiting-room with a prescription in his hand.

"What's all this, Doctor Manson! *Sixty* grain doses of KBr. for Evan Jones! And the Pharmacopœia says *five*."

"So does Aunt Kate's dream-book! Go ahead with sixty, Gadge. You know you'd really enjoy knocking off Evan Jones."

But Evan Jones, epileptic, was not knocked off. Instead he was seen, a week later, his fits lessened, taking walks in the Public Park.

The Committee ought to have cherished Doctor Manson tenderly, because his drug bill—despite explosive incidents—was less than half that of any other assistant. But alas! Manson cost the Committee three times as much in other directions, and often there was war because of it. He used vaccines and sera for instance, ruinous things which, as Ed Chenkin heatedly declared, none of them had ever heard of. When Owen, defending, instanced that winter month when Manson, using Bordet and Gengou vaccine, had arrested a raging epidemic of whooping cough in his district when all over the rest of the town children were going down of it, Ed Chenkin countered: "How do we know this newfangled thing did it? Why! When I tackled 'im myself, he said nobody could be *sure!*"

While Manson had many loyal friends, he also had enemies. There were those on the Committee who had never completely forgiven him for his outburst, those agonized words hurled at them, over that matter of the bridge, as they sat in full session three years before. They sympathized, of course, with Mrs. Manson and himself in their bereavement, but they could not hold themselves responsible. The Committee never did things in a hurry; Owen was then on holiday, and Len Richards, who had been given the job, was busy at the time with the new houses in Powis Street. It was preposterous to blame them.

As time went on Andrew had many heartburnings with the Committee, for he had a stubborn desire for his own way which the Committee did not like. In addition there was a certain clerical bias against him. Though his wife went to church, he was never seen there,—Doctor Oxborrow had been the first to point this out,—and he was reported to have laughed at the doctrine of total immersion. He had, moreover, a deadly enemy amongst "the chapel" folk—no less a person than the Reverend Edwal Parry, pastor of Sinai.

In the spring of 1926 the good Edwal, newly married, had sidled, late, into Manson's surgery with an air thoroughly Christian, yet ingratiatingly man of the world.

"How are you, Doctor Manson! I just happened to be passing. As a rule I attend with Doctor Oxborrow, he's one of my flock you know, and he's handy at the East Surgery also. But you're a very up-to-date doctor by all accounts and purposes. You're in the way of knowin' everything that's new. And I'd be glad—mind you I'll pay you a nice little fee too—if you could advise me." Edwal masked a faint priestly blush by show of worldly candour. "You see the wife and I don't want any children for a while yet anyhow, my stipend bein' what it is, like…"

Manson considered the minister of Sinai in a cold distaste. He said carefully:—

"Don't you realize there are people with a quarter of your stipend who would give their right hand to have children? What did you get married for?" His anger rose to a sudden white heat. "Get out—quick—you—you dirty little man of God!"

With a queer twist to his face Parry had slunk out. Perhaps Andrew had spoken too violently. But then Christine, since that fatal stumble, would never have children, and they both desired them with all their hearts.

Walking home from a call on this, the fifteenth of May, 1927, Andrew was inclined to ask himself why he and Christine had remained in Aberalaw since the death of their child. The answer was plain enough: his work on dust inhalation. It had absorbed him, fascinated him, bound him to the mines.

As he reviewed what he had done, considering the difficulties he had been obliged to face, he wondered that he had not taken longer to complete his findings. Those first examinations he had made—how far removed they seemed in time—yes, and in technique.

After he had made a complete clinical survey of the pulmonary conditions of all the workmen in the district and tabulated his findings, he had plain evidence of the marked preponderance of lung diseases amongst the anthracite workers. For example, he found that ninety per cent. of his cases of fibrosed lung came from the anthracite mines. He found also that the death rate from lung troubles amongst the older anthracite miners was nearly three times that of miners employed in all coal mines. He drew up a series of tables indicating the ratio-incidence of pulmonary disease, amongst the various grades of anthracite workmen.

Next, he set out to show that the silica dust he had found in his examinations of sputum was actually present in the anthracite headings. Not only did he demonstrate this conclusively, but, by exposing glass slides smeared with Canada balsam for varying periods in different parts of the mine, he obtained figures of the varying dust concentrations, figures which rose sharply during blasting and drilling.

He now had a series of exciting equations correlating excessive atmosphere concentrations of silica dust with excessive incidence of pulmonary disease. But this was not enough. He had actually to *prove* that the dust was harmful, that it was destructive to lung tissue and not merely an innocuous accessory after the fact. It was necessary for him to conduct a series of pathological experiments upon guinea pigs, to study the action of the silica dust upon their lungs.

Here, though his excitement rose, his real troubles began. He already had the spare room, the Lab. It was easy to procure a few guinea pigs. And the equipment required for his experiments was simple. But though his ingenuity was considerable he was not, and never would be, a pathologist. Awareness of this fact made him angry, more resolved than ever. He swore at a system which compelled him to work alone; and pressed Christine to his service, teaching her to cut and prepare sections, the mechanics of the trade which, in no time at all, she did better than he.

Next he constructed, very simply, a dust chamber in which for certain hours of the day the animals were exposed to concentrations of the dust, others being unexposed—the controls. It was exasperating work, demanding more patience than he possessed. Twice his small electric fan broke down. At a critical stage of the experiment he bungled his system of controls and was forced to begin all over again. But, in spite of mistakes and delays, he got his specimens, proving, in progressive stages, the deterioration of the lung and induction of fibrosis from the dust.

He drew a long breath of satisfaction, stopped scolding Christine and, for a few days, was fit to live with. Then another idea struck him and he was off again.

All his investigations had been conducted on the supposition that the damage to the lung was produced in response to mechanical destruction by the hard sharp silicate crystals inhaled. But now, suddenly, he asked himself if there was not some chemical action beyond the mere physical irritation of the particles. He was not a chemist but he was, by this time, too deeply immersed to allow himself to be defeated. He devised a fresh series of experiments.

He procured colloidal silica and injected it under the skin of one of his animals. The result was an abscess. Similar abscesses could, he found, be induced by the injection of aqueous solutions of amorphous silica, which was, physically, a nonirritant; while, in triumphant conclusion, he found that the injection of a mechanically irritating substance, such as particles of carbon, produced no abscess at all. The silica dust *was* chemically active.

He was now almost out of his mind with excitement and delight. He had done even more than he had set out to do. Feverishly he collected his data, drew up in compact form the results of his three years' work. He had decided, months ago, not only to publish his investigation but to send it in as his thesis for the degree of M.D. When the typescript came back from Cardiff, neatly bound in a pale blue folder, he read it exultantly, went out with Christine to post it, then slumped into a backwash of despair.

He felt worn-out and inert. He became aware, more vividly than ever, that he was no laboratory worker, that the best, the most valuable part of his work was that first phase of clinical research. He recollected, with a pang of compunction, how often he had raged at poor Christine. For days he was dispirited and listless. And yet, through it all, there were shining moments when he knew he had accomplished something after all.

XV

That May afternoon, when Andrew reached home, his mood of preoccupation, this oddly negative phase which had persisted since the dispatch of his thesis, caused him to miss the look of distress upon Christine's face. He greeted her absent-mindedly, went upstairs to wash, then came down to tea.

When he had finished, however, and lit a cigarette, he suddenly observed her expression. He asked, as he reached out for the evening paper:—

"Why? What's the matter?"

She appeared to examine her teaspoon for a moment.

"We had some visitors to-day—or rather I had—when you were out this afternoon."

"Oh? Who were they?"

"A deputation from the Committee, five of them, including Ed Chenkin, escorted by Parry—you know, the Sinai minister—and a man Davies."

An odd silence fell. He took a long pull at his cigarette, lowered the paper to gaze at her.

"What did they want?"

She met his scrutiny for the first time, fully revealing the vexation and anxiety in her eyes. She spoke hurriedly.

"They came about four o'clock—asked for you. I told them you were out. Then Parry said it didn't matter, they wanted to come in. Of course I was quite taken aback. I didn't know whether they wanted to wait for you, or what. Then Ed Chenkin said it was the Committee's house, that they represented the Committee and that in the name of the Committee they could and would come in." She paused, drew a quick breath. "I didn't budge an inch. I was angry—upset. But I managed to ask them *why* they wished to come in. Parry took it up then. He said it had come to his ears, and the ears of the Committee, in fact it was all over the town, that you were performing experiments on animals— vivisection, he had the cheek to call it. And because of that they had come to look at your workroom and brought Mr. Davies, the Prevention of Cruelty to Animals man, along with them."

Andrew had not moved, nor had his eyes left her face.

"Go on, dear," he said quietly.

"Well, I tried to stop them, but it was no use. They just pushed past, the seven of them, through the hall and into the Lab. Whenever they saw the guinea pigs Parry let out a howl—'Oh, the poor dumb creatures!' And Chenkin pointed to the stain on the boards—where I dropped the fuscine bottle, you remember, dear—and shouted out: ''Ave a look at that, *blood*!' They prowled round everything, went through our beautiful sections, the microtome, everything. Then Parry said, 'I'm not leavin' those poor suffering creatures to be tortured any more. I'd rather have them put out of their pain than that.' He took the bag Davies had with him and shoved them all into it. I tried to tell him there was no question of suffering, or vivisection, or any such rubbish. And in any case that those five guinea pigs were not going to be used for experiments, that we were going to give them to the Boland children, and to little Agnes Evans, for pets. But they simply wouldn't listen to me. And then they—they went away."

There was a silence. Andrew's face was now deeply flushed. He sat up.

"I never heard such rank impertinence in all my life. It—it's damnable you had to put up with it, Chris! But I'll make them pay for it!"

He reflected a minute, then started towards the hall to use the telephone. But just as he reached it the instrument rang. He snatched it from the hook.

"Hullo!" he said angrily, then his voice altered slightly. Owen was on the other end of the line. "Yes, it's Manson speaking. Look here, Owen—"

"I know, I know, Doctor," Owen interrupted Andrew quickly. "I've been trying to get in touch with you all afternoon. Now listen. No, no, don't interrupt me. We got to keep our heads over this. We're up against a nasty bit o' business, Doctor. Don't say any more on the telephone. I'm comin' down to see you now."

Andrew went back to Christine.

"What does he mean?" he fumed, when he had told her of the conversation. "Anyone would think we were to blame."

They waited for Owen's arrival, Andrew striding up and down in a passion of impatience and indignation, Chris sitting at her sewing with disquieted eyes.

Owen came. But there was nothing reassuring in his face.

Before Andrew could speak he said:—

"Doctor, did you have a licence?"

"A what?" Andrew stared at him. "What kind of licence?"

Owen's face now seemed more troubled. "You've got to have a licence from the Home Office for experimental work on animals. You knew that, didn't you?"

"But damn it all!" Manson protested hotly, "I'm not a pathologist; I never will be. And I'm not running a laboratory. I only wanted to do a few simple experiments to tie up with my clinical work. We didn't have more than a dozen animals altogether—did we, Chris?"

Owen's eyes were averted. "You ought to have had that licence, Doctor. There's a section of the Committee are tryin' to play you up pretty bad over this!" He went on quickly. "You see, Doctor, a chap like you, that's doin' pioneer work, who's honest enough to speak his mind, he's bound to—well, anyhow, it's only right you should know there's a section here that's dyin' to put a knife in you. But there now! It'll be all right. There'll be a regular old shindy with the Committee; you'll have to come before them, like. But you've had your troubles with them before. You'll come out on top again."

Andrew stormed. "I'll bring a counteraction. I'll sue them for—for illegal entry. No, damn it, I'll sue them for stealing my guinea pigs. I want them back, anyway."

A pale amusement twitched Owen's face. "You can't have them back, Doctor. Reverend Parry and Ed Chenkin they allowed they'd have to put them out their misery. In the cause of 'umanity they drowned them with their own hands."

Sorrowfully, Owen went away. And the following evening Andrew received a summons to appear before the Committee in one week's time.

Meanwhile the case had flared into prominence like a petrol blaze. Nothing so exciting, so scandalous, so savouring of the black arts had startled Aberalaw since Trevor Day, the solicitor, was suspected of killing his wife with arsenic. Sides were taken, violent factions formed. From his rostrum at Sinai, Edwal Parry thundered the punishment meted out, in this life and the hereafter, to those who tortured animals and little children. At the other end of the town, Reverend David Walpole, chubby minister of the Established Church, to whom Parry was as pig to good Mohammedan, bleated of progress and the feud between the Liberal Church of God and Science.

Even the women were aroused to action. Miss Myfanwy Bensusan, local president of the Welsh Ladies' Endeavour League, spoke to a crowded meeting in the Temperance Hall. It is true that Andrew had once offended Myfanwy by failing to take the chair at the W.L.E. Annual Rally. But her motives, otherwise, were unquestionably pure. After the meeting and on subsequent evenings, young lady members of the League—normally active in the streets only upon flag days—could be seen distributing gruesome antivivisection folders, each bearing an illustration of a partially disembowelled dog.

On Wednesday night Con Boland rang up with a joyous tale.

"How are ye, Manson, boy? Keepin' the old chin up? Good enough! I was thinking ye might be interested—our Mary was comin' home this evening from Larkin's when one of them simperin' flag sellers stopped her with a pamphlet—these cruelty falderals they've been shovin' around against ye. Do ye know—ha! ha!—Do ye know what the bold Mary did? She up with the pamphlet and tore it into bits. Then she up with her hand, boxed the flag-sellin' female's ears, tugged the hat off her head, and said—ha! ha! —what do you think our Mary said? 'If it's cruelty you're after,' says she—Ha! Ha!—'If it's cruelty you're after—*I'll give ye it!*'"

Physical combat was offered by others as loyal as Mary.

Though Andrew's district was solidly behind him, round the East Surgery there was a block of contrary opinion. Fights broke out in the pubs between Andrew's supporters and his enemies. Frank Davis came to the surgery on Thursday night, slightly battered, to inform Andrew that he had "knocked the block off two on Oxborrow's patients for saying as 'ow our man was a bloody butcher!"

Thereafter Doctor Oxborrow passed Andrew with a bouncing tread and eyes fixed a long way off. He was known to be working openly with the Reverend Parry against his undesirable colleague. Urquhart came back from the Masonic Club with the meaty Christian's comments, of which perhaps the choicest was: "Why should any doctor have to murder God's living creatures?"

Urquhart had few remarks to make himself. But once, squinting across at Andrew's constrained, tense face, he declared:—

"Dammit to hell! When I was your age I'd have enjoyed a scrap like this, too. But now—oh, dammit! I suppose I'm getting old."

Andrew could not help thinking that Urquhart misjudged him. He was far from enjoying the "scrap." He felt tired, irritable, worried. He asked himself fretfully if he was to spend all his life running his head into stone walls. Yet, although his vitality was low, he had a desperate desire to justify himself, to be openly vindicated before the squabbling town.

The week passed at last, and on Saturday afternoon the Committee assembled for what was specified in the agenda as "the disciplinary examination" of Doctor Manson. There was not a vacant place in the Committee room, and outside in the Square groups of people were hanging about as Andrew entered the offices and walked up the narrow stairs. He felt his heart bumping rapidly. He had told himself he must be calm and steeled. Instead, as he took his seat on that same chair which as a candidate he had occupied five years before, he was stiff, dry-lipped, nervous.

The proceedings began—not with prayer, as might have been expected from the sanctimony with which the opposition had conducted their campaign—but with a fiery speech from Ed Chenkin.

"I'm going to put the full facts of this case," said Chenkin, jumping up, "before my fellow members of this Committee." He proceeded, in a loud, illiterate speech to enumerate the complaints: Doctor Manson had no right to do this work. It was work done in the Committee's time, work done when he was being paid for doing the *Committee's* work, and work done on the Committee's property. Also it was vivisection, or near neighbour to it. And it was all done without the necessary permit, a very serious offence in the eye of the law!

Here Owen intervened swiftly:—

"As regards that last point, I must advise the Committee that if they report Doctor Manson's failure to secure this permit any subsequent action taken would involve the Medical Aid Society as a whole."

"What th'ell d'you mean?" Chenkin asked.

"As he is our assistant," Owen held, "we are legally responsible for Doctor Manson!"

There was a murmur of assent at this, and cries of: "Owen's right! We don't want any trouble on the Society. Keep it amongst ourselves."

"Never mind the bloody permit, then," bawled Chenkin, still upon his feet. "There's enough in the other charges to hang anybody."

"Hear! Hear!" called out someone at the back. "What about all them times he sneaked off to Cardiff on his motor bike—that summer three years back?"

"He don't give medicine," came the voice of Len Richards. "You can wait an hour outside his surgery and not get your bottle filled."

"Order! Order!" Chenkin shouted. When he had stilled them he proceeded to his final peroration. "All these complaints are bad enough! They show that Doctor Manson 'as never been a satisfactory servant to the Medical Aid. Besides which I might add that he don't give proper certificates to the men. But we got to keep our minds on the main item. Here we have an assistant that the whole town's up against for what ought by rights to be a police case, a man who has turned our property into a slaughter 'ouse—I swear by the Almighty, fellow members, I saw the blood on the floor with my own eyes —a man who's nothing but an experimenter and a crank. I ask you, fellow members, if you're goin' to stand it. No! say I. No! say you. Fellow members, I know you are with me one and all, when I say that here and now we demand Doctor Manson's resignation."

Chenkin glanced round at his friends and sat down amidst loud applause.

"Perhaps you'll allow Doctor Manson to state his case," Owen said palely, and turned to Andrew.

There was a silence. Andrew sat still for a moment. The situation was worse, even, than he had imagined. Put not your trust in Committees, he thought bitterly. Were these the same men who had smiled at him approvingly when they gave him the appointment? His heart burned. He would not, simply would not resign. He got to his feet. He was no speaker and he knew that he was no speaker. But he was angry now, his nervousness lost in a swelling indignation at the ignorance, the intolerant stupidity of Chenkin's accusation, and the acclamation with which the others had received it.

He began:—

"No one seems to have said anything about the animals Ed Chenkin drowned. That was cruelty if you like—useless cruelty. What I've been doing wasn't that! Why do you men take white mice and canaries down the mine? To test for black damp—you all know that. And when these mice get finished by a whiff of gas—do you call that cruelty? No you don't. You realize that these animals have been used to save men's lives, perhaps your *own* lives.

"That's what I've been trying to do for you! I've been working on these lung diseases that you get from the dust in the mine headings. You all know that you get chest trouble and that when you *do* get it you don't get compensation. For these last three years I've spent nearly every minute of my spare time on this inhalation problem. I've found out something which might improve your working conditions, give you a fairer deal, keep you in health—better than that stinking bottle of medicine Len Richards was talking about would have done! What if I did use a dozen guinea pigs? Don't you think it was worth it?

"You don't believe me, perhaps. You're prejudiced enough to think I would lie to you. Maybe you still think I've been wasting my time, *your* time as you call it, in a lot of cranky experiments." He was so worked up he forgot his stern resolution not to be dramatic. Diving into his breast pocket he produced the letter he had received earlier in the week. "But this'll show you what other people think of it, people who are qualified to judge."

He walked across to Owen and handed him the letter. It was an intimation from the Clerk of the Senate at St. Andrews that, for his thesis on Dust Inhalation, he had been awarded his M.D.

Owen read the crested, blue-typed letter with a sudden brightening of his face. Thereafter it was passed slowly from hand to hand.

It annoyed Andrew to observe the effect created by the Senate's communication. Although he was so desperately anxious to prove his case, he almost regretted his impulse in producing it. If they could not take his work without some sort of official bolstering they must be heavily prejudiced against him. Letter or no letter, he felt moodily, they were bent on making an example of him.

He was relieved when, after a few further remarks, Owen said:—

"Perhaps you'll leave us now, Doctor, please."

Waiting outside, while they voted on his case, he kicked his heels, simmering with exasperation. It was a wonderful ideal, this group of working men controlling the medical services of the community for the benefit of their fellow workers. But it was only an ideal. They were too biased, too unintelligent, ever to administer such a scheme progressively. It was perpetual labour for Owen to drag them along the road with him. And he had the conviction that, on this occasion, even Owen's good will would not save him.

But the secretary, when Andrew went in again, was smiling, briskly rubbing his hands. Others on the Committee were regarding him more favourably, at least without hostility.

And Owen immediately stood up and said:—

"I'm glad to tell you, Doctor Manson—I may even say that personally I'm delighted to tell you—that the Committee have decided by a majority to ask you to remain."

He had won, he had carried them after all. But the knowledge, after one swift throb of satisfaction, gave him no elation. There was a pause. They obviously expected him to express his relief, his gratitude. But he could not. He felt tired of the whole distorted business, of the Committee, Aberalaw, medicine, silica dust, guinea pigs and himself.

At last he said:—

"Thank you, Mr. Owen. I'm glad, after all I've tried to do here, that the Committee don't wish me to go. But, I'm sorry, I can't wait on in Aberalaw any longer. I give the Committee a month's notice from to-day." He spoke without feeling; then he spun round and walked out of the room.

There was a dead silence. Ed Chenkin was the quickest to recover himself.

"Good riddance," he called half-heartedly after Manson.

Then Owen startled them all with the first burst of anger he had ever shown in that Committee room.

"Shut your senseless mouth, Ed Chenkin." He flung down his ruler with intimidating violence. "We have lost the best man we ever had."

xvi

Andrew woke up in the middle of that night groaning:—

"Am I a fool, Chris? Chucking away our living—a sound job? After all, I *was* getting a few private patients lately. And Llewellyn has been pretty decent. Did I tell you? He half-promised to let me consult at the hospital. And the Committee,—they aren't a bad lot when you cut out the Chenkin crowd,—I believe in time when Llewellyn retired they might have made me head doctor in his place."

She comforted him, quiet, reasonable, lying beside him in the darkness.

"You don't really want us to stay in a Welsh mining practice all our lives, my dear. We've been happy here, but it's time for us to move on."

"But listen, Chris," he worried, "we haven't enough to buy a practice yet. We ought to have collected some more money before we hoofed it."

She answered sleepily: "What has money got to do with it? Besides we're going to spend all we've got—almost—on a real holiday. Do you realize you've hardly been away from these old mines for nearly four years?"

Her spirit infected him. Next morning the world seemed a gay and careless place. At breakfast, which he ate with new relish, he declared:—

"You're not a bad old girl, Chris. Instead of getting up on the platform and telling me you expect Big Things of me now, that it's time for me to go out and make my mark in the world, you just—"

She was not listening to him. Irrelevantly she protested:—

"Really, dear, I wish you wouldn't bunch the paper so! I thought it was only women did that. How do you expect me to read my gardening column?"

"Don't read it." On his way to the door he kissed her, smiling. "Think about me."

He felt adventurous, prepared to take his chance with life. Besides, the cautious side of him could not avoid glancing at the assets side of his balance sheet. He had his M.R.C.P., an honours M.D., and over three hundred pounds in the bank. With all this behind them surely they would not starve.

It was well that their intention stood firm. A revulsion of sentiment had swept upon the town. Now that he was going of his own free will, everybody wished him to remain.

The climax came a week after the meeting, when Owen unsuccessfully headed a deputation to Vale View to ask Andrew to reconsider his decision. Thereafter the feeling against Ed Chenkin swelled to the verge of violence. He was booed in the Rows. Twice he was played home from the mine by the penny whistle band, an ignominy usually reserved by the workmen for a blackleg.

In the face of all these local reverberations it was strange how lightly his thesis appeared to have shaken the outer world. It had gained him his M.D. It had been printed in the *Journal of Industrial Health* in England, and published as a brochure in the United States by the Association of American Hygiene. But beyond that, it earned him exactly three letters.

The first was from a firm in Brick Lane E.C. informing him that samples were being forwarded to him of their Pulmo-Syrup, the infallible lung specific for which they had hundreds of testimonials including several from prominent physicians. They hoped he would recommend Pulmo-Syrup amongst the miners in his practice. Pulmo-Syrup, they added, also cured rheumatism.

The second was from Professor Challis, an enthusiastic letter of congratulation and appreciation which ended by asking if Andrew could not call at the Institute in Cardiff sometime that week. In a P.S. Challis added: *Try and come Thursday.* But Andrew, in the hurry of these last few days, was unable to keep that appointment. Indeed, he mislaid the letter and for the time being forgot to answer it.

The third letter he did immediately answer, he was so genuinely thrilled to receive it. It was an unusual, stimulating communication which had crossed the Atlantic from Oregon. Andrew read and reread the typewritten sheets, then took them in excitement to Christine.

"This is rather decent, Chris!—this American letter—it's from a fellow called Stillman, Richard Stillman of Oregon—you've probably never heard of him, but I have—it's full of the most exact appreciation of my Inhalation stuff. More, much more than Challis— damn it, I should have answered his letter! This chap has absolutely understood what I was after, in fact he quietly puts me right on one or two points. Apparently the active destructive ingredient in my silicon is serecite. I hadn't enough chemistry to get to that. But it's a marvellous letter, congratulatory; and from Stillman!"

"Yes?" She peeped inquiringly. "Is he some doctor out there?"

"No, that's the amazing thing. He's a physicist, really. But he runs a clinic for disorders of the lungs, near Portland, Oregon. Look, it's on the notepaper. Some of them don't recognize him yet, but he's as big a man as Sphalinger in his own way. I'll tell you about him when we've time."

He showed how much he thought of Stillman's letter by sitting down to answer it on the spot.

They were now overwhelmed by preparations for their holiday, by arrangements for storing their furniture in Cardiff—the most convenient centre—and by the doleful processes of leave-taking. Their departure from Blaenelly had been abrupt, a heroic cleavage. But here they suffered much lingering sentiment. They were entertained by the Vaughans, the Bolands, even by the Llewellyns. Andrew developed "farewell-dyspepsia," symptomatic of these parting banquets. When the actual day arrived Jenny, in tears, told them—to their consternation—that they were to be given a "platform send-off!"

At the last moment, on top of this unsettling information, Vaughan came hastening round.

"Sorry to harass you people again. But look here, Manson, what have you been doing to Challis? I've just had a letter from the old boy. Your paper has sent him quite gaga— and incidentally, at least so I understand, the Metalliferous Board as well. Anyway he's asked me to get in touch with you. He wants you to see him in London without fail; says it's extremely important."

Andrew answered a trifle peevishly.

"We're going on holiday, man. The first real holiday we've had for years. How *can* I see him?"

"Let's have your address then. He'll obviously want to write to you."

Andrew glanced uncertainly at Christine. They had meant to keep their destination a secret, so that they should be free from all worries, correspondence, interference. But he gave Vaughan the information.

Then they were hurrying to the station, engulfed by the crowd from the district who waited there, shaken by the hand, shouted at, patted on the back, embraced, and finally hustled into their compartment of the moving train. As they steamed off their friends, massed on the platform, began lustily to sing "Men of Harlech."

"My God!" Andrew said, trying out his numb fingers. "That was the last straw." But his eyes were glistening, and a minute later he added, "I wouldn't have had us miss it for anything, Chris. Aren't people *decent*? And to think that a month ago half the town was after my blood! You can't get away from the fact—life's damn funny." He gazed at her humorously as she sat beside him. "And this, Mrs. Manson, though you are now an old woman, is your second honeymoon!"

They reached Southampton that evening, took their berths in the cross-channel steamer. Next morning they saw the sun rise behind St. Malo, and an hour later Brittany received them.

The wheat was ripening, the cherry trees were heavy with fruit, goats strayed on the flowering pastures. It had been Christine's idea to come here, to get close to the real France—not its picture galleries or palaces, not historic ruins or monuments, nothing which the tourist's guidebook insisted that they should see.

They reached Val André. Their little hotel was within sound of the sea, within scent of the meadows. Their bedroom had plain scrubbed boards and their morning coffee came to them steaming in thick blue bowls. They lazed the whole day long.

"Oh, Lord!" Andrew kept repeating. "Isn't this wonderful, darling? I never, never never want to look a lobar pneumonia in the face again." They drank cider, ate *langoustes*, shrimps, pastries, and whiteheart cherries. In the evenings Andrew played billiards with the proprietor on the antique octagonal table. Sometimes he only lost by fifty in the hundred.

It was lovely, wonderful, exquisite—the adjectives were Andrew's—all but the cigarettes, he would add.

A whole blissful month slipped past. And then, more frequently, and with unceasing restlessness, Andrew began to finger the unopened letter, now stained by cherry juice and chocolate, which had remained in his jacket for the past fortnight.

"Go on," Christine urged, at last, one morning. "We've kept our word! Open it."

He slit up the envelope studiously, read the letter lying upon his back in the sunlight, sat up slowly, then read it again. In silence he passed it over to Christine.

The letter was from Professor Challis. It stated that, as the direct result of his researches into dust inhalation, the C.M.M.F.B.—Coal Mines and Metalliferous Fatigue Board—had decided to open up the whole question with a view to reporting to the Parliamentary Committee. A whole-time medical officer was, for this purpose, to be appointed by the Board. And the Board on the strength of his recent investigations unanimously and without hesitation offered the appointment to him.

When she had read it, she looked at him happily.

"Didn't I tell you something would turn up?" She smiled. "Isn't it splendid?"

He was throwing stones quickly, nervously at a lobster pot on the beach.

"It's clinical work," he reflected aloud. "Couldn't be anything else. They *know* I'm a clinician."

She observed him with a deepening smile.

"Of course, darling, you remember our bargain: Six weeks here as a minimum, doing nothing, lying still. You won't let this interrupt our holiday?"

"No, no!"—looking at his watch. "We'll finish our holiday, but—anyhow—" he jumped up and gaily pulled her to her feet—"it won't do us any harm to run down to the telegraph office. And I wonder—I wonder if they've got a timetable there."

Book III

i

The Coal and Metalliferous Mines Fatigue Board—usually abbreviated to M.F.B.—was housed in a large impressive grey stone building on the Embankment, not far from Westminster Gardens, conveniently situated near the Board of Trade and the Mines Department,—both of which alternately forgot about, and fought fiercely for, a proprietary interest in the Board.

On the fourteenth of August, a fresh bright morning, in bustling health and immense spirits, Andrew ran up the steps of the building, the look in his eye that of a man about to conquer London.

"I'm the new Medical Officer," he told the commissionaire in the Office of Works uniform.

"Yes, sir, yes, sir," said the commissionaire, with a fatherly air. It was gratifying to Andrew that he seemed to be expected. "You'll want to see our Mr. Gill. Jones! Take our new doctor up to Mr. Gill's room."

The lift rose slowly, revealing green tiled corridors and many floors, on which the Office of Works uniform was again sedately visible. Then Andrew was ushered into a large, sunny room where he found himself shaking hands with Mr. Gill, who rose from his desk and put down his copy of the *Times* to welcome him.

"I'm a little late in getting in," Andrew declared with vigour. "Sorry! We just got back from France yesterday—but I'm absolutely ready to start."

"That's nice!" Gill was a jolly little man, in gold-rimmed glasses, a near-clerical collar, dark blue suit, dark blue tie held in place with a flat gold ring. He looked on Andrew with prim approval.

"Please sit down! Will you have a cup of tea, or a glass of hot milk? I usually have one about eleven. And yes—yes, it's nearly that now—"

"Oh, well—" said Andrew, hesitating; then, brightening: "Perhaps you can tell me about the work while we—"

Five minutes later the Office of Works uniform brought in a nice cup of tea and a glass of hot milk.

"I think you'll find that right, Mr. Gill. It 'as boiled, Mr. Gill."

"Thank you, Stevens." When Stevens had gone Gill turned to Andrew with a smile. "You'll find him a useful chap. He makes delicious hot buttered toast. It's rather awkward here—to get really first-class messengers. We're bits and pieces of all departments—Home Office, Mines Depart., Board of Trade—I myself," Gill coughed with mild pride, "am from the Admiralty."

While Andrew sipped his boiled milk and chafed for information about his job, Gill pleasantly discussed the weather, Brittany, the Civil Service pension scheme, and the efficacy of Pasteurization. Then, rising, he led Andrew to his room.

This also was a warmly carpeted, restful, sunny room with a superb view of the river. A large bluebottle was making drowsy nostalgic noises against the windowpane.

"I chose this for you," said Gill pleasantly. "Took a little bit of arrangement. That's an open coal fireplace, you'll see—nice for the winter. I—I hope you like it?"

"Why—it's a marvellous room, but—"

"Now I'll introduce you to your secretary, Miss Mason." Gill tapped, threw open a communicating door, revealing Miss Mason, a nice elderly girl, neat and composed, seated at a small desk. Rising, Miss Mason put down her *Times*.

"Good morning, Miss Mason."

"Good morning, Mr. Gill."

"Miss Mason, this is Doctor Manson."

"Good morning, Doctor Manson."

Andrew's head reeled slightly under the impact of these salutations, but he collected himself, joined in the conversation.

Five minutes later, as Gill stole pleasantly away, he remarked to Andrew, encouragingly:—

"I'll send you along some files."

The files arrived, borne tenderly by Stevens. In addition to his talents as toastmaker and dairyman, Stevens was the best file-bearer in the building. Every hour he entered Andrew's office, with cradled documents which he placed lovingly upon the desk of the japanned tin marked IN, while his eye, searching eagerly, besought something to take away from the tin marked OUT. It quite broke Stevens' heart when the OUT tin was empty. In this lamentable contingency he slunk away, defeated.

Lost, bewildered, irritated, Andrew raced through the files—minutes of past meetings of the M.F.B., dull, stodgy, unimportant. Then he turned urgently to Miss Mason. But Miss Mason—who came, she explained, from the Home Office Frozen Meat Investigation Department—proved a restricted source of enlightenment. She told him that the hours were from ten o'clock till four. She told him of the office hockey team —"the ladies' eleven of course, Doctor Manson"—of which she was vice-captain. She asked him if he would care to have her copy of the *Times*. Her gaze entreated him to be calm.

But Andrew was not calm. Fresh from his holiday, longing to work, he began to weave a pattern on the Office of Works' carpet. He gazed chafingly at the brisk river scene where tugs fussed about and long lines of coal barges went spattering against the tide. Then he strode down to Gill.

"When do I start?"

Gill jumped at the abruptness of the question.

"My dear fellow, you quite startled me. I thought I'd given you enough files to last you for a month." He looked at his watch. "Come along—it's time we had lunch."

Over his steamed sole, Gill tactfully explained, while Andrew battled with a chump chop, that the next meeting of the Board did not, and could not, take place until September the eighteenth; that Professor Challis was in Norway, Doctor Maurice Gadsby in Scotland, Sir William Dewar, Chairman of the Board, in Germany, and his own immediate chief, Mr. Blades, at Frinton with his family.

Andrew went back to Christine that evening with his thoughts in a maze. Their furniture was still in storage and, so that they might have time to look round and find a proper home, they had taken for a month a small furnished flat in Earl's Court.

"Could you believe it, Chris! They're not even *ready* for me. I've got a whole month to drink milk in, and read the Times, and initial files—oh! and have long intimate hockey talks with old girl Mason."

"If you don't mind, you'll confine your talks to your own old girl. Oh, really, darling, it's lovely here—after Aberalaw. I had a little expedition this afternoon, down to Chelsea. I found out where Carlyle's house is, and the Tate Gallery. Oh! I planned such lovely things for us to do. You can take a penny steamboat up to Kew. Think of the Gardens, darling. And next month Kreisler at the Albert Hall. Oh, and we must see the Memorial, to find out why everyone laughs at it. And there's a play on from the New York Theatre Guild; and wouldn't it be lovely if I could meet you someday for lunch?" She reached out a small vibrant hand. He had rarely seen her so excited. "Darling! Let's go out and have a meal. There's a Russian restaurant along this street. It looks *good.* Then, if you're not too tired, we might—"

"Here!" he protested as she led him to the door. "I thought you were supposed to be the matter-of-fact member of this family. But believe me, Chris, after my first day's 'toil' I could do with a lively evening."

Next morning he read every file on his desk, initialled them, and was ranging about his room by eleven o'clock. But soon the cage became too small to hold him and he set out, with violence, to explore the building. It proved uninteresting as a morgue without bodies until, reaching the top storey, he suddenly found himself in a long room, half-fitted as a laboratory, where, seated on a box which had once held sulphur, was a young man in a long dirty white coat, disconsolately trimming his fingernails, while his cigarette made yellower the nicotine stain upon his upper lip.

"Hello!" Andrew said.

A moment's pause, then the other answered uninterestedly:—

"If you've lost your way, the lift is the third on the right."

Andrew propped himself against the test bench and picked a cigarette from his packet. He asked:—

"Don't you serve tea here?"

For the first time the young man raised his head, jet-black and glossily brushed, singularly at variance with the upturned collar of his soiled coat.

"Only to the white mice," he answered with interest. "The tea leaves are particularly nourishing for them."

Andrew laughed, perhaps because the jester was five years younger than himself. He explained:—

"My name is Manson."

"I feared as much. So you've come to join the forgotten men." A pause. "I'm Doctor Hope! At least I used to think I was Hope. Now I am definitely Hope deferred."

"What are you doing here?"

"God only knows—and Billy Buttons—that's Dewar! Some of the time I sit here and think. But most of the time I sit. Occasionally they send me chunks of decomposed miners and ask me the cause of the explosion."

"And do you tell them?" Andrew inquired politely.

"No." Hope said rudely. "I fart!"

They both felt better after that extreme vulgarity and went out to lunch together. Going out to lunch, Doctor Hope explained, was the sole function of the day which enabled him to cling to reason. Hope explained other things to Manson. He was a Backhouse Research Scholar from Cambridge, *via* Birmingham, which probably—he grinned—accounted for his frequent lapses of good taste. He had been loaned to the Metalliferous Board through the pestering application of Professor Dewar. He had nothing to do but sheer mechanics, a routine which any lab. attendant could have tackled. He implied that he was surely going mad through indolence and the inertia of the Board, which he now referred to tersely as Maniac's Delight. It was typical of most of the research work in the country: controlled by a quorum of eminent mugs who were too engrossed by their own particular theories and too busy squabbling amongst themselves to shove the waggon in any one definite direction. Hope was pulled this way and that, told what to do instead of being allowed to do what he wished, and so interrupted he was never six months on the same job.

He gave Andrew thumbnail sketches of the council of Maniac's Delight. Sir William Dewar, the doddering but indomitable nonagenarian Chairman, he alluded to as "Billy Buttons" because of Sir William's propensity for leaving certain essential fastenings unlatched. Old Billy Buttons was chairman of almost every scientific committee in England, Hope told Andrew. In addition he gave those riotously popular wireless talks: Science for the Children.

Then there was Professor Whinney, aptly known to his students as the Nag; Challis, who wasn't bad when he forgot to dramatize himself as Rabelais Pasteur Challis; and Doctor Maurice Gadsby.

"Do you know Gadsby?" Hope asked.

"I've met the gentleman." Andrew related his examination experience.

"That's our Maurice," said Hope bitterly. "And he's such a damned little thruster. He's into everything. He'll stick himself into a Royal Apothecaryship one of these days. He's a clever little beast all right. But he's not interested in research. He's only interested in himself." Hope laughed suddenly. "Robert Abbey has a good one about Gadsby. Gadsby wanted to get into the Rumpsteak Club—that's one of those dining-out affairs that occur in London, and a pretty decent one, as it happens! Well, Abbey, who's an obliging pot, promised to do his best for Gadsby, though God knows why. Anyhow a week later Gadsby met Abbey. 'Am I in?' he asked. 'No,' Abbey said, 'You're not.' 'Good God,' blusters Gadsby. 'You don't mean I was blackballed.' 'Blackballed,' Abbey said. 'Listen, Gadsby! *Have you ever seen a plate of caviar*?'" Hope lay back and howled with laughter. A moment later he added: "Abbey happens to be on our Board as well. He's a white man. But he's got too much savvy to come often."

This was the first of many lunches which Andrew and Hope took together. Hope, despite his undergraduate humour and a natural tendency to flippancy, was well endowed with brains. His irreverence had a wholesome ring. Andrew felt that he might one day do something. Indeed, in his serious moments, Hope often exposed his eagerness to get back to the real work he had planned for himself, on the isolation of gastric enzymes.

Occasionally Gill came to lunch with them. Hope's phrase for Gill was characteristic: "a good little egg." Though veneered by his thirty years in the Civil Service—he had worked his way from boy clerk to principal—Gill was human underneath. In the office he functioned like a well oiled, easy-moving little machine. He arrived from Sunbury by the same train every morning, returned, unless he was "detained," by the same train every night. He had, in Sunbury, a wife and three daughters, and a small garden where he grew roses. He was superficially so true to type he might have stood as the perfect pattern of smug suburbia. Yet there existed, beneath, a real Gill who loved Yarmouth in winter and always spent his holiday there in December; who had a queer Bible, which he knew almost by heart, in a book named Hadji Baba; who—for fifteen years a fellow of the Society—was quite fatuously devoted to the penguins in the zoo.

Upon one occasion Christine made a fourth at this table. Gill surpassed himself in upholding the civility of the service. Even Hope behaved with admirable gentility. He confided to Andrew that he was a less likely candidate for the strait-jacket since meeting Mrs. Manson.

The days slipped past. While Andrew waited for the meeting of the Board, Christine and he discovered London. They took the steamboat trip to Richmond. They chanced upon a theatre named the Old Vic. They came to know the windy flutter of Hampstead Heath, the fascination of a coffee stall at midnight. They walked in the Row and rowed on the Serpentine. They solved the delusion of Soho. When they no longer had occasion to study the Underground maps before entrusting themselves to the Tube, they began to feel that they were Londoners.

ii

The afternoon of September the eighteenth brought the M.F.B. council together, and to Andrew, at last. Sitting beside Gill and Hope, conscious of the latter's flippant glances upon him, Andrew watched the members roll in to the long gilt-corniced Board room: Whinney, Doctor Lancelot Dodd-Canterbury, Challis, Sir Robert Abbey, Gadsby, and finally Billy Buttons Dewar himself.

Before Dewar's entry Abbey and Challis had spoken to Andrew—Abbey a quiet word, the professor an airy gush of graciousness—congratulating him upon his appointment. And when Dewar came in he veered upon Gill, exclaiming in his peculiar high-pitched voice:—

"Where is our new Medical Officer, Mr. Gill? Where is Doctor Manson?"

Andrew stood up, confounded at Dewar's appearance, which transcended even Hope's description. Billy was short, bowed, and hairy. He wore old clothes, his waistcoat much dropped upon, his greenish overcoat bulging with papers, pamphlets and the memoranda of a dozen different societies. There was no excuse for Billy, for he had much money and daughters, one of them married to a millionaire peer, but he looked now, and he always looked, like a neglected old baboon.

"There was a Manson at Queens with me in eighteen-eighty," he squeaked benevolently, by way of greeting.

"This is he, sir," murmured Hope, to whom the temptation was irresistible.

Billy heard him. "How would *you* know, Doctor Hope?" he squinted urbanely over the steel rimmed pince-nez on the end of his nose. "You weren't even in swaddling clothes then. Hee! Hee! Hee! Hee!"

He flapped away, chuckling, to his place at the head of the table. None of his colleagues, who were already seated, took any notice of him. Part of the technique of this Board was a proud unawareness of one's neighbours. But this did not dismay Billy. Pulling a wad of papers from his pocket he took a drink of water from the carafe, picked up the little hammer in front of him and hit the table a resounding thwack.

"Gentlemen, gentlemen! Mr. Gill will now read the minutes."

Gill, who acted as secretary to the Board, rapidly intoned the minutes of the last meeting, while Billy, giving to this chanting no attention whatsoever, alternately pawed amongst his papers and let his eye twinkle benevolently down the board towards Andrew whom he still vaguely associated with the Manson of Queens, 1880.

At last Gill finished. Billy immediately wielded the hammer.

"Gentlemen! We are particularly happy to have our new Medical Officer with us to-day. I remember, as recently as nineteen hundred and four, I emphasized the need of a permanent clinician who should be attached to the Board as a solid adjuvant to the pathologists whom we occasionally *filch*, gentlemen—Hee! Hee!—whom we occasionally filch from the Backhouse Research. And I say this with all respect to our young friend Hope, on whose charity—Hee! Hee!—on whose charity we have been so largely dependent. Now I well remember as recently as eighteen eighty-nine..."

Sir Robert Abbey interposed:—

"I'm sure, sir, the other members of the Board wish to join you wholeheartedly in congratulating Doctor Manson on his silicosis paper. If I may say so, I felt this to be a particularly patient and original piece of clinical research, and one which, as the Board well knows, may have the most far-reaching effects upon our industrial legislation."

"Hear, hear," boomed Challis, supporting his protégé.

"That is what I was about to say, Robert," said Billy peevishly. To him Abbey was still a young man, a student almost, whose interruptions demanded mild reproof. "When we decided at our last meeting that this investigation must be pursued, Doctor Manson's name immediately suggested itself to me. He has opened up this question and he must be given every opportunity to pursue it. We wish him, gentlemen,"—this being for Andrew's benefit he twinkled at him bushily along the table,—"to visit all the anthracite mines in the country, and possibly later we may extend this to all the coal mines. Also we wish him to have every opportunity for clinical examination of the miners in the industry. We will afford him every facility—including the skilled bacteriological services of our young friend Doctor Hope. In short, gentlemen, there is nothing we will *not* do to ensure that our new medical officer presses this all-important matter of dust inhalation to its ultimate scientific and administrative conclusion."

Andrew drew one quick and furtive breath. It was splendid, splendid—better than he had ever hoped. They were going to give him a free hand, back him up with their immense authority, turn him loose on clinical research. They were angels, all of them, and Billy was Gabriel himself.

"But, gentlemen," Billy suddenly piped, shuffling himself a new deal from his coat pockets, "*before* Doctor Manson goes on with this problem, before we can feel ourselves at liberty to allow him to concentrate his efforts upon it, there is another and more pressing matter which I feel he ought to take up."

A pause. Andrew felt his heart contract, and it began slowly to sink as Billy continued:—

"Doctor Bigsby of the Board of Trade has been pointing out to me the alarming discrepancy in the specifications of industrial first-aid equipments. There is, of course, a definition under the existing Act, but it is elastic and unsatisfactory. There are no precise standards, for example, as to the size and weave of bandages, the length, material, and type of splints. Now, gentlemen, this is an important matter and one which directly concerns this Board. I feel very strongly that our Medical Officer should conduct a thorough investigation and submit a report upon it before he begins upon the problem of inhalation."

Silence. Andrew glanced desperately round the table. Dodd-Canterbury, with his legs outstretched, had his eyes on the ceiling. Gadsby was drawing diagrams upon his blotter, Whinney frowning, Challis inflating his chest for speech.

But it was Abbey who said:—

"Surely, Sir William, this is matter either for the Board of Trade or the Mines Department."

"We are at the disposal of each of these bodies," squeaked Billy. "We are—Hee! Hee! —the orphan child of both."

"Yes, I know. But after all this—this bandage question is comparatively trivial, and Doctor Manson..."

"I assure you, Robert, it is far from trivial. There will be a question in the House presently. I had that from Lord Ungar only yesterday."

"Ah!" Gadsby said, lifting his ears. "If Ungar is keen, we have no choice." Gadsby could toady with deceptive brusqueness, and Ungar was a man he wished particularly to please.

Andrew felt driven to intervene.

"Excuse me, Sir William," he stumbled; "I—I understood I was going to do clinical work here. For a month I have been kicking about in my office, and now if I'm to..."

He broke off, looking round at them. It was Abbey who helped him.

"Doctor Manson's point is very just. For four years he's been working patiently at his own subject and now, having offered him every facility to expand it, we propose sending him out to count bandages."

"If Doctor Manson has been patient for four years, Robert," Billy squeaked, "he can be patient a little longer. Hee! Hee!"

"True, true," boomed Challis. "He'll be free for silicosis eventually."

Whinney cleared his throat. "Now," Hope muttered to Andrew, "the Nag is about to neigh."

"Gentlemen," Whinney said, "for a long time I have been asking this Board to investigate the question of muscular fatigue in relation to steam heat—a subject which, as you know, interests me deeply, and which, I venture to say, you have hitherto not given the consideration it so richly merits. Now it appears to me that, if Doctor Manson is going to be diverted from the question of inhalation, it would be an admirable opportunity to pursue this all-important question of muscular fatigue..."

Gadsby looked at his watch: "I have an appointment in Harley Street in exactly thirty-five minutes."

Whinney turned angrily to Gadsby. Co-Professor Challis supported him with a gusty: "Intolerable impertinence."

Tumult seemed about to break.

But Billy's urbane yellow face peered from behind his whiskers at the meeting. He was not disturbed. He had handled such meetings for forty years. He knew they detested him and wanted him to go. But he was not going—he was never going. His vast cranium was filled with problems, data, agenda, obscure formulae, equations; with physiology and chemistry; with facts and figments of research—a vaulted incalculable sepulchre, haunted by phantoms of decerebrated cats, illumined by polarized light and all rosy-hued by the great remembrance that when he was a boy, Lister had patted him upon the head.

He declared guilelessly:—

"I must tell you, gentlemen, I have already as good as promised Lord Ungar and Doctor Bigsby that we shall assist them in their difficulty. Six months ought to suffice, Doctor Manson. Perhaps a little longer. It will not be uninteresting. It will bring you into contact with people and things, young man. You remember Lavoisier's remark concerning the drop of water! Hee! Hee! And now, touching Doctor Hope's pathological examination of the specimen from Wendover Colliery in July last..."

At four o'clock, when it was all over, Andrew threshed the matter out with Gill and Hope in Gill's room. The effect of this Board, and perhaps of his increasing years, was to implant in him the beginnings of restraint. He neither raved nor furiously split his infinitives but contented himself merely with stabbing a neat pattern with a Government pen upon a Government desk.

"It won't be so bad," Gill consoled. "It means travelling all over the country, I know, but that can be rather pleasant. You might even take Mrs. Manson with you. There's Buxton now—that's a centre for all the Derbyshire coalfield. And at the end of six months you can begin your anthracite work."

"He'll never get the chance," Hope grinned. "He's a bandage counter—for life!"

Andrew picked up his hat. "The trouble with you, Hope, is—you're too *young.*"

He went home to Christine. And the following Monday, since she resolutely refused to miss the gay adventure, they bought a secondhand Morris for sixty pounds and started out together upon the Great First Aid Investigation. It is to be admitted they were happy as the car sped up the highway to the North, and Andrew, having given a simian impersonation of Billy Buttons steering the car with his feet, remarked:—

"Anyway! Never mind what Lavoisier said to the drop of water in eighteen thirty-two. We're together, Chris!"

The work was imbecile. It consisted of the inspection of the first-aid materials kept at different collieries throughout the country: splints, bandages, cotton wool, antiseptics, tourniquets and the rest. At the good collieries the equipment was good; and at poor collieries the equipment was poor. Underground inspection was no novelty to Andrew. He made hundreds of underground inspections, crawling miles along haulage-ways to the coal face, to view a box of bandages carefully planted there half an hour beforehand.

At small pits in hardy Yorkshire he overheard under-managers whisper aside:—

"Run down, Geordie, and tell Alex to go to the chemist's..." then: "Have a chair, Doctor, we'll be ready for ye in a minute!" In Nottingham he comforted temperance ambulance men by telling them cold tea was a superior stimulant to brandy. Elsewhere he swore by whisky. But mostly he did the work with alarming conscientiousness. He and Christine found rooms in a convenient centre. Thereafter he combed the district in the car. While he inspected Christine sat and knitted at a distance. They had adventures, usually with landladies. They made friends, chiefly among the mining inspectors. Andrew was not surprised that his mission provoked these hardheaded, hardfisted citizens to senseless laughter. It is to be regretted that he laughed with them.

And then, in March, they returned to London, resold the car for only ten pounds less than they had paid for it, and Andrew set about writing his report. He had made up his mind to give the Board value for its money, to offer them statistics by the tubful, pages of tables, charts, and divisional graphs showing how the bandage curve rose as the splint curve fell. He was determined, he told Christine, to show them how well he had done the work and how excellently they had all wasted their time.

At the end of the month when he had rushed a rough draft through to Gill, he was surprised to receive a summons from Doctor Bigsby of the Board of Trade.

"He's delighted with your report," Gill fluttered, as he escorted Andrew along Whitehall. "I shouldn't have let the cat out. But there it is—it's a lucky start for you, my dear fellow. You've no idea how important Bigsby is. He's got the whole factory administration in his pocket!"

It took them some time to reach Doctor Bigsby. They had to sit with their hats in two anterooms before gaining admission to the final chamber. But there was Doctor Bigsby, at last, thickset and cordial, with a dark grey suit and darker grey spats, double-breasted waistcoat and a bustling efficiency.

"Sit down, gentlemen. This report of yours, Manson. I've seen the draft and though it's early to speak I must say I like the look of it. Highly scientific. Excellent graphing. That's what we want in this department. Now as we're out to standardize equipment in factories and mines you ought to know my views. First of all I see you recommend a three-inch bandage as the major bandage of the specification. Now, I prefer the two-and-a-half-inch. You'll agree there, won't you?"

Andrew was irritated; it may have been the spats.

"Personally, so far as the mines are concerned, I think the bigger the bandage the better. But I don't think it makes a hell of a lot of difference!"

"Eh? What?" Reddening behind the ears. "No *difference*?"

"Not a bit."

"But don't you see—don't you realize—the whole principle of standardization is involved? If we suggest two-and-a-half-inch and you recommend three-inch there may be enormous difficulty."

"Then I'll recommend three-inch," Andrew said coolly.

Doctor Bigsby's hackles rose, it was possible to see them rising.

"Your attitude is difficult to understand. We've been working for years towards the two-and-a-half-inch bandage. Why... Don't you know how much this *matters*...?"

"Yes, I know!" Andrew equally lost his temper. "Have you ever been underground? I have. I've done a bloody operation, lying on my guts in a puddle of water, with one safety lamp and no headroom. And I tell you straight, any finicky half-inch difference in your bandage doesn't matter a tinker's curse."

He passed out of the building more swiftly than he had entered, followed by Gill, who wrung his hands and lamented the fracas all the way to the Embankment.

When he got back Andrew stood in his room, sternly regarding the traffic on the river, the bustling streets, the buses running, trams clanging over bridges, the movement of human people, all the pulsing vivid flow of life.

"I don't belong to this outfit in here," he thought with a surge of impatience. "I should be out there—out there!"

Abbey had given up attending the Board meetings. And Challis had disheartened Manson, even to the point of panic, by taking him to lunch the week before and warning him that Whinney was lobbying hard, would try to put him on to his muscular fatigue investigation before the silicosis question was touched.

Andrew reflected, with a despairing pretence at humour: "If *that* happens, on top of the bandages, I might as well take a reader's ticket for the British Museum."

Walking home from the Embankment he found himself peering enviously at the brass plates bolted on area railings outside the houses of doctors. He would stop, watch a patient mount to the door, ring the bell, be admitted—then, walking moodily on, he would visualize the ensuing scene, the interrogations, the swift production of stethoscope, the whole thrilling science of diagnosis. He was a doctor, too, wasn't he? At least, once upon a time...

Towards the end of May, in this frame of mind, he was walking up Oakley Street about five in the evening when he suddenly saw a crowd of people gathered round a man lying on the pavement. In the gutter alongside was a shattered bicycle and, almost on top of it, a drunkenly arrested motor lorry.

Five seconds later Andrew was in the middle of the crowd, observing the injured man, who, attended by a kneeling policeman, was bleeding from a deep wound in the groin.

"Here! Let me through. I'm a doctor."

The policeman, striving unsuccessfully to fix a tourniquet, turned a flustered face.

"I can't stop the bleeding, doctor. It's too high up."

Andrew saw that it was impossible to tourniquet. The wound was too high up in the iliac vessel, and the man was bleeding to death.

"Get up," he said to the policeman. "Put him flat on his back." Then, making his right arm rigid, he leaned over and thrust his fist hard into the man's belly over the descending aorta. The whole weight of his body, thus transmitted to the great vessel, immediately arrested the haemorrhage. The policeman removed his helmet and wiped his forehead. Five minutes later the ambulance arrived. Andrew went with it.

Next morning Andrew rang up the hospital. The house surgeon answered brusquely, after the fashion of his kind:—

"Yes, yes, he's comfortable. Doing well. Who wants to know?"

"Oh," mumbled Andrew from the public phone box, "nobody."

And that, he thought bitterly, was exactly what he was: nobody, doing nothing, getting nowhere. He endured it till the end of the week, then quietly, without fuss, he handed in his resignation to Gill for transmission to the Board.

Gill was upset, yet admitted that a premonition of this sad event had troubled him. He made a neat little speech which concluded:—

"After all, my dear fellow, I have realized that your place is—well, if I may borrow a wartime comparison—not at the base but—er—in the front line with the—er—troops."

Hope said:—

"Don't listen to the rose-cultivating penguin fancier! You're lucky. And I'll be after you if I keep my reason—as soon as my three years are up!"

Andrew heard nothing about the Board's activities on the question of dust inhalation until months later when Lord Ungar raised the question dramatically in the House, quoting freely from medical evidence afforded him by Doctor Maurice Gadsby.

Gadsby was acclaimed by the Press as a Humanitarian and a Great Physician. And silicosis was, in that year, scheduled as an industrial disease.

Book IV

i

They began their search for a practice. It was a jagged business—wild peaks of expectation followed by wilder plunges of despair. Stung by a consciousness of three successive failures—at least so he construed his departures from Blaenelly, Aberalaw, and the M.F.B.—Andrew longed to vindicate himself at last. But their total capital, increased by stringent saving during the last months of salaried security, was no more than six hundred pounds. Though they haunted the medical agencies and reached for every opportunity offered in the columns of the *Lancet*, it appeared that this sum was scarcely adequate as purchase money for a London practice.

They never forgot their first interview. Doctor Brent, of Cadogan Gardens, was retiring, and he offered a nice nucleus practice, suitable for a well-qualified gentleman. It seemed, on the face of it, an admirable chance. An extravagant taxi—for fear that someone speedier might snatch the plum—rushed them to Doctor Brent, whom they found to be a white-haired, pleasant, almost demure little man.

"Yes," Doctor Brent said modestly. "It's a pretty good pitch. Nice house, too. I want only seven thousand pounds for the lease. There's forty years to run, and the ground rent's only three hundred a year. As to the practice—I thought the usual—two years' premium for cash, eh, Doctor Manson?"

"Quite!" Andrew nodded gravely. "You'd give a long introduction, too? Thank you, Doctor Brent. We'll consider it."

They considered it over threepenny cups of tea in the Brompton Road Lyons.

"Seven thousand—for the lease!" Andrew gave a short laugh. He thrust his hat back from his corrugated brow, stuck his elbows on the marble table. "It's pretty damnable, Chris! The way these old fellows hang on with their back teeth. And you can't prise them loose unless you've got money. Isn't that an indictment of our system? But rotten as it is, I'll accept it. You wait! I'm going to attend to this money question from now on."

"I hope not," she smiled. "We've been moderately happy without it."

He grunted. "You won't say that when we start to sing in the streets. Check, miss, please."

Because of his M.D., M.R.C.P., he wanted a non-panel, non-dispensing practice. He wanted to be free of the tyranny of the card system. But as the weeks went on he wanted anything, anything that offered him a chance. He inspected practices in Tulse Hill, Islington, and Brixton, and one—the surgery had a hole in the roof—in Camden Town. He went to the length of debating with Hope—who assured him that on his capital it was suicide—the plan of taking a house and setting out his plate on chance.

And then, after two months, when they had reached the point of desperation, all at once Heaven relented and allowed old Doctor Foy to die, painlessly, in Paddington. Doctor Foy's obituary notice, four lines in the *Medical Journal*, caught Andrew's eye. They went, their enthusiasm all spent, to Number 9 Chesborough Terrace. They saw the house, a tall, leaden-hued sepulchre with a surgery at the side and a brick garage behind. They saw the books, which indicated that Doctor Foy had made perhaps five hundred pounds a year, mainly from consultations, with medicine, at the rate of three and six. They saw the widow, who assured them timidly that Doctor Foy's practice was sound and had once been excellent with many "good patients" coming to the "front door." They thanked her and left without enthusiasm.

"And yet I don't know," Andrew worried. "It's full of disadvantages. I hate the dispensing. It's a baddish locality. D'you notice all those moth-eaten boarding houses next door? But it's on the *fringe* of a decent neighbourhood. And a corner situation. And a main street. And near enough our price. One and a half years' purchase—and it was decent of her to say she'd fling in the old man's consulting room and surgery furniture as well—and all ready to step into—that's the advantage of a death vacancy. What do you say, Chris? It's now or never. Shall we chance it?"

Christine's eyes rested upon him doubtfully. For her, the novelty of London had worn off. She loved the country and now, in these drab surroundings, she longed for it with all her heart. Yet he was so set upon a London practice she could not bring herself to try, even, to persuade him from it.

She nodded slowly. "If you want to, Andrew."

The next day he offered Mrs. Foy's solicitors six hundred pounds in place of the seven hundred and fifty demanded. The offer was accepted, the cheque written. On Saturday, the tenth of October, they moved their furniture from storage and entered into possession of their new home.

It was Sunday before they extracted themselves from the frantic eruption of straw and sacking and wondered shakily how they stood. Andrew took advantage of the moment to launch one of those lectures, rare yet odious, which made him sound like a deacon of a nonconformist chapel.

"We are properly up against it here, Chris. We've paid out every stiver we've got. We've got to live on what we earn. Heaven only knows what that'll be. But we've got to do it. You've got to spruce things up, Chris, economize—"

To his dismay she burst into tears, standing palely there in the large, gloomy, dirty-ceilinged, and as yet uncarpeted, front room.

"For mercy's sake!" she sobbed. "Leave me alone. Economize. Don't I always economize for you? Do I cost you *anything*?"

"Chris!" he exclaimed aghast.

She flung herself frantically against him. "It's this house! I didn't realize. That basement, the stairs, the *dirt*—"

"But hang it all, it's the practice that really matters!"

"We might have had a little country practice, somewhere."

"Yes! With roses round the cottage door. Damn it all…"

In the end he apologized for his sermon. Then they went, his arm still round her waist, to fry eggs in the condemned basement. There he tried to cheer her by pretending that it was not a basement but a section of the Paddington Tunnel through which trains would at any minute pass. She smiled wanly at his attempted humour, but she was in reality looking at the broken scullery sink.

Next morning, at nine o'clock sharp—he decided: I must not be early or they will think I'm too eager!—he opened his surgery. His heart was beating with excitement and a greater, far greater expectation than on that almost-forgotten morning when he took the first surgery of all at Blaenelly.

Half-past nine came. He waited anxiously. Since the little surgery, which had its own door to the side street, was attached by a short passage to the house, he could equally control his consulting room—the main room on the ground floor, not badly equipped with Doctor Foy's desk, a couch, and a cabinet—to which the "good" patients, by Mrs. Foy's account, were admitted through the front door of the house. He had, in fact, a double net cast out. Tense as any fisherman, he waited for what that double cast might bring.

Yet it brought nothing, nothing! It was nearly eleven o'clock now and still no patient had arrived. The group of taxi drivers standing by their cabs at the rank opposite talked equally together. His plate shone on the door, beneath Doctor Foy's old battered one.

Suddenly, when he had almost abandoned hope, the bell on the surgery door tinkled sharply and an old woman in a shawl came in. Chronic bronchitis—he saw it, before she spoke, in every rheumy wheeze. Tenderly, tenderly he seated and sounded her. She was an old patient of Doctor Foy's. He talked to her. In the tiny cubbyhole of a dispensary, a mere lair halfway down the passage between the surgery and the consulting room, he made up her physic. He returned with it. And then, without question, as he prepared, tremblingly, to ask her for it, she handed him the fee, three and six.

The thrill of that moment—the joy, the sheer relief of these silver coins there in the palm of his hand—was unbelievable. It felt like the first money he had ever earned in his life. He closed the surgery, ran to Christine, thrust the coins upon her.

"First patient, Chris. It mightn't be a bad old practice after all. Anyhow, this buys us our lunch!"

He had no visits to make, for the old doctor had been dead nearly three weeks now, and no locum had kept the practice going in the interval. He must wait till the calls came in. Meanwhile, aware from her mood that Christine wished to wrestle with her domestic worries in solitude, he occupied the forenoon by walking round the district, prospecting, viewing the peeling houses, the long succession of drab private hotels, the sooted, grimly arborescent squares, the narrow mews converted into garages; then, at a sudden turn of North Street, a squalid patch of slum—pawnshops, hawkers' barrows, pubs, shop windows showing patent medicines, devices in gaudy rubber.

He admitted to himself that the district had come down in the world since those days when carriages had spun to the yellow-painted porticoes. It was dingy and soiled, yet there were signs of new life springing up amidst the fungus—a new block of flats in course of erection, some good shops and offices and, at the end of Gladstone Place, the famous Laurier's. Even he, who knew nothing of women's fashions, had heard of Laurier's, and it did not require the long line of elegant motor cars standing outside the windowless, immaculately white-stoned building to convince him that the little he knew of its exclusiveness was true. He felt it strange that Laurier's should stand incongruously amongst these faded terraces. Yet there it was, indubitable as that policeman opposite.

In the afternoon he completed his inaugural tour by calling upon the doctors in the immediate vicinity. Altogether he made eight such calls. Only three of them made any deep impression on him—Doctor Ince of Gladstone Place, a young man; Reeder, at the end of Alexandra Street; and at the corner of Royal Crescent an elderly Scotsman named

McLean.

But the way in which they all said: "Oh! It's poor old Foy's practice you've taken on," somehow depressed him. Why that "on"? he thought, a trifle angrily. He told himself that in six months' time they would change their manner. Though Manson was thirty now, and knew the value of restraint, he still hated condescension as a cat hates water.

That night in the surgery there were three patients, two of whom paid him the three and sixpenny fee. The third promised to return and settle up on Saturday. He had, in his first day's practice, earned the sum of ten and six.

But the following day he took nothing at all. And the day after, only seven shillings. Thursday was a good day; Friday just saved from being blank; and on Saturday, after an empty morning, he took seventeen and six at the evening surgery, though the patient to whom he had given credit on Monday failed to keep his promise to return and pay.

On Sunday, though he made no comment to Christine, Andrew morbidly reviewed the week. Had he made a horrible mistake in taking this derelict practice, in sinking all their savings in this tomblike house? What was *wrong* with him? He was thirty; yes, over thirty. He had an M.D., honours, and the M.R.C.P. He had clinical ability, and a fine piece of clinical research work to his credit. Yet here he was, taking barely enough three and sixpences to keep them in bread. It's the system, he thought savagely, it's *senile*. There ought to be some better scheme, a chance for everybody; say—oh, say State control! Then he groaned, remembering Doctor Bigsby and the M.F.B. No, damn it, that's hopeless; bureaucracy, chokes individual effort—it would suffocate me. I must succeed; damn it all, I *will* succeed!

Never before had the financial side of practice so obtruded itself upon him. And no subtler method of converting him to materialism could have been devised than those genuine pangs of appetite—the euphemism was his own—which he carried with him many days of the week.

About a hundred yards down the main bus route stood a small delicatessen shop kept by a fat little woman, a naturalized German, who called herself Smith but who, from her broken speech and insistent *s*'s, was obviously Schmidt. It was typically Continental, this little place of Frau Schmidt's, its narrow marble counter loaded with soused herrings, olives in jars, sauerkraut, several kinds of *wurst*, pastries, salami, and a delicious kind of cheese named Libtauer. Also it had the virtue of being very cheap. Since money was so scarce at 9 Chesborough Terrace and the cooking stove a choked and antique ruin, Andrew and Christine dealt a great deal with Frau Schmidt. On good days they had hot Frankfurters and "apfelstrudel"; on bad they would lunch on a soused herring and baked potatoes. Often at night they would drop into Frau Schmidt's, after scanning her display through the steamed window with a selective eye, and come away with something savoury in a string bag.

Frau Schmidt soon got to know them. She developed an especial liking for Christine. Her larded, pastry-cook's face would wrinkle up, almost closing her eyes, beneath her high dome of blond hair, as she smiled and nodded to Andrew:

"You will be all right. You will succeed. You have a good wife. She iss small, like me. But she iss good. Chust wait—I will send you patients!"

Almost at once, the winter was upon them and fogs hung about the streets, always intensified, it seemed, by the smoke from the great railway station near by. They made light of it, they pretended their struggles were amusing, but never in all their years at Aberalaw had they known such hardship.

Christine did her utmost with their chill barracks. She whitewashed the ceilings, made new curtains for the waiting room. She repapered their bedroom. By painting the panels black and gold, she transformed the senile folding doors which disfigured the first floor drawing-room.

Most of his calls, infrequent though these were, took him to the boarding houses of the neighbourhood. It was difficult to collect the fees from such patients—many of them were seedy, even doubtful characters, and adept in the art of bilking. He tried to make himself agreeable to the gaunt females who kept these establishments. He made conversation in gloomy hallways. He would say, "I'd no idea it was so cold! I should have brought my coat," or "It's awkward getting about. My car's laid up for the moment."

He struck up a friendship with the policeman who usually took point duty at the busy traffic crossing outside Frau Schmidt's delicatessen. Donald Struthers was the policeman's name, and there was kinship between them from the start, for Struthers, like Andrew, came from Fife. He promised, in his own style, to do what he could do to help his compatriot, remarking with a grim facetiousness:—

"If ever anybody gets run down and killed here, Doctor, I'll be sure and fetch them along to ye."

One afternoon, about a month after their arrival, when Andrew got home—he had been calling on the chemists of the district, inquiring brightly for a special 10cc. Voss syringe which he knew none of them would keep in stock, then, casually introducing himself as the new and vigorous practitioner of Chesborough Terrace—Christine's expression appraised him of some excitement.

"There's a patient in the consulting room," she breathed. "She came by the front door."

His face brightened. This was the first "good" patient who had come to him. Perhaps it was the beginning of better things. Preparing himself, he walked briskly into the consulting room.

"Good afternoon! What can I do for you?"

"Good afternoon, Doctor. Mrs. Smith recommended me."

She rose from her chair to shake hands with him. She was plump, good-natured, thickly made up, with a short fur jacket and a large handbag. He saw at once that she was one of the street-women who frequented the district.

"Yes?" he inquired, his expectation sinking a little.

"Oh, Doctor," she smiled diffidently. "My friend just give me a nice pair of gold earrings. And Mrs. Smith—I am customer there—she said you would pierce my ears for me? My friend, he's very anxious I don't get done with a dirty needle or something, Doctor."

He took a long steadying breath. Had it actually come to this? He said:—

"Yes, I'll pierce your ears for you."

He did this carefully, sterilizing the needle, spraying her lobes with ethyl chloride, even fitting the gold rings in for her.

"Oh, Doctor, that's lovely"—peering in the mirror of her handbag. "And I never felt a thing. My friend'll be pleased. How much, Doctor?"

The statutory fee for Foy's "good" patients, mythical though they might be, was seven and six. He mentioned this sum.

She produced a ten-shilling note from her bag. She thought him a kind, distinguished, and very handsome gentleman—she always liked them dark, somehow—and she also thought, as she accepted her change, that he looked hungry.

When she had gone he did not wear holes in the carpet, as he would once have done, raving that he, too, had prostituted himself by this petty, servile act. He was conscious of a strange humility. Holding the crumpled note, he went to the window, watching her disappear down the street, swaying her hips, swinging her handbag, proudly wearing her new earrings.

ii

Through the rigours of the battle he hungered for medical friendship. He had gone to a meeting of the local medical association without enjoying himself greatly. Denny was still abroad. Finding Tampico to his liking Philip had remained there, taking a post as surgeon to the New Century Oil Company. For the present, at least, he was lost to Andrew. While Hope, on a mission to Cumberland, was—as he phrased it in his rudely coloured postcard—counting corpuscles for Maniac's Delight.

Many times Andrew was taken by the impulse to get in touch with Freddie Hampton; but always, though he often got as far as the phone book, the reflection that he was still unsuccessful—not properly settled, he told himself—restrained him. Freddie was still in Queen Anne Street, though he had moved to a different number. Andrew found himself wondering more and more how Freddie had got on, recollecting the old adventures of their student days, until suddenly he found the compulsion too strong for him. He did ring Hampton.

"You've probably forgotten all about me," he grunted, half-prepared for a snub. "This is Manson—Andrew Manson. I'm in practice here in Paddington."

"Manson! Forgotten you! You old warhorse!" Freddie was lyrical on the other end of the line. "Good lord, man! *Why* haven't you rung me?"

"Oh, we've barely got settled," Andrew smiled into the receiver, warmed by Freddie's gush. "And before—on that Board job—we were rushing all over England. I'm married now, you know."

"So am I! Look here, old man, we've got to get together again. Soon! I can't get over it. You, here, in London. Marvellous! Where's my book—Look here, how about next Thursday? Can you come to dinner then? Yes, yes. That's great. So long then, old man, in the meantime I'll have my wife drop yours a line."

Christine seemed lacking in enthusiasm when he told her of the invitation.

"You go, Andrew," she suggested after a pause.

"Oh! that's nonsense! Freddie wants you to meet his wife. I know you don't care about him much, but there'll be other people there, other doctors probably. We may get a new slant on things there, dear. Besides, we've had no fun lately. Black tie, he said. Lucky I bought myself that dinner jacket for the Newcastle mines do. But what about you, Chris? You ought to have something to wear."

"I ought to have a new gas cooker," she answered a trifle grimly.

These last weeks had taken toll of her. She had lost a little of that freshness which had always been her greatest charm. And sometimes, as just now, her tone was short and jaded.

But on Thursday night, when they started out for Queen Anne Street, he could not help thinking how sweet she looked in the dress—yes, it was the white dress she had bought for that Newcastle dinner, altered in some way which made it seem newer, smarter. Her hair was done in a new style too, closer to her head, so that it lay darkly about her pale brow. He noticed this as she tied his bow for him, meant to tell her how nice it was, then forgot, in the sudden fear that they would be late.

They were not late, however, but early, so early that an awkward three minutes elapsed before Freddie came gaily in, both hands outstretched, apologizing and greeting them in the same breath, telling them he had just come in from hospital, that his wife would be down in a second, offering drinks, pounding Andrew on the back, bidding them be seated. Freddie had put on weight since that evening at Cardiff, there was heavy prosperity in the pink roll of flesh on the back of his neck, but his small eyes still glistened and not a single yellow plastered hair was out of its place. He was so well-groomed that he shone.

"Believe me!"—he elevated his glass—"it's wonderful to see you people again. This time we've got to keep it up. How do you like my place here, old man? Didn't I tell you at that dinner—and *what* a dinner!—I bet we'll do better to-night—that I'd do it? I've got the whole house here, of course—not just rooms; bought the freehold last year. And did it cost money?" He patted his tie approvingly. "No need to advertise the fact, of course, even if I am successful. But I don't mind you knowing, old man."

It looked an expensive background, there was no doubt: smooth modern furniture, deepset fireplace, a baby grand player-piano with artificial magnolia blossoms shaped from mother-of-pearl in a big white vase.

Andrew was preparing to voice admiration when Mrs. Hampton entered, tall, cool, with dark hair parted in the middle and clothes extraordinarily different from Christine's.

"Come along, my dear." Freddie greeted her with affection, even with deference, and darted to pour and offer her a glass of sherry. She had time negligently to wave away the glass before the other guests—Mr. and Mrs. Charles Ivory, Doctor and Mrs. Paul Freedman—were announced. Introductions followed, with much talk and laughter amongst the Ivorys, the Freedmans and the Hamptons. Then they went in—not too soon —to dinner.

The table appointments were rich and superfine. They closely resembled a costly display, complete with candelabra, which Andrew had seen in the window of Labin and Benn, the famous Regent Street jewellers. The food was unrecognizable as meat or fish, yet it tasted extremely well. And there was champagne. After two glasses Andrew felt more confident. He began to talk to Mrs. Ivory, who sat on his left, a slender woman in black with an extraordinary amount of jewellery around her neck and large protruding blue eyes which she turned upon him from time to time with an almost babyish stare.

Her husband was Charles Ivory, the surgeon—she laughed in answer to his question; she thought everyone knew Charles. They lived in New Cavendish Street round the corner, the whole house was theirs. It was nice being near Freddie and his wife. Charles and Freddie and Paul Freedman were all such good friends, all members of the Sackville Club. She was surprised when he admitted he was not a member. She thought everyone was a member of the Sackville.

Deserted, he turned to Mrs. Freedman on his other side, finding her softer, friendlier, with a pretty, almost oriental bloom. He encouraged her to talk of her husband also. He said to himself: "I want to *know* about these fellows, they're so damned prosperous and smart."

Paul, said Mrs. Freedman, was a physician, and though they had a flat in Portland Place, Paul's rooms were in Harley Street. He had a wonderful practice—she spoke too fondly to be bragging—chiefly at the Plaza Hotel; he must know the big new Plaza, overlooking the Park. Why, at lunchtime the Grill Room was crammed with celebrities. Paul was practically the official doctor for the Plaza Hotel. So many wealthy Americans and film stars and—she broke off smiling—oh, everybody came to the Plaza, which made it rather wonderful for Paul.

Andrew liked Mrs. Freedman. He let her run on until Mrs. Hampton rose, when he jumped up gallantly to draw back her chair.

"Cigar, Manson?" Freddie asked him with a knowledgeable air when the ladies had gone. "You'll find these pretty sound. And I advise you not to miss this brandy. Eighteen ninety-four. Absolutely no nonsense about it."

With his cigar going and a drain of brandy in the wide-bellied glass before him, Andrew drew his chair nearer to the others. It was this he had really been looking forward to, a close, lively medical palaver—straight cut shop, and nothing else. He hoped Hampton and his friends would talk. They did.

"By the way," Freddie said, "I ordered myself one of these new Iradium lamps to-day at Glickert's. Pretty stiff. Something around eighty guineas. But it's worth it."

"M'yes," said Freedman thoughtfully. He was slight, dark-eyed, with a clever Jewish face. "It ought to pay for its keep."

Andrew took an argumentative grip of his cigar.

"I don't think much of these lamps, you know. Did you see Abbey's paper in the *Journal* on bogus Heliotherapy? These Iradiums have got absolutely no infrared content."

Freddie stared, then laughed.

"They've got a hell of a lot of three-guinea content. Besides, they bronze nicely."

"Mind you, Freddie," Freedman cut in, "I'm not in favour of expensive apparatus. It's got to be paid for before you show a profit. Besides, it dates, loses its vogue. Honestly, old chap, you'll find nothing to beat the good old hypo."

"*You* certainly use it," said Hampton.

Ivory joined in. He was bulky, older than the others, with a pale, shaven jowl, and the easy style of a man about town.

"Talking of that, I booked a course of injections to-day. Twelve. You know, manganese. And I tell you what I did. And I think it pays these days. I said to the fellow —I said, 'Look here, you're a businessman. This course is going to cost you fifty guineas, but if you care to pay me now and be done with it I'll make it forty-five.' He wrote me the cheque there and then."

"Ruddy old poacher," Freddie expostulated. "I thought you were a surgeon."

"I am," Ivory nodded. "Doing a curettage at Sherrington's tomorrow."

"Love's labour lost," Freedman muttered absently to his cigar; then, returning to his original thought: "There's no getting away from it, though. Basically, it's interesting. In good class practice oral administration is definitely demoded. If I prescribed—oh, say an Omnipon powder, at the Plaza, it wouldn't cut one guinea's worth of ice. But if you give the same thing hypodermically, swabbing up the skin, sterilizing and all the rest of the game, your patient thinks, scientifically, that you are the cat's pyjamas!"

Hampton declared vigorously:—

"It's a damn good job for the medical profession that oral administration is off the map in the West End. Take Charlie's case here, as an example. Suppose he'd prescribed manganese—or manganese and iron, the good old bottle of physic—probably just as much use to the patient—all he knocks out of it is three guineas. Instead of that he splits the medicine into twelve ampules, and gets fifty—sorry, Charlie, I mean forty-five."

"Less twelve shillings," murmured Freedman gently. "The price of the ampules."

Andrew's head rocked. Here was an argument in favour of the abolition of the medicine bottle which staggered him with its novelty. He took another swig of brandy to steady himself.

"That's another point," reflected Freedman. "They don't know how little these things cost. Whenever a patient sees a row of ampules on your desk she thinks instinctively, 'Heavens! this is going to mean money!'"

"You'll observe," Hampton winked at Andrew, "how Freedman's parsing of the good word patient is usually feminine. By the way, Paul, I heard about that shooting yesterday. Dummett's willing to make up a syndicate if you, Charles, and I will go in with him."

For the next ten minutes they talked of shooting, golf,—which they played on various expensive courses around London,—and cars,—Ivory was having a special body built to his instructions on a new three-and-a-half-litre Rex,—while Andrew listened and smoked his cigar and drank his brandy. They all drank a deal of brandy. Andrew felt, a trifle muzzily, that they were extraordinarily good fellows. They did not exclude him from their conversation, but always managed to make him feel by a word or a look that he was with them. Somehow they made him forget that he had eaten a soused herring for his luncheon. And as they stood up Ivory clapped him on the shoulder.

"I must send you a card, Manson. It'd be a real pleasure to see a case with you—any time."

Back in the drawing-room the atmosphere seemed, by contrast, formal; but Freddie, in tremendous spirits, more shining than ever, hands in his pockets, linen spotlessly agleam, decided that the evening was still young, that they must finish it altogether at the Embassy.

"I'm afraid—" Christine threw a pale glance at Andrew—"we ought to be going."

"Nonsense, darling!" Andrew smiled roseately. "We couldn't dream of breaking up the party!"

At the Embassy, Freddie was obviously popular. He and his party were bowed and smiled to a table against the wall. There was more champagne. There was dancing. These fellows do themselves well, thought Andrew mistily, expansively.

"Oh! tha's a—tha's a splen'id tune they're playing—I won-woner if Chris would like t'dance."

In the taxi, returning at last to Chesborough Terrace, he proclaimed happily:—

"First-rate chaps these, Chris! 'Sbeen a wonderful evening, hasn't it?"

She answered in a thin, steady voice:

"It's been a hateful evening!"

"Eh—what?"

"I like Denny and Hope as—oh—as your medical friends, Andrew; not these, these flashy—"

He broke in. "But look here, Chris—Wha's wrong with—"

"Oh! Couldn't you see?" she answered in an icy fury. "It was everything. The food, the furniture, the way they talked—money, money all the time. Perhaps you didn't see the way she looked at my dress, Mrs. Hampton I mean. You could see her *realizing* that she spends more on one beauty treatment than I do on clothes in a whole year. It was almost funny in the drawing-room when she found out what a nobody I was. She of course is the daughter of Whitton—the whisky Whitton! You can't guess what it was like —the conversation—before you came in. Smart Set gossip, who's week-ending with whom, what the hairdresser told her, the latest society abortion, not one word of anything *decent*. Why! She actually hinted that she was 'sweet on'—as she put it—the danceband leader at the Plaza."

The sarcasm in her tone was diabolic. Mistaking it for jealousy, he babbled:—

"I'll make money for you, Chris. I'll buy you plenty of expensive clothes."

"I don't want money," she said tautly. "And I hate expensive clothes."

"But—darling!" Tipsily he reached for her.

"Don't!" Her voice struck him. "I love you, Andrew. But not when you're drunk."

He subsided in his corner, fuddled, furious. It was the first time she had ever repulsed him.

"All right, my girl," he muttered. "If that's the way of it."

He paid the taxi, let himself into the house before her. Then without a word he marched up to the spare bedroom. Everything seemed squalid and dismal after the luxury he had just quitted. The electric switch would not work properly—the whole house was imperfectly wired.

"Damn it," he thought as he flung himself into bed. "I'm going to get out of this hole. I'll show her. I *will* make money. What *can* you do without it?"

Until now, in all their married life, they had never slept apart.

iii

At breakfast next morning Christine behaved as though the whole episode were forgotten. He could see that she was trying to be especially nice to him. This gratified him and made him sulkier than ever. A woman, he reflected,—pretending absorption in the morning paper,—has got to be shown her place occasionally. But after he had grunted a few surly replies Christine suddenly stopped being nice to him and retired within herself, sitting at the table with compressed lips, not looking at him, waiting till he should finish the meal. Stubborn little devil, he thought, rising and walking out of the room; I'll show her!

His first action in his consulting room was to take down the *Medical Directory*. He was both curious and eager to have more precise information of his friends of the previous evening. Quickly he turned the pages, taking Freddie first. Yes, there it was—Frederick Hampton, Queen Anne Street, M.B., Ch.B., assistant to outpatients, Walthamwood.

Andrew's brows drew into a frown of perplexity. Freddie had talked a great deal last night about the hospital appointment—nothing like a hospital appointment for helping a fellow in the West End, he had said, gives the patients confidence to know he's a visiting physician. Yet surely this wasn't it: a poor-law institution—and at Walthamwood, one of the newer outer suburbs? There couldn't be a mistake, though, this was the current directory, he had bought it only a month ago.

More slowly, Andrew looked up Ivory and Freedman, then he rested the big red book on his knees, his expression puzzled, oddly reflective. Paul Freedman was, like Freddie, an M.B. but without Freddie's distinction. Freedman had no visiting appointment. And Ivory? Mr. Charles Ivory of New Cavendish Street had no surgical qualification but the lowest, the M.R.C.S., and no hospital appointment whatsoever. His record indicated a certain amount of experience in wartime and pensions hospitals. Beyond that—nothing.

Extremely thoughtful now, Andrew rose and put the book on its shelf, then his face drew into a sudden resolution. There was no comparison between his own qualifications and those of the prosperous fellows he had dined with last night. What they could do he could do also. Better. Despite Christine's outburst, he was more determined than ever to make a success of himself. But first he must get himself attached, not to Walthamwood or any such poor-law make-believe, but to one of the London hospitals. Yes! a real hospital—that must be his immediate objective. But how?

For three days he brooded, then he went shakily to Sir Robert Abbey. It was the most difficult task in the world for him to ask a favour, particularly as Abbey received him with such twinkling kindness.

"Well! How is our express bandage enumerator? Aren't you ashamed to look me in the eye? I'm told Doctor Bigsby has developed hypertension. Know anything about that? What is it you want, an argument with me, or a seat on the Board?"

"Well, no, Sir Robert. I was wondering—that's to say—could you help me, Sir Robert, to find an outpatients hospital appointment?"

"Hmm! That's much more difficult than the Board. Do you know how many young fellows there are walking the Embankment? All waiting on honorary appointments. You ought really to be going on with your lung work too—and that narrows the field."

"Well—I—I suppose—"

"The Victoria Chest Hospital. That's your target. One of our oldest London Hospitals. Suppose I make some inquiries. Oh! I don't promise anything, but I'll keep my eye scientifically open."

Abbey made him stay to tea. At four o'clock, unvaryingly, he had a ritual of drinking two cups of China tea in his consulting room, no milk or sugar, and nothing to eat. It was a special tea which tasted of orange blossoms. Abbey kept the conversation flowing easily on diverse topics, from Khang Hsi saucerless cups to the Pirquet reaction; then, as he showed Andrew to the door, he said:—

"Still quarrelling with the textbooks? Don't give that up. And don't—even if I do get you into the Victoria—for the love of Galen!—don't develop a bedside manner." His eyes twinkled. "That's what has ruined me."

Andrew went home treading the clouds. He was so pleased he neglected to maintain his dignity with Christine. He blurted out:—

"I've been to Abbey. He's going to try and fix me up at the Victoria Chest! That practically gives me a consultant's standing." The gladness in her eyes made him suddenly feel shamefaced, small. "I've been pretty difficult lately, Chris! We haven't been getting on too well, I suppose. Let's—oh! let's make it up, darling."

She ran to him, protesting it had all been her fault. Then, for some strange reason, it appeared entirely to be his. Only a small segment of his mind retained the fixed intention of confounding her, at some early date, by the greatness of his material success.

He flung himself into his work with renewed vigour, feeling that something fortunate would surely turn up soon. Meanwhile there was no doubt that his practice was increasing. It was not, he told himself, the class of practice he wanted, these three-and-sixpenny consultations and five-shilling visits. Yet it was genuine practice. The people who came to him or called him out were far too poor to dream of troubling the doctor unless they were really ill. Thus he met diphtheria in queer stuffy rooms above converted stables, rheumatic fever in damp servants' basements, pneumonia in the attics of lodging houses. He fought disease in that most tragic room of all, the single apartment where some elderly man or woman lived alone, forgotten by friends and relatives, cooking poor meals on a gas ring, neglected, unkempt, forsaken. There were many such cases. He came across the father of a well-known actress—whose name shone in bright lights in Shaftesbury Avenue—an old man of seventy, paralyzed, living in filthy squalor. He visited an elderly gentlewoman, gaunt, ludicrous, and starving, who could show him her photograph in her Court presentation dress, tell him of the days when she had driven down these same streets in her own carriage. In the middle of the night he pulled back to life—and afterwards hated himself for it—a wretched creature, penniless and desperate, who had preferred the gas oven to the workhouse.

Many of his cases were urgent—surgical emergencies which cried aloud for immediate admission to hospital. And here Andrew encountered his greatest difficulty. It was the hardest thing in the world to secure admission, even for the worst, the most dangerous case. These emergencies had a way of happening late at night. Returning, coat and jacket over his pyjamas, a scarf round his neck, hat still on the back of his head, he would hang over the telephone, ringing one hospital after another, entreating, imploring, threatening; but he always met with the same refusal, the curt, often insolent: "Doctor Who? Who? No, no! Sorry! We're full up!"

He went to Christine, livid, blaspheming. "They're not full up. They've plenty of beds at St. John's for their own men. If they don't know you they freeze you stiff. I'd like to wring that last young pup's neck! Isn't it *hell*, Chris? Here am I with this strangulated hernia and I can't get a bed. Oh! I suppose some of them *are* full up. And this is London! This is the heart of the bloody British Empire. This is our voluntary hospital system. And some banqueting bastard of a philanthropist got up the other day and said it was the most marvellous in the world. It means the workhouse again for the poor devil. Filling in forms—What do you earn? What's your religion? and was your mother born in wedlock?—and him with peritonitis! Oh, well! Be a good sort, Chris, and get the relieving officer on the phone for me."

Whatever his difficulties, no matter if he railed against the dirt and poverty which he often had to combat, she always had the same reply:—

"It's *real* work anyway. And that seems to me to make all the difference."

"Not enough to keep the bugs off me," he growled, going up to the bath to shake himself free.

She laughed; for she was back again to her old happiness. Though the fight had been formidable, she had at last subdued the house. Sometimes it would attempt to rear its head and strike at her, but in the main it lay clean, furbished, obedient to her eye. She had her new gas cooker, new shades for the lamps; she had the loose chair-covers freshly cleaned. And her stair-rods shone like a guardsman's buttons. After weeks of worry with servants who, in this district, preferred to work in the boarding houses because of the tips they earned there, Christine had chanced on Mrs. Bennett, a widow of forty, clean and hardworking, who, because of her daughter, a child of seven, had found it almost impossible to secure a "living in" position. Together Mrs. Bennett and Christine had attacked the basement. Now the former railway tunnel was a comfortable bed-sitting—room, with a highly floral wallpaper, furniture brought from "the barrows" and painted cream by Christine, where Mrs. Bennett and little Florrie—now departing regularly with her satchel to Paddington School—felt themselves secure. In return for this security and comfort—after months of straitened uncertainty—Mrs. Bennett could not do enough to prove her worth.

The early spring flowers which made the waiting-room so bright reflected the happiness of Christine's house. She bought them at the street market for a few pence, as she went on her round of morning shopping. Many of the hawkers in Mussleburgh Road knew her. It was possible to buy fruit and fish and vegetables cheaply there. She ought to have been more conscious of her standing as the wife of a professional man; but alas! she was not, and she often brought her purchases back in her neat string bag, stopping at Frau Schmidt's on the way back for a few minutes' conversation and a wedge of the Libtauer cheese which Andrew liked so well.

Frequently, in the afternoons, she walked round the Serpentine. The chestnut trees were breaking into green and the waterfowl went scurrying across the wind-ruffled water. It was a good substitute for the open countryside which she had always loved so much.

Sometimes in the evening Andrew would glance at her in that oddly jealous manner which meant that he was cross because the day had gone past without his noticing her.

"What have you been up to all day while I've been busy? If I ever do get a car you'll have to drive the damn thing. That'll keep you close to me."

He was still waiting for those "good" patients who did not come, longing to hear from Abbey about the appointment, fretful because their evening at Queen Anne Street had produced no subsequent opportunity. Secretly he was cut that he had seen nothing of Hampton or his friends since then.

In this condition he sat in his surgery one evening towards the end of April. It was nearly nine o'clock and he was about to close up, when a young woman entered.

She gazed at him uncertainly.

"I didn't know whether to come this way—or by the front door."

"It's exactly the same," he smiled sourly. "Except that it's half-price this end. Come along. What is it?"

"I don't mind paying the full fee." She came forward with a peculiar earnestness and sat down on the rexine-covered chair. She was about twenty-eight, he judged, stockily built, dressed in dark olive-green, with bunchy legs and a large plain serious face. To look at her was to have the instinctive thought: No nonsense here!

He relented, saying: "Don't let's talk about the fee! Tell me your trouble."

"Well, Doctor!" She still seemed to wish, gravely, to establish herself. "It was Mrs. Smith—in the little provision shop—who recommended me to come to you. I've known her a long time, I work at Laurier's, quite near. My name is Cramb. But I must tell you I've been to a great many doctors round here." She pulled off her gloves. "It's my hands."

He looked at her hands, the palms of which were covered by a reddish dermatitis, rather like psoriasis. But it was not psoriasis, the edges were not serpiginous. With sudden interest he took up a magnifying glass and peered more closely. Meanwhile she went on talking in her earnest, convincing voice.

"I can't tell you what a disadvantage this is to me in my work. I'd give anything to get rid of it. I've tried every kind of ointment under the sun. But none of them seem to be the slightest use."

"No! They wouldn't." He put down the glass, feeling all the thrill of an obscure yet positive diagnosis. "This is rather an uncommon skin condition, Miss Cramb. It's no good treating it locally. It's due to a blood condition and the only way to get rid of it is by dieting."

"No medicine?" Her earnestness gave way to doubt. "No one ever told me that before."

"I'm telling you now." He laughed and, taking his pad, drew out a diet for her, adding also a list of foods which she must absolutely avoid.

She accepted it hesitatingly. "Well! Of course I'll try it, Doctor. I'd try *anything.*" Meticulously she paid him his fee, lingered as though still dubious, then went away. He immediately forgot her.

Ten days later she returned, coming this time by the front door, and entering the consulting room with such an expression of suppressed fervour that he could barely keep from smiling.

"Would you like to see my hands, Doctor?"

"Yes." Now he did smile. "I hope you don't regret the diet."

"Regret it!" She surrendered her hands to him in a passion of gratitude. "Look! Completely cured. Not a single spot on them. You don't know how much it means to me—I can't tell you—such cleverness—"

"That's all right," he said lightly. "It's my job to know these things. You run away and don't worry. Keep off those foods I told you about and you'll never have it again."

She rose.

"And now let me pay you, Doctor?"

"You've already paid me." He was conscious of a mild aesthetic thrill. Right gladly would he have taken another three and six, or even seven and six, from her, but the temptation to dramatize the triumph of his skill proved irresistible.

"But, Doctor—" Unwillingly she allowed herself to be escorted to the door, where she paused for the final earnestness. "Perhaps I'll be able to show my gratitude some other way?"

Gazing at her upturned moon face, a ribald thought crossed his mind. But he merely nodded and closed the door upon her. Again he forgot about her. He was tired, already half-regretful at refusing the fee, and, in any case, he had little thought of what any shopgirl might do for him.

But here at least he did not know Miss Cramb. Moreover, he quite overlooked a possibility, emphasized by Aesop, which as a bad philosophizer he ought to have remembered.

iv

Martha Cramb was known as "the Halfback" to the "juniors" at Laurier's. Sturdy, unattractive, sexless, she seemed a strange person to be one of the senior assistants in this unique shop which dealt luxuriously in smart gowns, exquisite undergarments, and furs so rich their prices mounted to hundreds of pounds. Yet the Halfback was an admirable saleswoman, highly valued by her clients. The fact was that Laurier's, in its pride, employed a special system, each "Senior" collecting her own especial clients, a little group of the Laurier customers whom she served exclusively, studied, "dressed" and for whom she "laid aside" things when the new models came in. The relationship was intimate, often existed over many years, and was one to which the Halfback in her earnest sincerity was particularly suited.

She was the daughter of a Kettering solicitor. Many of the Laurier girls were daughters of small professional men in the provinces and outer suburbs. It was esteemed an honour to be allowed to enter Laurier's, to wear the dark green dress which was the uniform of the establishment. Sweated employment and the bad "living-in" conditions which ordinary shop assistants were sometimes made to endure simply did not exist at Laurier's, where the girls were admirably fed and housed and chaperoned. Mr. Winch, the only male buyer in the shop, especially saw to it that they were chaperoned. He particularly esteemed the Halfback, and often held sedate conference with her. He was a pink motherly old gentleman who had been in millinery for forty years. His thumb was worn flat from appraising material, his back permanently cricked in deferential greeting. Maternal though he might be, Mr. Winch, to the stranger entering Laurier's, exhibited the only trousers in a vast and frothy sea of femininity. He had an unsympathetic eye for those husbands who came with their wives to inspect the mannequins. He knew Royalty. He was almost as great an institution as Laurier's.

The incident of Miss Cramb's cure caused a mild sensation amongst the staff at Laurier's. And the immediate result was that from sheer curiosity a number of the Juniors dropped in to Andrew's surgery with mild complaints. Giggling, they told each other that they wanted to see "what the Halfback's doctor was like!"

Gradually however, more and more of the Laurier girls began to come to the surgery at Chesborough Terrace. All the girls were insurance patients. They were compelled by law to be "on the panel," but, with true Laurier arrogance, they repudiated the scheme. By the end of May it was not uncommon for half a dozen of them to be waiting in the surgery—very smart, modelled upon their customers, lipsticked, young. The result was a marked improvement in the surgery receipts. Also a laughing remark by Christine:—

"What *are* you doing with that beauty chorus, darling? Sure they haven't mistaken this for the stage door?"

But Miss Cramb's throbbing gratitude—oh, the ecstasy of those healed hands!—was only beginning to express itself. Hitherto Doctor McLean, safe and elderly, of Royal Crescent, had been regarded as the semi-official doctor of Laurier's, called upon when emergency demanded—as, for instance, when Miss Twig of the Tailoring burned herself badly with a hot iron. But Doctor McLean was on the verge of retiring, and his partner and immediate successor, Doctor Benton, was neither safe nor elderly. Indeed, more than once, Doctor Benton's ankle-roving eye and too tender solicitude for the prettier Juniors had caused Mr. Winch pinkly to frown. Miss Cramb and Mr. Winch discussed these matters at their little conferences together, Mr. Winch nodding gravely with hands clasped behind his back, as Miss Cramb dwelled upon Benton's inadequacy and the presence of another professional man at Chesborough Terrace, strict and ungaudy, who achieved brilliance without sacrifice to Thaïs. Nothing was settled, Mr. Winch always took his time, but there was a portentous gleam in his eye as he swam away to greet a duchess.

In the first week of June, when Andrew had already come to feel shame for his earlier contempt of her, still another manifestation of Miss Cramb's good offices fell in burning fire upon his head.

He received a letter, very neat and precise—no such informality as a phone call, he afterwards learned, would have befitted the writer—asking him to call on Tuesday, the following forenoon, as near eleven o'clock as possible, at 9 Park Gardens, to see Miss Winifred Everett.

Closing his surgery early, he left, with a rising sense of anticipation, to make this visit. It was the first time he had been called out of the drab neighbourhood which had, up till now, contained his practice. Park Gardens was a handsome block of flats, not altogether modern, but large and substantial, with a fine view of Hyde Park. He rang the bell of Number 9, expectant and tense, with the odd conviction that this was his chance at last.

An elderly servant showed him in. The room was spacious, with old furniture, books and flowers, reminding him of Mrs. Vaughan's drawing room. The moment he entered it he felt that his premonition was correct. He swung round as Miss Everett entered, finding her glance, level and composed, fixed appraisingly upon him.

She was a well-made woman of about fifty, dark-haired and sallow-skinned, severely dressed, with an air of complete assurance. She began immediately, in a measured tone:
—

"I have lost my doctor—unfortunately—for I had great faith in him. My Miss Cramb recommended you. She's a very faithful creature and I trust her. I've looked you up. You're well-qualified." She paused, quite openly inspecting him, weighing him up. She had the look of a woman well-fed, well-taken-care-of, who would not allow a finger near her without due inspection of the cuticle. Then, guardedly, "I think perhaps you might suit. I usually have a course of injections at this time of year. I'm subject to hay fever. You know all about hay fever, I presume?"

"Yes," he answered. "Which injections do you have?"

She mentioned the name of a well-known preparation. "My old doctor put me on that. I have great faith in it."

"Oh, that!" Nettled at her manner, he was on the point of telling her that the faithful remedy of her faithful doctor was worthless, that it had achieved its popularity through skilful advertising on the part of the firm who produced it and the absence of pollen in most English summers. But with an effort he restrained himself. There was a struggle between all that he believed and all he wished to have. He thought defiantly: If I let this chance slip, after all these months, I'm a fool.

He said, "I think I can give you the injection as well as anyone."

"Very well. And now about your fees. I never paid Doctor Sinclair more than one guinea a visit. May I take it that you will continue this arrangement?"

A guinea a visit—it was three times the largest fee he had ever earned! And more important still, it represented his first step into the superior class of practice he had coveted all these months. Again he stifled the quick protest of his convictions. What did it matter if the injections were useless? That was her look-out, not his. He was sick of failure, tired of being a three-and-sixpenny hack. He wanted to get on, succeed. And he would succeed at all costs.

He came again the following day at eleven o'clock sharp. She had warned him, in her severe way, against being late. She did not wish her forenoon walk interfered with. He gave her the first injection. And thereafter he called twice a week, continuing the treatment.

He was punctual, precise as she, and he never presumed. It was almost amusing the way in which she gradually thawed to him. She was a queer person, Winifred Everett, and a most decided personality. Though she was rich—her father had been a large manufacturer of cutlery in Sheffield and all the money that she had inherited from him was safely invested in the funds—she set herself out to get the utmost value from every penny. It was not meanness but rather an odd kind of egoism. She made herself the centre of her universe, took the utmost care of her body, which was still white and fine, went in for all sorts of treatments which she felt would benefit her. She must have everything of the best. She ate sparingly, but only the finest food. When on his sixth visit she unbent to offer him a glass of sherry, he observed that it was Amontillado of the year 1819. Her clothes came from Laurier's. Her bed linen was the finest he had ever seen. And yet, with all this, she never, according to her lights, wasted a farthing. Not for the life of him could he imagine Miss Everett flinging a half-crown to a taximan without first carefully looking at the meter.

He ought to have loathed her, yet strangely he did not. She had developed her selfishness to the point of a philosophy. And she was so eminently sensible. She exactly reminded him of a woman in an old Dutch picture, a Ter Borch which Christine and he had once seen. She had the same large body, the same smooth-textured skin, the same forbidding yet pleasure-loving mouth.

When she saw that he was, in her own phrase, really going to suit her, she became much less reserved. It was an unwritten law with her that the doctor's visit should last twenty minutes, otherwise she felt she had not had the value of it. But by the end of a month he was extending this to half an hour. They talked together. He told her of his desire for success. She approved it. Her range of conversation was limited. But the range of her relations was unlimited, and it was of them, mostly, that she talked. She spoke to him frequently of her niece, named Catharine Sutton, who lived in Derbyshire and who often came to town since her husband, Captain Sutton, was M.P. for Barnwell.

"Doctor Sinclair used to look after them," she remarked in a noncommittal voice. "I don't see why you shouldn't now."

On his last visit she gave him another glass of her Amontillado and, very pleasantly, she said:—

"I hate bills coming in. Please let me settle up now." She handed him a folded cheque for twelve guineas. "Of course, I shall have you in again soon. I usually have an anticoryza vaccine in the winter."

She actually accompanied him to the door of the flat and there she stood for a moment, her face drily illumined, the nearest approach to a smile he had ever seen there. But it passed quickly and, gazing at him forbiddingly, she said:

"Will you take the advice of a woman old enough to be your mother? Go to a good tailor. Go to Captain Sutton's tailor—Rogers, in Conduit Street. You've told me how much you wish to succeed. You never will, in that suit."

He strode down the road cursing her, the hot indignity still burning on his brow, cursing her in his old impassioned style. Interfering old bitch! What business was it of hers! What right had she to tell him how he should dress? Did she take him for a *lapdog*? That was the worst of compromise, of truckling to convention. His Paddington patients paid him only three and six, yet they did not ask him to be a tailor's dummy. In future he would confine himself to them and call his soul his own!

But somehow that mood passed. It was perfectly true that he had never taken the slightest interest in his clothes, a suit off the peg had always served him excellently, covered him, kept him warm without elegance. Christine, too, though she was always so neat, never bothered about clothes. She was happiest in a tweed skirt and a woollen jumper she had knitted herself.

Surreptitiously he took stock of himself: his nondescript, worsted, uncreased trousers, mud-spattered at the selvedge. Hang it all, he thought testily, she's perfectly right. How can I attract first-class patients if I look like this? Why didn't Christine tell me? It was *her* job; not old lady Winnie's. What was that name she gave me—Rogers of Conduit Street? Hell! I'm likely to go there!

He had recovered his spirits when he reached home. He flourished the cheque under Christine's nose.

"See that, my good woman! Remember when I came running in with that first wretched three and a bender from the surgery? Bah! That's what I say to it now—bah! This is real money, gen-u-ine fees, like a first-rate M.D., M.R.C.P. ought to be earning. Twelve guineas for talking nicely to Winnie the Pooh, and innocuously inoculating her with Glickert's Eptone."

"What's that?" she asked smiling; then suddenly she was doubtful. "Isn't that the stuff I've heard you run down so much?"

His face altered, he frowned at her, completely at a loss. She had made the one remark he did not wish to hear. All at once he felt angry, not with himself, but with her.

"Blast it, Chris! You're *never* satisfied!" He turned and banged out of the room. For the rest of that day he was in a sulky humour. But next day he cheered up. He went then to Rogers, in Conduit Street.

V

He was self-conscious as a schoolboy when, a fortnight later, he came down in one of his two new suits. It was a dark double-breasted grey, worn, on Rogers' suggestion, with a wing collar and a dark bow tie which picked up the shade of the grey. There was not the shadow of a doubt, the Conduit Street tailor knew his job; and the mention of Captain Sutton's name had made him do it thoroughly.

This morning, as it fell out, Christine was not looking her best. She had a slight sore throat and had wound her old scarf protectively around her throat and head. She was pouring his coffee when the radiance of his presence burst upon her. For a moment she was too staggered to speak.

"Why Andrew!" she gasped. "You look wonderful. Are you going anywhere?"

"Going anywhere? I'm going on my rounds, my work, of course!" Being self-conscious made him almost snappy. "Well! Do you like it?"

"Yes," she said, not quickly enough to please him. "It's—it's frightfully smart—but," she smiled, "somehow it doesn't quite seem *you*!"

"You'd rather keep me looking like a tramp, I suppose."

She was silent, her hand, raising her cup, suddenly contracted so that the knuckles showed white. Ah! he thought, I got her there. He finished breakfast and entered the consulting room.

Five minutes later she followed him there, scarf still round her throat, her eyes hesitant, pleading.

"Darling," she said, "please don't misunderstand me! I'm delighted to see you in a new suit. I want you to have everything, everything that's best for you. I'm sorry I said that a moment ago; but you see—I'm accustomed to you—oh! it's awfully hard to explain—but I've always identified you as—now *please* don't misunderstand me—as someone who doesn't give a hang about how he looks or how people think he looks. You remember that Epstein head we saw. That it wouldn't have looked quite the same if—oh!—if it had been trimmed and polished up?"

He answered abruptly.

"I'm not an Epstein head."

She made no reply. Lately, he had been difficult to reason with and, hurt at this misunderstanding, she did not know what to say. Still hesitating, she turned away.

Three weeks later, when Miss Everett's niece came to spend a few weeks in London, he was rewarded for his wise observance of the elder lady's hint. On a pretext Miss Everett summoned him to Park Gardens, where she scanned him with severe approval. He could almost see her passing him as a fit candidate for her recommendation. On the following day he received a call from Mrs. Sutton who, since the condition ran, apparently, in the family, wished the same hay-fever treatment as her aunt. This time he had no compunction about injecting the useless eptone of the useful Messrs. Glickert. He made an excellent impression upon Mrs. Sutton. And before the end of that same month he was called to a friend of Miss Everett's who also occupied a flat in Park Gardens.

Andrew was highly diverted with himself. He was winning, winning, winning. In his straining eagerness for success he forgot how contrary was his progress to all that he had hitherto believed. His vanity was touched. He felt alert and confident. He did not pause to reflect that this rolling snowball of his high-class practice had been started, in the first place, by a fat little German woman behind the counter of a ham-and-beef shop near that vulgar Mussleburgh Market. Indeed, almost before he had time to reflect at all, the snowball took a further downhill roll—another and more exciting opportunity was offered to his grasp.

One afternoon in June, the zero hour between two o'clock and four, when nothing of consequence normally occurred, he was sitting in the consulting room, totalling his receipts for the past month, when suddenly the phone rang. Three seconds and he was at the instrument.

"Yes, yes! This is Doctor Manson speaking."

A voice, anguished and palpitant, came back to him.

"Oh, Doctor Manson! I'm relieved to find you in. This is Mr. Winch! Mr. Winch of Laurier's. We've had a slight mishap to one of our customers. Could you come? Could you come at once?"

"I'll be there in four minutes." Andrew clicked back the receiver and sprang for his hat. A 33 bus, hurtling outside, solidly sustained his impetuous leap. In four minutes and a half he was inside the revolving doors of Laurier's, met by an anxious Miss Cramb, and escorted over swimming surfaces of green-piled carpet, past long gilt mirrors and satinwood panelling against which, as if by chance, there could be seen one small hat on its stand, a lacy scarf, an ermine evening wrap.

As they hastened, with rapid earnestness, Miss Cramb explained:—

"It's Miss le Roy, Doctor Manson. One of our customers. Not mine, thank goodness, she's always giving trouble. But, Doctor Manson, you see I spoke to Mr. Winch about you—"

"Thanks!"—brusquely—he could still on occasion be brusque. "What's happened?"

"She seems—oh, Doctor Manson—she seems to have had a fit in the fit-fitting-room!"

At the head of the broad staircase she surrendered him to Mr. Winch, pinkly agitated, who fluttered:—

"This way, Doctor—this way—I hope you can do something. It's most dreadfully unfortunate—"

Into the fitting-room,—warm, exquisitely carpeted in a lighter shade of green, with gilt-and-green-panelled walls,—a crowd of twittering girls, a gilt chair upturned, a towel thrown down, a spilled glass of water, pandemonium... And there, the centre of it all, Miss le Roy, the woman in the fit. She lay on the floor, rigid, with spasmodic clutchings of her hands and sudden stiffenings of her feet. From time to time a straining, intimidating crowing broke from her tense throat.

As Andrew entered with Mr. Winch one of the older assistants in the group burst into tears.

"It wasn't my fault," she sobbed. "I only pointed out to Miss le Roy it was the design she chose herself—"

"Oh, dear. Oh, dear," muttered Mr. Winch. "This is dreadful, dreadful. Shall I—shall I ring for the ambulance?"

"No, not yet," Andrew said in a peculiar tone. He bent down beside Miss le Roy. She was very young, about twenty-four, with blue eyes and washed-out silky hair all tumbled under her askew hat. Her rigidity, her convulsive spasms were increasing.

On the other side of her knelt another woman, with dark concerned eyes, apparently her friend. "Oh, Toppy, Toppy," she kept murmuring.

"Please clear the room," said Andrew suddenly. "I'd like everyone out but—" his eye fell upon the dark young woman—"but this lady here."

The girls went, a trifle unwillingly—it had been pleasurable diversion assisting at Miss le Roy's fit. Miss Cramb, even Mr. Winch, removed themselves from the room. The moment they had gone the convulsions became terrifying.

"This is an extremely serious case," Andrew said, speaking very distinctly. Miss le Roy's eyeballs rolled towards him. "Get me a chair, please."

The fallen chair was righted, in the centre of the room, by the other woman. Then slowly and with great sympathy, supporting her by the armpits, Andrew helped the convulsed Miss le Roy upright into the chair. He held her head erect.

"There," he said with greater sympathy. Then, taking the flat of his hand, he hit her a resounding smack upon the cheek. It was his most courageous action for many months, and remained so—alas!—for many months to come.

Miss le Roy stopped crowing, the spasm ceased, her rolling eyeballs righted themselves. She gazed at him in pained, in infantile bewilderment. Before she could relapse he took his hand again and struck her on the other cheek. Smack! The anguish in Miss le Roy's face was ludicrous. She dithered, seemed about to crow again, and then began, gently, to cry.

Turning to her friend she wept: "Darling, I want to go home."

Andrew gazed apologetically at the dark young woman, who now regarded him with restrained yet singular interest.

"Sorry," he muttered. "It was the only way. Bad hysteria—carpopedal spasms. She might have harmed herself—I hadn't an anaesthetic or anything. And anyway—it worked."

"Yes, it worked."

"Let her cry this out," Andrew said. "Good safety-valve. She'll be all right in a few minutes."

"Wait though—" quickly. "You must see her home."

"Very well," Andrew said, in his busiest professional tone.

In five minutes' time Toppy le Roy was able to make good her face, a lengthy operation punctuated by a few desultory sobs.

"I don't look too foul, do I, darling?" she inquired of her friend. Of Andrew she took no notice whatsoever.

They left the fitting room thereafter, and their progress through the long showroom was sheer sensation. Wonder and relief left Mr. Winch almost speechless. He did not know, he would never know how this had come about, how the writhing paralytic had been made to walk. He followed, babbling deferential words. As Andrew passed through the main entrance behind the two women he wrung him fervently with a spongy hand.

The taxi took them along Bayswater Road in the direction of Marble Arch. There was not even pretence of speech. Miss le Roy was sulking now, like a spoiled child who has been punished, and she was still jumpy—from time to time, her hands and the muscles of her face gave slight involuntary twitches. She was, now that she could be seen more normally, very thin and almost pretty in a scrawny little way. Her clothes were beautiful yet, despite them, she seemed to Andrew exactly like a young pulled chicken, through which traces of electric current periodically passed. He was himself nervous, conscious of the awkward situation, yet determined in his own interests to take advantage of it to the full.

The taxi rounded the Marble Arch, ran alongside Hyde Park, and, wheeling to the left, they drew up before a house in Green Street. Then, almost immediately, they were inside. The house took Andrew's breath away; he had never imagined anything so luxurious—the wide soft-pinewood hall, the cabinet gorgeous with jade, the strange single painting set in a costly panel, the reddish-gold lacquer chairs, the wide settees, the skin-thin faded rugs.

Toppy le Roy flung herself down on a satin cushioned sofa, still ignoring Andrew, and tugged off her little hat which she flung on the floor.

"Press the bell, darling, I must have a drink. Thank God, Father isn't home."

Quickly, a manservant brought cocktails. When he had gone Toppy's friend considered Andrew thoughtfully—almost, but not quite, smiling.

"I think we ought to explain ourselves to you, Doctor. It's all been rather hurried. I'm Mrs. Lawrence. Toppy here—Miss le Roy—had rather a row over a dress she's having specially designed for the Arts Charity Ball and—well! she's been doing too much lately, she's a very nervy little person—and the long and the short of it is that although Toppy's very cross with you we're frightfully indebted to you for getting us back here. And I'm going to have another cocktail."

"Me too," said Toppy peevishly. "That bloody Laurier woman. I'll tell Father to ring up and get her sacked! Oh, no I won't!" As she tilted her second cocktail a smile of gratification slowly overspread her face. "I did give them something to think about, though, didn't I, Frances! I simply went *wild*! That look on old Mamma Winch's face was too, too funny." Her scraggy little frame shook with laughter. She met Andrew's eyes without ill-will. "Go on, Doctor. Laugh! It was priceless."

"No, I don't think it was so amusing." He spoke quickly, anxious to explain himself, establish his position, convince her she was ill. "You really had a bad attack. I'm sorry I had to treat you as I did. If I'd had an anaesthetic I'd have given you that. Much less—less annoying for you. And please don't imagine that I think you tried to bring on that attack. Hysteria—well, that's what it was—is a definite syndrome. People oughtn't to be unsympathetic about it. It's a condition of the nervous system. You see, you're extremely run-down, Miss le Roy, all your reflexes are on edge; you're in a very nervous state."

"That's perfectly true," Frances Lawrence nodded. "You've been doing far too much lately, Toppy."

"Would you really have given me chloroform?" Toppy asked Andrew in childish wonder. "That would have been fun."

"But seriously, Toppy," Mrs. Lawrence said, "I wish you'd take yourself up."

"You sound like Father," Toppy said, losing her good humour.

There was a pause. Andrew had finished his cocktail. He put the glass down on the carved pine mantelpiece behind him. There seemed nothing more for him to do.

"Well!" he said effectively, "I must get on with my work. Please take my advice, Miss le Roy. Have a light meal, go to bed, and—since I cannot be of any further service to you—call in your own doctor to-morrow. Good-by."

Mrs. Lawrence accompanied him into the hall, her manner so unhurried that he was obliged to restrain the busy briskness of his exit. She was tall and slim, with rather high shoulders and a small elegant head. In her dark, beautifully waved hair a few iron-grey strands gave her a curious distinction. Yet she was quite young; not more than twenty-seven, he was sure. Despite her height she had fine bones; her wrists especially were small and fine; indeed, her whole figure seemed flexible, exquisitely tempered, like a fencer's. She gave him her hand, her greenish hazel eyes fixed upon him in that faint, friendly, unhurried smile.

"I only wished to tell you how I admired your new line of treatment." Her lips twitched. "Don't give it up on any account. I foresee you making it a crashing success."

Walking down Green Street to pick up a bus he saw to his amazement that it was nearly five o'clock. He had spent three hours in the company of these two women. He ought to be able to charge a really big fee for that! And yet, despite this elevating thought—so symptomatic of his brave new outlook—he felt confused, strangely dissatisfied. Had he really made the most of his chance? Mrs. Lawrence had seemed to like him. But you never could tell with people like that. What a marvellous house, too!

Suddenly he gritted his teeth in angry exasperation. Not only had he omitted to leave his card; he had forgotten even to tell them who he was. As he took his seat in the crowded bus beside an old workman in soiled overalls he blamed himself bitterly for missing a golden opportunity.

vi

The following morning, at quarter-past eleven, as he was on the point of taking his departure on a round of cheap visits centred about the Mussleburgh Market, the telephone rang. A manservant's voice, gravely solicitous, purred at him.

"Doctor Manson, sir! Ah! Miss le Roy wishes to know, sir, what time you will be calling on her to-day. Ah! Excuse me sir, hold on—Mrs. Lawrence will speak to you herself."

Andrew hung on, with a quick throbbing excitement, while Mrs. Lawrence talked to him in friendly fashion, explaining that they were expecting him to call, without fail.

As he came away from the phone he told himself exultantly that he hadn't missed the opportunity yesterday; he hadn't—no, he hadn't missed it after all.

He dropped all his other calls, urgent or otherwise, and went straight to the house in Green Street. And here, for the first time, he met Joseph le Roy. He found Le Roy impatiently awaiting him in the jade-bedizened hall, a bald thickset figure, downright and bejowled, who abused his cigar like a man who has no time to lose. In one second his eyes bored into Andrew, a swift surgical operation which ended to his satisfaction. He then spoke forcibly in a colonial tongue.

"See here, doc, I'm in a hurry. Mrs. Lawrence had a hell of a bother tracking you down this morning. I understand you're a clever young fellow and you don't stand any nonsense. You're married too, aren't you? That's good. Now you take my girl in hand. Get her right, get her strong, get all this damn hysteria out of her system. Don't spare anything. I can pay. Good-by."

Joseph le Roy was a New Zealander. And despite his money, his Green Street house, and his exotic little Toppy, it was not difficult to believe the truth—that his great-grandfather was one Michael Cleary, an illiterate farm hand on the lands around Greymouth Harbour, who was known colloquially to his fellow "scrubbies" as Leary. Joseph le Roy had certainly faced up to life as Joe Leary, a boy whose first job was that of "milker" on the great Greymouth farms. But Joe was born, as he said himself, to milk more than cows. And thirty years later, in the top-floor office of the first Auckland skyscraper, it was Joseph le Roy who put his signature to the deal unifying the Island dairy farms into a great dried milk combine.

It was a magic scheme—the Cremogen Combine. At this time dried milk goods were unknown, commercially unorganized. It was Le Roy who saw their possibility, who led their attack on the world market, advertising them as God-given nourishment for infants and invalids. The cream of the achievement lay, not in Joe's products, but in his own rich audacity. The surplus skim milk, which had been poured down the drain or given to the pigs in hundreds of New Zealand farms, was now sold in the cities of the world, in Joe's neat brightly papered tins, as Cremogen, Cremax, and Cremefat, at three times the price of pure fresh milk.

Co-director in the Le Roy Combine, and manager of the English interests, was Jack Lawrence, who had been, illogically enough, a Guards officer before he went into business in the city. Yet it was more than the bare association of commerce which drew Mrs. Lawrence and Toppy together. Frances, rich in her own right and far more at home in the smart society of London than Toppy—who occasionally betrayed her brushwood antecedents—had an amused affection for the *enfant gâté*. When Andrew went upstairs after his interview with Le Roy she was waiting for him outside Toppy's room.

Indeed, on subsequent days Frances Lawrence was usually present at the time of his visit, helping him with his exciting, wilful patient, ready to see an improvement in Toppy, insistent that she continue with the treatment, asking when they might expect his next call.

Grateful to Mrs. Lawrence, he was still diffident enough to feel it strange that this patrician, self-admittedly selective person whom, before he came to see her photographs in the illustrated weeklies, he knew to be exclusive, should have even this mild interest in him. Her wide and rather sulky mouth usually expressed hostility towards people who were not her intimates, yet for some reason she was never hostile to him. He had an extraordinary desire, greater than curiosity, to fathom her character, her personality. He seemed to know nothing of the real Mrs. Lawrence. It was a delight to watch the controlled actions of her limbs, as she moved about the room. She was always at ease, watchful in everything she did, with a mind behind her friendly guarded eyes, despite the graceful casualness of her speech.

He hardly realized that the suggestion was hers, yet—though he said nothing to Christine, who still contentedly balanced her housekeeping budget in shillings and pence—he began to ask himself impatiently how any doctor could develop a high-class practice without a smart car? It was ridiculous to think of him stepping along Green Street, carrying his own bag, with dust on his shoes, facing the slightly superior manservant, without a car. He had the brick garage at the back of his house, which would considerably reduce the cost of upkeep, and there were firms who specialized in supplying cars to doctors, admirable firms who did not mind graciously deferring the terms of payment.

Three weeks later a brown folding-roof coupé, brand new and darkly glittering, drew up at 9 Chesborough Terrace. Easing himself from the driving seat, Andrew ran up the stairs of his house.

"Christine!" he called out, trying to suppress the gloating excitement in his voice. "Christine! Come and see something!"

He had meant to stagger her. And he succeeded.

"Goodness!" She clutched his arm. "Is it *ours*? Oh! what a beauty!"

"Isn't she? Look *out*, dear, don't handle the paintwork! It's—it's liable to mark the varnish!" He smiled at her in quite his old way. "Pretty good surprise, eh, Chris? Me getting it and licencing it and everything and never saying a word to you. Step in, lady, and I'll demonstrate. She goes like a bird."

She could not admire the little car enough as he took her, bareheaded, on an easy spin round the Square. Four minutes later they were back, standing on the pavement, while he still feasted his eyes upon the treasure. Their moments of intimacy, of understanding and happiness together, were so rare now that she was loath to relinquish this one.

She murmured: "It'll be so easy for you to get about now, dear." Then again, diffidently: "And if we could get out a little bit into the country, say on Sundays, into the woods—oh, it would be *wonderful*."

"Of course," he answered absently. "But it's really for the practice. We can't go gadding about, getting mud all over it!" He was thinking of the effect this dashing little coupé would have upon his patients.

The main effect, however, was beyond his expectation. On Thursday of the following week, as he came out of the heavy glass and iron-grilled door of Number 17a Green Street, he ran straight into Freddie Hampton.

"Hello, Hampton," he said casually. He could not repress a thrill of satisfaction at the sight of Hampton's face. At first Hampton had barely recognized him, and as he did so, his expression, falling through various degrees of surprise, was still frankly nonplussed.

"Why, hello!" said Freddie. "What are you doing here?"

"Patient," Andrew answered, jerking his head backwards in the direction of Number 17a. "I've got Joe le Roy's daughter on my hands."

"Joe le Roy!"

That exclamation alone was worth a lot to Manson. He put a proprietary hand on the door of his beautiful new coupé.

"Which way are you going? Can I drop you anywhere?"

Freddie revived himself quickly. He was seldom at a loss, and never for any length of time. Indeed, in thirty seconds, his opinion of Manson, his whole idea of Manson's usefulness to him, had undergone a swift and unexpected revolution.

"Yes," he smiled companionably. "I was going along to Bentinck Street—to Ida Sherrington's Home. Walking to keep the old figure down. But I'll step in with you."

There was a pause for a few minutes while they ran across Bond Street. Hampton was thinking hard. He had welcomed Andrew effusively to London because he hoped Manson's practice might occasionally provide him with a three-guinea consultation at Queen Anne Street. But now the change in his old classmate, the car, and above all the mention of Joe le Roy—the name had for him infinitely more worldly significance than it had for Andrew—showed him his mistake. There were Manson's ideal qualifications, too—useful, extremely useful. Looking astutely ahead, Freddie saw a better, an altogether more profitable basis for cooperation between Andrew and himself. He would go carefully of course, for Manson was a touchy, uncertain devil.

He said:—

"Why don't you come in with me and meet Ida? She's a useful person to know, though she keeps the worst nursing home in London. Oh! I don't know! She's probably as good as the rest of them. And she certainly charges more."

"Yes?"

"Come in with me and see my patient. She's harmless—old Mrs. Raeburn. Ivory and I are doing a few tests on her. You're strong on lungs, aren't you? Come along and examine her chest. It'll please her enormously. And it'll be five guineas for you."

"What! You mean...? But what's the matter with her chest?"

"Nothing much," Freddie smiled. "Don't look so stricken! She's probably got a touch of senile bronchitis! And she'd love to see you! That's how we do it here. Ivory and Freedman and I. You really ought to be in on it, Manson. We won't talk about it now—yes, round that first corner there!—but it would amaze you how it works out."

Andrew drew up the car at the house indicated by Hampton, an ordinary town dwelling-house, tall and narrow, which had obviously never been intended for its present purpose. Indeed, gazing at the busy street, along which the traffic racketed and hooted, it was difficult to imagine how any sick person could find peace here. It looked precisely the place to provoke rather than to cure a nervous breakdown. Andrew mentioned this to Hampton as they mounted the steps to the front door.

"I know, my dear fellow," Freddie agreed with ready cordiality. "But they're all the same. This little bit of the West End is jammed with them. You see, we must have them convenient to ourselves." He grinned. "Ideal if they were out somewhere quiet, but—for instance—what surgeon would drive ten miles every day to see his case for five minutes? Oh! You'll get to know about our little West End sick bays in due course." He drew up in the narrow hall into which they passed. "They've all got three smells, you observe—anaesthetics, cooking, and excreta—logical sequence—forgive me, old man! And now meet Ida."

With the air of a man who knows his way about, he led the way into a constricted office on the ground floor, where a little woman in a mauve uniform and a stiff white headdress sat at a small desk.

"Morning, Ida," Freddie exclaimed between flattery and familiarity. "Doing your sums?"

She raised her eyes, saw him, and smiled good-naturedly. She was short, stout, and extremely full-blooded. But her bright red face was so thickly covered with powder that the result was a mauve complexion almost the colour of her uniform. She had a look of coarse bustling vitality, of knowing humour, of pluck. Her teeth were false and ill-fitting. Her hair was grizzled. Somehow, it was easy to suspect her of a strong vocabulary, to imagine her performing admirably as the keeper of a second-rate night club.

Yet Ida Sherrington's nursing home was the most fashionable in London. Half the peerage had been to Ida; and society women, racing men, famous barristers, and diplomats. You had only to pick up the morning paper to read that yet another bright young person famous on stage or screen had left her appendix safely in Ida's motherly hands. She dressed all her nurses in a delicate shade of mauve, paid her wine butler two hundred pounds and her chef twice that sum a year. The prices which she charged her patients were fantastic. Forty guineas for a room each week was not an uncommon figure. And on top of that came extras, the chemist's bill—often a matter of pounds—the special night nurse, the theatre fee. But when argued with, Ida had one answer which she often adorned with a free and easy adjective. She had her own worries, with cuts and percentages to be paid out, and often she felt it was she who was being bled.

Ida had a soft side for the younger members of the profession and she greeted Manson agreeably as Freddie babbled:—

"Take a good look at him. He'll soon be sending you so many patients you'll overflow into the Plaza Hotel."

"The Plaza overflows into me." Ida nodded her headdress meaningly.

"Ha! Ha!" Freddie laughed. "That's pretty good—I must tell old Freedman that one. Paul'll appreciate it. Come on Manson. We'll go up top."

The cramped lift, just wide enough to hold a wheeled stretcher diagonally, took them to the fourth floor. The passage was narrow; trays stood outside the doors, and vases of flowers wilting in the hot atmosphere. They went into Mrs. Raeburn's room.

She was a woman of over sixty, propped up on her pillows, expectant of the doctor's visit, holding in her hand a slip of paper on which she had written certain symptoms experienced during the night, together with questions which she wished to ask. Andrew placed her unerringly as the elderly hypochondriac, Charcot's *malade au petit morceau de papier.*

Seated on the bed, Freddie talked to her, felt her pulse—no more—listened to her and gaily reassured her. He told her Mr. Ivory would be calling with the results of some highly scientific tests in the afternoon. He asked her to allow his colleague, Doctor Manson, whose speciality was lungs, to examine her chest. Mrs. Raeburn was flattered. She enjoyed it all very much. It emerged that she had been in Hampton's hands for two years. She was wealthy, without relatives, and spent her time equally between exclusive private hotels and West End nursing homes.

"Lord!" Freddie exclaimed as they left the room. "You've no idea what a gold mine that old woman has been to us. We've taken nuggets out of her."

Andrew did not answer. The atmosphere of this place slightly sickened him. There was nothing wrong with the old lady's lungs, and only her touching look of gratitude towards Freddie saved the matter from being downright dishonest. He tried to convince himself. Why should he be such a stickler? He would never make a success of himself if he continued intolerant, opinionative. And Freddie had meant it kindly, giving him the chance to examine this patient.

He shook hands amicably enough with Hampton before stepping into his coupé. And at the end of the month, when he received a neatly written cheque from Mrs. Raeburn— with her best thanks—for five guineas, he was able to laugh at his silly scruples. He enjoyed receiving cheques now, and to his extreme satisfaction more and more of them were coming his way.

vii

The practice, which had shown a promising increase, now began a rapid, almost electrifying expansion in all directions, the effect of which was to sweep Andrew more swiftly with the stream. In a sense he was the victim of his own intensity. He had always been poor. In the past, his obstinate individualism had brought him nothing but defeat. Now he could justify himself with the amazing proofs of his material success.

Shortly after his emergency call to Laurier's he had a highly gratifying interview with Mr. Winch, and thereafter more of the Laurier Juniors, and even some of the Seniors, came to consult him. They came chiefly for trivial complaints, yet once the girls had visited him it was strange how frequently they reappeared—his manner was so kind, so cheering, so brisk. His surgery receipts soared. Soon he managed to have the front of the house repainted, and with the help of one of those firms of surgical outfitters—all of them burning to assist young practitioners to enlarge their incomes—he was able to refurnish his surgery and consulting room with a new couch, a padded swing chair, a dinky rubber tyred trolley, and sundry elegantly scientific cabinets in white enamel and glass.

The manifest prosperity of the freshly cream-painted house, of his car, of this glitteringly modern equipment, soon traversed the neighbourhood, bringing back many of the "good" patients who had consulted Doctor Foy in the past but had gradually dropped off when the old doctor and his consulting room became progressively dingy.

The days of waiting, of hanging about, were finished for Andrew. At the evening surgeries it was as much as he could do to keep going—the front bell purring, the surgery door *pinging*, patients waiting for him back and front, causing him to dash between the surgery and the consulting room. The next step came inevitably. He was forced to evolve a scheme to save his time.

"Listen, Chris," he said one morning. "I've just struck on something that's going to help me a lot in these rush hours. You know—when I've seen a patient in the surgery I come back into the house to make up the medicine. Takes me five minutes usually. And it's a shocking waste of time—when I might be using it to polish off one of the 'good' patients waiting to see me in the consulting room. Well, d'you get my scheme? From now on, you're my dispenser!"

She looked at him with a startled contraction of her brows.

"But I don't know anything about making up medicine."

He smiled reassuringly.

"That's all right, dear. I've prepared a couple of nice stock mixtures. All you have to do is fill the bottles, label and wrap them."

"But—" Christine's perplexity showed in her eyes. "Oh, I want to help you Andrew, only—do you really believe—"

"Don't you see I've *got* to?" His gaze avoided hers. He drank the rest of his coffee irritably. "I know I used to talk a lot of hot air about medicine at Aberalaw. All theories! I'm—I'm a practical physician now. Besides, all these Laurier girls are anaemic. A good iron mixture won't do them any harm."

Before she could answer the sound of the surgery bell had pulled him away.

In the old days she would have argued, taken a firm stand. But now, sadly, she reflected on the reversal of their earlier relationship. She no longer influenced, guided him. It was he who drove ahead.

She began to stand in the cubbyhole of the dispensary during those hectic surgery periods, waiting for his tense exclamation, in his rapid transit between "good" and surgery patients—"Iron!" or "Alba!" or "Carminative!" or sometimes, when she would protest that the iron mixture had run out, a strung-up, significant bark: "Anything! Damn it! *Anything at all!*"

Often the surgery was not over until half-past nine. Then they made up the book, Doctor Foy's heavy ledger, which had only been half used when they took over the practice.

"My God! What a day, Chris!" he gloated. "D'you remember that first measly three and six I took, like a shaky schoolboy? Well, to-day—to-day, we took over eight pounds *cash.*"

He tucked the money, heavy piles of silver and a few notes, into the little Afrikander tobacco sack which Doctor Foy had used as his moneybag, and locked it in the middle drawer of the desk. As with the ledger, he kept on using this old bag in order to continue his luck.

Now, indeed, he forgot all about his early doubts and praised his acumen in taking over the practice.

"We've got it absolutely gilt-edged every way, Chris," he exulted. "A paying surgery and a sound middle-class connection. And on top of that I'm building up a first-rate consultant practice on my own. You just watch where we're going."

On the first of October he was able to tell her to refurnish the house. After his morning surgery he said—with impressive casualness, his new manner:—

"I'd like you to go up West to-day, Chris. Go to Hudson's—or to Ostley's if you like it better. Go to the best place. And get all the new furniture you want. Get a couple of new bedroom suites, drawing-room suite, get *everything*."

She glanced at him in silence as he lit a cigarette, smiling.

"That's one of the joys of making money, being able to give you everything you want. Don't think I'm mean. Lord, no! You've been a little brick, Chris, the whole way through our bad times. Now we're just beginning to enjoy our good times."

"By ordering expensive shiny furniture and—and hair-stuffed three-piece suites from Ostley's."

He missed the bitterness in her tone. He laughed.

"That's right, dear. It's high time we got rid of our old Regency junk."

Tears sprang to her eyes. She flashed:—

"You didn't think it was junk at Aberalaw. And it isn't, either. Oh! those were real days, those were happy days!"

With a choking sob she spun round and left the room.

He stared after her in blank surprise. Her moods had been queer recently—uncertain and depressed, with sudden bursts of incomprehensible bitterness. He sensed that they were drifting away from each other, losing that mysterious unity, that hidden bond of comradeship which had always existed between them. Well! It was not his fault. He was doing his best, his utmost. He thought angrily, my getting on means nothing to her, nothing. But he could not dwell upon the unreasonableness, the injustice of her behaviour. He had a full list of calls before him and, since it was Tuesday, his usual visit to the bank.

Twice a week, regularly, he dropped in at the bank to make payments into his account, for he knew it was unwise to let cash accumulate in his desk. He could not but contrast these pleasant visits with his experience in Blaenelly when, as a down-at-heel assistant, he had been humiliated by Aneurin Rees. Here Mr. Wade, the manager, always gave him a warmly deferential smile and often an invitation to smoke a cigarette in his private room.

"If I may say so, Doctor, without being personal, you're doing remarkably nicely. Round here we can do with a go-ahead doctor, who's just got the right amount of conservatism. Like yourself, Doctor, if I may say so. Now these Southern Railway Guaranteed we were discussing the other day..."

Wade's deference was merely one instance of the general upswing of opinion. He now found the other doctors of the district giving him a friendly salute as their coupés went past his own. At the autumn divisional meeting of the Medical Association, in that same room where, on his first appearance, he had been made to feel himself a pariah, he was welcomed, made much of, given a cigar by Doctor Ferrie, vice president of the division.

"Glad to see you with us, Doctor," fussed little red-faced Ferrie. "Did you approve of my speech? We've got to hold out for our fees. On night calls especially, I am taking a firm stand. The other night I was knocked up by a boy—a mere child of twelve, if you please. 'Come round quick Doctor,' he blubbers. 'Father's at work and my mother's taken awful bad.' You *know* that 2 A.M. conversation. And I'd never seen the kid in my life before. 'My dear boy,' says I, 'your mother's no patient of mine! Away and fetch me my half guinea and *then* I'll come.' Of course he never came back. I tell you, Doctor, this district is *terrible...*"

On the week after the divisional meeting Mrs. Lawrence rang him up. He always enjoyed the graceful inconsequence of her telephone conversations, but to-day, after mentioning that her husband was fishing in Ireland, that she might possibly be going later to join him there, she asked him, dropping out her invitation as though it were of no importance, to luncheon on the following Friday.

"Toppy'll be there. And one or two people—less dull, I think, than one usually meets. It might do you some good, perhaps, to know them."

He hung up the receiver between satisfaction and an odd irritation. In his heart he was piqued that Christine had not been invited too. Then, gradually, he came to see that it was not a social but really a business occasion. He must get about and make contacts, particularly amongst the class of people who would be present at this luncheon. And, in any case, Christine need know nothing at all of the affair. When Friday came he told her that he had a luncheon engagement with Hampton and jumped into his car, relieved. He forgot that he was an extremely bad liar.

Frances Lawrence's house was in Knightsbridge, in a quiet street, between Hans Place and Wilton Crescent. Though it had not the splendour of the Le Roy mansion, its restrained taste conveyed an equal sense of opulence. Andrew was late in arriving and most of the guests were already there: Toppy; Rosa Keane the novelist; Sir Dudley

Rumbold-Blane, M.D., F.R.C.P., famous physician and member of the board of Cremo Products; Nicol Watson, traveller and anthropologist, and several others of less alarming distinction.

He found himself at table beside a Mrs. Thornton, who lived, she told him, in Leicestershire, and who came up periodically to Brown's Hotel for a short season in town. Though he was now able calmly to sustain the ordeal of introductions, he was glad to regain his assurance under cover of her chatter, a maternal account of a foot injury received at hockey by her daughter Sybil, a schoolgirl at Roedean.

Giving one ear to Mrs. Thornton, who took his mute listening for interest, he still managed to hear something of the suave and witty conversation around him—Rosa Keane's acid pleasantries, Watson's fascinatingly graceful account of an expedition he had recently made through the Paraguayan interior. He admired also the ease with which Frances kept the talk moving, at the same time sustaining the measured pedantry of Sir Rumbold, who sat beside her. Once or twice he felt her eyes upon him, half-smiling, interrogative.

"Of course," Watson concluded his narrative with a deprecatory smile, "easily one's most devastating experience was to come home and run straight into an attack of influenza."

"Ha!" said Sir Rumbold. "So you've been a victim too." By the device of clearing his throat and placing his pince-nez upon his richly endowed nose, he gained the attention of the table. Sir Rumbold was at home in this position—for many years now the attention of the great British Public had been focussed upon him. It was Sir Rumbold who, a quarter of a century before, had staggered humanity by the declaration that a certain portion of man's intestine was not only useless but definitely harmful. Hundreds of people had rushed straight away to have the dangerous section removed and, though Sir Rumbold was not himself amongst this number, the fame of the operation, which the surgeons named the Rumbold-Blane excision, established his reputation as a dietician. Since then he had kept well to the front, successfully introducing to the nation bran food, Yourghout, and the lactic acid bacillus. Later he invented the Rumbold-Blane Mastication, and now, in addition to his activities on many company boards, he wrote the menus for the famous Railey chain of restaurants: *Come, Ladies and Gentlemen, Let Sir Rumbold-Blane, M.D., F.R.C.P., Help You Choose Your Calories!* Many were the muttered grumbles amongst more legitimate healers that Sir Rumbold should have been scored off the *Register* years ago: to which the answer manifestly was—what would the *Register* be without Sir Rumbold?

He now said, glancing paternally at Frances:—

"One of the most interesting features of this recent epidemic has been the spectacular therapeutic effect of Cremogen. I had occasion to say the same thing at our Company meeting last week. We have—aha!—no cure for influenza. And in the absence of cure, the only way to resist its murderous invasion is to develop a high state of resistance, a vital defence of the body against the inroads of the disease. I happened to say, I flatter myself rather aptly, that we had proved incontestably, not on guinea pigs—aha! aha!—like our laboratory friends—but on *human beings*, the phenomenal power of Cremogen in organizing and energizing the vital antagonism of the body."

Watson turned to Andrew with his odd smile. "What do you think of Cremo production, Doctor?"

Caught unawares, Andrew found himself saying:—

"It's as good a way of taking skim milk as any other."

Rosa Keane, with a swift approving side-glance, was unkind enough to laugh. Frances was smiling too. Hurriedly, Sir Rumbold passed to a description of his recent visit, as a guest of the Northern Medical Union, to the Trossachs.

Otherwise the luncheon was harmonious. Andrew eventually found himself joining freely in the conversation. Before he took his leave from her drawing-room Frances had a word with him.

"You really do shine," she murmured, "out of the consulting room. Mrs. Thornton hasn't been able to drink her coffee for telling me about you. I have a strange presentiment that you've bagged her—is that the phrase?—as a patient."

With that remark ringing in his ear, he went home feeling that he was much the better, and Christine none the worse, for the adventure.

On the following morning, however, at half-past ten, he had an unpleasant shock.

Freddie Hampton rang him to inquire briskly: "Enjoy your lunch yesterday? How did I know? Why, you old dog, haven't you seen this morning's *Tribune*?"

Dismayed, Andrew went directly into the waiting-room, where the papers were laid out when Christine and he had finished with them. For the second time he went through the *Tribune*, one of the better-known pictorial dailies. Suddenly he started. How had he missed it before? There, on a page devoted to society gossip, was a photograph of Frances Lawrence with a paragraph describing her luncheon party of the day before, his name amongst the guests.

With a chagrined face he slipped the sheet from the others, crushed it into a ball, flung it in the fire. Then he realized that Christine had already read the paper. He frowned in an access of vexation. Though he felt sure that she had not seen this confounded paragraph, he went scowling into his consulting room.

But Christine had seen the paragraph. And, after a momentary bewilderment, the hurt of it struck her to the heart. Why had he not told her? Why? Why? She would not have minded his going to this stupid lunch. She tried to reassure herself—it was all too trivial to cause her such anxiety and pain. But she saw, with a dull ache, that its implications were not trivial.

When he went out on his round she attempted to go on with her work in the house. But she could not. She wandered into his consulting room, from there into his surgery, with the same heavy oppression in her breast. She began in a desultory fashion to dust the surgery. Beside the desk lay his old medical bag, the first he had ever possessed, which he had used at Blaenelly, carrying it along the Rows, using it in his emergency calls down the mine. She touched it with a strange tenderness. He had a new bag now, a finer one. It was part of this new, this finer practice which he was striving after so feverishly, and which, deep in her heart, she so distrusted. She knew it was useless to attempt to speak to him about her misgivings on his behalf. He was so touchy now—the sign of his own conflict—a word from her would set him off, instantly provoke a quarrel. She must do her best in other ways.

It was Saturday forenoon and she had promised to take Florrie with her when she set out to do her shopping. Florrie was a bright little girl and Christine had become attached to her. She could hear her waiting now, at the head of the basement stairs, sent up by her mother, very clean and wearing a fresh frock, in a state of great preparedness. They often went out together like this on a Saturday.

She felt better in the open air with the child holding her hand, walking down the Market, talking to her friends amongst the hawkers, buying fruit, flowers, trying to think of something especially nice to please Andrew.

Yet the wound was still open. Why, why had he not told her? And why had she not been there? She recollected that first occasion at Aberalaw, when they had gone to the Vaughans and it had taken all her efforts to drag him with her. How different was the position now! Was she to blame? Had she changed, withdrawn into herself, become in some way antisocial? She did not think so. She still liked meeting and knowing people, irrespective of who or what they were. Her friendship with Mrs. Vaughan still persisted in their regular exchange of letters.

But actually, though she felt hurt and slighted, her main concern was less for herself than for him. She knew that rich people could be ill as well as poor, that it was possible for him to be as fine a doctor in Green Street, Mayfair, as in Cefen Row, Aberalaw. She did not demand the persistence of such heroic effects as leggings and his old Red Indian motorcycle. Yet she did feel with all her soul that in those days his idealism had been pure and wonderful, illuminating both their lives with a clear white flame. Now the flame had turned yellower and the globe of the lamp was smudged.

As she went into Frau Schmidt's she tried to erase the lines of worry from her brow. Nevertheless she found the woman looking at her sharply.

And presently Frau Schmidt grumbled: "You don't eat enough, my dear! You don't look as you should! And you haf a fine car now and money and everything. Look! I will make you taste this. It iss good!"

The long thin knife in her hand, she cut a slice of her famous boiled ham and made Christine eat a soft bread sandwich. At the same time Florrie was provided with an iced pastry. Frau Schmidt kept talking all the time.

"And now you want some Libtauer. Herr Doctor—he has eaten pounds of my cheese and he never grows tired of it. Some day I will ask him to write me a testimonial to put in my window. This is the cheese what has made me famous..."

Chuckling, Frau Schmidt ran on until they left her.

Outside, Christine and Florrie stood on the kerb waiting for the policeman on duty— it was their old friend Struthers—to signal them across. Christine kept a restraining hand on the impulsive Florrie's arm.

"You must always watch out for the traffic here," she cautioned. "What would your mother say if you were to get run over?"

Florrie, her mouth stuffed with the end of her pastry, considered this an excellent joke.

They were home at last and Christine began to undo the wrappings from her purchases. As she moved about the front room, putting the bronze chrysanthemums she had bought into a vase, she felt sad again.

Suddenly the telephone rang.

She went to answer it, her face still, her lips slightly drooping. For perhaps five minutes she was absent. When she returned her expression was transfigured. Her eyes were bright, excited. From time to time she glanced out of the window, eager for Andrew's return, her despondency forgotten in the good news she had received, news which was so important to him; yes, important to both of them. She had a happy conviction that nothing could have been more propitious. No better antidote to the poison of a facile success could ever have been decreed. And it was such an advance, such a real step up for him as well. Eagerly she went to the window again.

When he arrived she could not contain herself to wait but ran to meet him in the hall.

"Andrew! I've got a message for you from Sir Robert Abbey. He's just been on the telephone."

"Yes?" His face, which had drawn into sudden compunction at the sight of her, cleared.

"Yes! He rang up himself, wanted to speak to you. I told him who I was—oh! he was terribly nice—oh—oh! I'm telling you so badly. Darling! You're to be appointed to outpatients at the Victoria Hospital—immediately!"

His eyes filled slowly with excited realization.

"Why—that's good news, Chris."

"Isn't it, isn't it," she cried, delighted. "Your own work again—chances for research—everything you wanted on the Fatigue Board and didn't get!" She put her arms round his neck and hugged him.

He looked down at her, indescribably touched by her love, her generous unselfishness. He had a momentary pang.

"What a good soul you are, Chris! And—and what a lout I am!"

viii

Upon the fourteenth of the following month, Andrew began his duties in the outpatients department of the Victoria Chest Hospital. His days were Tuesdays and Thursdays, the hours from three until five o'clock in the afternoon. It was exactly like his old surgery days in Aberalaw, except that now all the cases which came to him were specialized lung and bronchial conditions. And he was, of course, to his great and secret pride, no longer a medical aid assistant but an honorary physician in one of the oldest and most famous hospitals in London.

The Victoria Hospital was unquestionably old. Situated in Battersea in a network of mean streets close to the Thames, it seldom caught, even in summer, more than a stray gleam of sunshine; while in winter its balconies, onto which the patients' beds were intended to be wheeled, were more often than not blanketed in river fog. Upon the gloomy, dilapidated façade was a great placard in red and white, which seemed obvious and redundant: VICTORIA HOSPITAL IS FALLING DOWN.

The outpatients department, where Andrew found himself, was, in part, a relic of the eighteenth century. Indeed, a pestle and mortar used by Doctor Lintel Hodges, honorary physician to the same section of the hospital from 1761 to 1793, was proudly exhibited in a glass case in the entrance hall. The untiled walls were painted a peculiar shade of dark chocolate, the uneven passages, though scrupulously clean, were so ill-ventilated that they sweated, and throughout all the rooms there hung the musty odour of sheer old age.

On his first day, he went round with Doctor Eustace Thoroughgood, the Senior Honorary, an elderly, pleasantly precise man of fifty, well under the middle height, with a small grey imperial and a kindly manner, rather like an agreeable churchwarden. Doctor Thoroughgood had his own wards in the hospital and under the existing system, a survival of old tradition—in which he was interestingly erudite—he was "responsible" for Andrew and for Doctor Milligan, the other Junior Honorary.

After their tour of the hospital he took Andrew to the long basement common room where, although it was barely four o'clock, the lights were already on. A fine fire blazed in the steel grate and on the linenfold walls there hung portraits of distinguished physicians to the hospital—Doctor Lintel Hodges, very pursy in his wig, in the place of honour above the mantelpiece. It was a perfect survival of a venerable and spacious past, and from the delicate dilation of his nostrils Doctor Thoroughgood—bachelor and churchwarden though he was—loved it as his own child.

They had a pleasant tea and much hot buttered toast with the other members of the staff. Andrew thought the house physicians very likeable youngsters. Yet as he noted their deference to Doctor Thoroughgood and himself he could not refrain from smiling at the recollection of his clashes with other "insolent pups," not so many months ago, in the frequent struggles to get his patients into hospital.

Seated next to him was a young man, Doctor Vallance, who had spent twelve months studying under the Mayo Brothers in the United States. Andrew and he began to talk about the famous Clinic and its system; then Andrew, with sudden interest, asked him if he had heard of Stillman while he was in America.

"Yes, of course," said Vallance. "They think a lot of him out there. He has no diploma of course, but the State has recognized him, making an exception in his case because of his accomplishments. He gets the most amazing results."

"Have you seen his clinic?"

"No," Vallance shook his head. "I didn't get as far as Oregon."

Andrew paused for a moment, wondering if he should speak. "I believe it's a most remarkable place," he said at length. "I happen to have been in touch with Stillman over a period of years—he first wrote me about a paper of mine published by the Association of American Hygiene. I've seen photographs and details of his clinic. One couldn't wish for a more ideal place to treat one's cases. High up, in the centre of a pine wood; isolated; glassed balconies, a special air-conditioning system to ensure perfect purity and constant temperature in winter..." Andrew broke off, deprecating his own enthusiasm, for a break in the general conversation made everything he said audible to the entire table. "When one thinks of our conditions in London, it seems an unattainable ideal."

Doctor Thoroughgood smiled with dry asperity.

"Our London physicians have always managed to get along very well in these same London conditions, Doctor Manson. We may not have the exotic devices of which you speak. But I venture to suggest that our solid, well-tried methods—though less spectacular—bring equally satisfactory and probably more lasting results."

Andrew, keeping his eyes lowered, did not answer. He felt that as a new member of the staff he had been indiscreet in voicing his opinion so openly. And Doctor Thoroughgood, to show that he had intended no snub, went on very pleasantly to turn the conversation. He talked about the art of cupping. This history of medicine had long been his special hobby and he had a mass of information on the subject of the surgeon-barbers of ancient London.

As they rose he declared agreeably to Andrew:—

"I actually have an authentic set of cups. I must show you them one day. It really is a shame cupping has gone out. It was—still is—an admirable way of inducing counterirritation."

Beyond that first slight breeze, Doctor Thoroughgood set himself out to be a sympathetic and helpful colleague. He was a sound physician, an almost unerring diagnostician, and he was always glad to have Andrew round his wards. But in treatment, his tidy mind resented the intrusion of the new. He would have nothing to do with tuberculin, holding that its therapeutic value was still completely unproved. He was chary of using pneumothorax and his percentage of inductions was the lowest in the hospital. He was, however, extremely liberal in the matter of cod-liver oil and malt. He prescribed it for all his patients.

Andrew forgot about Thoroughgood in beginning his own work. It was wonderful, he told himself, after months of waiting, to find himself starting again. He gave, at the outset, quite a good imitation of his old ardour and enthusiasm.

Inevitably his past work on the tubercular lesions induced by dust inhalation had brought him forward to the consideration of pulmonary tuberculosis as a whole. He planned vaguely, in conjunction with the Pirquet test, to investigate the earliest physical signs of the primary lesion. He had a wealth of material available in the undernourished children brought by their mothers in the hope of benefiting by Doctor Thoroughgood's well-known liberality with extract of malt.

And yet, though he tried very hard to convince himself, his heart was not in the work. He could not recapture the spontaneous enthusiasm of his inhalation investigations. He had far too much upon his mind, too many important cases in his practice, to be able to concentrate upon obscure signs which might not even exist. No one knew better than he how long it took to examine a case properly. And he was always in a hurry. This argument was unanswerable. Soon he fell into an attitude of admirable logic—humanly speaking, he simply could not do it.

The poor people who came to the dispensary did not demand much of him. His predecessor had, it appeared, been something of a bully, and so long as he prescribed generously and made an occasional joke his popularity was never in doubt. He got on, well, too, with Doctor Milligan, his opposite number, and it was not long before he found himself adopting Milligan's method of dealing with the regular patients. He would have them up, in a bunch, to his desk at the beginning of dispensary, and rapidly initial their cards. As he scribbled *Rep. Mixt.*—"the mixture as before"—he had no time to recollect how he had once derided this classic phrase. He was well on the way to being an admirable honorary physician.

ix

Six weeks after he had taken over at the Victoria, as he sat at breakfast with Christine, he opened a letter which bore the Marseilles postmark. Gazing at it unbelievingly for a moment, he gave a sudden exclamation:—

"It's from Denny! He's sick of Mexico at last! Coming back to settle down, he says—I'll believe that when I see it! But Lord! It'll be good to see him again. How long has he been away? It seems ages. Have you got the paper there, Chris? Look up when the *Oreta* gets in."

She was as pleased as he at the unexpected news, but for a rather different reason. There was a strong maternal strain in Christine, a queer Calvinistic protectiveness towards her husband. She had always recognized that Denny, and indeed, in a lesser degree, Hope, exerted a beneficial effect upon him. Now, especially, when he seemed changing, she was more anxiously alert. No sooner had this letter arrived than her mind was at work planning a meeting which would bring these three together.

The day before the *Oreta* was due at Tilbury she broached the matter.

"I wonder if you'd mind, Andrew—I thought I might give a little dinner next week—just for you and Denny and Hope."

He gazed at her in some surprise. In view of the vague undercurrent of constraint between them, it was strange to hear her talk of entertaining.

He answered:—

"Hope's probably at Cambridge. And Denny and I might as well go out somewhere." Then, seeing her face, he relented quickly. "Oh! All right. Make it Sunday though, that's the best night for all of us."

On the following Sunday Denny arrived, stockier and more brick-red of face and neck than ever. He looked older, seemed less morose, more contented, in his manner. Yet he was the same Denny, his greeting to them being:—

"This is a very grand house. Sure I haven't made a mistake?" Half-turning gravely to Christine: "This well-dressed gentleman *is* Doctor Manson, isn't he? If I'd known I'd have brought him a canary."

Seated, a moment later, he refused a drink.

"No! I'm a regular lime-juicer now. Strange as it may seem, I'm going to set to and get a real pull on the collar. I've had about enough of the wide and starry sky. Best way to get to like this blamed country is to go abroad."

Andrew considered him with affectionate reproof.

"You really ought to settle down, you know, Philip," he said. "After all you're on the right side of forty. And with your talents—"

Denny shot him an odd glance from beneath his brows.

"Don't be so smug, Professor. I may still show you a few tricks one of these days."

He told them he had been lucky enough to be appointed Surgical Registrar of the South Hertfordshire Infirmary, three hundred a year and all found. He did not consider it a permanency, of course, but there was a considerable amount of operative work to be done there and he would be able to refresh his surgical technique. After that he would see what could be done.

"Don't know how they gave me the job," he argued. "It must be another case of mistaken identity."

"No," said Andrew rather stolidly, "it's your M.S., Philip. A first-class degree like that will get you anywhere."

"What have you been doing to him?" Denny groaned. "He don't sound like the bloke what blew up that sewer with me."

At this point Hope arrived. He had not met Denny before. But five minutes was enough for them to understand one another. At the end of that time, as they went in to dinner, they were agreeably united in being rude to Manson.

"Of course, Hope," Philip sadly remarked as he unfolded his napkin, "you needn't expect much food here. Oh, no! I've known these people a long time. Knew the Professor before he turned into a woolly West-Ender. They were thrown out their last home for starving their guinea pigs."

"I usually carry a rasher in my pocket," said Hope. "It's a habit I acquired from Billy Buttons on the last Kitchenguenga expedition. But unfortunately I'm out of eggs. Mother's hens are not laying at the moment."

There was more of this as the meal went on,—Hope's facetiousness seemed especially provoked by Denny's presence,—but gradually they settled down to talk. Denny related some of his experiences in the Southern States—he had one or two Negro stories which made Christine laugh—and Hope detailed for them the latest activities of the Board. Whinney had at last succeeded in steering his long-contemplated muscular fatigue experiments into action.

"That's what I'm doing now," Hope gloomed. "But thank heaven my scholarship has only another nine months to run. Then I'm going to *do* something. I'm tired of working out other people's ideas, having old men stand over me." His tone dropped into ribald mimicry. "'How much sarcolactic acid did you find for me this time, Mr. Hope?' I want to do something for myself. I wish to God I had a little lab of my own!"

Then, as Christine had hoped, the talk became violently medical. After dinner,— despite Denny's melancholy prognostication, they had stripped a brace of ducks,—when coffee was brought in, she pleaded to remain. And though Hope assured her that the language would not be ladylike she sat, her elbows on the table, chin upon her hands, listening silently, forgotten, her eyes fixed earnestly on Andrew's face.

At first he had appeared stiff and reserved. Though it was a joy to see Philip again he had the feeling that his old friend was a little casual towards his success, unappreciative, even mildly derisive. After all, he had done pretty well for himself, hadn't he? And what had Denny—yes, what had Denny done? When Hope had chipped in with his attempts of humour he had almost told them, pretty sharply, to stop being funny at his expense.

Yet now that they were talking shop he was drawn into it, unconsciously. Momentarily, whether he wished it or not, he caught the infection from the other two and, with not a bad copy of his old rapture, he made himself heard.

They were discussing hospitals, which caused him suddenly to express himself upon the whole hospital system.

"The way I look at it is this." He took a long breath of smoke—it was not now a cheap Virginian cigarette but a cigar, from the box which he had, braving the devil in

Denny's eye, self-consciously produced. "The whole lay-out is obsolete. Mind you, I wouldn't for anything have you think I'm knocking my own hospital. I love it down there at the Victoria and I can tell you we do great work. But it's the system. Nobody but the good old apathetic B.P. would put up with it—like our roads, for instance, a hopeless out-of-date chaos. The Victoria is falling down. So is St. John's; half the hospitals in London are shrieking that they're falling down! And what are we doing about it? Collecting pennies. Getting a few quid out of the advertisement hoardings we stick up on our frontage. *Brown's Beer Is Best.* Isn't that sweet? At the Victoria, if we're lucky, in ten years' time we'll start to build a new wing, or a nurses' home—incidentally you should see where the nurses *sleep*! But what's the use of patching up the old carcass? What *is* the use of a lung hospital in the centre of a noisy foggy city like London—damn it all, it's like taking a pneumonia down a coal mine. And it's the same with most of the other hospitals, *and* the nursing homes too. They're bang in the middle of roaring traffic, foundations shaken by the Underground; even the patients' beds rattle when the buses go past. If I went in there, *healthy*, I'd want ten grains of barbitone every night to get to sleep. Think of patients lying in that racket after a serious abdominal, or running a temperature of a hundred and four with meningitis!"

"Well, what's the remedy?" Philip lifted an eyebrow in that new irritating fashion. "A joint hospital board with you as director in chief?"

"Don't be an ass, Denny," Andrew answered irritably. "Decentralization is the remedy. No, that isn't just a word out of a book, it's the result of all that I've gone through since I came to London. Why shouldn't our big hospitals stand in a green belt outside London, say fifteen miles outside? Take a place like Benham, for instance, only ten miles out, where there's still green country, fresh air, quiet. Don't think there would be any transportation difficulties. The tube—and why not a specially run hospital service—one straight, silent line?—could take you out to Benham in exactly eighteen minutes. Considering that it takes our fastest ambulance forty minutes on the average to bring in an emergency, that sounds to me an improvement. You might say if we moved the hospitals we'd denude each area of its medical services. That's rot! The dispensary stops in the area, the hospital moves out. And while we're talking about it, this question of area service is just one large hopeless muddle. When I came here at first, I found here in *West* London that the only place I could get in my patient was the *East* London Hospital. Down at the Victoria too, we get patients from all over the shop—Kensington, Ealing, Muswell Hill. There's no attempt to delimit special areas—everything comes pouring in to the centre of the city. I'm telling you fellows straight, the confusion is often unbelievable. And what's being done? Zero, absolute zero. We just drag on in the old, old way, rattling tin boxes, holding flag days, making appeals, letting students clown for pennies in fancy dress. One thing about these new European countries—they get things *done*. Lord, if I had my way I'd raze the Victoria flat and have a new Chest Hospital setting out at Benham with a straight line of communication. And by God! I'd show a rise in our recovery rate!"

This was merely by way of introduction. The crescendo of discussion rose.

Philip got on to his old contention—the folly of asking the general practitioner to pull everything out of the one black bag, the stupidity of making him carry every case on his shoulders until that delightful moment when, for five guineas, some specialist he had never seen before drove up to tell him it was too late to carry anything at all.

Hope, without mildness or restraint, expressed the case of the young bacteriologist, sandwiched between commercialism and conservatism—on the one hand, the bland firm of chemists who would pay him a wage to make proprietary articles, on the other a Board of blithering dotards.

"Can you imagine," Hope hissed, "the Marx brothers sitting in a rickety motor car with four independent steering wheels and an unlimited supply of motor horns? That's us at the M.F.B."

They did not stop until after twelve o'clock and then, unexpectedly, they found sandwiches and coffee before them on the table.

"Oh I say, Mrs. Manson," Hope protested with a politeness which showed that, in Denny's gibe, he was a Nice Young Man at Heart. "We must have bored you stiff. Funny how hungry talking makes one. I'll suggest that to Whinney as a new line of investigation—effect upon the gastric secretions of hot-air fatigue. Ha! Ha! That's a perfect Nag-ism!"

When Hope had gone, with fervent protestations that he had enjoyed the evening, Denny remained a few minutes longer, exacting the privilege of his older friendship. Then, Andrew having left the room to ring for a taxi, Philip apologetically brought out a small, very beautiful Spanish shawl.

"The Professor will probably slay me," he said. "But this is for you. Don't tell him till I'm safely out of the way." He arrested her gratitude, always for him the most embarrassing emotion. "Extraordinary how all these shawls come from China. They're not really Spanish. I got that one via Shanghai."

A silence fell. They could hear Andrew coming back from the telephone in the hall.

Denny got up, his kind, wrinkled eyes avoiding hers.

"I wouldn't worry too much about him, you know." He smiled. "But we must try, mustn't we, to get him back to Blaenelly standards?"

X

At the beginning of the Easter school holidays Andrew received a note from Mrs. Thornton asking him to call at Brown's Hotel to see her daughter. She told him briefly, in the letter, that Sybil's foot had not improved and, since she had been much struck by his interest at Mrs. Lawrence's, she was anxious to have his advice. Flattered by this tribute to his personality, he made the visit promptly.

The condition which he found upon examination was perfectly simple. Yet it was one which demanded an early operation. He straightened himself, with a smile to the solid, bare-legged Sybil now seated upon the edge of the bed, pulling on her long black stocking, and explained this to Mrs. Thornton.

"The bone has thickened. Might develop into a hammer toe, if it's left untreated. I suggest you have it seen to at once."

"That's what the school doctor said." Mrs. Thornton was not surprised. "We are really prepared. Sybil can go into a home here. But—well! I've got confidence in you, Doctor. And I want you to undertake all the arrangements. Whom do you suggest should do it?"

The direct question placed Andrew in a dilemma. His work being almost entirely medical he had met many of the leading physicians, yet he knew none of the London surgeons.

Suddenly he thought of Ivory. He said pleasantly:—

"Mr. Ivory might do this for us—if he's available."

Mrs. Thornton had heard of Mr. Ivory. Of course! Wasn't he the surgeon who had been in all the newspapers the month before through having flown to Cairo to attend a case of sunstroke? An extremely well-known man! She thought it an admirable suggestion that he should undertake her daughter's case. Her only stipulation was that Sybil should go to Miss Sherrington's Home. So many of her friends had been there she could not think of letting her go anywhere else.

Andrew went home and rang up Ivory, with all the hesitation of a man making a preliminary approach. But Ivory's manner—friendly, confident, charming—reassured him. They arranged to see the case together on the following day; and Ivory asserted that, though he knew Ida to be bunged up to the attics, he could persuade her to make room for Miss Thornton should this be necessary.

Next morning, when Ivory had agreed emphatically in Mrs. Thornton's presence with all that Andrew had said—adding that immediate operation was imperative—Sybil was transferred to Miss Sherrington's Home; and two days later, giving her time to settle down, the operation was performed.

Andrew was there. Ivory insisted that he be present, in the most genuine and friendly fashion imaginable.

The operation was not difficult,—indeed in his Blaenelly days Andrew would have tackled it himself,—and Ivory, though he seemed disinclined to speed, accomplished it with imposing competence. He made a strong cool figure in his big white gown, above which his face showed firm, massive, dominant-jawed. No one more completely resembled the popular conception of the great surgeon than Charles Ivory. He had the fine supple hands with which popular fiction always endows the hero of the operating theatre. In his handsomeness and assurance he was dramatically impressive. Andrew, who had himself slipped on a gown, watched him from the other side of the table with grudging respect.

A fortnight later, when Sybil Thornton had left the home, Ivory asked him to lunch at the Sackville Club. It was a pleasant meal. Ivory was a perfect conversationalist, easy and entertaining, with a fund of up-to-the-minute gossip, which somehow placed his companion on the same intimate, man-of-the-world footing as himself. The high dining-room of the Sackville, with its Adam ceilings and rock-crystal chandeliers, was full of famous—Ivory named them "amusing"—people. Andrew found the experience flattering, as no doubt Ivory intended it to be.

"You must let me put your name up at the next meeting," the surgeon remarked. "You'd find a lot of friends here, Freddie, Paul, myself—by the way, Jackie Lawrence is a member. Interesting marriage that; they're perfectly good friends, and they each go their own way! Honestly, I'd love to put you up. I've rather felt, you know, that you've just been a shade suspicious of me, old fellow. Your Scottish caution, eh? As you know I don't visit any of the hospitals. That's because I prefer to free-lance. Besides, my dear boy, I'm too *busy*. Some of these hospital fogies don't have one private case a month. I average ten a week! By the by, we'll be hearing from the Thorntons presently. You leave all that to me. They're first-class people. And incidentally, while I speak of it, don't you think Sybil ought to have her tonsils seen to? Did you look at them?"

"No—no, I didn't."

"Oh, you ought to have done, my boy. Absolutely pocketed, no end of septic absorption. I took the liberty—hope you don't mind—of saying we might do them for her when the warm weather comes in."

On his way home Andrew could not help reflecting what a charming fellow Ivory had turned out to be—actually, he ought to be grateful to Hampton for the introduction. This case had passed off superbly. The Thorntons were particularly pleased. Surely there could be no better criterion.

Three weeks later, as he sat at tea with Christine, the afternoon post brought him a letter from Ivory.

My dear Manson—

Mrs. Thornton has just come nicely to scratch. As I am sending the anaesthetist his bit I may as well send you yours—for assisting me so splendidly at the operation. Sybil will be coming to see you at the end of this term. You remember those tonsils I mentioned. Mrs. Thornton is delighted.

Ever cordially yours,—

C.I.

Enclosed was a cheque for twenty guineas.

Andrew stared at the cheque in astonishment,—he had done nothing to assist Ivory at the operation,—then gradually the warm feeling which money always gave him now stole round his heart. With a complacent smile he handed over the letter and the cheque for Christine's inspection.

"Damned decent of Ivory, isn't it, Chris? I bet we'll have a record in our receipts this month."

"But I don't understand." Her expression was perplexed. "Is this your bill to Mrs. Thornton?"

"No—silly," he chuckled. "It's a little extra—merely for the time I gave up to the operation."

"You mean Mr. Ivory is giving you part of his fee."

He flushed, suddenly up in arms.

"Good lord, no! That's absolutely forbidden. We wouldn't dream of that. Don't you see I earned this fee for assisting, for being *there*, just as the anaesthetist earned his fee for giving the anaesthetic. Ivory sends it all in with his bill. And I'll bet it was a bumper."

She laid the cheque upon the table, subdued, unhappy.

"It seems a great deal of money."

"Well, why not?" He closed the argument in a blaze of indignation. "The Thorntons are tremendously rich. This is probably no more to them than three and six to one of our surgery patients."

When he had gone, her eyes remained fastened upon the cheque with strained apprehension. She had not realized that he had associated himself professionally with Ivory. Suddenly all her former uneasiness swept back over her. That evening with Denny and Hope might never have taken place for all its effect upon him. How fond he now was, how terribly fond, of money. His work at the Victoria seemed not to matter beside this devouring desire for material success. Even in the surgery she had observed that he was using more and more stock mixtures, prescribing for people who had nothing wrong with them, urging them to call and call again. The worried look deepened upon her face, making it pinched and small, as she sat there, confronted by Charles Ivory's cheque. Tears welled slowly to her eyes. She must speak to him, oh, she must, she must.

That evening, after surgery, she approached him diffidently. "Andrew, would you do something to please me? Would you take me out to the country on Sunday in the car? You promised me when you got it. And of course—all winter we haven't been able to go."

He glanced at her queerly.

"Well—Oh, all right!"

Sunday came fine, as she had hoped, a soft spring day. By eleven o'clock he had done what visits were essential and with a rug and a picnic basket in the back of the car they set off. Christine's spirits lifted as they ran across Hammersmith Bridge and took the Kingston By-Pass for Surrey. Soon they were through Dorking, turning to the right on the road to Shere. It was so long since they had been together in the country that the sweetness of it, the vivid green of the fields, the purple of the budding elms, the golden dust of drooping catkins, the paler yellow of primroses clumped beneath a bank, suffused her being, intoxicating her.

"Don't drive so fast, dear," she murmured in a tone softer than she had used for weeks. "It's so lovely here." He seemed intent upon passing every car upon the road.

Towards one o'clock they reached Shere. The village, with its few red-roofed cottages and its stream quietly wandering amongst the watercress beds, was as yet untroubled by the rush of summer tourists. They reached the wooded hill beyond, and parked the car near one of the close-turfed bridle-paths. There, in the little clearing where they spread the rug, was a singing solitude which belonged only to them and to the birds.

They ate their sandwiches in the sunshine, drank the coffee from the thermos. Around them, in the alder clumps, the primroses grew in great profusion. Christine longed to gather them, to bury her face in their cool softness. Andrew lay with half-closed eyes, his head resting near her. A sweet tranquillity settled upon the dark uneasiness of her soul. If their life together could always be like this!

His drowsy gaze had for some moments been resting on the car. Suddenly he said:—

"Not a bad old bus, is she, Chris? I mean, for what she cost us. But we shall want a new one at the Show."

She stirred—her disquiet renewed by this fresh instance of his restless striving.

"But we haven't had her any time! She seems to me all that we could wish for."

"Hum! She's sluggish. Didn't you notice how that Buick kept ahead of us? I want one of these new Vitesse saloons."

"But why?"

"Why not? We can afford it. We're getting on, you know, Chris. Yes!" He lit a cigarette and turned to her with every sign of satisfaction. "In case you may not be aware of the fact, my dear little schoolmarm from Blaenelly, we are rapidly getting rich."

She did not answer his smile. She felt her body, peaceful and warm in the sunshine, chill suddenly. She began to pick at a tuft of grass, to twine it foolishly with a tassel of the rugs. She said slowly:—

"Dear, do we really want to be rich? I know I don't. Why all this talk about money? When we had scarcely any we were—oh! we were deliriously happy. We never talked of it, then. But now we never talk of anything else."

He smiled again, in a superior manner.

"After years of tramping about in slush, eating sausage and soused herrings, taking dog's abuse from pigheaded committees, and attending miners' wives in dirty back bedrooms, I propose, for a change, to ameliorate our lot. Any objections?"

"Don't make a joke of it, darling. You usen't to talk that way. Oh! Don't you see, don't you see, you're falling a victim to the very system you used to run down, the thing you used to hate?" Her face was pitiful in its agitation. "Don't you remember how you used to speak of life, that it was an attack on the unknown, as assault uphill—as though you had to take some castle that you knew was there, but couldn't see, on the top—"

He muttered uncomfortably:—

"Oh! I was young then—foolish. That was just romantic talk. You look round; you'll see that everybody's doing the same thing—getting together as much as they can! It's the only thing to do."

She took a shaky breath. She knew that she must speak now or not at all.

"Darling! It isn't the only thing. Please listen to me. Please! I've been so unhappy at this—the change in you. Denny saw it too. It's dragging us away from one another. You're not the Andrew Manson I married. Oh! If only you'd be as you used to be!"

"What have I done?" he protested irritably. "Do I beat you, do I get drunk, do I commit murder? Give me one example of my *crimes*."

Desperately, she replied:—

"It isn't the obvious things; it's your whole attitude, darling. Take that cheque Ivory sent you, for instance. It's a small matter, on the surface perhaps, but underneath—oh, if you take it underneath it's cheap and grasping and dishonest."

She felt him stiffen; then he sat up, offended, glaring at her.

"For God's sake! Why bring that up again? What's wrong with my taking it?"

"Can't you see?" All the accumulated emotion of the past months overwhelmed her, stifling her arguments, causing her suddenly to burst into tears. She cried hysterically: "For God's sake, darling. Don't, don't sell yourself!"

He ground his teeth, furious with her. He spoke slowly, with cutting deliberation.

"For the last time, I warn you to stop making a neurotic fool of yourself. Can't you try to be a help to me, instead of a hindrance, nagging me every minute of the day?"

"I haven't nagged you," she sobbed. "I've wanted to speak before, but I haven't."

"Then don't." He lost his temper and suddenly shouted: "Do you hear me? *Don't*. It's some complex you've got. You talk as if I was some kind of dirty crook. I only want to get on. And if I want money it's only as a means to an end. People judge you by what you are, what you have. If you're one of the have-nots you get ordered about. Well, I've had enough of that in my time. In future I'm going to do the ordering. Now do you understand? Don't even mention this damned nonsense to me again."

"All right, all right," she wept. "I won't. But I tell you—some day you'll be sorry."

The excursion was ruined for them, and most of all for her. Though she dried her eyes and gathered a large bunch of primroses, though they spent another hour on the sunny slope and stopped on the way down at the *Lavender Lady* for tea, though they spoke, in apparent amity, of ordinary things, all the rapture of the day was dead. Her face, as they drove through the early darkness, was pale and stiff.

His anger turned gradually to indignation. Why should Chris of all people set upon him? Other women, and charming women too, were enthusiastic at his rapid rise.

A few days later Frances Lawrence rang him up. She had been away, spending the winter at Jamaica—he had several times in the past two months had letters from the Myrtle Bank Hotel; but now she was back, eager to see her friends, radiating the sunshine she had absorbed. She told him gaily she wanted him to see her before she lost her sunburn.

He went round to tea. As she had implied, she was beautifully tanned, her hands and slender wrists, her spare interrogative face, strained as a faun's. The pleasure of seeing her again was intensified extraordinarily by the welcome in her eyes, those eyes which were indifferent to so many persons and which, with their high points of light, so friendly to him.

Yes, they talked as old friends. She told him of her trip, of the coral gardens, the fishes seen through the glass-bottomed boats, of the heavenly climate. He gave her, in return, an account of his progress.

Perhaps some indication of his thoughts crept into his words, for she answered lightly: "You're frightfully solemn and disgracefully prosy. That's what happens to you when I'm away. No! Frankly I think it's because you're doing too much. *Must* you keep on with all this surgery work? For my part I should have thought it time for you to take a room up West—Wimpole Street or Welbeck Street for instance—and do your consulting there."

At this point her husband entered, tall, lounging, mannered. He nodded to Andrew, whom he now knew fairly well—they had once or twice played bridge at the Sackville Club—and gracefully accepted a cup of tea.

Though he protested cheerfully that he would not for anything disturb them, Lawrence's entrance interrupted the serious turn of the conversation. They began to discuss, with considerable amusement, the latest junketing of Rumbold-Blane.

But half an hour later, as Andrew drove back to Chesborough Terrace Mrs. Lawrence's suggestion firmly occupied his mind. Why shouldn't he take a consulting room in Welbeck Street? The time was clearly ripe for it. He wouldn't give up anything of his Paddington practice—the surgery was far too profitable a concern to abandon lightly. But he could easily combine it with a room up West, use the better address for his correspondence, have the heading on his notepaper, his bills.

The thought sparkled within him, nerved him to greater conquest. What a good sort Frances was, just as helpful as Miss Everett and infinitely more charming, more exciting! Yet he was on excellent terms with her husband. He could meet his eye steadily. He needn't come skulking out of the house like some low boudoir hound. Oh! friendship was a great thing!

Without saying anything to Christine, he began to look for a convenient consulting room up West. And when he found one, about a month later, it gave him great satisfaction to declare, in assumed indifference, over the morning paper:

"By the way—you might care to know—I've taken a place in Welbeck Street now. I shall use it for my better-class consultations."

xi

The room at Number 57a Welbeck Street gave Andrew a new surge of triumph. I'm there, he secretly exulted. I'm there at last! Though not large, the room was well lit by a bay window and situated on the ground floor, a distinct advantage, since most patients hated to climb stairs. Moreover, although he shared the waiting-room with several other consultants whose neat plates shone beside his own on the front door, this consulting room was exclusively his own.

On the nineteenth of April, when the lease was signed, Hampton accompanied him as he went round to take possession. Freddie had proved extraordinarily helpful in all the preliminaries and had found him a useful nurse, a friend of the woman whom he employed at Queen Anne Street. Nurse Sharp was not beautiful. She was middle-aged, with a sour, vaguely ill-used yet capable expression. Freddie explained Nurse Sharp concisely:—

"The last thing a fellow wants is a pretty nurse. You know what I mean, old man. Fun is fun. But business is business. And you can't combine the two. We none of us are in this for our health. As a damned hardheaded fellow, you'll appreciate that. As a matter of fact I've got a notion you and I are going to come pretty close together now you've moved alongside me."

While Freddie and he stood discussing the arrangement of the room Mrs. Lawrence unexpectedly appeared. She had been passing and came in, gaily, to investigate his choice. She had an attractive way of turning up casually, of never appearing to obtrude herself. To-day she was especially charming in a black coat and skirt with a necklet of rich brown fur about her throat. She did not stay long but she had ideas, suggestions for decoration, for the window hangings and the curtains behind his desk, far more tasteful than the crude plannings Freddie and he had arranged.

Bereft of her vivacious presence the room was suddenly empty.

Freddie gushed: "You're a lucky devil, if ever I met one. She's a nice thing." He grinned enviously. "What did Gladstone say in eighteen ninety about the surest way to advance a man's career?"

"I don't know what you're driving at."

Nevertheless when his room was finished he had to agree with Freddie, and with Frances, who arrived to view her complete scheme, that it struck exactly the right note—advanced yet professionally correct. Consultations in these surroundings made three guineas seem a right and reasonable fee.

He had not many patients at the start. But by dint of writing politely to every doctor who sent cases to him at the Chest Hospital—letters relating, naturally, to these hospital cases and their symptoms—he soon had a network of filaments reaching out all over London which began to bring private patients to his door. He was a busy man these days, dashing in his new Vitesse saloon between Chesborough Terrace and the Victoria, between the Victoria and Welbeck Street, with a full round of visits in addition and always his packed surgery, often running as late as ten o'clock at night.

The tonic of success braced him for everything, tingled through his veins like a gorgeous elixir. He found time to run round to Rogers to order another three suits, then to a shirtmaker in Jermyn Street whom Hampton had recommended. His popularity at the hospital was increasing. True, he had less time to devote to his work in the outpatient department, but he told himself that what he sacrificed in time he made up in expertness. Even to his friends he developed a speedy brusqueness, rather taking, with his ready smile: "I must go, old fellow, simply rushed off my legs."

One Friday afternoon, five weeks after his installation at Welbeck Street, an elderly woman came to consult him about her throat. Her condition was no more than a simple laryngitis, but she was a querulous little person and she seemed anxious for a second opinion. Mildly injured in his pride, Andrew reflected to whom he should send her. It was ridiculous to think of her wasting the time of a man like Sir Robert Abbey. Suddenly his face cleared as he thought of Hampton round the corner. Freddie had been extremely kind to him lately. He might as well "pick up" the three guineas as some ungrateful stranger. Andrew sent her along with a note to Freddie.

Three quarters of an hour later she came back, in quite a different humour, soothed and apologetic, satisfied with herself, with Freddie and—most of all—with him.

"Excuse me for coming back, Doctor. I only wanted to thank you for the trouble you've taken with me. I saw Doctor Hampton and he confirmed everything you said. And he—he told me the prescription you gave me simply couldn't be improved on."

In June Sybil Thornton's tonsils came out. They were, to a certain extent, enlarged, and lately, in the *Journal,* suspicion had been thrown upon tonsillar absorption in its bearing upon the etiology of rheumatism. Ivory did the enucleation with tedious care.

"I prefer to go slow with these lymphoid tissues," he said to Andrew as they washed up. "I daresay you've seen people whip them out. *I* don't work that way."

When Andrew received his cheque from Ivory—again it came by post—Freddie was with him. They were frequently in and out of each other's consulting rooms. Hampton had promptly returned the ball by sending Andrew a nice gastritis in return for the laryngitis case. By this time, in fact, several patients had found their way, with notes, between Welbeck and Queen Anne Street.

"You know, Manson," Freddie now remarked, "I'm glad you've chucked your old dog-in-the-manger, holy-willy attitude. Even now, you know," he squinted across Andrew's shoulder at the cheque, "you're not getting all the juice out of the orange. You hang in with me, my lad, and you'll find your fruit more succulent."

Andrew had to laugh.

That evening, as he drove home, he was in an unusually lighthearted mood. Finding himself without cigarettes he drew up and dashed into a tobacconist's in Oxford Street. Here, as he came through the door, he suddenly observed a woman loitering at an adjacent window. It was Blodwen Page.

Though he recognized her at once, she was sadly altered from the bustling mistress of Bryngower. No longer stout, her figure had a listless droop, and the eye which she turned upon him when he addressed her was apathetic, cowed.

"It is Mrs. Page." He went up to her. "I ought to say Mrs. Rees now, I suppose. Don't you remember me? Doctor Manson."

She took him in, his well-dressed and prosperous air. She sighed: "I remember you, Doctor. I hope you're very well." Then, as though afraid to linger, she turned to where a few yards along the pavement a long bald-headed man impatiently awaited her. She concluded apprehensively, "I'll have to go now, Doctor. My husband's waiting."

Andrew observed her hurry off, saw Rees's thin lips shape themselves to the rebuke, "What d'you mean—keeping me waiting?" while she submissively bent her head. For an instant he was conscious of the bank manager's cold eye directed blankly upon himself. Then the pair moved off and were lost in the crowd.

Andrew could not get the picture out of his head. When he reached Chesborough Terrace and entered the front room he found Christine knitting there, with his tea— which she had rung for at the sound of his car—set out upon a tray. He glanced at her quickly, sounding her. He wanted to tell her of the incident, longed suddenly to end their period of strife.

But when he had accepted a cup of tea, and before he could speak, she said quietly:— "Mrs. Lawrence rang you again this afternoon. No message."

"Oh!" He flushed. "How do you mean—again?"

"This is the fourth time she's rung you in a week."

"Well, what of it?"

"Nothing. I didn't say anything."

"It's how you look. Can *I* help it if she rings me?"

She was silent, her eyes downcast, upon her knitting. If he had known the tumult in that still breast he would not have lost his temper as he did.

"You would think I was a bigamist, the way you go on. She's a perfectly nice woman. Why, her husband is one of my best friends. They're charming people. They don't hang about looking like a sick pup. Oh, hell—"

He gulped down the rest of his tea and got up. Yet the moment he was out of the room he was sorry. He flung into the surgery, lit a cigarette, reflecting wretchedly that things were going from bad to worse between Christine and himself. And he did not want them to get worse. Their growing estrangement depressed and irritated him; it was the one dark cloud in the bright sky of his success.

Christine and he had been ideally happy in their married life. The unexpected meeting with Mrs. Page had brought back a rush of tender memories of his courtship in Blaenelly. He did not idolize his wife as he once had done, but he was—oh, damn it all! —he was *fond* of her. Perhaps he had hurt her once or twice lately. As he stood there he had a sudden desire to make up with her, to please, propitiate her. He thought hard. Suddenly his eye brightened. He glanced at his watch, found that he had just half an hour before Laurier's closed. The next minute he was in his car and on his way to interview Miss Cramb.

Miss Cramb, when he mentioned what he desired, was immediately and fervently at his service. They fell into serious conversation together, then walked into the fur department where various "skins" were modelled for Doctor Manson. Miss Cramb stroked them with expert fingers, pointing out the lustre, the silvering, all that one should look for in this special pelt. Once or twice she disagreed gently with his views, earnestly indicating what was *quality* and what was not. In the end he made a selection which she cordially approved. Then she departed in search of Mr. Winch, and presently returned to state glowingly:—

"Mr. Winch says you're to have them *at cost*." No such word as "wholesale" had ever sullied the lips of a Laurier employee. "That brings them out at fifty-five pounds; and you can take it from me, Doctor, it's genuine value. They're beautiful skins, beautiful. Your wife will be proud to wear them."

On the following Saturday at eleven o'clock Andrew took the dark olive-green box, with the inimitable mark artistically scrawled upon its lid, and went into the drawing-room.

"Christine!" he called. "Here a moment!"

She was upstairs with Mrs. Bennett helping to make the beds, but she came at once, slightly out of breath, her eyes wondering a little at his summons.

"Look, dear!" Now that the climax approached he felt an almost suffocating awkwardness. "I bought you this. I know—I know we haven't been getting on so well lately. But this ought to show you—" He broke off and like a schoolboy, handed her the box.

She was very pale as she opened it. Her hands trembled upon the string.

Then she gave a little overwhelmed cry:—

"What lovely, lovely furs!"

There, in the tissue paper, lay a double stole of silver fox, two exquisite skins shaped fashionably into one. Quickly he picked them up, smoothing them as Miss Cramb had done, his voice excited now.

"Do you like them, Chris? Try them on. The good old Halfback helped me choose them. They're absolutely first-class quality. Couldn't have better. And value too. You see that sheen on them and the silver marking on the back—that's what you want specially to look for!"

Tears were running down her cheeks. She turned to him quite wildly.

"You do love me, don't you, darling? That's all that matters to me in the world!"

Reassured at last, she tried on the furs. They were magnificent.

He could not admire them enough. He wanted to make the reconciliation complete. He smiled.

"Look here, Chris. We might as well have a little celebration while we're about it. We'll go out to lunch to-day. Meet me one o'clock at the Plaza Grill."

"Yes, darling," she half-questioned. "Only—I've got some shepherd's pie for lunch to-day—that you used to like so much."

"No, no." His laugh was gayer than it had been for months. "Don't be an old stay-at-home. One o'clock. Meet the dark handsome gentleman at the Plaza. You needn't wear a red carnation. He'll know you by the furs."

All morning he was in a mood of high satisfaction. Fool that he'd been!—neglecting Christine. All women liked to have attention paid to them, to be taken out, given a good time. The Plaza Grill was just the place—all London, or most of it that mattered, could be seen there between the hours of one and three.

Christine was late, an unusual occurrence which caused him to fret slightly, as he sat in the small lounge facing the glass partition, watching all the best tables become quickly occupied. He ordered himself a second Martini. It was twenty minutes past one when she came hurrying in, flustered by the noise, the people, the ornate flunkeys and the fact that, for the last half-hour, she had been standing in the wrong lounge.

"I'm so sorry, darling," she gasped. "I really did ask. I waited and waited. And then I found it was the restaurant lounge."

They were given a bad table wedged against a pillar beside the service. The place was grotesquely crowded, the tables so close together people seemed to be sitting on each other's laps. The waiters moved like contortionists. The heat was tropical. The din rose and fell like a transpontine college yell.

"Now, Chris, what would you like?" Andrew said determinedly.

"You order, darling," she answered faintly.

He ordered a rich, expensive lunch: caviar, *soupe prince de Galles*, *poulet riche*, asparagus, *fraises des bois* in syrup. Also a bottle of Liebfraumilch, 1929.

"We didn't know much about this in our Blaenelly days." He laughed, determined to make merry. "Nothing like doing ourselves well, old girl."

Nobly she tried to respond to his mood. She praised the caviar, made an heroic effort with the rich soup. She pretended interest when he pointed out Glen Roscoe, the cinema star, Marvis Yorke, an American woman celebrated for her six husbands, and other cosmopolitans equally distinguished. The smart vulgarity of the place was hateful to her. The men were overgroomed, smooth and oiled. Every woman visible to her was a blonde, dressed in black, smart, made-up, carelessly hard.

All at once Christine felt herself turn a little giddy. She began to lose her poise. Usually her manner was one of natural simplicity. But lately the strain upon her nerves had been great. She became conscious of the discrepancy between her new furs and her inexpensive dress. She felt other women staring at her. She knew she was as out of place here as a daisy in an orchid house.

"What's the matter?" he asked suddenly. "Aren't you enjoying yourself?"

"Yes, of course," she protested, wanly trying to smile. But her lips were stiff now. She could barely swallow, let alone taste, the heavily creamed chicken on her plate.

"You're not listening to a thing I say," he muttered resentfully. "You haven't even touched your wine. Damn it all, when a man takes his wife out—"

"Could I have a little water?" she asked feebly. She could have screamed. She didn't belong to a place like this. Her hair wasn't bleached, her face not made-up; no wonder even the waiters watched her now. Nervously she lifted an asparagus stalk. As she did so the head broke and fell, dripping with sauce, on the new fur.

The metallic blonde at the next table turned to her companion with a smile of amusement. Andrew saw that smile. He gave up the attempt at entertainment. The meal ended in a dreary silence.

They went home more drearily. Then he departed, summarily, to do his calls. They were wider apart than before. The pain in Christine's heart was intolerable. She began to lose faith in herself, to ask herself if she was really the right wife for him. That night she put her arms round his neck and kissed him, thanking him again for the furs and for taking her out.

"Glad you enjoyed it," he said flatly, and went to his own room.

xii

At this point an event occurred which, for the time being, diverted Andrew's attention from his difficulties at home. He came upon a paragraph in the *Tribune*, which announced that Mr. Richard Stillman, the well known health expert of Portland, Oregon, U.S.A., had arrived on the *Imperial* and was staying at Brooks Hotel.

In the old days he would have rushed excitedly to Christine with the paper in his hand: "Look here, Chris! Richard Stillman has come over. You remember—I corresponded with him all that time. I wonder if he'd see me—honestly, I'd love to meet him."

But now he had lost the habit of running to Christine. Instead he pondered maturely over the *Tribune*, glad that he could approach Stillman, not as a medical aid assistant, but with the standing of a Welbeck Street consultant. Methodically he typed a letter recalling himself to the American and asking him to lunch at the Plaza Grill on Wednesday.

The following morning Stillman rang him up. His voice was quiet, friendly, alertly efficient.

"Glad to be talking to you, Doctor Manson. I'd be pleased for us to lunch. But don't let's make it the Plaza. I hate that place already. Why don't you come here and lunch with me?"

Andrew found Stillman in the sitting-room of his suite at Brooks, a quietly select hotel which put the racket of the Plaza to shame. It was a hot day, the morning had been a rush, and at the first sight of his host Andrew almost wished he had not come. The American was about fifty, small and slight, with a disproportionately large head and an undershot jaw. His complexion was a boyish pink-and-white, his light-coloured hair thin and parted in the middle. It was only when Andrew saw his eyes, pale, steady, and glacially blue, that he realized—almost felt the impact of—the driving force behind this insignificant frame.

"Hope you don't mind coming here," said Richard Stillman in the quiet manner of one to whom many have been glad to come. "I know we Americans are supposed to like the Plaza." He smiled, revealing himself human. "But it's a lousy crowd that goes there." He paused. "And now I've seen you, let me really congratulate you on that splendid inhalation paper. You didn't mind my telling you about serecite? What have you been doing lately?"

They descended to the restaurant, where the head of many waiters gave Stillman his attention.

"How about you? I'm going to have orange juice," Stillman said then, promptly, without looking at the French menu, "and two mutton cutlets with peas. Then coffee."

Andrew gave his order and turned with increasing respect to his companion. It was impossible to remain in Stillman's presence long without acknowledging the compelling interest of his personality. His history, which Andrew knew in outline, was in itself unique.

Richard Stillman came of an old Massachusetts family which had, for generations, been connected with the law, in Boston. But young Stillman, despite this continuity, evinced a strong desire to enter the medical profession, and at the age of eighteen at last persuaded his father to allow him to begin his studies at Harvard with that end in view. For three years he had followed the science curriculum at this University when his father died suddenly leaving Richard, his mother, and his only sister in unexpectedly poor circumstances.

At this point, when some means of support had to be found for the family, old John Stillman, Richard's grandfather, insisted that he attend a law school, following the family tradition. Arguments proved useless—the old man was implacable—and Richard was forced to take, not the medical degree he had hoped for, but a legal one. Then he entered the family offices in Boston and for four years devoted himself to the law.

It was, however, a half-hearted devotion. Bacteriology, in particular, microbiology, had fascinated him from his earliest student days, and in the attic of his Beacon Hill home he set up a small laboratory and devoted every spare moment to the pursuit of his passion. This attic was in fact the beginning of the Stillman Institute. Richard was no amateur. On the contrary he displayed not only the highest technical skill but an originality amounting almost to genius. And when, in the winter of 1908, his sister Mary, to whom he was much attached, died of rapid consumption, he began the concentration of his forces against the tubercule bacillus. He picked up the early work of Pierre Louis and Louis's American disciple, James Jackson, Jr. His examination of Laënnac's life work on auscultation brought him to the physiological study of the lungs. He invented a new type of stethoscope. He commenced, with the limited apparatus at his disposal, his first attempts to produce a blood serum.

In the year 1910, when old John Stillman died, Richard had at last succeeded in curing tuberculosis in guinea pigs. The results of this double event were immediate. Stillman's mother had all along sympathized with his scientific work. He needed little urging to dispose of the Boston law connection, and, with his inheritance from the old man's estate, to purchase a farm near Portland, Oregon, where he at once flung himself into the real business of his life.

So many valuable years had already been wasted he made no attempt to take a medical degree. He wanted progress, results. Soon he produced a serum from bay horses, succeeded with a bovine vaccine in the mass immunization of a herd of Jersey cows. At the same time he was applying the fundamental observations of Helmholtz and Willard Gibbs of Yale, and of later physicists like Bisaillon and Zinks, to the treatment of the damaged lung through immobilization. From this he launched straight into therapeutics.

His curative work at the new Institute soon brought him into prominence with triumphs greater than his laboratory victories. Many of his patients were ambulant consumptives, wandering from one sanatorium to another, reputably adjudged incurable. His success with these cases immediately earned for him disparagement, accusation, and the determined antagonism of the medical profession.

There now began for Stillman a different and more protracted struggle, the battle for recognition of his work. He had sunk every dollar he possessed in establishing his Institute and the cost of maintaining it was heavy. He hated publicity and resisted all inducements to commercialize his work. Often it seemed as though material difficulties, allied to the bitterness of the opposition, must submerge him. Yet Stillman with magnificent courage survived every crisis—even a national newspaper campaign conducted against him.

The era of misrepresentation passed, the storm of controversy subsided. Gradually Stillman won a grudging recognition from his opponents. In 1925 a Washington Commission visited and reported glowingly upon the work at the Institute. Stillman, now recognized, began to receive large donations from private individuals, from trust executives, and even from public bodies. These funds he devoted to the extension and perfection of his Institute, which became, with its superb equipment and situation, its herds of Jersey cattle and pure-bred Irish serum horses, a show place in the state of Oregon.

Though Stillman was not entirely free from enemies—in 1929, for instance, the grievances of a dismissed laboratory attendant set alight another flare of scandal—he had at least secured immunity to pursue his life work. Unchanged by success, he remained the same quiet and restrained personality who, nearly twenty-five years before, had grown his first cultures in the attic on Beacon Hill.

And now, seated in the restaurant of Brooks Hotel, he gazed across at Andrew with quiet friendliness.

"It's very pleasant," he said, "to be in England. I like your countryside. Our summers aren't so cool as this."

"I suppose you've come over on a lecture tour?" Andrew said.

Stillman smiled.

"No! I don't lecture now. Is it vanity to say that I let my results lecture for me? As a matter of fact I'm over here very quietly. It so happens your Mr. Cranston—I mean Herbert Cranston, who makes those marvellous little automobiles—came to me in America about a year back. He'd been a martyr to asthma all his life and I—well, at the Institute we managed to set him right. Ever since then he's been bothering me to come over and start a small clinic here on the lines of our place at Portland. Six months ago I agreed. We passed the plans and now the place—we're calling it Bellevue—is pretty near completion, out on the Chilterns near High Wycombe. I'm going to get it started, then I'll turn over to Marland—one of my assistants. Frankly, I look upon it as an experiment, a very promising experiment with my methods, particularly from the climatic and racial angles. The financial aspect is unimportant!"

Andrew leaned forward.

"That sounds interesting. What are you specially concentrating on? I'd like to look over your place."

"You must come when we are ready. We shall have our radical asthma régime. Cranston wants that. And then I have particularly specified for a few early tuberculosis cases. I say a few because," he smiled, "mind you, I don't forget I am just a biophysicist who knows a little about the respiratory apparatus—but in America our difficulty is to keep ourselves from being swamped. What was I saying? Ah, yes. These early T.B.'s. This will interest you. I have a new method of inducing pneumothorax. It is really an advance."

"You mean the Emile-Weil?"

"No, no. Much better. Without the disadvantages of negative fluctuation." Stillman's face lighted up. "You appreciate the difficulty of the fixed bottle apparatus—that point when the intrapleural pressure balances the fluid pressure and the flow of gas ceases altogether? Now, at the Institute, we've devised an accessory pressure chamber—I'll show you when you come out—through which we can introduce gas at a decided negative pressure, right at the start."

"But what about gas embolism?" Andrew said quickly.

"We eliminate the risk entirely. Look! It's quite a dodge. By introducing a small bromoform manometer close to the needle we avoid rarefaction. A fluctuation of -14 c.m. provides only 1 c.c. of gas at the needle-joint. Incidentally our needle has a four-way adjustment that goes a little better than Sangman's."

Andrew, in spite of himself—and his honorary appointment at the Victoria—was impressed.

"Why," he said, "if that is so, you're going to diminish pleural shock right down to nothing. You know, Mr. Stillman—well, it seems strange, quite startling to me, that all this should have come from you. Oh! forgive me, I've said that badly, but you know what I mean—so many doctors, going on with the old apparatus—"

"My dear physician," Stillman answered with amusement in his eyes, "don't forget that Carson, the first man to urge pneumothorax, was only a physiological essayist!"

After that they plunged into technicalities. They discussed apicolysis and phrenicotomy. They argued over Brauer's four points, passed on to oleothorax and Bernon's work in France—massive intrapleural injections in tuberculous empyema. They ceased only when Stillman looked at his watch and realized, with an exclamation, that he was half an hour late for an appointment with Cranston.

Andrew left Brooks Hotel with a stimulated and exalted mind. But, on the heels of that, came a queer reaction of confusion, dissatisfaction with his own work. I let myself get carried away by that fellow, he told himself, annoyed.

He was not in a particularly amiable frame of mind when he arrived at Chesborough Terrace; yet, as he drew up opposite his house, he composed his features into a noncommittal mould. His relations with Christine had come to demand this blankness, for she now presented to him a face so acquiescent and expressionless he felt, however much he raged internally, that he must answer it in kind.

It seemed to him that she had retired within herself, fallen back upon an inner life where he could not penetrate. She read a great deal, wrote letters. Once or twice when he came in he found her playing with Florrie—childish games, played with coloured counters, which they bought at the Stores. She began also, with unobtrusive regularity, to go to church. And this exasperated him most of all.

At Blaenelly she had accompanied Mrs. Watkins every Sunday to the parish church and he had found no reason for complaint. But now, unsympathetic and estranged from her, he saw it only as a further slight upon himself, a gesture of pietism directed at his suffering head.

This evening as he entered the front room she was seated alone in the room with her elbows on the table, wearing the glasses she had recently taken to, a book before her, a small occupied figure like a scholar at her lesson. An angry swell of exclusion swept over him. Reaching over her shoulders he picked up the book which, too late, she attempted to conceal. And there, at the head of the page, he read: *The Gospel According to St. Luke.*

"Good God!" He was staggered, somehow furious. "Is this what you've come to? Taken to Bible-thumping now?"

"Why not? I used to read it before I met you."

"Oh, you did, eh?"

"Yes." A queer look of pain was in her eyes. "Possibly your Plaza friends wouldn't appreciate the fact. But it is at least good literature."

"Is that so! Well, let me tell you this, in case you don't know it—you're developing into a blasted neurotic woman!"

"Quite probably. That again is entirely my fault. But let me tell you this. I'd rather be a blasted neurotic woman and be spiritually alive than a blasted successful man—and spiritually dead!"

She broke off suddenly, biting her lip, forcing back her tears. With a great effort she took control of herself. Looking at him steadily, with pain in her eyes, she said, in a low contained voice:—

"Andrew! Don't you think it would be a good thing for us both if I went away for a little while? Mrs. Vaughan has written me, asking me to spend a fortnight or three weeks with her. They've taken a house at Newquay for the summer. Don't you think I ought to go?"

"Yes! Go! Damn it all! Go!"

He swung round and left her.

xiii

Christine's departure for Newquay was a relief, an exquisite emancipation—for three whole days. Then he began to brood, to wonder what she was doing and whether she was missing him, to fret jealously as to when she would return. Though he told himself he was now a free man, he had the same sense of incompleteness which had kept him from his work at Aberalaw when she had gone to Bridlington, leaving him to study for his examination.

Her image rose before him, not the fresh young features of that earlier Christine, but a paler, maturer face with cheeks faintly drawn and eyes shortsighted behind their round glasses. It was not a beautiful face but it had some enduring quality which haunted him.

He went out a great deal, played bridge with Ivory, Freddie, and Freedman at the club. Despite his reaction to their first meeting he frequently saw Stillman, who was moving between Brooks Hotel and the nearly completed clinic at Wycombe. He wrote asking Denny to meet him in London, but it was impossible at this early stage of his appointment for Philip to get to town. Hope was inaccessible in Cambridge.

Fitfully he tried to concentrate on his clinical research at the hospital. Impossible. He was too restless. With this same restless intensity he went over his investments with Wade, the bank manager. All satisfactory; all going well. He began to thresh out a scheme for buying a freehold house in Welbeck Street—a heavy investment, but one which should prove highly profitable—of selling the Chesborough Terrace house, merely retaining the surgery at the side. One of the building societies would help him. He woke during the still hot nights, his mind seething with schemes, with his work in the practice, his nerves overwrought, missing Christine, his hand reaching automatically to his bedside table for a cigarette.

In the middle of it all he rang up Frances Lawrence.

"I'm all alone here at present. You wouldn't care to run out somewhere in the evening? It's so hot in London."

Her voice was collected, oddly soothing to him. "That would be frightfully nice. I was hoping somehow you might ring. Do you know Crossways? Flood-lit Elizabethan, I'm afraid. But the river is too perfect there."

The following evening he cleared his surgery in three quarters of an hour. Well before eight, he had picked her up at Knightsbridge and set the car in the direction of Chertsey.

They ran due west, through the flat market gardens outside Staines, into a great flood of sunset. She sat beside him, as he drove, saying little yet filling the car with her alien, charming presence. She wore a coat and skirt of some thin fawn material, a dark hat close to her small head. He was overwhelmingly conscious of her gracefulness, her perfect finish. Her ungloved hand, near to him, was curiously expressive of this quality—white, slender. Each long finger tipped by an exquisite scarlet oval. Fastidious.

Crossways, as she had implied, was an exquisite Elizabethan house set in perfect gardens on the Thames, with age-long topiary work and lovely formal lily ponds all outraged in the conversion from mansion to roadhouse by modern conveniences and an infamous jazz band. But although a fake lackey sprang to the car as they ran into the courtyard, already filled by expensive cars, the old bricks glowed behind the wistaria vine and the tall angled chimneys clustered serenely against the sky.

They went into the restaurant. It was smart, full, with tables placed round a square of polished floor and a head waiter who might have been brother to the grand vizier of the Plaza. Andrew hated and feared head waiters. But that, he now discovered, was because he had never faced them with a woman like Frances. One swift glance and they were ministered, with reverence, to the finest table in the room—surrounded by a corps of servitors, one of whom unflicked Andrew's napkin and placed it holily upon his knees.

Frances wanted very little: a salad, toast melba, no wine, only iced water. Undisturbed, the head waiter seemed to see in this frugality a confirmation of her caste. Andrew realized with a sudden qualm of dismay that, had he walked into this sanctuary with Christine and ordered such a trivial repast, he would have been hounded forth upon the highway with scorn.

He recollected himself to find Frances smiling at him.

"Do you realize we've known each other for quite a period of time now? And this is the first occasion you have asked me to come out with you?"

"Are you sorry?"

"Not noticeably so, I hope." Again the charming intimacy of her faintly smiling face elevated him, caused him to feel wittier, more at ease, of a superior status. It was no mere pretentiousness, no silly snobbishness. The stamp of her breeding was somehow extended until it caught up and included him. He was aware of people at the adjoining tables viewing them with interest, of masculine admiration to which she was calmly oblivious. He could not help visualizing the stimulus of a more constant association with her.

She said:—

"Would it flatter you too much if I told you I had put off a previous theatre engagement to come here? Nicol Watson—do you remember him? He was taking me to the Ballet—one of my favourites—what will you think of my infantile taste? Massine in *La Boutique Fantastique.*"

"I remember Watson. And his ride through Paraguay. Clever fellow."

"He's frightfully nice."

"But you felt it would be too hot at the Ballet?"

She smiled without answering, took a cigarette from a flat enamel box on which was depicted in faded colours an exquisite Boucher miniature.

"Yes, I heard Watson was running after you," he persisted with sudden vehemence. "What does your husband think of that?"

Again she did not speak, merely lifting an eyebrow as if mildly deprecating some lack of subtlety.

After a moment she said:—

"Surely you understand? Jackie and I are the best of friends. But we each have our own friends. He's at Juan at present. But I don't ask him why." Then lightly, "Shall we dance—just once?"

They danced. She moved with that same extraordinary fascinating grace, light in his arms, impersonal.

"I'm not altogether good," he said when they returned. He was even falling into her idiom—gone, gone were the days when he would have grunted, "Damn it, Chris, I'm no hoofer."

Frances did not reply. That again he felt to be eminently characteristic of her. Another woman would have flattered, contradicted him, made him feel clumsy. Driven by a sudden impulsive curiosity he exclaimed:—

"Please tell me something. Why have you been so kind to me? Helping me the way you've done—all those months?"

She looked at him, faintly amused yet without evasion.

"You are extraordinarily attractive to women. And your greatest charm is that you do not realize it."

"No, but, really—" he protested, flushed; then he muttered, "I hope I'm some kind of a doctor as well."

She laughed, slowly fanning away the cigarette smoke with her hand. "You will not be convinced. Or I should not have told you. And of course you're an excellent doctor. We were talking of you only the other night at Green Street. Le Roy is getting a little tired of our company dietician. Poor Rumbold! He wouldn't have enjoyed hearing Le Roy bark, 'We must put the skids under Grandpa.' But Jackie agrees. They want someone younger, with more drive, on the board,—shall I use the cliché?—a coming man. Apparently they plan a big campaign in the medical journals, they want really to interest the profession—from the scientific angle, as Le Roy put it. And of course Rumbold is just a joke amongst his colleagues. But why am I talking of this? Such a waste of a night like this. Now don't frown as though you were about to assassinate me, or the waiter, or the band-leader—I wish you would actually, isn't he odious? You look exactly as you did that first day—when you came into the fitting-room—very haughty and proud and nervous—even a little ridiculous. And then—poor Toppy! By the ordinary convention it is *she* who should be here."

"I'm very glad she's not," he said with his eyes upon the table.

"Please don't think me banal. I couldn't bear that. We are fairly intelligent I hope—and we—well, I for one—just do not believe in the *grand passion*. Isn't the phrase enough? But I do think life is so much gayer if one has—a friend—to go a bit of the way with one." Her eyes showed high points of amusement again. "Now I sound completely Rossetti-ish, which is too frightful." She picked up her cigarette case. "And anyhow it's stuffy here and I want you to see the moon on the river."

He paid the bill and followed her through the long glass windows which an act of vandalism had inset in the fine old wall. On the balustered terrace the music of the dance band came faintly. Before them a wide avenue of turf led down to the river between dark borders of clipped yew. As she had said, there was a moon which splashed great shadows from the yews and glinted palely upon a group of archery targets standing on the bottom lawns. Beyond lay the silver sheen of water.

They strolled down to the river, seated themselves upon a bench that stood beside the verge. She took off her hat and gazed silently at the slowly moving current, its eternal murmur strangely blended with the muted hum of a high-powered car travelling at speed into the distance.

"What queer night sounds," she said. "The old and the new. And searchlights across the moon there. It's our age."

He kissed her. She gave no sign either way. Her lips were warm and dry. In a minute she said:—

"That was very sweet. And very badly done."

"I can do better," he mumbled, staring in front of him, not moving. He was awkward, without conviction, ashamed and nervous. Angrily he told himself that it was wonderful to be here on such a night with such a graceful, charming woman. He ought by all the canons of moonshine and the magazines to have swept her madly into his arms. As it was he became aware of his cramped position, of a desire to smoke, of the vinegar in the salad touching up his old indigestion.

And Christine's face in some unaccountable way was mirrored in the water before him, a jaded and rather harassed face, on her cheek a plaintive smudge of paint from the brush with which she had painted the heavy folding doors, when they first came to Chesborough Terrace. It worried and exasperated him. He was here, bound by the obligation of the circumstances. And he was a man, wasn't he—not a candidate for Voronoff? Defiantly, he kissed Frances again.

"I thought possibly you were taking another twelve months to make up your mind." Her eyes held that high affectionate amusement. "And now, don't you think we should go, Doctor? These night airs—aren't they rather treacherous to the Puritanical mind?"

He helped her to her feet and she retained his hand, holding it lightly as they walked to the car. He flung a shilling to the baroque retainer, started the engine for London. As he drove her silence was eloquently happy.

But he was not happy. He felt himself a hound and a fool. Hating himself, disappointed in his own reactions, he still dreaded the return to his sultry room, his restless solitary bed. His heart was cold, his brain a mass of tormenting thoughts. The recollection swept before him of the agonizing sweetness of his first love for Christine, the beating ecstasy of those early days at Blaenelly. He pushed it away from him furiously.

They were at her house and his mind still struggled with the problem. He got out of the car and opened the door for her. They stood together on the pavement while she opened her bag and took out her latchkey.

"You'll come up, won't you? I'm afraid the servants are in bed."

He hesitated, stammered.

"It's very late, isn't it?"

She did not seem to hear him but went up the few flagstone steps with her key in her hand. As he followed, sneaking after her, he had a fading vision of Christine's figure walking down the market, carrying her old string bag.

xiv

Three days later Andrew sat in his Welbeck Street consulting room. It was a hot afternoon and, through the screen of his open window, there came the pestering drone of traffic, borne upon the exhausted air. He was tired, overworked, fearful of Christine's return at the end of the week, expectant yet nervous of every telephone ring, sweating under the task of coping with six three-guinea patients in the space of one hour, and the knowledge that he must rush his surgery to take Frances out to supper. He glanced up impatiently as Nurse Sharp entered, more than usual acrimony on her patchy features.

"There's a man called to see you, a dreadful person. He's not a patient and he says he's not a traveller. He's got no card. His name's Boland."

"Boland?" Andrew echoed blankly; then his face cleared suddenly. "Not Con Boland? Let him in, Nurse! Straightaway."

"But you have a patient waiting. And in ten minutes Mrs. Roberts—"

"Oh! never mind Mrs. Roberts!" he threw out irritably. "Do as I say."

Nurse Sharp flushed at his tone. It was on her tongue to tell him she was not used to being spoken to like that. She sniffed and went out with her head in the air. The next minute she showed Boland in.

"Why, Con!" said Andrew jumping up.

"Hello, hello, he*llo,*" shouted Con, as he bounded forward with a broad and genial grin. It was the redheaded dentist himself, no different, as real and untidy in his oversize shiny blue suit and large brown boots as if he had that moment walked out of his wooden garage; a shade older perhaps, but with no less violence in the beaded brush of his red moustache, still undaunted, wildhaired, exclamatory. He pounded Andrew vehemently on the back. "In the name of God, Manson! It's great to see ye again. Ye're lookin' marvellous, marvellous. I'd have known ye in a million. Well! Well! To think of this now. It's a high-class place you have here and all." He turned his beaming gaze upon the acidulous Sharp, who stood watching scornfully. "This lady nurse of yours wasn't for lettin' me in till I told her I was a professional man, myself. It's the God's truth, Nurse. This swanky-lookin' fella ye work for was in the same wan-horse medical scheme as myself not so long ago. Up in Aberalaw. If ever ye're passin' that way, drop in on the missus and me and we'll give ye a cup of tea. Any friend of my old friend Manson is welcome as the day!"

Nurse Sharp gave him one look and walked out of the room. But it was wasted on Con, who gushed and bubbled with a pure and natural joy, swinging round to Andrew irrepressibly:—

"No beauty, eh, Manson, my boy? But a decent woman I'll be bound. Well, well, well! How are ye, now? How *are* ye?"

He refused to relinquish Andrew's hand, but pumped it up and down, grinning away in sheer delight.

It was a rare tonic to see Con again on this devitalizing day. When Andrew at last freed himself, he flung himself into his swing chair, feeling himself human again, shoving over the cigarettes to Con. Then Con, with one grubby thumb in an armhole, the other pressing the wet end of a freshly lit cigarette, sketched the reason of his coming.

"I had a bit of a holiday due to me, Manson, my boy, and a couple of matters to attend to, so the wife just told me to pack off and hit it. Ye see, I've been workin' on a sort of a spring invention for tightenin' up slack brakes. Off and on I've been devotin' the full candlepower of the old grey mather to th' idee. But devil take them, there's nobody'll look at the gadget! But never mind, never mind, we'll let it go. It's not important besides the other thing." Con cast his cigarette ash upon the carpet and his face took a more serious turn. "Listen, Manson, my boy! It's Mary—you'll remember Mary surely, for I can tell you she remembers you! She's been poorly lately—not up to the mark at all. We've had her to Llewellyn and devil the bit of good he's doin' her." Con grew heated suddenly; his voice was thick. "Damn it all, Manson, he's got the sauce to say she's got a touch of T.B.—as if that wasn't all finished and done with in the Boland family when her Uncle Dan went to the sanatorium fifteen years ago. Now look here, Manson, will ye do something for old friendship's sake? We knew ye're a big man now; sure ye're the talk of Aberalaw. Will ye take a look at Mary for us? Ye can't tell what confidence that girl has in you; we've got it ourselves—Mrs. B. and me—for that matter. That's why she says to me she says, 'You go to Doctor Manson when you're in the way of meetin' him. And if he'll see the daughter sure we'll send her up any time that's likely to be convenient.' Now what do you say, Manson? If you're too busy ye've only got to say so and I can easy sling my hook."

Andrew's expression had turned concerned.

"Don't talk that way, Con. Can't you see how delighted I am to see you? And Mary, poor kid—you know I'll do everything I can for her, everything."

Unmindful of Nurse Sharp's significant inthrustings he squandered his precious time in conversation with Con until at last she could bear it no longer.

"You have five patients waiting now, Doctor Manson. And you're more than an hour behind your appointment times. I can't make any more excuses to them, I'm not used to treating patients this way."

Even then, he still clutched at Con, and accompanied him to the front door, pressing hospitality upon him.

"I'm not going to let you rush back home, Con. How long are you up for? Three or four days? That's fine! Where are you staying? The Westland—out Bayswater way! That's no good! Why don't you come and stop with me instead; you're near us already. And we've bag-loads of room. Christine'll be back on Friday. She'll be delighted to see you, Con, delighted. We can talk over old times together."

On the following day Con brought his bag round to Chesborough Terrace. After the evening surgery they went together to the second house of the Palladium Music Hall. It was amazing how good every turn seemed in Con's company. The dentist's ready laugh rang out, dismaying at first, then infecting the immediate vicinity. People twisted round to smile at Con in sympathy.

"In the name of God!" Con rolled in his seat. "D'y' see that fella? With the bicycle? D'y' mind the time, Manson—"

In the interval they stood in the bar, Con with his hat on the back of his head, froth on his moustache, brown boots, happily planted.

"I can't tell ye, Manson, my boy, what a treat this is for me. Sure you're kindness itself!"

In the face of Con's genial gratitude Andrew somehow felt himself a tarnished hypocrite.

Afterwards they had a steak and beer at the Cadero; then they returned, stirred up the fire in the front room and sat down to talk. They talked and smoked and drank further bottles of beer. Momentarily Andrew forgot the complexities of supercivilized existence. The straining tension of his practice, the prospect of his adoption by Le Roy, the chance of promotion at the Victoria, the state of his investments, the soft-textured nicety of Frances Lawrence, the dread of an accusation in Christine's distant eyes—these all faded as Con bellowed:—

"D'you mind the time we fought Llewellyn? And Urquhart and the rest drew back on us—Urquhart's still goin' strong by the same token, sends his best regards—and then we set to, the both of us, and finished the beer?"

But the next day came. And it brought, inexorably, the moment of reunion with Christine. Andrew dragged the unsuspecting Con to the end of the platform, irritably aware of the inadequacy of his self-possession, realizing that Boland was his salvation. His heart was beating in painful expectation as the train steamed in. He knew one shattering moment of anguish and remorse at the sight of Christine's small familiar face advancing amongst the crowd of strangers, straining in expectation towards his own. Then he lost everything in the effort to achieve cordial unconcern.

"Hello, Chris! Thought you were never coming! Yes, you may well look at him. It's Con all right! Himself and no other! And not a day older. He's staying with us, Chris—we'll tell you all about it in the car. I've got it outside. Did you have a good time? Oh, look here! *Why* are you carrying your case?"

Swept away by the unexpectedness of this platform reception—when she had feared she might not be met at all—Christine lost her wan expression, and colour flowed back nervously into her cheeks. She also had been apprehensive, nervously keyed, longing for a new beginning. She felt almost hopeful now. Ensconced in the back of the car with Con she talked eagerly, stealing glances at Andrew's profile in the driving seat.

"Oh, it is good to be home." She took a long breath inside the front door of the house; then, quickly, wistfully, "You have missed me, Andrew?"

"I should think I have. We *all* have. Eh, Mrs. Bennett? Eh, Florrie? Con! What the devil are you doing with that luggage?"

He was out in a second, giving Con a hand, performing unnecessarily with suitcases. Then, before anything more could be done or said, he had to leave on his rounds. He insisted that they could expect him for tea.

As he slumped into the seat of his car he groaned:—

"Thank God that's over! She doesn't look a lot the better of the holiday. Oh, hell! I'm sure she didn't notice. And that's the main thing at present."

Though he was late in returning, his briskness, his cheerfulness were excessive. Con was enraptured with such spirits.

"In the name of God! Ye've more go in ye than ever ye had in the old days, Manson, my boy."

Once or twice he felt Christine's eye upon him, half-pleading for a sign, a look of understanding. He perceived that Mary's illness was distracting her—a conflicting anxiety. She explained, in an interval of conversation, that she had asked Con to wire Mary to come through at once, to-morrow if possible. She was worried about Mary. She hoped that something, or rather everything, would be done without delay.

It fell out better than Andrew had expected. Mary wired back that she would arrive on the following day before lunch, and Christine was fully occupied in preparing for her. The stir and excitement in the house masked even his hollow heartiness.

But when Mary appeared he suddenly became himself again. It was evident at first sight that she was not well. Grown in these intervening years to a lanky young woman, with a slight droop to her shoulders, she had that almost unnatural beauty of complexion which spoke an immediate warning to Andrew.

She was tired out by her journey and though she wished, in her pleasure at seeing them again, to sit up and continue talking, she was persuaded to bed about six o'clock. It was then that Andrew went up to auscultate her chest.

He remained upstairs for only fifteen minutes, but when he came down to Con and Christine in the drawing-room his expression was, for once, genuinely disturbed.

"I'm afraid there's no doubt about it. The left apex. Llewellyn was perfectly right, Con. But don't worry. It's in the primary stage. We can do something with it!"

"You mean," said Con, gloomily apprehensive, "you mean it can be cured?"

"Yes. I'd go so far as to say that. It means keeping an eye on her, constant observation, every care." He reflected, frowning deeply. "It seems to me, Con, that Aberalaw's about the worst place for her—always bad for early T.B. at home. Why don't you let me get her into the Victoria? I've got a pull with Doctor Thoroughgood. I'd get her into his ward for a certainty. I'd keep my eye on her."

"Manson!" Con exclaimed impressively. "That's one true act of friendship. If ye only knew the trust that girl of mine has in ye! If any man'll get her right it's yourself."

Andrew went immediately to telephone Thoroughgood. He returned in five minutes with the information that Mary could be admitted to the Victoria at the end of the week. Con brightened visibly and, his bounding optimism responding to the idea of the Chest Hospital, of Andrew's attention, and Thoroughgood's supervision, Mary was for him as good as cured.

The next two days were fully occupied. By Saturday afternoon when Mary was admitted and Con had boarded his train at Paddington, Andrew's self-possession was at last equal to the occasion. He was able to press Christine's arm, and exclaim lightly on his way to the surgery:—

"Nice to be together again, Chris! Lord! What a week it has been."

It sounded perfectly in key. But it was as well he did not see the look upon her face. She sat down in the room, alone, her head bent slightly, her hands in her lap, very still.

She had been so hopeful when first she came back. But now, within her, was the dreadful foreboding: *Dear God! When and how is this going to end?*

XV

On and on rushed the spate of his success, a bursting dam sweeping him irresistibly forward in an ever-sounding, ever-swelling flood.

His association with Hampton and Ivory was now closer and more profitable than ever. Moreover, Freedman had asked him to deputize for him at the Plaza, while he flew to Le Touquet for seven days' golf, and, by way of acknowledgment, to split the fees. Usually it was Hampton who acted as Freedman's locum, but lately Andrew suspected a rift between these two.

How flattering for Andrew to discover that he could walk straight into the bedroom of a paroxysmal film star, sit on her satin sheets, palpate her sexless anatomy with sure hands, perhaps smoke a cigarette with her if he had time!

But even more flattering was the patronage of Joseph Le Roy. Twice in the last month he had lunched with Le Roy. He knew there were important ideas working in the other man's mind. At their last meeting Le Roy had tentatively remarked:—

"You know, Doc, I've been feeling my way with you. It's a pretty large thing I'm going on to, and I'll need a lot of clever medical advice. I don't want any more double-handed big hats—old Rumbold isn't worth his own calories, we're going to pin the crape on him right away! And I don't want a lot of so-called experts goin' into a huddle and pulling me round in circles. I want one level-headed medical adviser, and I'm beginning to think you're about it. You see, we've reached a wide section of the public with our products on a popular basis. But I honestly believe the time has come to expand our interests and go in for more scientific derivatives. Split up the milk components, electrify them, irradiate them, tabloid them. Cremo with vitamin B, Cremofax and lecithin for malnutrition, rickets, deficiency insomnia—you get me, Doc. And further, I believe if we tackle this on more orthodox professional lines we can enlist the help and sympathy of the whole medical profession, make every doctor, so to speak, a potential salesman. Now this means scientific advertising, Doc, scientific approach; and that's where I believe a young scientific doctor on the inside could help us all along the road. Now I want you to get me straight. This is all perfectly open and *scientific*. We are actually raising our own status. And when you consider the worthless extracts that doctors do recommend, like Marrobin C and Vegatog and Bonebran, why, I consider in elevating the general standard of health we are doing a great public service to the nation."

Andrew did not pause to consider that there was probably more vitamin value in one fresh green pea than in several tins of Cremofax. He was excited, not by the fee he would receive for acting on the board, but at the thought of Le Roy's interest.

It was Frances who told him how he might profit by Le Roy's spectacular market operations. Ah! it was pleasant to drop in to tea with her, to feel that this charming sophisticated woman had a special glance for him, a swift provoking smile of intimacy! Association with her gave him sophistication too, added assurance, a harder polish. Unconsciously he absorbed her philosophy. Under her guidance he was learning to cultivate the superficial niceties and let the deeper things go hang.

It was no longer an embarrassment to face Christine; he could come into his house quite naturally, following an hour spent with Frances. He did not stop to wonder at this astounding change. If he thought of it at all it was to argue that he did not love Mrs. Lawrence, that Christine knew nothing of it, that every man came to this particular *impasse* some time in his life. Why should he set himself up to be different?

By way of recompense he went out of his way to be nice to Christine, spoke to her with consideration, even discussed his plans with her. She was aware that he proposed to buy the Welbeck Street house next spring, that they would be leaving Chesborough Terrace whenever the arrangements were complete. She never argued with him now, never threw recriminations at his head, and if she had moods he never saw them. She seemed altogether passive. Life moved too swiftly for him to pause long for reflection. The pace exhilarated him. He had a false sensation of strength. He felt vital, increasing in consequence, master of himself and of his destiny.

And then, out of high heaven, the bolt fell.

One evening the wife of a neighbouring petty tradesman came to his consulting room at Chesborough Terrace. She was Mrs. Vidler, a small sparrow of a woman, middle-aged, but bright-eyed and spry, a regular Londoner who had all her life never been further from Bow Bells than Margate. Andrew knew the Vidlers well; he had attended the little boy for some childish complaint when he first came to the district. In those early days, too, he had sent his shoes there to be mended, for the Vidlers, respectable, hard-working tradespeople, kept a double shop at the head of Paddington Street named, rather magnificently, "Renovations Ltd."—one half devoted to boot repairs and the other to the cleaning and pressing of wearing apparel. Harry Vidler himself might often be seen, a sturdy pale-faced man, collarless and in his shirt sleeves, with a last between his knees or, though he kept a couple of helpers, using a damping-board if work in the other department was urgent.

It was of Harry that Mrs. Vidler now spoke.

"Doctor," she said in her brisk way, "my husband isn't well. For weeks now he's been poorly. I've been at him and at him to come, but he wouldn't. Will you call to-morrow, Doctor? I'll keep him in bed."

Andrew promised that he would call.

Next morning he found Vidler in bed, giving a history of internal pain and growing stoutness. His girth had increased extraordinarily in these last few months and inevitably, like most patients who have enjoyed good health all their lives, he had several ways of accounting for it. He suggested that he had been taking a drop too much ale, or that perhaps his sedentary life was to blame.

But Andrew, after his investigation, was obliged to contradict these elucidations. He was convinced that the condition was cystic and, although not dangerous, it was one which demanded operative treatment. He did his best to reassure Vidler and his wife by explaining how a simple cyst such as this might develop internally and cause no end of inconvenience which would all disappear when it was removed. He had no doubt at all in his mind as to the upshot of the operation, and he proposed that Vidler should go into hospital at once.

Here, however, Mrs. Vidler held up her hands.

"No, sir, I won't have my Harry in a hospital!" She struggled to compose her agitation. "I've had a kind of feeling this was coming—the way he's been overworking in the business. But now it 'as come, thank God we're in a position as can deal with it. We're not well-off people, Doctor, as you know, but we 'ave got a little bit put by. And now's the time to use it. I won't have Harry go beggin' for subscribers' letters, and standin' in queues, and goin' into a public ward like he was a pauper."

"But, Mrs. Vidler, I can arrange—"

"No! You can get him in a private home, sir. There's plenty round about here. And you can get a private doctor to operate on him. I can promise you, sir, so long as I'm here, no public hospital shall 'ave Harry Vidler."

He saw that her mind was firmly made up. And indeed Vidler himself, since this unpleasant necessity had arisen, was of the same opinion as his wife. He wanted the best treatment that could be had.

That evening Andrew rang up Ivory. It was automatic now for him to turn to Ivory; the more so as, in this instance, he had to ask a favour.

"I'd like you to do something for me, Ivory. I've an abdominal here, that wants doing —decent hard-working people but not rich, you understand. There's nothing much in it for you, I'm afraid. But it would oblige me if you did it for—shall we say a third of the usual fee?"

Ivory was very gracious. Nothing would please him more than to do his friend Manson any service within his power. They discussed the case for several minutes and at the end of that discussion Andrew telephoned Mrs. Vidler.

"I've just been on to Mr. Charles Ivory, a West End surgeon who happens to be a particular friend of mine. He's coming to see your husband with me to-morrow, Mrs. Vidler, at eleven o'clock. That all right? And he says—are you there?—he says, Mrs. Vidler, that if the operation has to be undertaken he'll do it for thirty guineas. Considering that his usual fee would be a hundred guineas—perhaps more—I think we're not doing too badly."

"Yes, Doctor, yes." Her tone was worried, yet she made the effort to sound relieved. "It's very kind of you, I'm sure. I think we can manage that some'ow."

Next morning Ivory saw the case with Andrew and on the following day Harry Vidler moved into the Brunsland Nursing Home in Brunsland Square.

It was a clean, old-fashioned home not far from Chesborough Terrace, one of many in the district where the fees were moderate and the equipment scanty. Most of its patients were medical cases, hemiplegics, chronic cardiacs, bedridden old women with whom the main difficulty was the prevention of bedsores. Like every other home which Andrew had entered in London it had never been intended for its present purpose. There was no lift, and the operating theatre had once been a conservatory. But Miss Buxton, the proprietress, was a qualified Sister and a hard working woman. Whatever its defects, the Brunsland was spotlessly aseptic—and even to the furthest corner of its shining linoleumed floors.

The operation was fixed for Friday and, since Ivory could not come early, it was set for the unusually late hour of two o'clock.

Though Andrew was at Brunsland Square first, Ivory arrived punctually. He drove up with the anaesthetist and stood watching while his chauffeur carried in his large bag of instruments—so that nothing might interfere with his subsequent delicacy of touch. And, though he plainly thought little of the home, his manner remained as suave as ever.

Within the space of ten minutes he had reassured Mrs. Vidler, who waited in the front room, made the conquest of Miss Buxton and her nurses; then, gowned and gloved in the little travesty of a theatre, he was imperturbably ready.

The patient walked in with determined cheerfulness, slipped off his dressing-gown, which one of the nurses then whipped away, and climbed upon the narrow table. Realizing that he must go through with the ordeal, Vidler had come to face it with courage. Before the anaesthetist placed the mask over his face he smiled at Andrew.

"I'll be better after this is over." The next moment he had closed his eyes and was almost eagerly drinking in deep draughts of ether. Miss Buxton removed the bandages. The iodined area was exposed, unnaturally tumescent, a glistening mound. Ivory commenced the operation.

He began with some spectacular deep injections into the lumbar muscles.

"Combat shock," he threw out gravely to Andrew. "I always use it."

Then the real work began.

His medial incision was large, and immediately, almost ludicrously, the trouble was revealed. The cyst bobbed through the opening like a fully inflated wet rubber football. The justification of his diagnosis added, if anything, to Andrew's self-esteem. He reflected that Vidler would do nicely when detached from this uncomfortable accessory and with an eye on his next case he surreptitiously looked at his watch.

Meanwhile Ivory, in his masterly manner, was playing with the football, imperturbably trying to get his hands round it to its point of attachment and imperturbably failing. Every time he attempted to control it the ball slithered away from him. If he tried once he tried twenty times.

Andrew glanced irritably at Ivory, thinking, What is the man doing? There was not much space in the abdomen in which to work, but there was space enough. He had seen Llewellyn, Denny, a dozen others at his old hospital manipulate expertly with far less latitude. It was a surgeon's job to fiddle through cramped positions. Suddenly he realized that this was the first abdominal operation Ivory had ever done for him. Insensibly, he dropped his watch back into his pocket, drew nearer, rather rigidly, to the table.

Ivory was still straining to get behind the cyst, still calm, incisive, unruffled. Miss Buxton and a young nurse stood trustfully by, not knowing very much about anything. The anaesthetist, an elderly grizzled man, was stroking the end of the stoppered bottle contemplatively with his thumb. The atmosphere of the bare little glass-roofed theatre was flat, supremely uneventful. There was no high sense of tension or steam-heated drama, merely Ivory raising one shoulder, manœuvring with his gloved hands, trying to get behind the smooth rubber ball. But for some reason a sense of coldness fell on Andrew.

He found himself frowning, watching tensely. What was he dreading? There was nothing to be afraid of, nothing. It was a straightforward operation. In a few minutes it would be finished.

Ivory, with a faint smile, as of satisfaction, gave up the attempt to find the cyst's point of attachment. The young nurse gazed at him humbly as he asked for a knife. Ivory took the knife in slow motion. Probably never in his career had he looked more exactly like the great surgeon of fiction. Holding the knife, before Andrew knew what he was about, he made a generous puncture in the glistening wall of the cyst.

After that everything happened at once.

The cyst burst, exploding a great clot of venous blood into the air, vomiting its contents into the abdominal cavity. One second there was a round tight sphere, the next a flaccid purse of tissue lay in a mess of gurgling blood. Frantically Miss Buxton felt in the drum for swabs.

The anaesthetist sat up abruptly. The young nurse looked like fainting. Ivory said gravely:—

"Clamp, please."

A wave of horror swept over Andrew. He saw that Ivory, failing to reach the pedicle to ligature it, had blindly, wantonly, incised the cyst. And it was a haemorrhagic cyst.

"Swab, please," Ivory said in his impassive voice. He was fiddling about in the mess, trying to clamp the pedicle, swabbing out the blood-filled cavity, packing, failing to control the haemorrhage. Realization broke on Andrew in a blinding flash. He thought: God Almighty! He can't operate, he can't operate at all!

The anaesthetist, with his finger on the carotid, murmured in a gentle, apologetic voice: "I'm afraid—he seems to be going, Ivory."

Ivory, relinquishing the clamp, stuffed the belly cavity full of blooded gauze. He began to suture up his great incision.

There was no swelling now. Vidler's stomach had a caved-in, pallid, empty look, the reason being that Vidler was dead.

"Yes, he's gone now," said the anaesthetist finally.

Ivory put in his last stitch, clipped it methodically and turned to the instrument tray to lay down his scissors. Paralyzed, Andrew could not move. Miss Buxton, with a clay-coloured face, was automatically packing the hot bottles outside the blanket. By great force of will she seemed to collect herself. She went outside. The porter, unaware of what had happened, brought in the stretcher. Another minute and Harry Vidler's body was being carried upstairs to his bedroom.

Ivory spoke at last.

"Very unfortunate," he said in his collected voice as he stripped off his gown. "I imagine it was shock. Don't you think so, Gray?"

Gray, the anaesthetist, mumbled an answer. He was busy packing up his apparatus.

Still Andrew could not speak. Amidst the dazed welter of his emotion he suddenly remembered Mrs. Vidler, waiting downstairs. It seemed as if Ivory read that thought. He said, "Don't worry, Manson. I'll attend to the little woman. Come. I'll get it over for you now."

Instinctively, like a man unable to resist, Andrew found himself following Ivory down the stairs to the waiting-room. He was still stunned, weak with nausea, wholly incapable of telling Mrs. Vidler. It was Ivory who rose to the occasion, rose almost to the heights.

"My dear lady," he said, compassionate and upstanding, placing his hand gently on her shoulder, "I'm afraid—I'm afraid we have bad news for you."

She clasped her hands, in worn brown kid gloves, together. Terror and entreaty were mingled in her eyes.

"What?"

"Your poor husband, Mrs. Vidler, in spite of everything which we could do for him —"

She collapsed into the chair, her face ashen, her gloved hands still working together.

"Harry!" she whispered in a heartrending voice. Then again, "Harry!"

"I can only assure you," Ivory went on, sadly, "on behalf of Doctor Manson, Doctor Gray, Miss Buxton, and myself, that no power on earth could have saved him. And even if he had survived the operation..." He shrugged his shoulders significantly. She looked up at him, sensing his meaning, aware, even at this frightful moment, of his condescension, his goodness to her.

"That's the kindest thing you could have told me, Doctor." She spoke through her tears.

"I'll send down Sister to you. Do your best to bear up. And thank you, thank you for your courage."

He went out of the room and once again Andrew went with him. At the end of the hall was the empty office, the door of which stood open. Feeling for his cigarette case, Ivory walked into the office. There he lit a cigarette and took a long pull at it. His face was perhaps a trifle paler than usual but his jaw was firm, his hand steady, his nerve absolutely unshaken.

"Well, that's over," he reflected coolly. "I'm sorry, Manson. I didn't dream that cyst was haemorrhagic. But these things happen in the best-regulated circles, you know."

It was a small room with the only chair pushed underneath the desk. Andrew sank down on the leather-covered club fender that surrounded the fireplace. He stared feverishly at the aspidistra in the yellowish green pot placed in the empty grate. He was sick, shattered, on the verge of a complete collapse. He could not escape the vision of Harry Vidler, walking unaided to the table—"I'll be better after this is over"—and then ten minutes later, sagging on the stretcher, a mutilated, butchered corpse. He gritted his teeth together, covered his eyes with his hand.

"Of course," Ivory inspected the end of his cigarette, "he didn't die on the table. I finished before that—which makes it all right. No necessity for an inquest."

Andrew raised his head. He was trembling, infuriated by the consciousness of his own weakness in this awful situation which Ivory had sustained with such cold-blooded nerve.

He said, in a kind of frenzy:—

"For Christ's sake stop talking. You know you killed him. You're not a surgeon. You never were; you never will be a surgeon. You're the worst butcher I've ever seen in all my life."

There was a silence. Ivory gave Andrew a pale, hard glance. "I don't recommend that line of talk, Manson."

"You don't?" A painful, hysterical sob shook Andrew. "I know you don't! But it's the truth. All the cases I've given you up till now have been child's play. But this—the first real case we've had—Oh, God! I should have known—I'm just as bad as you—"

"Pull yourself together, you hysterical fool. You'll be heard."

"What if I am?" Another weak burst of anger seized Andrew. He choked: "You know it's the truth as well as I do. You bungled so much—it was almost murder!"

For an instant it seemed as if Ivory would knock him senseless off the fender, a physical effort which, with his weight and strength, the older man could easily have accomplished. But with a great struggle he controlled himself. He said nothing, simply turned and walked out of the room. But there was an ugly look on his cold, hard face which spoke, icily, of unforgiving fury.

How long Andrew remained in the office, his forehead pressed against the cold marble of the mantelpiece, he did not know. But at last he rose, realizing dully that he had work which he must do. The dreadful shock of the calamity had caught him with the destructive violence of an explosive shell. It was as though he, also, were eviscerate and empty. Yet he still moved automatically, advancing as might a horribly wounded soldier, compelled by machinelike habit to perform the duties expected of him.

In this fashion he managed, somehow, to drag round his remaining visits. Then, with a leaden heart and an aching head, he came back home. It was late, nearly seven o'clock. He was just in time for his surgery and evening consultations.

His front waiting-room was full, his surgery packed to the door. Heavily, like a dying man, he took stock of them: his patients, gathered, despite the fine summer evening, to pay tribute to his manner, his personality. Mostly women, a great many of them Laurier's girls, people who had been coming to him for weeks, encouraged by his smile, his tact, his suggestion that they persevere with their medicine; the old gang, he thought numbly, the old game!

He dropped into his surgery swing chair, began with a mask-like face the usual evening rite.

"How are you? Yes, I think you're looking a shade better! Yes. Pulse has much more tone. The physic is doing you good. Hope it's not too nasty for you, my dear girl."

Out to the waiting Christine, handing her the empty bottle, forward along the passage to the consulting room, stringing out the same interrogative platitudes there, the same bogus sympathy; then back along the passage, picking up the full bottle, back into the surgery again. So it went on, this infernal circus of his own damnation.

It was a sultry night. He suffered abominably, but still he went on, half to torture himself and half in empty deadness because he could not stop. As he passed backwards and forwards in a daze of pain he kept asking himself: Where am I going? Where, in the name of God, am I going?

At last, later than usual, at quarter to ten, it was finished. He locked the outer door of the surgery, came through to the consulting room where, according to routine, Christine waited, ready to call out the lists, to help him make up the book.

For the first time in many weeks he really looked at her, gazed deeply into her face as, with lowered eyes, she studied the list in her hand. Piercing even his numbness, the change in her shocked him. Her expression was still and fixed, her mouth drooped. Though she did not look at him there was a mortal sadness in her eyes.

Seated at the desk before the heavy ledger he felt a frightful straining in his side. But his body, that outer covering of deadness, allowed nothing of that inner throbbing to escape. Before he could speak she had begun to call out the list.

On and on he went, marking the book, a cross for a visit, a circle for a consultation, marking the total of his iniquity.

When it was finished she asked, in a voice whose wincing satire he only then observed:—

"Well! How much to-day?"

He did not, could not answer. She left the room. He heard her go upstairs to her room, heard the quiet sound of her closing the door. He was alone: dry, stricken, bemused.

Where am I going? Where in the name of God am I going?

Suddenly his eyes fell upon the tobacco sack, full of money, bulging with his cash takings for the day. Another wave of hysteria swept over him. He took up the bag and flung it into the corner of the room. It fell with a dull and senseless sound.

He jumped up. He was stifling, he could not breathe.

Leaving the consulting room, he rushed into the little back yard of the house, a small well of darkness beneath the stars. Here he leaned weakly against the brick dividing-wall. He began, violently, to retch.

xvi

He tossed restlessly in bed all through the night until, at six in the morning, he at last fell asleep. Awakening late he came down after nine o'clock, pale and heavy-eyed, to find that Christine had already breakfasted and gone out. Normally this would not have upset him. Now, with a pang of anguish, it made him feel how far they were apart.

When Mrs. Bennett brought him his nicely cooked bacon and egg he could not eat it, the muscles of his throat refused to work. He drank a cup of coffee; then, on an impulse, he mixed himself a stiff whisky-and-soda, drank that too. He then prepared to face the day.

Though the machine still held him, his movements were less automatic than before. A faint gleam, a haggard shaft of light had begun to penetrate his dazed uncertainty. He knew that he was on the verge of a great, a colossal breakdown. He knew also that if he once fell into that abyss he would never crawl out of it. Cautiously holding himself in, he opened the garage and took out his car. The effort made the sweat spring out on his palms.

His main purpose this morning was to reach the Victoria. He had made an appointment with Doctor Thoroughgood to see Mary Boland. That, at least, was an engagement he did not wish to miss. He drove slowly to the hospital. Actually he felt better in the car than when he walked—he was so used to driving that it had become automatic, reflex.

He reached the hospital, parked his car, went up to the ward. With a nod to Sister he passed along to Mary's bed, picking up her chart on the way. Then he sat down on the red blanketed edge of the bed, aware of her welcoming smile, of the big bunch of roses beside her, but all the while studying her chart. The chart was not satisfactory.

"Good morning," she said. "Aren't my flowers beautiful? Christine brought them yesterday."

He looked at her. No more flushed, but a little thinner than when she came in.

"Yes, they're nice flowers. How do you feel, Mary?"

"Oh! All right." Her eyes avoided his momentarily, then swept back full of warm confidence. "Anyway I know it won't be for long. You'll soon have me better."

The trust in her words and, above all, her gaze, sent a great throb of pain through him. He thought: If anything goes wrong here it will be the final smash.

At that moment Doctor Thoroughgood arrived to make his round of the ward. As he came in, he saw Andrew, and at once advanced towards him.

"Morning, Manson," he said pleasantly. "Why? What's the matter? Are you ill?"

Andrew stood up.

"I'm quite well, thank you."

Doctor Thoroughgood gave him an odd glance; then he turned to Mary's bed.

"I'm glad you asked to see this case with me. Let's have the screens, Sister."

They spent ten minutes together examining Mary, then Thoroughgood went over to the alcove by the end window, where, though in full view of the ward, they could not be overheard.

"Well?" he said.

Out of the haze Andrew heard himself speak.

"I don't know how you feel, Doctor Thoroughgood, but it seems to me that the progress of this case isn't quite satisfactory."

"There are one or two features..." Thoroughgood pulled at his narrow little beard.

"It seems to me that there's some slight extension."

"Oh, I don't think so, Manson."

"The temperature is more erratic."

"'M, perhaps."

"Excuse me for suggesting it—I appreciate our relative positions perfectly, but this case means a great deal to me—under the circumstances would you not consider pneumothorax? You remember I was very anxious we should use it when Mary—when the case came in."

Thoroughgood glanced sideways at Manson. His face altered, set into stubborn lines.

"No, Manson. I'm afraid I don't see this as a case for induction. I didn't then, and I don't now."

There was a silence. Andrew could not utter another word. He knew Thoroughgood, his crotchety obstinacy. He felt spent, physically and morally, unable to pursue an argument which must be fruitless. He listened with an immobile face while Thoroughgood ran on, airing his own views about the case. When the other concluded and started to go round the remaining beds he went over to Mary, told her he would call again soon, and left the ward. Before he drove away from the hospital he asked the lodge porter to ring up his house to say he would not be in for lunch.

It was now not far off one o'clock. He was still distressed, wrapped in painful self-contemplation, and faint for want of food. Near Battersea Bridge he stopped outside a small cheap tea-room. Here he ordered coffee and some hot buttered toast. But he could only drink the coffee, his stomach revolted at the toast. He felt the waitress gazing at him curiously.

"Ain't it right?" she said. "I'll change it."

He shook his head, asked her for his check. As she wrote it he caught himself stupidly counting the shiny black buttons on her dress. Once, a long time ago, he had gazed at three pearly buttons in a Blaenelly schoolroom. Outside, a yellow glare hung oppressively above the river. As from a distance he remembered that he had two appointments this afternoon at Welbeck Street. He drove there slowly.

Nurse Sharp was in a bad temper, her usual humour when he asked her to come in on Saturdays. Yet she also inquired if he felt ill. Then, in a softer voice, for Doctor Hampton was a particular object of her regard, she told him that Freddie had rung him twice since lunchtime.

When she went out of the consulting room he sat at his desk staring straight in front of him. The first of his patients arrived at half-past two—a heart case, a young clerk from the Mines Department who had come to him through Gill, who was genuinely suffering from a valvular complaint. He found that he was spending a long time over this case, taking especial pains, detaining the young man earnestly while he carefully went over the details of the treatment.

At the end, as the other fumbled for his thin pocketbook he said quickly: "Please don't pay me now. Wait until I send your bill."

The thought that he would never send the bill, that he had lost his thirst for money and could once again despise it, comforted him strangely.

Then the second case came in, a woman of forty-five, Miss Basden, one of the most faithful of his followers. His heart sank at the sight of her. Rich, selfish, hypochondriacal, she was a younger, a more egotistic replica of that Mrs. Raeburn he had once seen with Hampton in Sherrington's home.

He listened wearily, his hand on his brow, while, smiling, she launched into an account of all that had happened to her constitution since her visit to him a few days before.

Suddenly he raised his head.

"Why do you come to me, Miss Basden?"

She broke off in the middle of a sentence, the pleased expression still fixed upon the upper part of her face, but her mouth dropping slowly open.

"Oh, I know I'm to blame," he said. "I told you to come. But there's nothing really wrong with you."

"Doctor Manson!" she gasped, unable to believe her ears.

It was quite true. He realized, with cruel insight, that all her symptoms were due to money. She had never done a day's work in her life, her body was soft, pampered, overfed. She did not sleep because she did not exercise her muscles. She did not even exercise her brain. She had nothing to do but cut coupons and think about her dividends and scold her maid and wonder what she, and her pet Pomeranian, would eat. If only she would walk out of his room and do something real; stop all the little pills and sedatives and hypnotics and cholagogues and every other kind of rubbish; give some of her money to the poor; help other people and stop thinking about herself! But she would never, never do that, it was useless even to demand it of her. She was spiritually dead and, God help him, so was he!

He said heavily:—

"I'm sorry I can't be of any further service to you, Miss Basden. I—I may be going away. But I've no doubt you'll find other doctors, round about here, who will be only too happy to pander to you."

She opened her mouth several times like a fish gasping for air. Then an expression of positive apprehension came upon her face. She was sure, quite sure, that he had gone out of his mind. She did not wait to reason with him. She rose, hastily gathering her belongings together, and hurried from the room.

He prepared to go home, shutting the drawers of his desk with an air of finality. But before he got up Nurse Sharp bounced into the room, smiling.

"Doctor Hampton to see you! He's come round himself instead of telephoning."

The next minute Freddie was there, airily lighting a cigarette, flinging himself into a chair with an air of purpose in his eye. His tone had never been friendlier.

"Sorry to bother you on a Saturday, old man. But I knew you were here, so I brought round the old mountain to Mahomet. Now look here, Manson. I've heard all about the operation yesterday and I don't mind telling you I'm darn well glad. It's about high time you had an inside slant on dear friend Ivory."

Hampton's voice took on a sudden vicious twist. "I think you ought to know, old chap, that I've been rather falling out with Ivory and Freedman lately. They haven't been playing the game with me. We've been running a little pool together, and very profitable it was, but now I'm pretty well sure these two are twisting me out of some of my share. Besides which, I'm about sick of Ivory's bloody side. He's no surgeon. You're damned well right. He's nothing but a damned abortionist. You didn't know that, eh? Well, take it from me as gospel. There's a couple of nursing homes not one hundred miles from this house where they do nothing else—all very pretty and above-board of course—and Ivory's the head scraper! Freedman isn't much better. He's nothing but a sleek dope peddler and he isn't so smart as Ivory. One of these days he's going to get it in the neck from the D.D.A. Now you listen to me, old man, I'm speaking to you for your own good. I'd like you to know the whole inside story about those fellows because I want you to throw them over and come in with me. You've been too damn green. You haven't been getting your proper whack. Don't you know that when Ivory gets a hundred guineas for an operation he hands back fifty?—that's how he gets them, you see! And what has he been handing you? A measly fifteen or maybe twenty. It isn't good enough, Manson! And after this bit of botching yesterday I damn well wouldn't stand for it. Now I've said nothing to *them* yet, I'm too smart for that; but here's my scheme, old man: Let's ditch them altogether, you and me, and start a tight little partnership of our own. After all we were old pals at college, weren't we? I like you. I've always liked you. And I can show you a hell of a lot."

Freddie broke off to light another cigarette, then he smiled agreeably, expansively, exhibiting his possibilities as a potential partner. "You wouldn't believe the stunts I've pulled. D'you know my latest? Three-guineas-a-time injections—*of sterile water*! Patient came in one day for her vaccine; I'd forgotten to order the damn thing; so, rather than disappoint, pumped in the H_2O. She came back the next day to say she'd had a better reaction than from any of the others. So I went on. And why not? It all boils down to faith and the bottle of coloured water. Mind you I can plug the whole pharmacopoeia into them when it's necessary. I'm not unprofessional—Lord, no! It's just that I'm wise, and if you and I really got together, Manson,—you with your degrees and me with my savvy,—we'd simply skim the pool. There's got to be two of us, you see. You want second opinions all the time. And I've got my eye on a smart young surgeon—hell of a lot better than Ivory! We might snaffle him later. Eventually we might even have our own nursing home. And *then* we'd be in Klondike."

Andrew remained motionless and stiff. He had no anger against Hampton, only a bitter loathing of himself. Nothing could have shown him more blastingly how he stood, what he had done, where he had been going, than this suggestion of Hampton's.

At last, seeing that some answer was demanded of him, he mumbled:—

"I can't go in with you, Freddie. I've—I've suddenly got sick of it. I think I'll chuck it here for a bit. There are too many jackals in this square mile of country. There's a lot of good men, trying to do good work, practising honestly, fairly, but the rest of them are just jackals. It's the jackals who give all these unnecessary injections, whip out tonsils and appendices that aren't doing any harm, play ball amongst one another with their patients, split fees, perform abortions, back up pseudoscientific remedies, chase the guineas all the time."

Hampton's face had slowly reddened.

"What the hell!" he spluttered. "What about yourself?"

"I know, Freddie," Andrew said heavily. "I'm just as bad. I don't want any ill-feeling between us. You used to be my best friend."

Hampton jumped up.

"Have you gone off your rocker, or what?"

"Perhaps. But I'm going to try and stop thinking of money and material success. That isn't the test of a good doctor. When a doctor earns five thousand a year he's not healthy. And why—why should a man try to make money out of suffering humanity?"

"You bloody fool," said Hampton distinctly. He swung round and went out of the room.

Again Andrew sat woodenly at his desk, alone, desolate. He got up at last and drove home. As he approached his house he was conscious of the rapid beating of his heart. It was now after six o'clock. The whole trend of his weary day seemed working upwards to its climax. His hand trembled violently as he turned his latchkey in the door.

Christine was in the front room. The sight of her pale still face sent a great shiver through him. He longed for her to ask, to show some concern as to how he had spent these hours away from her.

But she merely said, in that even noncommittal voice: "You've had a long day. Will you have some tea before the surgery?"

He answered: "There won't be any surgery to-night."

She glanced at him.

"But Saturday—it's your busiest night!"

His answer was to write out a notice stating that the surgery was closed to-night. He walked along the passage, pinned it upon the surgery door. His heart was now thumping so violently he felt that it must burst. When he returned along the passage she was in the consulting room, her face paler still, her eyes distraught.

"What is the matter?" she asked in a strange voice.

He looked at her. The anguish in his heart tore at him, broke through in a great rush that swept him beyond all control.

"Christine!" Everything within him went into that single word. Then he was at her feet, kneeling, weeping.

xvii

Their reconciliation was the most wonderful thing that had happened to them since they first fell in love. Next morning, which was Sunday, he lay beside her, as in those days at Aberalaw, talking, talking and, as though years had slipped from him, pouring out his heart to her. Outside the quiet of Sunday was in the air, the sound of bells, soothing and peaceful. But he was not peaceful.

"How did I come to do it?" he groaned restlessly. "Was I mad, Chris, or what? I can't believe it when I look back on it. Me—getting in with that crowd—after Denny, and Hope—God! I should be executed."

She soothed him. "It all happened with such a rush, dear. It would have swept anyone off his feet."

"No, but honestly, *Chris*. I feel like going off my head when I think about it. And what a hell of a time it must have been for you! Lord! it ought to be a *painful* execution!"

She smiled, actually smiled. It was the most marvellous experience to see her face stripped of that frozen blankness, tender, happy, solicitous of him. Oh! God, he thought: we're both *living* again.

"There's only one thing to be done," he brought his brows together determinedly. Despite his nervous brooding he felt strong now, freed from a haze of illusion, ready to act. "We've got to clear out of here. I'm in too deep, Chris, far too deep. I'd only be reminded at every turn of the fake stuff I'd been doing; yes, and maybe get pulled back. We can easily sell the practice. And oh! Chris, I've got a wonderful idea."

"Yes, darling?"

He relaxed his nervous frown to smile at her diffidently, tenderly.

"How long is it since you called me that? I like it. Yes, I know, I deserved it—oh, don't let me start thinking again, Chris! This idea, this scheme—it hit me when I woke up this morning. I was worrying all over again about Hampton having asked me to join up with his rotten team idea—then suddenly it struck me, why not a genuine team? It's the sort of thing they have amongst doctors in America—Stillman always cracks it up to me, even though he isn't a doctor himself—but we just don't seem to have gone in for it here much. You see, Chris, even in quite a small provincial town you could have a clinic, a little team of doctors, each doing his own stuff. Now listen, darling, instead of sticking in with Hampton and Ivory and Freedman why don't I get Denny and Hope together and form a genuine threesome? Denny does all the surgical work,—and you know how good he is!—I handle the medical side, and Hope is our bacteriologist! You see the benefit of that, we're each specializing in our own province and pooling our knowledge. Perhaps you remember all Denny's arguments—and mine too—about our hidebound G.P. system—how the general practitioner is made to stagger along, carrying everything on his shoulders, an impossibility? Group medicine is the answer to that, the perfect answer. It comes between state medicine and isolated, individual effort. The only reason we haven't had it here is because the big men like keeping everything in their own hands. But oh! wouldn't it be wonderful, dear, if we could form a little front-line unit, scientifically and—yes, let me say it—spiritually intact, a kind of pioneer force to try to break down prejudice, knock out the old fetishes, maybe start a complete revolution in our whole medical system?"

Her cheek pressed against the pillow, she gazed at him with shining eyes.

"It's like old times to hear you talk that way. I can't tell you how I love it. Oh! it's like beginning all over again. I am happy, darling, *happy*."

"I've got a lot to make up for," he reasoned sombrely. "I've been a fool. And worse." He pressed his brow with his hands. "I can't get poor Harry Vidler out of my head. And I won't, either, till I do something really to make up for it." He groaned suddenly. "I was to blame there, Chris, as much as Ivory. I can't help feeling I've got off too easily. It doesn't seem right that I should get away with it. But I'll work like hell, Chris. And I believe Denny and Hope will come in with me. You know their ideas. Denny's really dying to get back into the rough-and-tumble of a practice again. And Hope—if we give him a little lab, where he can do original stuff between making our sera—he'll follow us anywhere."

He jumped out of bed and began to pace up and down the room in his old impetuous style, torn between elation for the future and remorse for the past, turning things over in his head, worrying, hoping, planning.

"I've so much to settle up, Chris," he cried; "and one thing I must see about. Look, dear! When I've written some letters—and we've had lunch—how about taking a little run into the country with me?"

She looked at him questioningly.

"But if you're busy?"

"I'm not too busy for this. Honestly, Chris, I have a fearful weight on my mind over Mary Boland. She's not getting on well at the Victoria and I haven't taken near enough notice. Thoroughgood is most unsympathetic and he doesn't properly understand her case, at least not to my way of thinking. God! If anything happened to Mary after me making myself responsible to Con for her I would just about go crazy. It's an awful thing to say of one's own hospital, but she'll *never* recover at the Victoria. She ought to be out in the country, in the fresh air, in a good sanatorium."

"Yes?"

"That's why I want us to run out to Stillman's. Bellevue's the finest, the most marvellous little place you could ever hope to see. If only I could persuade him to take Mary in—Oh! I'd not only be satisfied, I'd feel I'd really done something worth while."

She said with decision:—

"We'll leave the minute you're ready."

When he had dressed he went downstairs, wrote a long letter to Denny and another to Hope. He had only three serious cases on his hands and on his way to visit them he posted the letters. Then, after a light meal, he and Christine set out for Wycombe.

The journey, despite the emotional tension persisting in his mind, was a happy one. More than ever it was borne upon him that happiness was an inner state, wholly spiritual, independent—whatever the cynics might say—of worldly possessions. All this time, when he had been striving and tearing after wealth and position and succeeding in every material sense, he had imagined himself happy. But he had not been happy. He had been existing in a kind of delirium, craving more after everything he got. Money, he thought bitterly, it was all for dirty money! First he had told himself he wanted to make a thousand pounds a year. When he reached that income he had immediately doubled it, and set that figure as his maximum. But that maximum, when achieved, found him dissatisfied. And so it had gone on. He wanted more and more. It would in the end have destroyed him.

He glanced sideways at Christine. How she must have suffered because of him! But now, if he had wished for any confirmation of the sanity of his decision, the sight of her altered glowing face was evidence enough. It was not now a pretty face, for there were marks of the wear and tear of life drawn upon it, a little dark of lines about the eyes, a faint hollowing of the cheeks which had once been firm and blooming. But it was a face which had always worn an aspect of serenity and truth. And this re-animation which kindled it was so bright and moving he felt a fresh pang of compunction strike deeply into him. He swore he would never again in all his life do anything to make her sad.

They reached Wycombe towards three o'clock, then took a side road uphill which led along the crest of the ridge past Lacey Green. The situation of Bellevue was superb, upon a little plateau which though sheltered on the North afforded an outlook over both valleys.

Stillman was cordial in his reception. He was a self-contained, undemonstrative little man seldom given to enthusiasm; yet he showed his pleasure in Andrew's visit by demonstrating the full beauty and efficiency of his creation.

Bellevue was intentionally small, but of its perfection there could be no question. Two wings, angled to a southwestern exposure, were united by a central administrative section. Above the entrance hall and offices was a lavishly equipped treatment room, its south wall entirely of Vitaglass. All the windows were of this material, the heating and ventilating system the last word in modern efficiency. As Andrew walked round he could not help contrasting this ultramodern perfection with the antique buildings, built a hundred years before, which served as many of the London hospitals, and with those old dwelling-houses, badly converted and ill-equipped, which masqueraded as nursing homes.

Afterwards, when he had shown them round, Stillman gave them tea. And here Andrew brought out his request with a rush.

"I hate asking you a favour, Mr. Stillman." Christine had to smile at the almost-forgotten formula. "But I wonder if you'd take in a case for me here? Early T.B. Probably requires pneumothorax. You see she's the daughter of a great friend of mine, a professional man—dentist—and she's not getting on where she is—"

Something like amusement gathered behind Stillman's pale blue eyes.

"You don't mean you're proposing to send me a case? Doctors don't send me cases here—though they do in America. You forget that here I'm a fake healer running a quack sanatorium, the kind that makes his patients walk barefooted in the dew before leading them in to a grated carrot breakfast!"

Andrew did not smile.

"I didn't ask you to pull my leg, Mr. Stillman. I'm dead-serious about this girl. I'm— I'm worried about her."

"But I'm afraid I am full up, my friend. In spite of the antipathy of your medical fraternity I have a waiting list as long as my arm. Strange!" Stillman did at last impassively smile. "People want me to cure them in spite of the doctors."

"Well!" Andrew muttered. Stillman's refusal was a great disappointment to him. "I was more or less banking on it. If we could have got Mary in here—oh! I'd have felt *relieved.* Why, you've got the finest treatment centre in England. I'm not trying to flatter you. I know! When I think of that old ward in the Victoria where she's lying now, listening to the cockroaches scramble behind the skirting—"

Stillman leaned forward and picked up a thin cucumber sandwich from the low table before them. He had a characteristic, almost finicky way of handling things as though he had just, with the utmost care, washed his hands and went in fear of soiling them.

"So! It's a little ironic comedy you are arranging. No, no, I mustn't talk that way, I see you are worried. And I will help you. Although you *are* a doctor I'll take your case." Stillman's lip twitched at the blank expression on Andrew's face. "You see, I'm broad-minded. I don't mind dealing with the profession when I'm obliged to. Why don't you smile? That's a joke. Never mind. Even if you've no sense of humour you're a darn sight more enlightened than most of the brethren. Let me see. I have no room vacant till next week. Wednesday, I think. Bring your case to me a week from Wednesday, and I promise you I'll do the best for her I can!"

Andrew's face reddened with gratitude.

"I—I can't thank you enough—I—"

"Then don't. And don't be so polite. I prefer you when you look like throwing things about. Mrs. Manson, does he ever throw the china at you? I have a great friend in America, he owns sixteen newspapers, and every time he gets in a temper he breaks a five-cent plate. Well, one day, it so happened..."

He went on to tell them a long, and, to Manson, quite pointless story.

But, driving home in the cool of the evening Andrew meditated to Christine:—

"That's one thing settled anyway, Chris—a big load off my mind. I'm positive it's the right place for Mary. He's a great chap is Stillman. I like him a lot. He's nothing to look at, but underneath he's just pressed steel. I wonder if ever we could have a clinic on these lines—miniature replica—Hope and Denny and me. That's a wild dream, eh? But you never know. And I've been thinking, if Denny and Hope do come in with me and we pitch out in the provinces—we might be near enough one of the coal fields for me to pick up my inhalation work again. What d'you think, Chris?"

By way of answer she leaned sideways and, greatly to the common danger on the public highway, she soundly kissed him.

xviii

Next morning he rose early, after a good night's rest. He felt tense, keyed for anything. Going straight to the telephone, he put the practice in the hands of Fulger and Turner, medical transfer agents, of Adam Street. Mr. Gerald Turner, present head of that old, established firm answered personally and, in response to Andrew's request, he came out promptly to Chesborough Terrace. After a scrutiny of the books lasting all that forenoon he assured him that he would have not the slightest difficulty in effecting a quick sale.

"Of course, we shall have to state a reason, Doctor, in our advertisements," said Mr. Turner gently tapping his teeth with his cased pencil. "Any purchaser is bound to ask himself, Why should any doctor give up a gold-mine like this? And excuse me for saying so, Doctor, it *is* a gold-mine. I've never seen such spot-cash receipts for many a day. Shall we say on account of ill-health?"

"No," said Andrew brusquely. "Tell them the truth. Say—" he checked himself. "Oh, say for personal reasons."

"Very well, Doctor." And Mr. Gerald Turner wrote, against his draft advertisement: "Relinquished from motives purely personal and unconnected with the practice."

Andrew concluded:—

"And remember, I don't want a fortune for this thing—only a good price. There's a lot of tame cats who mightn't follow the new man around."

At lunchtime Christine produced two telegrams which had come for him. He had asked both Denny and Hope to wire him in reply to the letters he had written the day before.

The first, from Denny, said simply:—
IMPRESSED. EXPECT ME TO-MORROW EVENING.

The second declared with typical flippancy:—
MUST I SPEND ALL MY LIFE WITH LUNATICS? FEATURE OF ENGLISH PROVINCIAL TOWNS PUBS STOCKS CATHEDRALS AND PIG MARKETS. DID YOU SAY LABORATORY? SIGNED INDIGNANT RATEPAYER.

After lunch Andrew ran down to the Victoria. It was not Doctor Thoroughgood's visiting hour, but that suited his purpose admirably. He wanted no fuss or unpleasantness, least of all did he wish to upset his senior who, for all his obstinacy and prim concern with the barber-surgeons of the past, had always treated him well.

Seated beside Mary's bed he explained privately to her what he wished to do.

"It was my fault to begin with." He patted her hand reassuringly. "I ought to have foreseen this wasn't quite the place for you. You'll find a difference when you get to Bellevue—a big difference, Mary. But they've been very kind to you here; there's no need to hurt anybody's feelings. You must just say you want to go out the fifteenth; discharge yourself. If you don't like to do it yourself I'll get Con to write and say he wants you out. They've so many people waiting for beds it'll be easy. Then on Wednesday I'll take you out myself by car to Bellevue. I'll have a nurse with me and everything. Nothing could be simpler—or better for you."

He returned home with a sense of something further accomplished, feeling that he was beginning to clear up the mess into which his life had fallen. That evening in his surgery he set himself sternly to weed out the chronics, ruthlessly to sacrifice his charm school. A dozen times in the course of an hour he declared firmly:—

"This must be your last visit. You've been coming a long time. You're quite better now. And it doesn't do to go on drinking medicine!"

It was amazing, at the end of it, how much lighter he felt. To be able to speak his mind, honestly and emphatically, was luxury he had long denied himself. He went into Christine with a step almost boyish.

"Now I feel less like a salesman for bath salts!" He groaned: "God! How can I talk that way? I'm forgetting what's happened—Vidler—everything I've done!"

It was then that the telephone rang. She went to answer it, and it seemed to him that she was a longish time absent and when she returned her expression was oddly strained.

"Someone wants you on the phone."

"Who...?" All at once he realized that Frances Lawrence had called him up. There was a bar of silence in the room. Then, hurriedly, he said, "Tell her I'm not in. Tell her I've gone away. No, wait!" His expression strengthened, he took an abrupt movement forward. "I'll speak to her myself."

He came back in five minutes to find that she had seated herself with some work in her familiar corner where the light was good. He glanced at her covertly, then glanced away, walked to the window and stood there moodily looking out with his hands in his pockets. The quiet click of her knitting needles made him feel inordinately foolish, a sad and stupid dog, cringing home limp-tailed and bedraggled from illicit foray. At last he could contain himself no longer.

Still with his back to her he said:—

"That's finished too. It may interest you to know it was only my stupid vanity—that and self-interest. I loved you all the time." Suddenly he ground out: "Damn it, Chris. It was all my fault. These people don't know any better, but I do. I'm getting out of this too easy—too easy. But let me tell you: While I was at the 'phone I rang up Le Roy; thought I might as well make one job of it. Cremo products won't be interested in me any more. I've wiped myself off their slate, too, Chris. And, God! I'll see that I stay off!"

She did not answer but the click of her needles made, in the silent room, a brisk and cheerful sound. He must have remained there a long time, his shamed eyes upon the movement of the street outside, upon the lights springing up through the summer darkness. When at length he turned, the invading dusk had crept into the room, but she still sat there, almost invisible in the shadowed chair, a small slight figure occupied with her knitting.

That night he woke up sweating and distressed, turning to her blindly, still anguished by the terrors of his dream.

"Where are you, Chris? I'm sorry. I'm truly sorry. I'll do my best to be decent to you in future." Then quieted, already half-asleep: "We'll take a holiday when we sell out here. God! my nerves are rotten—to think I once called you neurotic! And when we settle down, wherever it is, you'll have a garden, Chris. I know how you love it. Remember—remember at Vale View, Chris?"

Next morning he brought her home a great bunch of chrysanthemums. He strove with all his old intensity to show his affection for her, not by that showy generosity which she had hated—the thought of that Plaza luncheon still made him shiver!—but in small, considerate, almost forgotten ways.

At teatime when he came home with a special kind of sponge cake that she liked and on top of that silently brought in her house slippers from the cupboard at the end of the passage, she sat up in her chair, frowning, mildly protesting:—

"Don't, darling, *don't*—or I'm sure to suffer for it. Next week you'll be tearing your hair and kicking me round the house—like you used to in those old days."

"Chris!" he exclaimed, his face shocked, pained. "Can't you see that's all changed? From now on I'm going to make things up to you."

"All right, all right, my dear." Smiling she wiped her eyes. Then with a sudden tensity of which he had never suspected her, "I don't mind how it is, so long as we're *together*. I don't want you to run after me. All I ask is that you don't run after anybody else!"

That evening Denny arrived, as he had promised, for supper. He brought a message from Hope, who had rung him on the toll line from Cambridge, to say that he would be unable to get to London that evening.

"He said he was detained on business," Denny declared, knocking out his pipe. "But I strongly suspect friend Hope will shortly be taking unto himself a bride. Romantic business—the mating of a bacteriologist!"

"Did he say anything about my idea?" Andrew asked quickly.

"Yes, he's keen—not that it matters, we could just pocket him and take him along with us! And I'm keen too." Denny unfurled his napkin and helped himself to salad. "I can't imagine how a first-class scheme like this came out of your fool head. Especially when I fancied you'd tucked yourself up as a West End soap merchant. Tell me about it."

Andrew told him, fully, and with increasing emphasis. They began to discuss the scheme in its more practical details.

They suddenly realized how far they had progressed when Denny said:—

"My view is that we don't want to pick too large a town. Under twenty thousand inhabitants—that's ideal. We can make things hum there. Look at a map of the West Midlands. You'll find scores of industrial towns served by four or five doctors who are politely at each other's throats, where the good old M.D. drags out half a tonsil one morning and sludges *mist. alba* the next. It's just there that we can demonstrate our idea of specialized cooperation. We won't buy ourselves in. We just so to speak arrive. Lord! I'd like to see their faces, Doctor Brown and Jones and Robinson, I mean. We'll have to stand wagonloads of abuse—incidentally, we may be lynched. Seriously, though, we want a central clinic—as you say—with Hope's lab attached. We might even have a couple of beds upstairs. We won't be very grand at first—it means conversion rather than building, I suppose—but I've a feeling we'll take root." Suddenly aware of Christine's glistening eyes as she sat following their talk he smiled. "What do you think about it, ma'am? Crazy, isn't it?"

"Yes," she answered a trifle huskily. "But it's—it's the crazy things that matter."

"That's the word, Chris! By God! This does matter."

Andrew bounced the cutlery as he brought down his fist. "The scheme's good. But it's the ideal behind the scheme! A new interpretation of the Hippocratic oath; an absolute allegiance to the scientific ideal, no empiricism, no shoddy methods, no stock prescribing, no fee-snatching, no proprietary muck, no soft-soaping of hypochondriacs, no—Oh! for the Lord's sake, give me a drink! My vocal cords won't stand up to this, I ought to have a drum."

They talked on until one o'clock in the morning. Andrew's tense excitement was a stimulus felt even by the stoic Denny. His last train had long since departed. That night he occupied the spare room and as he hurried off after breakfast on the following day he promised to come to town again on the following Friday. Meanwhile he would see Hope and—final proof of his enthusiasm—buy a large-scale map of the West Midlands.

"It's on Chris, it's on!" Andrew came back triumphant from the door. "Philip's as keen as mustard. He doesn't say much. But *I know*."

That same day they had the first inquiry for the practice. A prospective buyer arrived, and he was followed by others. Gerald Turner came in person with the more likely purchasers. He had a beautiful flow of elegant language which he even directed upon the architecture of the garage. On Monday, Doctor Noel Lowry called twice, alone in the morning and escorted by the agent in the afternoon. Thereafter Turner rang up Andrew, suavely confidential:—

"Doctor Lowry is interested, Doctor; *very* interested I may say. He's particularly anxious we don't sell till his wife has a chance to see the house. She's at the seaside with the children. She's coming up Wednesday."

This was the day on which Andrew had arranged to take Mary to Bellevue but he felt the matter could be left in Turner's hands. Everything had gone as he anticipated at the hospital. Mary was due to leave at two o'clock. He had fixed up with Nurse Sharp to accompany them in the car.

It was raining heavily as, at half-past one, he started off by driving to Welbeck Street to pick up Nurse Sharp. She was in a sulky humour, waiting but unwilling, when he reached Number 57a. Since he had told her he must dispense with her services at the end of the month her moods had been even more uncertain. She snapped an answer to his greeting and stepped into the car.

Fortunately he had no difficulty with Mary. He drew up as she came through the porter's lodge and the next moment she was in the back of the saloon with Nurse Sharp, warmly wrapped in a rug with a hot bottle at her feet. They had not gone far, however, before he began to wish he had not brought the sulky and suspicious nurse. It was evident that she considered the expedition far beyond the scope of her duties. He wondered how he had managed to put up with her so long.

At half-past three they reached Bellevue. The rain had now ceased, and a burst of sun came through the clouds as they ran up the drive. Mary leaned forward, her eyes fastened nervously, a little apprehensively, upon the place from which she had been led to expect so much.

Andrew found Stillman in the office. He was anxious to see the case with him at once, for the question of pneumothorax induction weighed heavily on his mind. He spoke of this as he smoked a cigarette and drank a cup of tea.

"Very well," Stillman nodded as he concluded. "We'll go up right now."

He led the way to Mary's room. She was now in bed, pale from her journey and still inclined to apprehensiveness, gazing at Nurse Sharp who stood at one end of the room folding up her dress. She gave a little start as Stillman came forward.

He examined her meticulously. His examination was an illumination to Andrew, quiet, silent, absolutely precise. He had no bedside manner. He was not impressive. He did not, indeed, resemble a physician at work. He was like a business man engaged with the complications of an adding machine which has gone wrong. Although he used the stethoscope, most of his investigation was tactile, a palpation of the inter-rib and supra-clavicular spaces as if, through his smooth fingers, he could actually sense the condition of the living, breathing lung cells beneath.

When it was over he said nothing to Mary but took Andrew beyond the door. "Pneumothorax," he said. "There's no question. That lung should have been collapsed weeks ago. I'm going to do it right away. Go back and tell her."

While he went off to see to the apparatus Andrew returned to the room and informed Mary of their decision. He spoke as lightly as he could, yet it was evident that the immediate prospect of the induction upset her further.

"You'll do it?" she asked in an uneasy tone. "Oh! I'd much rather you did it."

"It's nothing, Mary. You won't feel the slightest pain. I'll be here. I'll be helping him! I'll see that you're all right."

He had meant actually to leave the whole technique to Stillman. But as she was so nervous, so palpably depending upon him, and as, indeed, he felt himself responsible for her presence here he went to the treatment room and offered his assistance to Stillman.

Ten minutes later they were ready. When Mary was brought in he gave her the local anaesthesia. He then stood by the manometer, while Stillman skilfully inserted the needle, controlling the flow of sterile nitrogen gas into the pleura. The apparatus was exquisitely delicate and Stillman undoubtedly a master of the technique. He had an expert touch with the cannula, driving it deftly forward, his eye fixed upon the manometer for the final "snap" which announced perforation of the parietal pleura. He had his own method of deep manipulation to prevent the occurrence of surgical emphysema.

After an early phase of acute nervousness Mary's anxiety gradually faded. She submitted to the operation with increasing confidence and at the end she could smile at Andrew, completely relaxed. Back again in her room she said:—

"You were right. It was nothing. I don't feel as if you'd done anything at all."

"No?" He lifted an eyebrow; then laughed: "That's how it should be—no fuss, no sense of anything terrible happening to you—I wish every operation could go that way! But we've immobilized that lung of yours all the same. It'll have a rest now. And when it starts breathing again—believe me!—it will be healed."

Her glance rested upon him, then wandered round the pleasant room, through the window to the view of the valley beyond.

"I'm going to like it here, after all. He doesn't try to be nice—Mr. Stillman, I mean— but somehow you feel he is nice. Do you think I could have my tea?"

xix

It was nearly seven o'clock when he left Bellevue. He had remained longer than he had anticipated, talking to Stillman on the lower verandah, enjoying the cool air and the quiet conversation of the other man. As he drove off he was pervaded by an extraordinary sense of placidity, of tranquillity. He derived that benefit from Stillman, whose personality, with its repose, its indifference to the trivialities of life, reacted favourably upon his own impetuous disposition. Moreover he was now easy in his mind about Mary. He contrasted his previous hurried action, her summary dispatch into an out-of-date hospital, with all that he had done for her this afternoon. It had caused him inconvenience, a great deal of troublesome arrangement. It was quite unorthodox. Though he had not discussed the question of payment with Stillman, he realized that Con was in no position to meet the Bellevue fees and that, in consequence, the settlement of the bill would fall upon himself. But all this became as nothing beside the glowing sense of real achievement which pervaded him. For the first time in many months he felt that he had done something which, to his own belief, was worthy. It pervaded him warmly, a cherished thought, the beginning of his vindication.

He drove slowly, enjoying the quiet of the evening. Nurse Sharp once again sat in the back seat of the car but she had nothing to say and he, with his own thoughts, was almost unconscious of her. When they drove into London, however, he asked where he should drop her and, on her reply, drew up at Notting Hill Tube Station. He was glad to be rid of her. She was a good nurse but her nature was repressed and unhappy. She had never liked him. He decided to post her month's salary the next day. Then he would not see her again.

Strangely, his mood had altered as he came along Paddington Street. It always affected him to pass the Vidlers' shop. Out of the corner of his eye he saw it—Renovations Ltd. One of the assistants was pulling down the shutters. The simple action was so symbolic it sent a shiver through him. Subdued, he reached Chesborough Terrace and ran the car into his garage. He went into his house with a curious sadness pressing upon him.

Christine met him joyfully in the hall. Whatever his mood might be, hers was vivid with success. Her eyes were shining with her news.

"Sold!" she declared gaily. "Knocked down lock, stock, and basement. They waited and waited for you, darling—they've only just gone. Doctor and Mrs. Lowry, I mean. He got so agitated," she laughed, "because you weren't here for the surgery, that he set to and did it himself. Then I gave them supper. Then we made more conversation. I could almost see Mrs. Lowry deciding that you'd had a motor smash. Then *I* began to worry! But now you are here, dear! And it's all *right*. You've to meet him at Mr. Turner's office tomorrow at eleven to sign the contract. And... Oh! yes—he's given Mr. Turner a deposit."

He followed her into the front room, where the supper had been cleared from the table. He was pleased, naturally, that the practice should be sold, yet he could not, at present, summon any great show of elation.

"It is good, isn't it," Christine went on, "that it should all be settled up so quickly? I don't think he expects a very long introduction. Oh! I've been thinking so much before you came in. If only we could have a little holiday at Val André again, before we start work.... It was so lovely there..." She broke off, gazing at him. "Why, what's the matter, dear?"

"Oh, nothing," he smiled, sitting down. "I'm a little tired, I think. Probably because I missed my dinner—"

"What?" she exclaimed, aghast. "I was certain you'd have it at Bellevue, before you left." Her glance swept around. "And I've cleared everything away, and let Mrs. Bennett out to the pictures."

"It doesn't matter."

"But it *does*. No wonder you didn't jump when I told you about the practice. Now you just sit there one minute and I'll bring up a tray. Is there anything you'd especially like? I could heat up some soup—or make you some scrambled eggs—or *what?*"

He considered.

"The egg, I think, Chris. Oh! but don't bother. Well, if you like, then—and perhaps a bit of cheese afterwards."

She was back in no time with a tray on which stood a plate of scrambled eggs, a glass of celery heart, bread, biscuits, butter and the cheese dish. She placed the tray upon the table. As he pulled in his chair she brought out a bottle of ale from the sideboard cupboard.

While he ate she watched him solicitously. She smiled.

"You know, dear, I've often thought—if we'd lived in Cefen Row, say a kitchen and one bedroom, we'd have fitted in perfectly. High life doesn't agree with us. Now I'm going to be a workingman's wife again I'm awfully happy."

He went on with his scrambled egg. The food was certainly making him feel better.

"You know, darling," she continued, placing her hands beneath her chin in her characteristic way, "I've thought such a lot these last few days. Before that my mind was stiff, somehow, all closed up. But since we're together—oh, since we're ourselves again everything has seemed so clear. It's only when you've got to fight for things that they really become worth while. When they just drop into your lap there's no satisfaction in them. Don't you remember those days at Aberalaw—they've been living, simply living in my mind all day—when we had to go through all those rough times together? Well! Now I feel that the same thing is starting for us all over again. It's our kind of life, darling. It's us! And oh! I'm so happy about it."

He glanced towards her.

"You're really happy, Chris?"

She kissed him lightly.

"Never happier in my life than I am at this moment."

There was a pause. He buttered a biscuit and lifted the lid of the dish to help himself to cheese. But there was anticlimax in the action which revealed, not his favourite Libtauer but no more than a barren end of cheddar, which Mrs. Bennett used for cooking. The instant she saw it Christine gave a self-reproachful cry.

"And I meant to call at Frau Schmidt's to-day!"

"Oh! it's all right, Chris."

"But it isn't all right." She whipped the dish away before he could help himself.

"Here am I mooning like a sentimental school-girl, giving you no dinner at all—when you come in tired—starving you. Fine sort of workingman's wife I'd be!" She jumped up, her eye upon the clock. "I've just time to rush across for it now before she closes."

"Don't bother, Chris—"

"*Please*, darling." She silenced him gaily. "I *want* to do it. I want to—because you love Frau Schmidt's cheese and I—I love you."

She was out of the room before he could protest again. He heard her quick step in the hall, the light closing of the outer door. His eyes still were faintly smiling—it was so like her to do this. He buttered another biscuit, waiting for the arrival of the famous Libtauer, waiting for her return.

The house was very still: Florrie sleeping downstairs, he reflected, and Mrs. Bennett at the cinema. He was glad Mrs. Bennett was coming with them on their new venture. Stillman had been great this afternoon. Mary would be all right now, right as rain. Marvellous how the rain had cleared off this afternoon—beautiful it had been coming home through the country, so fresh and quiet. Thank God! Christine would soon have her garden again. He and Denny and Hope might get themselves lynched by the five doctors in Muddletown. But Chris would always have her garden!

He began absently to eat one of the buttered biscuits. He'd lose his appetite if she didn't hurry up. She must be talking to Frau Schmidt. Good old Frau; sending him his first cases. If he'd only gone on decently instead of—oh, well, that was finished with now, thank God! They were together again, Christine and he, happier than ever they had been. Wonderful to hear her say that a minute ago. He lit a cigarette.

Suddenly the doorbell rang violently. He glanced up, laid down his cigarette, went into the hall. But not before the bell had been wrenched again. He opened the front door.

Immediately he was conscious of the commotion outside, a crowd of people on the pavement, faces and heads interwoven with the darkness. But before he could resolve the mingling pattern, the policeman who had rung the bell loomed up before him. It was Struthers, his old Fife friend, the pointsman. What seemed strange about Struthers was the staring whiteness of his eyes.

"Doctor," he breathed with difficulty like a man who has been running. "Your wife's got hurted. She ran—Oh! God Almighty!—she ran right out the shop in front of the bus."

A great hand of ice enclosed him. Before he could speak the commotion was upon him. Suddenly, dreadfully, the hall was filled with people, Frau Schmidt weeping, a bus conductor, another policeman, strangers, all pressing in, forcing him back, into the consulting room. And then, through the crowd, carried by two men, the figure of his Christine. Her head dropped backwards upon the thin white arch of her neck. Still entwined by its string in the fingers of her left hand was the little parcel from Frau Schmidt. They laid her upon the high couch of his consulting room.

She was quite dead.

XX

He broke down completely and for days was out of his mind. Moments of lucidity there were when he became aware of Mrs. Bennett, of Denny, and, once or twice, of Hope. But for the most part he went through life, performed the actions demanded of him, in sheer automatism, his whole being concentrated deep within himself in one long nightmare of despair. His frayed-out nervous system intensified the agony of his loss by creating morbid fancies and terrors of remorse, from which he awoke, sweating, crying out in anguish.

Dimly he was conscious of the inquest, the drab formality of the coroner's court, of the evidence given so minutely, so unnecessarily by the witnesses. He stared fixedly at the squat figure of Frau Schmidt upon whose plump cheeks the tears kept rolling, rolling down.

"She was laughing, laughing all the time she came into my shop. Hurry, please—she kept on telling me—I don't want to keep my husband waiting—"

When he heard the coroner expressing sympathy with Doctor Manson in his sad bereavement he knew that it was over. He stood up mechanically, found himself walking upon grey pavements with Denny.

How the arrangements for the funeral were made he did not know, they all came mysteriously to pass without his knowledge. As he drove to Kensal Green his thoughts kept darting hither and thither, backwards through the years. In the dingy confines of the cemetery he remembered the wide and windswept uplands behind Vale View where the mountain ponies raced and reared their tangled manes. She had loved to walk there, to feel the breeze upon her cheeks. And now she was being laid in this grimy city graveyard.

That night in the stark torture of his neurosis he tried to drink himself insensible. But the whisky only seemed to goad him to fresh anger against himself. He paced up and down the room, late into the night, muttering aloud, drunkenly apostrophizing himself.

"You thought you could get away with it. You thought you *were* getting away with it. But by God! you weren't. Crime and punishment, crime and punishment! You're to blame for what happened to her. You've *got* to suffer." He walked the length of the street, hatless, swaying, to stare, wild-eyed at the blank shuttered windows of the Vidler shop. He came back muttering, through bitter maudlin tears, "God is not mocked! Chris said that once—God is not mocked, my friend."

He staggered upstairs, hesitated, went into her room, silent, cold, deserted. There on the dressing table lay her bag. He picked it up, pressed it against his cheeks, then fumblingly opened it. Some coppers and loose silver lay inside, a small handkerchief, a bill for groceries. And then, in the middle pocket he came upon some papers—a faded snapshot of himself taken at Blaenelly and—yes, he recognized them with a throbbing pang—those little notes he had received at Christmas from his patients at Aberalaw: *With grateful thanks*—she had treasured them all those years. A heavy sob broke from his breast. He fell on his knees by the bed in a passion of weeping.

Denny made no effort to stop his drinking. It seemed to him that Denny was about the house almost every day. It was not because of the practice, for Doctor Lowry was doing that now. Lowry was living out somewhere but coming in to consult and pick up the calls. He knew nothing whatever of what was going on, he did not wish to know. He kept out of Lowry's way. His nerves had gone to pieces. The sound of the doorbell made his heart palpitate madly. A sudden step made the sweat break out on the palms of his hands. He sat upstairs in his room with a rolled up handkerchief between his fingers, wiping his sweating palms from time to time, staring at the fire, knowing that when night came he must face the spectre of insomnia.

This was his condition when Denny walked in one morning and said:—

"I'm free at last, thank God. Now we can go away."

There was no question of refusal, his power of resistance was completely gone. He did not even ask where they were going. In silent apathy he watched Denny pack a suitcase for him. Within an hour they were on their way to Paddington Station.

They travelled all afternoon through the southwest counties, changed at Newport and struck up through Monmouthshire. At Abergavenny they left the train and here, outside the station, Denny hired a car. As they drove out of the town across the River Usk and through the rich autumnal tinted countryside he said:—

"This is a small place I once used to come to—fishing. Llantony Abbey. I think it ought to suit."

They reached their destination, through a network of hazelfringed lanes, at six o'clock. Round a square of close green turf lay the ruins of the abbey, smooth grey stones, a few arches of the cloisters still upstanding. And adjoining was the guest house, built entirely from the fallen stones. Near at hand a small stream flowed with a constant soothing ripple. Wood smoke rose, straight and blue, into the quiet evening air.

Next morning Denny dragged Andrew out to walk. It was a crisp dry day but Andrew, sick from a sleepless night, his flabby muscles failing on the first hill, made to turn back when they had gone only a short way. Denny, however, was firm. He walked Andrew eight miles that first day and on the next he made it ten. By the end of the week they were walking twenty miles a day and Andrew, crawling up to his room at night, fell immediately into insensibility upon his bed.

There was no one to worry about them at the Abbey. Only a few fisherman remained, for it was now close to the end of the trout season. They ate in the stone-flagged refectory at a long oak table before an open log fire. The food was plain and good.

During their walks they did not speak. Often they walked the whole day long with no more than a few words passing between them. At the beginning Andrew was quite unconscious of the countryside through which they tramped, but as the days passed the beauty of its woods and rivers, of its sweeping bracken-covered hills, penetrated gradually, imperceptibly through his numbed senses.

The progress of his recovery was not sensationally swift—yet by the end of the first month he was able to stand the fatigue of their long marches and face the future without cowering. He saw that no better place could have been chosen for his recovery than this isolated spot, no better routine than this Spartan, this monastic existence. When the first frost bit hard into the ground he felt the joy of it instinctively in his blood.

He began unexpectedly to talk. The topics of their discussion were inconsequential at the outset. His mind, like an athlete performing simple exercises before approaching greater feats, was guarded in its approach to life. But imperceptibly he learned from Denny the progress of events.

His practice had been sold to Doctor Lowry, not for the full amount which Turner had stipulated—since under the circumstances no introduction had been given—but for a figure near enough that sum. Hope had at last completed the full term of his scholarship and was now at his home in Birmingham. Denny also was free. He had given up his registrarship before coming to Llantony. The inference was so clear that Andrew suddenly lifted up his head.

"I ought to be fit for work at the beginning of the year."

Now they began to talk in earnest, and within a week his hardfaced listlessness was gone. He felt it strange and sad that the human mind should be capable of recovering from such a mortal blow as that which had struck him. Yet he could not help it, the recovery was there. Previously he had trudged with stoic indifference, a perfectly functioning machine. Now he breathed the sharp air with real vigour, switched at the bracken with his stick, took his correspondence out of Denny's hands, and cursed when the post did not bring the *Medical Journal.*

At night Denny and he pored over a large-scale map. With the help of an almanac they made a list of towns, weeded out that list, then narrowed their selection down to eight. Two of the towns were in Staffordshire, three in Northamptonshire, and three in Warwickshire.

On the following Monday Denny took his departure, and was away a week. During these seven days Andrew felt the rushing return of his old desire for work, his own work, the real work he could do with Hope and Denny. His impatience become colossal. On Saturday afternoon he walked all the way to Abergavenny to meet the last train of the week. Returning, disappointed, to endure two further nights and one whole day of this intensifying delay, he found a small dark Ford drawn up at the guest house. He hurried through the door. There in the lamp-lit refectory, Denny and Hope sat at a ham-and-egg tea with whipped cream and tinned peaches on the sideboard.

That week end they had the place entirely to themselves. Philip's report, delivered at that richly composite meal, was a fiery prelude to the excitement of their discussions. Outside rain and hail battered on the windows. The weather had finally broken. It made no difference to them.

Two of the towns visited by Denny—Franton and Stanborough—were, in Hope's phrase, ripe for medical development. Both were solid semi-agricultural towns upon which recently a new industry had been grafted. Stanborough had a freshly erected plant for the manufacture of motor engine bearings, Franton a large sugar-beet factory. Houses were springing up on the outskirts, the population increasing. But in each case the medical services had lagged behind. Franton had only a cottage hospital and Stanborough none at all. Emergency cases were sent to Coventry, fifteen miles away.

These bare details were enough to set them off like hounds upon a scent. But Denny had information even more stimulating. He produced a plan of Stanborough torn from an A.A. Midland Route itinerary. He remarked:—

"I regret to say I stole it from the hotel at Stanborough. Sounds like a good beginning for us there."

"Quick," impatiently declared the once facetious Hope, "what's this mark here?"

"That," Denny said, as they bent their heads over the plan, "is the market square—at least, that's what it amounts to, only for some reason they call it the Circle. It's bang in the centre of the town, high up, too, with a fine situation. You know the kind of thing, a ring of houses and shops and offices, half-residential, half old established businesses, rather a Georgian effect, with low windows and porticoes. The chief medico of the place—a whale of a fellow, I saw him, important red face and mutton chops; incidentally he employs two assistants—has his house in the Circle." Denny's tone was gently ironic. "Directly opposite, on the other side of the charming granite fountain in the middle of the Circle, are two empty houses, large rooms, sound floors, good frontage *and* for sale. It seems to me—"

"And to me," said Hope with a catch of his breath, "off-hand I should say there's nothing I should like better than a little lab, opposite that fountain."

They went on talking. Denny unfolded further details, interesting details.

"Of course," he concluded, "we are probably all quite mad. This idea has been brought to perfection in the big American cities by thorough organization and tremendous outlay. But here—in Stanborough! And we none of us have a lot of cash! We shall also probably fight like hell amongst ourselves. But somehow—"

"God help Old Mutton-Chops!" said Hope, rising and stretching himself.

On Sunday they took their plans a stage further, arranging that Hope should make a détour to include Stanborough on his way home on Monday. Denny and Andrew would arrive on Wednesday, meet him at Stanborough hotel, when one of them would make discreet inquiry at the local house-agent's.

With the prospect of a full day before him Hope left early next morning, dashing off in his Ford in a spatter of mud before the others had finished breakfast. The sky was still heavily overcast but the wind was high, a gusty exhilarating day. After breakfast Andrew went out by himself for an hour. It was good to feel fit again, with his work reaching out to him once more in the high adventure of the new clinic. He had not realized how much his scheme meant to him until now, quite suddenly, it was near fruition.

When he returned at eleven o'clock the post had come in, a pile of letters forwarded from London. He sat down at the table with a sense of anticipation to open them. Denny was beside the fire behind the morning paper.

His first letter was from Mary Boland. As he scanned the closely written sheets his face warmed to a smile. She began by sympathizing with him, hoping he had now recovered fully. Then briefly she told him about herself. She was better, infinitely better, almost well again. Her temperature had been normal for the last five weeks. She was up, taking graduated exercise. She had put on so much weight he would scarcely recognize her. She asked him if he could not come to see her. Mr. Stillman had returned to America for several months, leaving his assistant Mr. Marland in charge. She could not thank him sufficiently for having sent her to Bellevue.

Andrew laid down the letter, his expression still bright with the thought of Mary's recovery. Then, throwing aside a number of circulars and advertising literature, all in flimsy envelopes with halfpenny stamps, he picked up his next letter. This was a long official-looking envelope. He opened it, drew out the stiff sheet of notepaper within.

Then the smile left his face. He stared at the letter with disbelieving eyes. His pupils widened. He turned deadly pale. For a full minute he remained motionless—staring, staring at the letter.

"Denny," he said, in a low voice. "Look at this."

xxi

Eight weeks before, when Andrew set down Nurse Sharp at Notting Hill Station, she went on by tube to Oxford Circus and from there walked rapidly in the direction of Queen Anne Street. She had arranged with her friend Nurse Trent, who was Doctor Hampton's receptionist, to spend the evening at the Queen's Theatre where Louis Savory, whom they both adored, was appearing in "The Duchess Declares." But since it was now quarter-past eight and the performance began at eight forty-five the margin of time left for Nurse Sharp to call for her friend and be in the upper circle of the Queen's was narrow. Moreover, instead of having leisure for a nice hot meal at the Corner House as they had planned, they would be obliged to snatch a sandwich on the way down or perhaps do without altogether. Nurse Sharp's mood, as she thrust her way along Queen Anne Street, was that of a woman bitterly ill-used. As the events of the afternoon kept turning in her mind she seethed with indignation and resentment. Mounting the steps of Number 17c she hurriedly pressed the bell.

It was Nurse Trent who opened the door, her expression patiently reproachful. But before she could speak Nurse Sharp pressed her arm.

"My dear," she said, speaking rapidly, "I'm ever so sorry. But *what* a day I've had! I'll tell you later. Just let me pop in to leave my things. If I come as I am I think we can just do it."

At that moment, as the two nurses stood together in the passage Hampton came down the stairs, groomed, shining, and in his evening clothes. Seeing them, he paused. Freddie could never resist an opportunity to demonstrate the charm of his personality. It was part of his technique, making people like him, getting the most out of them.

"Hello, Nurse Sharp!"—rather gaily, as he picked a cigarette from his gold case. "You look weary. And why are you both so late? Didn't I hear something from Nurse Trent about a theatre to-night?"

"Yes, Doctor," said Nurse Sharp. "But I—I was detained over one of Doctor Manson's cases."

"Oh?" Freddie's tone held just a hint of interrogation.

It was enough for Nurse Sharp. Rankling from her injustices, disliking Andrew and admiring Hampton, she suddenly let herself go.

"I've never had such a time in all my life, Doctor Hampton. Never. Taking a patient from the Victoria and sneaking her out to that Bellevue place, and Doctor Manson keeping me there all hours while he does a pneumothorax with an unqualified man..." She poured out the whole story of the afternoon, repressing her smarting tears of vexation with difficulty.

There was a silence when she concluded. Freddie's eyes held an odd expression.

"That was too bad, Nurse," he said at length. "But I hope you won't miss your theatre. Look, Nurse Trent—you must take a taxi and charge it to me. Put it on your expense sheet. Now if you'll excuse me, I must go."

"*There's* a gentleman," Nurse Sharp murmured, following him admiringly with her eyes. "Come, dear, get the taxi."

Freddie drove thoughtfully to the club. Since his quarrel with Andrew he had almost of necessity pocketed his pride and fallen back to a closer association with Freedman and Ivory. To-night, the three were dining together. And as they dined, Freddie, less in malice than from a desire to interest the other two, to pull himself up with them again, airily remarked:—

"Manson seems to be playing pretty parlour tricks since he left us. I hear he's started feeding patients to that Stillman fellow."

"What!" Ivory laid down his fork.

"And co-operating, I understand." Hampton sketched a graceful version of the story. When he finished Ivory demanded with sudden harshness:—

"Is this true?"

"My dear fellow," Freddie answered in an aggrieved tone, "I had it from his own nurse not half an hour ago."

A pause followed. Ivory lowered his eyes and went on with his dinner. Yet beneath his calm he was conscious of a savage elation. He had never forgiven Manson for that final remark after the Vidler operation. Though he was not thin-skinned, Ivory had the sultry pride of a man who knows his own weakness and guards it jealously. He knew deep in his heart that he was an incompetent surgeon. But no one had ever told him with such cutting violence the full extent of his incompetence. He hated Manson for that bitter truth.

The others had been talking a few moments when he raised his head. His voice was impersonal.

"This nurse of Manson's—can you get her address?"

Freddie broke off, gazing at him across the table.

"Absolutely."

"It seems to me," Ivory reflected coolly, "that something ought to be done about this. Between you and me, Freddie, I never had much time for this Manson of yours, but that's neither here nor there. I'm thinking purely of the ethical aspect. Gadsby happened to be speaking to me about this Stillman only the other evening—we were guests at the Mayfly Dinner. He's getting into the papers—Stillman, I mean. Some ignorant jackass in Fleet Street has got together a list of alleged cures by Stillman, cases where doctors had failed; you know, the usual twaddle. Gadsby is pretty hot about it all. I believe Cranston was a patient of his at one time—before he ditched him for this quack. Now! Just what is going to happen if members of the profession are going to *support* this rank outsider? Gad! The more I think about it the less I like it. I'm going to get in touch with Gadsby straight off the handle. Waiter! Find out if Doctor Maurice Gadsby is in the Club. If not, have the porter ring up and find out if he's at his house."

Hampton, for once, looked uncomfortable about his collar. He had no rancour in his disposition and no ill-will towards Manson, whom, in his easy, egotistic fashion he had always liked.

He muttered: "Don't bring me into it."

"Don't be a fool, Freddie. Are we going to let that fellow sling mud at us and then get away with *this*?"

The waiter returned to say that Doctor Gadsby was at home. Ivory thanked him.

"I'm afraid this means the end of my bridge, you fellows. Unless Gadsby happens to be engaged."

But Gadsby was not engaged and later that evening Ivory called upon him. Though the two were not exactly friends, they were good enough acquaintances for the physician to produce his second best port and a reputable cigar. Whether or not Doctor Gadsby knew something of Ivory's reputation he was at least aware of the surgeon's social standing, which ranked high enough for Maurice Gadsby, aspirant to fashionable honours, to treat him with adequate good-fellowship.

When Ivory mentioned the object of his visit Gadsby had no need to assume interest. He leaned forward in his chair, his small eyes fastened upon Ivory, listening intently to the story.

"Well! I'm damned!" he exclaimed with unusual vehemence at the end of it. "I know this Manson. We had him for a short time on the M.F.B. and I assure you we were extremely relieved to see the end of him. A complete outsider; hasn't the manners of an errand boy. And do you actually mean to tell me that he took a case from the Victoria— it must have been one of Thoroughgood's cases, we'll hear what Thoroughgood has to say about *that*—and turned it over to Stillman?"

"More than that, he actually assisted Stillman at the operation."

"If that is true," Gadsby said, carefully, "the case is one for the G.M.C."

"Well—" Ivory hesitated becomingly. "That was precisely my own view. But I rather held back. You see I knew this fellow at one time rather better than you. I didn't really feel like lodging the complaint myself."

"I will lodge it," said Gadsby authoritatively. "If what you tell me is indeed a fact I will lodge it personally. I should consider myself failing in my duty if I did not take immediate action. The point at issue is a vital one, Ivory. This man Stillman is a menace, not so much to the public, as to the profession. I think I told you my experience of him the other night at dinner. He threatens our status, our training, our tradition. He threatens everything that we stand for. Our only remedy is to ostracize him. Then, sooner or later, he runs into disaster over the question of certification. Observe that, Ivory! Thank God! We have kept that in the hands of the profession. We alone can sign a death certificate. But if—mark you—if this fellow and others like him can secure professional collaboration, then we're lost. Fortunately the G.M.C. have always come down like a ton of bricks upon that sort of thing in the past. You remember the case of Jarvis, the manipulator, several years ago, when he got some cad of a doctor to anaesthetize for him. *He* was struck off, *instanter*. The more I think of that bounder Stillman the more I'm determined to make an example of this. If you'll excuse me one minute now I'll ring Thoroughgood. And then to-morrow I shall want to interrogate that nurse."

He rose and telephoned Doctor Thoroughgood. On the following day, in Doctor Thoroughgood's presence, he took a signed statement from Nurse Sharp. So conclusive was her testimony he immediately put himself in touch with his solicitors, Messrs. Boon and Everton of Bloomsbury Square. He detested Stillman, of course. But he had already a soothing premonition of the benefit likely to accrue to a public upholder of the medical morality.

When Andrew, oblivious, went to Llantony, the process raised against him was moving steadily upon its way. It is true that Freddie, coming, in dismay, on a paragraph reporting the inquest upon Christine's death, had telephoned Ivory to try to stop the case. But by then it was too late. The complaint had been lodged.

Later the Penal Cases Committee considered that complaint and upon its authority a letter was dispatched summoning Andrew to attend the November meeting of the Council to answer the charge laid against him.

This was the letter which he now held in his hand, white with anxiety, confronted by the menace of its legal phrasing:—

That you, Andrew Manson, knowingly and wilfully, on August 15th, assisted one Richard Stillman, an unregistered person practicing in a department of medicine, and that you associated yourself in a professional capacity with him in carrying out such practice. And that in relation thereto you have been guilty of infamous conduct in a professional respect.

xxii

The case was to be heard on November tenth and Andrew was in London a full week before that date. He was alone, for he had asked Hope and Denny to leave him entirely to himself. And he stayed, with a bitter, melancholy sentiment, at the Museum Hotel.

Though outwardly controlled, his state of mind was desperate. He swung between dark fits of bitterness and an emotional suspense which came not only from his doubts about the future but from the vivid remembrance of every past moment of his medical career. Six weeks ago this crisis would have found him still benumbed by the agony of Christine's death, heedless, uncaring. But now, recovered, eager and ready to begin work again, he felt the shock of it with cruel intensity.

He realized, with a heavy heart, that if all his reborn hopes were killed then he too might just as well be dead.

These and other painful thoughts perpetually thronged his brain, producing at times a state of bewildering confusion. He could not believe that he, Andrew Manson, was in this horrible situation, really facing the dreaded nightmare of every doctor. Why was he called before the Council? Why did they wish to strike him off the register? He had done nothing disgraceful. He was guilty of no felony, no misdemeanour. All that he had done was to cure Mary Boland of consumption.

His defence was in the hands of Horner and Co., of Lincoln's Inn Fields, a firm of solicitors Denny had strongly recommended to him. At first sight Thomas Horner was not impressive, a small red-faced man with gold-rimmed glasses and a fussy manner. Through some defect in his circulation he was subject to attacks of suffusion of his skin, which gave him a self-conscious air, a peculiarity that certainly did not serve to inspire confidence. Nevertheless Horner had decided views upon the conduct of the case. When Andrew, in his first burst of agonized indignation, had wished to rush to Sir Robert Abbey, his one influential friend in London, Horner had wryly pointed out that Abbey was a member of the Council. With equal disapproval the fussy little solicitor had vetoed Andrew's frantic plea that they cable Stillman to return immediately from America. They had all the evidence that Stillman could give them and the actual presence of the unqualified practitioner could serve only to exasperate the Council members. For the same reason Marland, now acting at Bellevue, must stay away.

Gradually Andrew began to see that the legal aspect of the case was utterly different from his own. His frenzied logic as, in Horner's office, he protested his innocence, caused the solicitor disapprovingly to wrinkle up his brow. At last Horner was forced to declare:—

"There is one thing I must beg of you, Doctor Manson,—*not* to express yourself in such terms during the hearing on Wednesday. I assure you nothing would be more fatal to our case."

Andrew stopped short, his hands clenched, his eyes burning.

"But I want them to know the *truth*. I want to show them that getting this girl cured was the best thing I'd done for years. After mucking about for months doing ordinary material practice I'd actually done something fine and that—*that's* what they're having me up for."

Horner's eyes, behind his glasses, were deeply concerned. In his vexation the blood rushed into his skin.

"Please, *please*, Doctor Manson. You don't *understand* the gravity of our position! I must take this opportunity to tell you frankly that at the *best* I consider our chances of —of success to be slender. Precedent is dead against us: Kent in nineteen nine, Louden in nineteen twelve, Foulger in nineteen nineteen; they were all deleted for unprofessional associations. And of course, in the famous Hexam case, in nineteen twenty-one, Hexam was struck off for administering a general anaesthetic for Jarvis the bonesetter. Now, what I wish to entreat of you is this—answer questions in the affirmative or negative or, failing that, as briefly as possible. For I solemnly warn you that if you launch into one of these digressions which you have recently been offering me we will unquestionably lose our case, and you will be struck off the register as sure as my name is Thomas Horner."

Andrew saw dimly that he must try to hold himself in check. Here he must, like a patient laid upon the table, submit to the formal operations of the Council. But it was difficult for him to reach that passive state. The mere idea that he must forgo all attempt at self-exoneration and dully answer "Yes" or "No" was more than he could bear.

On the evening of Tuesday, November ninth, when his febrile expectation of what the next day would bring had reached its zenith, he found himself unaccountably in Paddington, walking in the direction of the Vidlers' shop, driven by a strange subconscious impulse. Deeply buried in his mind lay the morbid, still unconquered fancy that all the calamity of these last months came in punishment for Harry Vidler's death. The inference was involuntary, unadmitted. Yet it was there, springing from the deep roots of his earliest belief. He was drawn irresistibly to Vidler's widow as though the mere sight of her might help him—give him, in some strange manner, appeasement from his suffering.

It was a wet dark night and there were few people in the streets. He had a sense of queer unreality, walking unrecognized in this district where he had been known so well. His own dark figure became a shadow amongst other phantoms, all hurrying, hurrying through the teeming rain. He reached the shop just before closing time, hesitated; then, as a customer came out, hurriedly he went in.

Mrs. Vidler was alone, behind the counter of the cleaning and pressing department, folding a woman's coat which had just been left with her. She wore a black skirt and an old blouse, dyed black, gaping a little at the neck. Her mourning made her somehow smaller. Suddenly she lifted her eyes and saw him.

"It's Doctor Manson," she exclaimed, her face lighting up. "How are you, Doctor?"

His answer came stiffly. He saw that she knew nothing of his present trouble. He remained standing in the doorway, rigid, gazing at her, the rain dripping slowly from his hat brim.

"Come in, Doctor. Why, you're drenched. It's a wicked night—"

He interrupted her, his voice strained, unreal.

"Mrs. Vidler, I've wanted to come and see you for a long time. I've often wondered how you were getting on."

"I'm managing, Doctor. Not so bad. I've a new young man in the cobbling. He's a good worker. But come in and let me give you a cup of tea."

He shook his head.

"I'm—I'm just passing." Then he went on, almost desperately.

"You must miss Harry very much."

"Well, yes, I do. At least, at first I did. But it's wonderful,"—she even smiled at him, —"how you come to get used to things."

He said rapidly, confusedly:—

"I reproach myself—in a way. Oh! It all happened so suddenly for you, I've often felt you must blame me—"

"Blame you!" She shook her head. "How can you say such a thing, when you done everything, even to the home, and getting the finest surgeon—"

"But you see," he persisted huskily, a rigid coldness in all his body, "if you had done differently, perhaps if Harry had gone to hospital—"

"I wouldn't have had it any different, Doctor. My Harry had the best that money could give him. Why, even his funeral, I wish you could have seen it, the wreaths. As for _blaming_ yourself—why, many's the time I've said in this shop Harry couldn't have had a better nor a kinder nor a cleverer doctor than yourself..."

As she went on talking he saw with a conclusive pang that, though he made open confession, she would never believe him. She had her illusion of Harry's peaceful, inevitable, costly passing. It would be cruelty to shake her from this pillar to which she clung so happily. He said, after a pause:

"I'm very glad to have seen you again, Mrs. Vidler. As I've said, I wanted to look you up."

He broke off, shook hands with her, bade her good night and went out.

The encounter, far from reassuring or consoling him, served only to intensify his wretchedness. His mood underwent a complete revulsion. What had he expected? Forgiveness, in the best fictional tradition? Condemnation? He reflected bitterly that now she probably thought more highly of him than ever. As he tramped back through the sopping streets he had the sudden conviction that he must lose his case to-morrow. The conviction deepened to a terrifying certainty.

Not far from his hotel, in a quiet side street, he passed the open doorway of a church. Once again impulse caught him, caused him to stop, retrace his steps and enter. It was dark inside, empty and warm, as though a service had not long ended. He did not know what church it was, nor did he care. He simply sat down in the back seat of all and fixed his haggard gaze upon the dark enshrouded apse. He reflected that Christine in their estrangement had fallen back upon the thought of God. He had never been a churchgoer, but now here he was, in this unknown church. Tribulation brought people here, brought people to their senses, brought people to the thought of God.

There he sat, bowed, like a man resting at the end of a journey. His thoughts flowed outwards, not in any considered prayer, but winged with the longing of his soul. God! don't let me be struck off. Oh, God! don't let me be struck off. For perhaps half an hour he remained in this strange meditation, then he rose and went straight to his hotel.

Next morning, though he had slept heavily, he woke to an even greater sense of sick anxiety. As he dressed his hands trembled slightly. He blamed himself for having come to this hotel with its associations of his membership examination. The feeling he now experienced was exactly that pre-examination dread, intensified a hundredfold.

Downstairs he could eat no breakfast. The time of his case was eleven o'clock and Horner had asked him to be early. He estimated it would take him not more than twenty minutes to get to Hallam Street, and he fretted, in nervous pretence, with the newspapers in the hotel lounge until half-past ten. But when he started his taxi was caught in a long traffic jam due to an obstruction in Oxford Street. It was striking eleven when he reached the G.M.C. offices.

He hurried into the Council Chamber with only a disturbed impression of its size, of the high table where the council sat with the President, Sir Jenner Halliday, in the chair. Seated at the far end were the participants in his own case, oddly like actors waiting for their cue. Horner was there; Mary Boland, accompanied by her father; Nurse Sharp, Doctor Thoroughgood, Mr. Boon, Ward Sister Myles—his glance travelled along the line of chairs. Then hastily he seated himself beside Horner.

"I thought I told you to be early," the solicitor said in an aggrieved tone. "This other case is almost over. With the Council it's fatal to be late."

Andrew made no answer. As Horner had said, the President was even now pronouncing judgment on the case before his own, an adverse judgment, erasure from the register. Andrew could not keep his eye from the doctor convicted of some drab misdemeanour, a seedy down-at-heel individual who looked as though he had struggled hard to make a living. His utterly hopeless expression, as he stood condemned by this august body of his fellows, sent a shiver over Andrew.

But he had no time for thought, for more than a passing wave of pity. The next minute his own case was called. His heart contracted as the proceedings began.

The charge was formally read through. Then Mr. George Boon, the prosecuting solicitor, rose to open. He was a thin, precise frock-coated figure, clean-shaven, with a wide black ribbon to his eyeglasses. His voice came deliberately.

"Mr. President, gentlemen, this case which you are about to consider has, I submit, nothing to do with any theory of medicine as defined under Section Twenty-eight of the Medical Act. On the contrary, it exhibits a clear-cut instance of professional association with an unregistered person, a tendency which, I may perhaps observe, the Council has recently had cause to deplore.

"The facts of the case are these. The patient, Mary Boland, suffering from apical phthisis, was admitted to the wards of Doctor Thoroughgood at the Victoria Chest Hospital on July the eighteenth. There she remained under the care of Doctor Thoroughgood until August the fifteenth, when she discharged herself on the pretext that she wished to return to her home. I say 'pretext' because, on the day of her discharge, instead of returning home, the patient was met at the lodge of the hospital by Doctor Manson, who immediately took her to an institution by the name of Bellevue which purports, I believe, to undertake the cure of pulmonary disorders.

"On arrival at this place, Bellevue, the patient was put to bed and examined by Doctor Manson in conjunction with the proprietor of the establishment, Mr. Richard Stillman, an unqualified person and—er—I understand, an alien. Upon examination, it was decided in consultation,—I particularly call the Council to mark that phrase,—in consultation, by Doctor Manson and Mr. Stillman, to operate upon the patient and to induce the condition of pneumothorax. Thereupon Doctor Manson administered the local anaesthetic and the induction was performed by Doctor Manson and Mr. Stillman.

"Now, gentlemen, having briefly outlined the case I propose with your permission to call further evidence. Doctor Eustace Thoroughgood, please."

Doctor Thoroughgood rose and came forward. Removing his eyeglasses, and holding them in readiness to emphasize his points, Boon began his interrogation.

"Doctor Thoroughgood, I have no wish to embarrass you. We are well aware of your reputation, I might say your eminence, as a consulting physician upon diseases of the lungs and I have no doubt you may be actuated by a sense of leniency towards your junior colleague; but, Doctor Thoroughgood, is it not the fact that on Saturday the morning of August the fourth, Doctor Manson pressed you to a consultation upon this patient Mary Boland?"

"Yes."

"And is it not also the fact that in the course of this consultation he pressed you to adopt a line of treatment which you thought to be unwise?"

"He wished me to perform A.P.T."

"Exactly! And in the best interests of the patient you refused."

"I did."

"Was Doctor Manson's manner in any way peculiar when you refused?"

"Well—" Thoroughgood hesitated.

"Please, Doctor Thoroughgood! We respect your natural reluctance."

"He didn't seem altogether himself that morning. He seemed to disagree with my decision."

"Thank you, Doctor Thoroughgood. You had no reason to imagine that the patient was dissatisfied with her treatment at the hospital,—" at the mere idea a watery smile touched Boon's arid face,—"that she had any grounds for complaint against you or the staff?"

"None whatever. She always seemed well pleased, happy and contented."

"Thank you, Doctor Thoroughgood." Boon picked up his next paper. "And now, Ward Sister Myles, please."

Doctor Thoroughgood sat down. Ward Sister Myles came forward. Boon resumed:—

"Sister Myles, on the forenoon of Monday, August the sixth, the next day but one after this consultation between Doctor Thoroughgood and Doctor Manson, did Doctor Manson call to see the patient?"

"He did."

"Was it a usual hour for him to call?"

"No."

"Did he examine the patient?"

"No. We had no screens that morning. He just sat and talked with her."

"Exactly, Sister—a long and earnest conversation, if I may use the wording of your statutory declaration. But tell us, Sister, in your own words now, what took place immediately subsequent to Doctor Manson's departure."

"About half an hour after, Number Seventeen—that's to say, Mary Boland—said to me: 'Sister, I've been thinking things over and I've made up my mind to go. You've been very kind to me. But I want to leave a week from Wednesday.'"

Boon interrupted quickly.

"'A week from Wednesday.' Thank you, Sister. It was that point I wished to establish. That will be all at present."

Ward Sister Myles stepped back.

The solicitor made a politely satisfied gesture with his beribboned eyeglasses.

"And now—Nurse Sharp, please." A pause. "Nurse Sharp, you are in a position to bear out the statement relating to Doctor Manson's movements on the afternoon of Wednesday, August the fifteenth."

"Yes, I was there!"

"I gather from your tone, Nurse Sharp, that you were there unwillingly."

"When I found out where we were going and who this man Stillman was, not a doctor or anything, I was—"

"Shocked," Boon suggested.

"Yes, I was," shot out Nurse Sharp. "I've never had to do with anybody but proper doctors, real specialists, all my life."

"Exactly," Boon purred. "Now, Nurse Sharp, there is just one point which I wish you to make quite clear once again for the benefit of the Council. Did Doctor Manson actually co-operate with Mr. Stillman in—in performing this operation?"

"He did," Nurse Sharp answered vindictively.

At this point Abbey leaned forward and put a question suavely, through the President.

"Is it not the case, Nurse Sharp, that when the events in question took place you were under notice to Doctor Manson?"

Nurse Sharp reddened, violently, lost her composure and stammered: "Yes, I suppose so."

As she sat down a minute later Andrew was conscious of a faint spark of warmth— Abbey, at least, remained his friend.

Boon turned to the Council table, mildly aggrieved at the interruption.

"Mr. President, gentlemen, I might continue to call witnesses but I am too sensible of the value of the Council's time. Moreover, I submit that I have proved my case conclusively. There seems not the slightest doubt that the patient Mary Boland was removed, entirely through the connivance of Doctor Manson, from the care of an eminent specialist in one of the best hospitals in London to this questionable institute— which in itself constitutes a grave breach of professional conduct—and that there Doctor Manson deliberately associated himself with the unqualified proprietor of this institute in the performance of a dangerous operation, already stated to be contra-indicated by Doctor Thoroughgood, the specialist ethically responsible for the case. Mr. President, gentlemen, here, I submit, we are not dealing, as might appear at first sight, with an isolated instance, an accidental misconduct, but with a planned, preconceived, and almost systematic infringement of the medical code."

Mr. Boon sat down, well-pleased, and began to polish his glasses. There was a moment's silence. Andrew kept his eyes firmly upon the floor. It had been torture for him to endure the biased presentation of the case. Bitterly he told himself that they were treating him like some hole-and-corner criminal. Then his solicitor came forward and prepared to address the Council.

As usual, Horner seemed flustered, his face was red, and he had difficulty in arranging his papers. Yet, strangely, this seemed to gain him the indulgence of the Council. The

A.J. Cronin

President said:—

"Yes, Mr. Horner?"

Horner cleared his throat.

"May it please you, Mr. President, gentlemen—I am not in dispute with the evidence brought by Mr. Boon. I have no wish to go behind the facts. But the manner of their interpretation gravely concerns us. There are, besides, certain additional points which throw a complexion upon the case much more favourable to my client.

"It has not yet been stated that Miss Boland was primarily Doctor Manson's patient, since she consulted him, previous to seeing Doctor Thoroughgood, on July the eleventh. Further, Doctor Manson was personally interested in the case. Miss Boland is the daughter of a close friend. Thus, all along, he regarded her as his own responsibility. We must frankly admit that Doctor Manson's action was completely misguided. But I suggest respectfully it was neither dishonourable nor malicious.

"We have heard of this slight difference of opinion over the question of treatment between Doctor Thoroughgood and Doctor Manson. Bearing in mind Doctor Manson's great interest in the case, it was not unnatural for him to wish to take it back into his own hands. Naturally, he wished to cause his senior colleague no distress. That, and nothing more, was the reason of the subterfuge upon which Mr. Boon has laid such stress." Here Horner paused, pulled out a handkerchief and coughed. He had the air of a man approaching a more difficult hurdle. "And now we come to the matter of association, of Mr. Stillman and Bellevue. I assume members of the Council are not ignorant of Mr. Stillman's name. Although unqualified, he enjoys a certain reputation and is even reported to have brought about certain obscure cures."

The President interrupted gravely:—

"Mr. Horner, what can you, a layman, know of these matters?"

"I agree, sir," Horner said hurriedly. "My real point is that Mr. Stillman would appear to be a man of character. It so happens that he introduced himself to Doctor Manson many years ago through a letter complimenting Doctor Manson upon some research work he had done upon the lungs. The two met later on a purely unprofessional footing when Mr. Stillman came here to establish his clinic. Thus, though it was ill-considered, it was not unnatural that Doctor Manson, seeking a place where he could himself give treatment to Miss Boland, should avail himself of the convenience offered him at Bellevue. My friend Mr. Boon has referred to Bellevue as a 'questionable' establishment. On that point I feel the Council might be interested to hear evidence. Miss Boland, please."

As Mary rose the scrutiny of the Council members fell upon her with marked curiosity. Though she was nervous and kept her gaze on Horner, not once glancing at Andrew, she seemed well, in normal health.

"Miss Boland," said Horner, "I want you to tell us frankly—did you find anything to complain of while you were a patient of Bellevue?"

"No! Quite the reverse." Andrew saw at once that she had been carefully instructed beforehand. Her answer came with guarded moderation.

"You suffered no ill effects?"

"On the contrary. I am better."

"In fact, the treatment carried out there was really the treatment Doctor Manson suggested for you at your first interview with him on—let me see—on July the eleventh."

"Yes."

"Is this relevant?" the President asked.

"I have finished with this witness, sir," Horner said quickly. As Mary sat down he threw out his hands towards the Council table in his deprecatory style. "What I am venturing to suggest, gentlemen, is that the treatment effected at Bellevue was in actuality Doctor Manson's treatment carried out—unethically perhaps—by other persons. There was, I contend, within the meaning of the act, no professional co-operation between Stillman and Doctor Manson. I should like to call Doctor Manson."

Andrew stood up, acutely conscious of his position, of every eye directed towards him. He was pale and drawn. A sense of cold emptiness lay in the pit of his stomach. He heard Horner address him.

"Doctor Manson, you received no financial gain in respect of this alleged co-operation with Mr. Stillman?"

"Not a penny."

"You had no ulterior motive, no base objective, in doing as you did?"

"No."

"You meant no reflection on your senior colleague Doctor Thoroughgood?"

"No. We got on well together. It was just—our opinions did not coincide on this case."

"Exactly," Horner intervened rather hastily. "You can assure the Council, then, honestly and sincerely, that you had no intention of offending against the medical code, nor the remotest idea that your conduct was in any degree infamous."

"That is the absolute truth."

Horner suppressed a sigh of relief as, with a nod, he dismissed Andrew. Though he had felt himself obliged to produce this evidence he had feared his client's impetuosity. But now it was safely over, and he felt that, if his summing-up were brief, they might now possibly have a slender chance of success.

He said with a contrite air:—

"I have no wish to keep the Council further. I have tried to show that Doctor Manson made merely an unhappy mistake. I appeal, not only to the justice, but to the mercy of the Council. And I should like finally to draw the Council's attention to my client's attainments. His past history is one of which any man might be proud. We are well aware of cases in which brilliant men have been guilty of a single error, and, failing to secure mercy, their careers were eclipsed. I hope, and indeed I pray, that this case which you are about to judge may not be such as these."

The apology and humility in Horner's tone were quite admirable in their effect upon the Council. But almost at once Boon was on his feet again, craving the indulgence of the President.

"With your permission, sir, there are one or two questions I should like to put to Dr. Manson." He swung round, inviting Andrew to his feet by an upward movement of his eyeglasses.

"Doctor Manson, your last answer was scarcely clear to me. You say you had no knowledge that your conduct was in any degree infamous. Yet you *did* know that Mr.

Stillman was not a qualified gentleman."

Andrew considered Boon from beneath his brows. The attitude of the finicky solicitor had, during the entire hearing, made him feel guilty of some disgraceful act. A slow spark kindled in the chilly void within him.

He said distinctly:—

"Yes, I knew he was not a doctor."

The little wintry smirk of satisfaction showed on Boon's face. He said goadingly:—

"I see. I see. Yet even that did not deter you."

"Even that didn't," echoed Andrew with sudden bitterness. He felt his control going. He took a long breath. "Mr. Boon, I've listened to you asking a great many questions. Will you allow me to ask you one? Have you heard of Louis Pasteur?"

"Yes," Boon was startled into the reply. "Who hasn't?"

"Exactly! Who hasn't? You are probably unaware of the fact, Mr. Boon, but perhaps you will allow me to tell you that Louis Pasteur, the greatest figure of all in scientific medicine, was *not* a doctor. Nor was Ehrlich—the man who gave medicine the best and most specific remedy in its entire history. Nor was Haffkine—who fought the plague in India better than any *qualified gentleman* has ever done. Nor was Metchnikoff, inferior only to Pasteur in his greatness. Forgive me for reminding you of these elementary facts, Mr. Boon. They may show you that every man fighting disease who hasn't got his name on the register isn't necessarily a knave or a fool."

Electric silence. Hitherto the proceedings had dragged along in an atmosphere of pompous dreariness, a musty staleness, like a secondhand law court. But now every member at the Council table sat erect; Abbey, in particular, had his eyes upon Andrew with a strange intentness. A moment passed.

Horner, with his hand before his face, groaned in dismay. Now, indeed, he knew the case was lost. Boon, though horribly discomfited, made an effort to recover himself.

"Yes, yes, these are illustrious names, we know. Surely you don't compare Stillman with them?"

"Why not?" Andrew rushed on in burning indignation. "They're only illustrious because they're dead. Virchow laughed at Koch in his lifetime—abused him! We don't abuse him now. We abuse men like Sphalinger and Stillman. There's another example for you—Sphalinger—a great and original scientific thinker. He's not a doctor. He has no medical degree. But he's done more for medicine than thousands of men *with* degrees, men who ride about in motor cars and charge their fees, free as air, while Sphalinger is opposed and disparaged and accused, allowed to spend his fortune in research and treatment, and then left to struggle on in poverty."

"Are we to take it," Boon managed a sneer, "that you have an equal admiration for Richard Stillman?"

"Yes. He's a great man, a man who has devoted his whole life to benefiting mankind. He's had to fight jealousy and prejudice, and misrepresentation, too. In his own country he has overcome it. But apparently not here. Yet I'm convinced that he's done more against tuberculosis than any man living in this country. He's outside the profession. Yes! But there are plenty inside it who have been running up against T.B. all their lives and have never done an atom of good in fighting it."

There was sensation in the long high room. Mary Boland's eyes, now fixed on

Andrew, were shining between admiration and anxiety. Horner, slowly and sadly, was gathering his papers, slipping them into his leather case.

The President intervened.

"Do you realize what you are saying?"

"I do." Andrew gripped the back of his chair tensely, aware that he had been carried into grave indiscretion but determined to stand by his opinions. Breathing quickly, strung to breaking pitch, a queer kind of recklessness took hold of him. If they were going to strike him off, let him give them cause to do so.

He rushed on: "I've listened to the pleading that's been going on to-day on my behalf and all the time I've been asking myself what harm I've done. I don't want to work with quacks. I don't believe in bogus remedies. That's why I don't open half the highly scientific advertisements that come pouring into my letter box by every post. I know I am speaking more strongly than I should, but I can't help it. We're not nearly liberal enough. If we go on trying to make out that everything's wrong outside the profession and everything is right within, it means the death of scientific progress. We'll just turn into a tight little trade protection society. It's high time we started putting our own house in order, and I don't mean the superficial things either. Go to the beginning, think of the hopelessly inadequate training doctors get. When I qualified I was more of a menace to society than anything else. All I knew was the names of a few diseases and the drugs I was supposed to give for them. I couldn't even lock a pair of midwifery forceps. Anything I know I've learned since then. But how many doctors do learn anything beyond the ordinary rudiments they pick up in practice? They haven't got time, poor devils; they're rushed off their feet. That's where our whole organization is rotten. We ought to be arranged in scientific units. There ought to be compulsory post-graduate classes. There ought to be a great attempt to bring science into the front line, to do away with the old bottle-of-medicine idea, give every practitioner a chance to study, to co-operate in research. And what about commercialism? The useless guinea-chasing treatments, the unnecessary operations, the crowds of worthless pseudo-scientific proprietary preparations we use—isn't it time some of these were eliminated? The whole profession is far too intolerant and smug. Structurally, we're static. We never think of advancing, altering our system. We say we'll do things, and we don't. For years we've been bleating about the sweated conditions under which our nurses work, the wretched pittances we pay them. Well? They're still being sweated, still paid their pittances. That's just an example. What I really mean is deeper than that. We don't give our pioneers a chance. Doctor Hexam, the man who was brave enough to give anaesthetics for Jarvis, the manipulator, when he was beginning his work, got struck off the register. Ten years later when Jarvis had cured hundreds of cases which had baffled the best surgeons in London, when he had been given a knighthood, when all the 'best people' proclaimed him a genius, then we crawled back and gave him an honorary M.D. By that time Hexam was dead of a broken heart. I know I have made plenty of mistakes, and bad mistakes, in practice. And I regret them. But I made no mistake with Richard Stillman. And I don't regret what I did with him. All I ask you to do is to look at Mary Boland. She had apical phthisis when she went to Stillman. Now she's cured. If you want any justification of my infamous conduct here it is, in this room, before you."

Quite abruptly he ended and sat down. At the high council table there was queer light upon Abbey's face. Boon, still upon his feet, gazed at Manson with mixed feelings. Then, reflecting vengefully that he had at least given this upstart doctor enough rope to hang himself with, he bowed to the President and took his chair.

For a minute a peculiar silence filled the chamber, then the President made the customary declaration.

"I ask all strangers to withdraw."

Andrew went out with the rest. Now his recklessness was gone and his head, his whole body, was throbbing like an overtaxed machine. The atmosphere of the council chamber stifled him. He could not endure the presence of Horner, Boland, Mary, and the other witnesses. He dreaded especially that melancholy reproach on the face of his solicitor. He knew he had behaved like a fool, a wretched declamatory fool. Now he saw his honesty as sheer madness. Yes, it was madness to attempt to harangue the Council as he had done. He ought to have been not a doctor but a stump orator in Hyde Park. Well! Soon he would cease to be a doctor. They would simply wipe him off the list.

He went into the cloakroom, desiring only to be alone, and sat on the edge of one of the washbasins, mechanically feeling for a cigarette. But the smoke was tasteless on his parched tongue and he crushed the cigarette beneath his heel. It was strange, despite the hard things, the true things he had said of the profession a few moments ago, how miserable he should feel at being cast out from it. He realized that he might find work with Stillman. But this was not the work he wanted. No! He wished to be with Denny and Hope, to develop his own bent, drive the spearhead of his scheme into the hide of apathy and conservatism. But all this must be done from within the profession; it could never, in England, never, never, be accomplished from outside. Now Denny and Hope must man the Trojan horse alone. A great wave of bitterness swept over him. The future stretched out before him desolately. He had already that most painful sense of all, the feeling of exclusion; and allied to it, the knowledge that he was finished, done for—this was the end.

The sound of people moving in the corridor brought him wearily to his feet. As he joined them and re-entered the council chamber, he told himself sternly that only one thing remained to him. He must not grovel. He prayed that he would give no sign of subservience, of weakness. With his eyes fixed firmly on the floor immediately before him, he saw no one, gave no glance towards the high table, remained passive, motionless. All the trivial sounds of the room re-echoed maddeningly about him—the scraping of chairs, the coughing, whispering, even the incredible sound of someone tapping idly with a pencil.

But suddenly there was silence. A spasm of rigidity took hold of Andrew. Now, he thought, now it is coming!

The President spoke. He spoke slowly, impressively.

"Andrew Manson, I have to inform you that the Council has given very careful consideration to the charge brought against you and to the evidence brought in support of it. The Council is of opinion that, despite the peculiar circumstances of the case and your own particularly unorthodox presentation of it, you were acting in good faith and were sincerely desirous of complying with the spirit of the law demanding a high standard of professional conduct. I have to inform you, accordingly, that the Council has not seen fit to direct the Registrar to erase your name."

For one dazed second he did not comprehend. Then a sudden shivering thrill passed over him. They had not struck him off. He was free, clear, vindicated.

He raised his head shakily towards the Council table. Of all the faces, strangely blurred, turned towards his own, the one he saw most distinctly was that of Robert Abbey. The understanding in Abbey's eyes distressed him even more. He knew, in one illuminating flash, that it was Abbey who had got him off.

Gone now was his pretence of indifference. He muttered feebly—and though he addressed the President it was to Abbey that he spoke:—

"Thank you, sir."

The President said: "That terminates the case."

Andrew stood up, instantly surrounded by his friends, by Con, Mary, the astounded Mr. Horner, by people he had never seen before, who now shook him warmly by the hand. Somehow he was in the street outside, still being beaten about the shoulders by Con, oddly reassured in his nervous confusion by the passing buses, the normal stream of traffic, recapturing every now and then, with a start of joy, the unbelievable ecstasy of his release.

He looked down unexpectedly to see Mary gazing up at him, her eyes still filled with tears.

"If they'd done anything to you—after all you've done for me I'd—Oh! I'd have killed that old President."

"In the name of God!" Con irrepressibly declared. "I don't know what ye were worrying about! The minute old Manson started to get goin'—sure, I knew he would knock the stuffing outa them."

Andrew smiled weakly, doubtfully, joyously.

The three reached the Museum Hotel after one o'clock. And there, waiting in the lounge, was Denny. He sauntered towards them, gravely smiling. Horner had telephoned the news.

But he had no comment to make. He merely said:—

"I'm hungry. But we can't feed here. Come along, all of you, and lunch with me."

They lunched at the Connaught Restaurant. Though no flicker of emotion crossed Philip's face, though he talked mainly of motor cars to Con, he made it a happy celebration.

Afterwards he said to Andrew:—

"Our train leaves at four o'clock. Hope's in Stanborough—at the hotel, waiting on us. We can get that property dirt cheap. I've got some shopping to do. But I'll meet you at Euston at ten to four!"

Andrew gazed at Denny, conscious of his friendship, of all that he owed him since the first moment of their meeting in the little Blaenelly surgery.

He said suddenly:—

"Supposing I'd been struck off?"

"You're not." Philip shook his head. "And I'll see to it that you never will be."

When Denny left to make his purchases Andrew accompanied Con and Mary to their train at Paddington. As they waited on the platform, rather silent now, he repeated the invitation he had already given them.

"You must come and see us at Stanborough."

"We will that," Con assured him. "In the spring—whenever I get the little bus tuned up."

When their train steamed out Andrew still had an hour to spare. But there was no doubt in his mind as to what he wished to do. Instinctively, he boarded a bus, and soon he was in Kensal Green. He entered the cemetery, stood a long time at Christine's grave, thinking of many things. It was a bright, fresh afternoon, with that crispness in the breeze which she had always loved. Above him, on the branch of a grimy tree, a sparrow chirped merrily.

When at last he turned away, hastening for fear he should be late, there in the sky before him a bank of cloud lay brightly, bearing the shape of battlements.

About the Author

Archibald Joseph (A.J.) Cronin was a Scottish author and physician born in 1896. He is known for such popular works as *The Citadel, The Stars Look Down,* and *The Keys of the Kingdom.* *The Citadel* inspired social change in the United Kingdom by helping to promote conversations about ethics in medicine and paved the way for the eventual formation of the National Health Service. His novels and novellas have been widely adapted for radio, film, and television, including the Oscar-nominated 1938 film adaptation of *The Citadel* starring Robert Donat, Rosalind Russell, Ralph Richardson, and Rex Harrison, and the long-running BBC radio drama *Country Doctor.*

Called "uncannily like Dickens" by *The New York Times*, Cronin received his medical degree from Glasgow University in 1925 and was appointed Medical Inspector of Mines for Great Britain in 1925. During this tenure, Cronin inspected mining outfits across South Wales, an experience that would heavily influence his writing career. Although Cronin went on to practice medicine in both Glasgow and London, his first novel, written in 1931 and titled *Hatter's Castle*, became a bestseller in England, after which he devoted his time entirely to writing. He continued to enjoy widespread success as a novelist into the 1940s and '50s, with many of his novels becoming bestsellers. By the late 1950s, Cronin's total sales in the U.S. had passed seven million, and his works had been widely translated across the globe. Cronin is still considered one of the English-speaking world's most successful and appreciated authors today. Cronin continued to write into his eighties, and passed away at the age of 84 in Montreux, Switzerland in 1981.